UNCERTAIN TIMES

Alan Reynolds

Fisher King Publishing

UNCERTAIN TIMES

Copyright © Alan Reynolds 2024

Print ISBN 978-1-916776-10-4
Epub ISBN 978-1-916776-11-1

All rights reserved. No part of this publication may be
reproduced or distributed in any form or by any means, or
stored in a database or electronic retrieval system without
the prior written permission of Fisher King Publishing Ltd.
Thank you for respecting the author of this work.

This is a work of fiction. Names, characters, businesses,
places, events and incidents are either the products of the
author's imagination or used in a fictitious manner. Any
resemblance to actual persons, living or dead, or actual
events is purely coincidental.

Published by

Fisher King Publishing

fisherkingpublishing.co.uk

A huge thanks to Rick Armstrong for his
unstinting support, guidance, and friendship,
also, to Samantha Richardson, Rachel Topping and all
the team at Fisher King Publishing.

My thanks also to my very talented niece, Karen Paxton
for her superb cover painting and to Jane Wheater
for editorial and proof-reading support.

Dedicated to my family and friends, and to all
those who have supported me in my writing –
your encouragement has been inspirational.
Much love

Also by Alan Reynolds

Also by Alan Reynolds

Playing with Kings
Traitors End
Breaking the Bank
The Scorn Pillar
The Tinker
The Coat
Smoke Screen
Valley of The Serpent
Another – a video with narration
Exile
Treat Island
The Boxer's Story
Brother's Box
The Trial Poppy
Double Canopy

"You cannot simultaneously prevent and prepare for war."

Albert Einstein

> "

Chapter One

Thursday, January 5th, 1939.

A meeting took place in Obersalzberg, Germany, between Adolf Hitler and Polish Foreign Minister, Józef Beck, to discuss the Polish port of Danzig. Poland, as a country, was still only twenty years old, established after The Great War. Danzig was previously a German port but was given to Poland by the Allies to allow the country access to the Baltic. It is reported that the meeting between the pair was heated as Hitler demanded the return of the port. However, the Poles refused to back down - Danzig was an issue over which they would fight. To Hitler, it was like a festering wound, an itch that couldn't be scratched, while the British looked on, impotent, locked into their policy of appeasement. The French were tied up with domestic matters.

In Keighley, Yorkshire, this meeting would have little interest in daily conversation, however the implications would have a lasting effect on the Marsden family – and the world.

Friday, January 6th.

Friday's were always busy in the James Street bakery, an establishment which had been in the Marsden family for over a hundred years.

Six a.m., and fourth-generation baker William Marsden was already mixing the dough ready for the first batch of bread; his seventeen-year-old younger brother, Robert, was assisting. Early January, and it was cold; their breath visible in the morning air as they toiled by the illumination of the two lightbulbs which lit the bread-making area. It was dark outside.

Gone were the days of Buxton's daily delivery and his friendly banter. With flour in more plentiful supply, William bought his ingredients weekly in bulk, and had constructed a storeroom behind the bakery which was piled high with hundredweight bags. Early closing due to flour shortages was a thing of the past.

William had completely transformed the operation in the two years since he had taken over running the business from his father, who's health issues had prevented him from working. William had modernised not just the equipment, but the shop and bakery layout. There were also new product lines. He'd recently read about a new bread-slicing machine in a trade magazine which was being used by the Wonderloaf Bakery in London. He was certain that it was going to be the future direction of bread retailing and had discussed buying one with his father, Arthur, who still owned the business. His reaction was predictable, resisting any attempt of change. "We've always done it this way; it's what people expect," was the extent of his argument.

The old oven had gone, replaced with a modern version. It was still traditional brick-built, with an iron door, but without the cracks that had started to appear in the hundred-year-old version used by William's father, and grandfather.

As a result of these changes the business was now profitable, and they no longer relied on Arthur's mother, Mildred, for subsidies.

William had inherited many of his father's characteristics, including his stubbornness, but whereas Arthur at the same age was gangly, William, now twenty-four, had filled out and was much stronger, certainly physically, mostly due to the better diet he had enjoyed growing up. Robert was more like Ivy, his mother. Customers would call him a 'kind' person, and he tended to live in his brother's shadow.

"Eh up, our Daisy," said William, seeing his nineteen-year-old sister appear at the door of the baking shed. "Tha ready to start on cakes?"

Daisy Marsden had inherited her mother's looks and spirit; she was hard-working and independent. She would be considered a 'modern' woman, and was more than a match for her brothers, or any man for that matter.

"Aye, 'appen I'll do some breadcakes and scones; eggs need using today."

"'As tha ordered some more?"

"Aye, don't fret, William, delivery's s'afternoon."

A further customisation of the baking shed included the installation of an industrial gas oven capable of turning out cakes, scones, and breadcakes, which were very popular with customers, and had become an important part of the bakery's product range. Once a week, Daisy also produced homemade biscuits, which had become a best-seller. There was a small storeroom next to the oven where the ingredients were kept.

"What about biscuits?"

"Aye, I made some yesterday; should last us today." She turned to Robert. "Can tha give us hand, Robert, this morning?"

"Aye, Daisy, as soon as we've first mix in t'oven."

By eight-thirty, the two shop assistants had arrived and were arranging the bread, rolls, and cakes in trays below the counter. William had installed a glass front and top to the serving area which enabled the customers to view the produce while they waited.

Ruth Danby, who had been recruited in 1914, while William's father was serving in France, was still there, and part of the fabric of the bakery. Her colleague at the time,

Betty Granger, married Douglas Tanner, brother of Samuel Tanner, one of Arthur's pals from the Malt Shovel who was killed in the trenches, in 1915. Their fifteen-year-old daughter, Doris, was now the other full-time assistant.

There was an air of industry as the bakery prepared itself for the coming day's trading.

Upstairs, William's mother, Ivy, was making breakfast; Arthur was still in bed. He had had another bad night, waking up unable to catch his breath.

She heard the toilet flush and her husband appeared at the kitchen door. He was stooped and held onto the doorframe; he was coughing violently.

"Sit thaself down, Arthur, I've done tha a bit of bacon and some toast." Arthur had lost the energy to argue.

"Aye," he replied, and shuffled to the small table in the parlour.

The living quarters had also been transformed since Arthur's childhood. Ivy was instrumental in that. Following their marriage in 1915, Ivy had been living at Springfield Hall, the palatial residence owned by Arthur's mother, Mildred, while he was serving in Egypt. Unfortunately, whilst there, he contracted Black Water Fever, which left his lungs severely weakened, and he was eventually discharged from the army on medical grounds.

Following a lengthy recuperation, he was determined to return to his former home and resume his role as master baker. Ivy refused to move unless changes were made. The apartment now had a proper bathroom with toilet and bath, as well as the two additional bedrooms. The kitchen, too, had received a makeover, with a modern gas oven, replacing the old range, running water, and new storage cupboards.'

With the three children labouring away in the shop below,

the parlour was quiet. The occasional trolleybus trundled by, but the noise had become ambient; it was part of daily life. Arthur was at the table reading The Daily Mirror, his newspaper of choice since his return to the bakery, primarily because of its support for the Labour Party.

Ivy brought in a tray with two cups and saucers and a teapot covered in a woollen tea cosy, then returned with the breakfast. She sat down opposite Arthur who was still engrossed with his newspaper.

"Anything interesting?" she asked.

"Aye, looks like old Adolf's at it again, says here he's after some of Poland he reckons belongs to Germany."

"What does that mean?"

"I reckon he'll invade. I wouldn't trust him as far as I could throw him. There'll be a war if we're not careful; you mark my words."

"Surely not, not after the last one. I can't imagine anyone would want to go through that again."

"He's brainwashed 'em, all of 'em, even the workers. They'll do what he says. Everybody's cow-towing to him. Chamberlain's too weak; he won't stand up to him. Peace in our time... who's he kidding? There's even people supporting that Oswald Moseley and he's nowt but a Fascist. 'Appen folk can't see what's going on in front of their own eyes."

Arthur started coughing violently again and was struggling to get his breath. His face changed colour from red to blue. Ivy went behind him and started rubbing his back.

He took out his handkerchief and coughed into it. His sputum was flecked with red. Arthur gradually calmed down; his breathing was shallow but recovering.

"I'll call Doctor Adams; you're not right, Arthur, tha coughing's getting worse."

"Nay, tha don't want to be calling 'im. There's nowt they can do, and he'll end up sending us a bill."

"Aye, but tha can't go on like this."

"I'll be alreet, woman, don't fret; pour us some tea, that'll help."

Arthur was unable to speak and paused while he recovered. After a few minutes, his colour gradually returned but his chest ached. He slumped forward.

"Here, drink this," said Ivy, presenting him with a cup of tea.

Tea leaves floated around the top and Arthur fished them out with his teaspoon.

"Are tha still going down to t'Shovel today?"

"Aye, why not? It'll get me out of 'ere for a bit."

"Are tha sure tha's well enough?"

"Aye, I'll be reet."

Midday, and James Street was busy. There were queues at most of the emporia. The greengrocer's store was doing a good trade, the pallets of produce neatly laid out in front of the shop. Old Walter Nugent, the previous owner, had long since passed and, in the absence of family succession, the business had been taken over by a husband and wife, the Pattersons. That was over fifteen years ago. Ivy and Joyce Patterson had become good friends.

Further along, the butcher's had hardly changed at all. The Stonehouse family continued to provide the good folk of Keighley with their meat. Violet Stonehouse, Ivy's mother, was now in her seventies and not in the best of health, However, she continued to play the role of Matriarch to the family. Despite her outwardly 'steely' persona, she had never really got over the death of her eldest son, Wilfred, who had died in 1915 trying to escape from the mental institution where he had been sent following his neurosis.

She could not equate the term 'deserter' to him and was bitter at not receiving a war pension. She had made many representations to the Military hierarchy and to the Government for payment. Unfortunately, they would not countenance being seen to reward 'cowardice', as it had said in one of their replies.

After the war, she, unsurprisingly, suffered periods of depression, but gradually recovered, recognising she needed to be strong for her family.

Following Wilfred's death, Ernest, the next eldest had assumed the role of master butcher, and it was his energy that had kept the business going with the help of Ronald, Lillian, and Gladys, the remaining family.

Phyllis had also continued to work at the butcher's but on a part time basis, having raised three children. Her husband worked in one of the mills and they lived in a small, terraced house the other side of town.

Ronald Stonehouse eventually left butchery in the early twenties, as the business could not financially sustain the staff numbers and trained as a motor engineer working at Pease's Garage.

Gladys still lived above the shop in the flat and was Violet's principle carer. Ronald and Lillian were both married with children and lived a trolleybus ride away.

Granger's Store on the corner continued to dominate the top of James Street. It was another shop that had maintained its traditional service and had changed little since the war years. The product lines had naturally become more diverse with food generally being more plentiful. If anything, the store had become more up-market in its clientele. George Granger died in 1925 and the business passed to his nephew,

Philip.

The park opposite seemed different. It used to be the place where picknickers would spend some time, children would let off steam playing 'catch me', or people would just pass the time on one of the benches. Today, it was merely used as a pleasant short cut or dog walk. Very few would use it for recreational purposes. Some of the trees had been cut down as they had become safety hazards and the grass area had become stained with yellow patches where dogs had been.

The taxi rank was still there. Two blue Morris Super-six cabbies were parked up waiting patiently for custom, their drivers at their steering wheels reading newspapers. The vehicles were much improved from their 1914 cousins, but there was still the muscle-tearing need to swing the handle to start them.

Arthur Marsden left the parlour and slowly descended the stairs, one at a time. He shuffled out of the shop, prompting whispers among the waiting queue. At forty-four years of age, he looked like someone in his sixties and was unrecognisable from the uncompromising master baker of 1914.

He still bore the scars of the conflict, the red weal on his chest from spiteful flying shrapnel, the missing lobe on his left ear taken as a meal by a rat while Arthur was lay in a flooded shell crater.

He left the bakery and stopped on the corner to let a car go by and catch his breath. The adjoining road, West Street, was much clearer these days, absent of the horse droppings that in the past presented a hazard to the unwary. The blacksmith's shop, which had provided farrier services just down the street for over fifty years, had also gone, along with the Victorian cobbles. The occasional horse and cart was the exception rather than the rule.

The bank on the corner was still there. No longer the Bank of Liverpool, but since 1928, Martins Bank. It was where the Marsden family still had their accounts.

Arthur crossed the road and immediately stopped again to catch his breath. There was a streetlamp on the corner, and he held onto it for balance. A trolleybus went by, almost full; one or two downstairs were stood up holding the leather straps attached to the ceiling. Arthur was unable to ride on the trolleybus anymore. With so many smokers the fumes irritated his lungs.

The welcoming sign of the Malt Shovel hung above him. The familiar smell of ale and tobacco greeted him as he entered the pub, turned right, and made his way to the bar. For some reason, the smoke didn't seem to cause the same irritation. It was a larger room than the downstairs compartment of a trolleybus.

"Usual Duggie," said Arthur as the landlord approached.

Arthur placed a sixpence on the counter.

"Ah do, Arthur, 'ow be tha?"

"Aye, not complaining,"

'Duggie' Douglas and his wife Sally had taken over the tenancy of the pub from Thomas and Maisy Fielding when Thomas retired to Scarborough in 1924. It had subsequently been modernised by the brewery with new pumps and optics, but, otherwise, it had maintained the character of yesteryear. The clientele, though, had changed. The pub was no longer the domain of the foundrymen and millworkers 'wetting up' before their shift; now it was mostly passing trade and locals.

Duggie put the pint on the counter in front of Arthur together with his penny change.

"Ta, Duggie."

He looked around the bar. Friday lunchtime wasn't as

busy as the old days. A thin layer of cigarette smoke hung in the air from the ten or so customers. There were no women in the bar; that hadn't changed. Any frequenting the alehouse would be in the 'snug', a small room on the left-hand side opposite the entrance to the bar.

Every now and then, Arthur could still see his millworker pals, Samuel Tanner and Henry King, and his best pal Wilfred, the master butcher, seated at the table in the corner putting the world to rights, ghosts of times gone by.

Arthur was still wracked with guilt, wondering why he had been spared from the carnage of the trenches while his best friends had perished. He took his drink to blank out his life, but the reality was, it did the opposite, changing his mood into someone angry with the world. Ivy had borne the brunt of his ire.

He took another gulp of his ale, then stopped. Something was wrong. Arthur started choking uncontrollably. Beer sprayed from his mouth and nose.

He was holding on to the bar trying to catch his breath.

"Hey up, Arthur, are tha alreet?" said the landlord, seeing Arthur struggling to breathe.

Arthur's face had turned red.

"Sally, quick give us a hand here," shouted Duggie. Other drinkers had noticed what was happening and tried to help. His wife came out from the back and took over.

"Lay him on the floor. We need to get him to the Victoria."

Sally started pressing hard on Arthur's chest.

"He's stopped breathing," said Duggie, looking at his wife.

"I'll get a cabbie," said Jim Stride, one of the customers, and dashed out of the bar.

Sally kept pressing down rhythmically on Arthur's chest. "I don't know if this is helping," said Sally.

"He's still not breathing," said the landlord. "Wait, stop a moment, I think you've done it."

Duggie checked again. "Yes, I think he's breathing, but we need to get him to hospital."

It was five minutes before the cabbie arrived. Duggie and one of the customers lifted the unconscious Arthur off the floor, taking an arm each, and half-carried/half-dragged Arthur out to the vehicle. Between them they managed to get him slumped into the back. Duggie, the landlord, sat alongside, holding onto him to prevent Arthur from falling forward.

It was only a short drive the Victoria Hospital on Highfield Lane, but time was of the essence. Arthur had been unconscious now for over ten minutes, although he still appeared to be breathing.

The cabbie pulled up outside the main entrance, and Duggie ran into the reception and shouted for a doctor. A man in a white coat with a stethoscope around his neck was talking to one of the nurses in the reception area, and quickly joined the landlord to the waiting taxicab.

"What happened?" asked the doctor.

"He had a coughing fit and couldn't get his breath. He stopped breathing, but I think he's got a pulse now."

Arthur was lay on the back seat.

The doctor quickly leaned into the vehicle and listened to Arthur's chest. "We need to get him inside. Can you lift him?"

The cab driver joined them and between the three of them, they managed to negotiate Arthur into the hospital entrance. "Quick get a trolley," shouted the doctor to the nurse.

There was frantic activity as they struggled to get Arthur onto a trolley. The doctor placed an oxygen mask over Arthur's nose and mouth.

"That should help," he said, looking at Duggie who was alongside.

Chapter Two

Meanwhile, back at the Malt Shovel, Sally asked one of the customers to run up to the bakery to explain what had happened.

The bakery was busy as the messenger from the Malt Shovel leaned across the counter to Ruth. "Quick, it's Arthur, he's had a turn; they've taken him to The Victoria. Can you let Mrs Marsden know?"

The man left.

Ruth excused herself from the next customer, much to their annoyance, and went into the baking shed where William and Robert were preparing another batch of bread.

"Your Da's had one of his turns; they've taken him to the Victoria," said Ruth with an expression of concern.

William stopped what he was doing. "What...? When was this?"

"I don't know, just now, someone from the pub just came in and said your Da had been taken to the Victoria."

"Thanks, Ruth, I better go and tell Ma." He turned to Robert. "Can tha look after things? I'll go and find out what's happening."

Ivy was in the kitchen when William came into the flat. "Mam, mam," he called. "It's Da, he's in the Victoria."

Ivy came out of the kitchen wiping her hands with a towel.

"What's happened?" said Ivy with a look of concern.

"I don't know. Someone from the Shovel just came into the shop to say Da had had one of his turns and was in the Victoria."

"Oh, my Lord. Can you get a cabbie? I'll be down

directly."

Five minutes later, Ivy and William were in the taxi heading for the hospital. It drew up outside the entrance of the huge Victorian edifice. As the name suggests, the medical facility dated back to the previous century as a cottage hospital but had received many makeovers and additions since its inception.

Ivy paid the cabbie, then headed inside and rushed to the reception desk.

"My husband's here; I need to see him," said Ivy to the receptionist.

"What's his name?"

"Arthur... Arthur Marsden."

She checked the list of those admitted.

"Ah, yes, the doctor's with him. Please take a seat, someone will be with you shortly."

"How is he? Do you know?"

"No, I'm sorry, I don't. Please take a seat. The doctor shouldn't be long."

Time dragged as Ivy and William patiently waited for news of Arthur, and it was almost three quarters of an hour before a doctor walked into the reception area. His facial expression wasn't exhibiting good news.

"How is he, doctor?"

"Would you like to follow me?" he replied, without making eye contact.

He led Ivy and William down one of the corridors to a room on the right-hand side.

As they entered, they feared the worse. The room was decked out in flowers; there was a cross on the wall and comfortable seats. The atmosphere was restful.

The doctor invited the pair to sit down.

"I'm really sorry, Mrs Marsden, but despite our best efforts, we were unable to save Arthur. His lungs were in such a bad shape."

"Oh, no, no!" Ivy immediately started crying. William did his best to console her.

"I'll let you have a moment. You can see him when you're ready if you wish to say goodbye."

"Yes, thank you," replied Ivy.

Ivy composed herself and they followed the doctor back into reception.

Just then, a familiar figure came through the entrance and rushed towards them. "Ivy, William, what's the news? Robert telephoned me and I came straightaway."

"He's passed, Mam." Ivy started crying again.

Arthur's mother, Mildred, placed a consoling arm around her, then turned to the doctor.

"What happened?"

"His lungs gave in; there was nothing we could do."

"It was the war, you know, that did for him. He was never the same after he came back," said Mildred.

"Yes, like so many sons before him. I'm so sorry. Would you like to say goodbye?" said the doctor.

"Yes please," replied Mildred, and the three followed the doctor to the ward where screens had been placed around one of the beds.

Ten days later, the funeral of Arthur Albert Marsden took place at the Methodist Church; the same church that had hosted his father's funeral in 1914.

It was a simple affair, something Arthur had insisted on; he didn't believe in wasting good money while others were struggling to put food on the table.

Nevertheless, all the family were there, including

Arthur's sisters, Agnes and Grace who had travelled up from London with their husbands, Alistair and Matthew. Agnes's daughter, Gwendoline, also attended, while Matthew and Grace's children, old enough to look after themselves, stayed in London.

Mildred had paid for the cortege of three cars to follow the hearse to the church and then to the graveyard where he was buried next to his pals in Utley cemetery.

Ivy agreed to host the wake in the flat over the bakery. William had closed the bakery at one o'clock as a mark of respect; notices to that effect were displayed on the window.

By four o'clock, the old parlour was filled with family and friends wishing to pay their last respects. It was a sad occasion, although many expressed the view that Arthur's death was welcome release, given the state of his health in recent years. It was little comfort to Ivy who had still not yet come to terms with her loss.

Mildred Marsden had taken charge of proceedings as she was inclined to do. Now in her sixty-nineth year, her white hair evidenced her advancing years. Nevertheless, she still walked with purpose and indomitable presence.

Matthew and Alistair knew each other well and were regular mutual house guests, living only two miles from each other in London. Both were wearing dark suits and ties as befitting a funeral. Agnes and Grace were wearing smart dresses.

The two men shared a keen interest in politics and were in deep conversation as the sisters consoled each other.

Alistair still walked with a slight limp, a reminder of his war-time experiences. He had lost most of his hair and looked the part of a concert pianist. Matthew on the other hand was an impressive man, not quite in his fifties, his various officer roles in the military had given him a confidence and bearing. His dark hair was flecked with grey, but he could be mistaken for a film star with his rugged looks.

"So, do you think anything will come of last week's Chamberlain and Halifax's mission to Rome?" asked Alistair.

"No, I don't, not for one minute; it was a total waste of time. According to reports I've seen, Count Galeazzo Ciano, he's Mussolini's son-in-law, called the meeting, and I quote, 'a big lemonade'; that translates into 'farce'," said Matthew.

"As bad as that?"

"Yes, I'm afraid Chamberlain is perceived as weak, and the Italian's believe we, the British, don't have the stomach for a war."

"Yes," replied Alistair. "I can see that. Certainly, Chamberlain seems hell-bent on this emollient crusade."

"Yes, true. The problem is, this will all get reported back to Ribbentrop, and of course will embolden Hitler even further. At the moment he can do whatever he wants and knows he'll be unopposed."

"That's worrying."

"It's worse than that, Alistair, Germany has been building up its naval capabilities. Between you and me, it's not looking good for Czechoslovakia either. The view is that he will annex the rest of the country in the not-too-distant future."

"But I thought that was all settled... the Sudetenland, last year."

"Unfortunately not, Hitler will want the rest, and Poland could be next, you mark my words, and the world will just watch and let it happen."

"What about the French?"

"They are as weak as the British. No one has the stomach

for another war; that's the reality of it."

"So, we sit around and let Hitler do what he wants?"

"Yes, it seems so. We need Churchill in charge."

"Churchill? Bit of a loose cannon, I heard."

"There's nothing wrong with that. At least he would stand up to Hitler, but he's a voice in the wilderness at the moment."

Alistair was holding a China cup of tea and took a sip, contemplating Matthew's remarks.

Ivy's voice cut through the hubbub of conversation. "Matthew, there's a telephone call for you."

Matthew waved and followed Ivy into the bedroom where Ivy had the black Bakelite equipment.

She passed the heavy phone receiver to Matthew and left him to take the call.

"Yes, Commander, I can be back later this evening."

Matthew hung up and headed back to the parlour. He spotted his wife deep in conversation with Freda, the youngest of the Marsden siblings.

"Grace, darling, I've just been called back to London; it's an emergency."

"Oh dear, how are you going to get back?" asked Grace.

"I can take the train. Are you staying on for a couple of days?"

"That depends. I'll telephone you tonight."

"I could be late. Telephone in the morning; if your mother doesn't mind."

"No, she won't mind, of course I will. We'll need to go back to Blossom Cottage to get your stuff," said Grace.

"Yes, I'll take a taxi."

"I better come with you."

Grace approached Ivy. "Matthew's got to return to London, some emergency or another."

Matthew joined Alistair. "Sorry, I've got to go, Alistair, bit of an emergency."

"Nothing serious, I hope."

"Not sure. There's been some bombings in London. It'll be all over the newspapers tomorrow."

"The Irish?"

"I don't know exactly, could be. That's why I have to go back."

Matthew thanked Ivy and expressed his condolences again. "I hope you didn't mind me giving the department your telephone number. I gave them your mother's too, in case of emergencies. There's always something happening these days."

"No, of course not. Thank you for coming; I know Arthur would have appreciated it," replied Ivy.

While Matthew said his farewells and offered his apologies, Grace retrieved the house keys from her mother. They left the gathering and walked across the road to the taxi rank. Grace would return later.

By seven o'clock, it was just family members sitting in the parlour swapping 'Arthur' anecdotes. The Marsdens were on one side of the room; Ivy's family, the Stonehouses, the other,

There was a sadness; Arthur had not had the happiest of lives. Being wrongly arrested for a public order offence whilst returning from a protest march led to his enforced conscription. His experiences in the war were to shape his later life, not just physically but mentally. The man who went to France to fight in 1914 was not the same man that returned.

Arthur was always principled, refusing to join the rest of the family at Springfield Hall, the palatial home his mother had purchased from his father's surprise legacy, was an example. He believed the money was tainted. The injuries he had sustained in the trenches, followed by his illness contracted in the Middle East, were to severely limit his capabilities. He became a bitter and angry man.

Despite his various ills, Ivy had become his rock. In recent years she had moved from wife to carer, but never complained, even when she had cause.

There were practical matters to consider. Arthur hadn't made a will despite encouragement from Mildred; he didn't trust anyone to do with the law, he said. The bakery therefore passed to Ivy. This was not going to be an issue. Ivy had no intention of interfering with the business and would continue under William's management.

Freda, Arthur's youngest sister, approached Agnes and Alistair.

"When are you going back to London, Agnes?" she enquired.

Agnes and Alistair were stood together, drinking tea with their daughter Gwendoline. Agnes looked the very essence of 'chic', but not overdressed. She had a very good sense of style. Alistair was wearing a dark business suit.

Agnes looked at her husband, then answered the question. "Tomorrow, late morning, Alistair has work, and Gwendoline has school."

"Do you enjoy teaching, Alistair?" asked Freda.

"Very much, and you? How long have you been teaching?"

"It will be twelve years come September. Yes, very much," she replied.

"What ages do you teach?" asked Agnes.

"Infants, five to seven."

"Goodness, that must be a handful."

"It's only a small village school so classes are small. It's not difficult." She looked at Agnes. "Will you be going back to performing?"

"I've no plans at the moment; there never seems enough time in the day; what with looking after the house and my family." Agnes looked at Alistair and smiled.

"I thought you would have a housekeeper."

"Well, I do have an assistant, Mary, but that's mainly to look after the letters; I still get so many. Oh, and she manages the houses."

"Houses?" asked Freda with some surprise.

"Yes, Cameron, you remember, my manager, invested a lot of my money in buying houses. He thought they would be a safe investment."

"And he's been proved right," interjected Alistair.

"He died, didn't he?" said Freda, with a sad expression.

"Yes, not long after he retired to Scotland," replied Agnes. "I think he found giving up work difficult. He was always so active. I was surprised when he left London; he was very much part of the theatrical community. He lived and breathed it. There are still two of his productions running."

Freda turned to Gwendoline. "And how is school, Gwen?"

"Hard work. I've got exams shortly. I'm trying to get into the London School of Music."

Gwendoline had inherited her mother's looks, and spoke with an air of confidence, her accent displaying not a hint of her Yorkshire heritage. Agnes had long shaken off her northern tones.

"Oh, that's excellent. We do seem to be blessed with such a talented family," said Freda.

"Yes, she's very talented; we are so proud of her. She's certainly a better pianist than I was at her age," said Alistair.

Just then Grace joined them, having returned from Oakworth.

"Hello Grace, did Matthew get off alright?" asked Freda.

"Yes, he sends his apologies. This is quite a regular thing. He gets called up at all hours."

"It must be a worry."

"I think you get used to it. Mind you, he never tells me what he's up to; his work at the Ministry's all very hush, hush."

Mildred's third daughter, Molly, walked across and joined the group.

"Hello Molly," said Agnes. "We were just saying what a nice service."

"Yes, it was."

"How's the rag trade?" asked Grace.

At the end of 1918, Molly was working full time with seamstress and designer, Kitty Bluet, at her atelier in Blossom Cottage, her house in Oakworth, a small town around ten miles from Keighley. Molly had shown a flair for fabric and Kitty had taken her on as an apprentice. Molly married John Taylor in 1923 and moved into a new house with her husband on the outskirts of Bradford, paid for by her father-in-law, a wool merchant.

After the birth of her son Daniel in 1925, she left Kitty's employ and continued to work from home in her studio. Her designs became so popular there was typically a six-week waiting list for completion of garments. On the back of this popularity, in 1928, she and her husband started a fashion business, employing a number of local girls.

"It's fine at the moment; I've got lots of orders," replied Molly. "Getting the right cloth is the main issue, but we're managing."

"I'm not surprised; I love your designs. I was going to

ask if you could design something for me before we leave," said Agnes.

"Yes, of course; I can call round to Ma's tomorrow morning and take some measurements," said Molly. "What time will you be going back to London?"

"Lunchtime, or thereabouts, we have a train at one o'clock."

"What about you, Grace? What time will you be leaving?"

"I'll be on the same train; it's much easier."

"Matthew had to leave, I noticed," said Molly.

"Yes, some problem at work," replied Grace.

"Oh, that's such a shame; it's ages since we've had the time to talk. So, what do you think? Is there going to be a war?"

Alistair gave his views. "Well, it depends. I think Chamberlain and Halifax are trying to prevent one, but if it means appeasing Hitler, then I think that would be wrong; we need to stand up to him."

"But surely no-one wants another war; not after the last one. Look what it did to poor Arthur," replied Molly.

"And millions of others," added Freda.

Mildred walked across from the kitchen. "I'm going back to the cottage. Do you want to share a cabbie, or are you staying a bit longer?"

Agnes looked at Grace. "I think we'll join you. Will there be enough room for all of us?"

"Yes, I'm sure we can all squeeze in," replied Mildred.

Mildred had been residing at Springfield Hall in Oakworth since 1914, but with the children off her hands, it had become much too big for her and was expensive to run. Like many, her investments had been adversely affected by the financial crash of 1930, and she had been looking for a suitable smaller residence. The opportunity came from a tragedy. Her best friend, and Molly's mentor, Kitty Bluet, succumbed to breast cancer in 1931. Her son, Freddie, inherited Blossom Cottage, but agreed to sell it to Mildred; there were too many memories.

Grace, Agnes, Alistair, and Gwendoline were all staying with Mildred, and, having said their farewells, made their way across James Street to the taxi rank, leaving Ivy with her family.

Chapter Three

Following a distinguished career in Military Intelligence during the war, Matthew Keating's move into the Secret Service was a natural progression and had earned him promotion to the rank of Major.

It was around ten-thirty, when he arrived back in London. He took a taxi from St Pancras to the headquarters of the Secret Intelligence Service in Broadway Buildings, near to St James's Park Underground Station. It was going to be a long night.

The streets were still busy. Matthew looked out of the window at the double-decker buses with their sides plastered with advertisements, Dunlop Tyres, Lipton Tea, Black and White cigarettes, dodging their way to their destinations packed with travellers. Traffic police with their white arm bands were still directing traffic even at this hour. The largest city in the world was buzzing.

The taxi pulled up outside the austere building that was home to the SIS.

Matthew walked through the double doors and presented his pass to the security guard. He took the stairs to the basement floor, a secure area, well below street level.

He entered the room; it was alive with activity. Noise levels were high with over twenty typists click-clacking away at their machines. Around the sides, listening machines attended by personnel wearing black, Bakelite, headsets. Metal brackets enabled them to be placed over the head. As messages were intercepted, notes were taken to be passed to the analysts for assessment.

No-one reacted to Matthew's presence as he walked through the organised chaos to his office. He took off his overcoat and stowed it in the small wardrobe in the corner, picked up his telephone, and called his boss.

"Colonel...? Keating... just arrived, sir."

"Ah, Major, good. Come on through."

Matthew headed out of his office, through the decryption room. As he left the mayhem, it was markedly quiet; his footsteps the only sound as he walked down the corridor. He reached his boss's room, knocked and went in.

There was little formality, no saluting.

"Ah, Major, come in, take a seat. Sorry to drag you away from your funeral but something big has turned up. That ultimatum from the IRA." He was holding a piece of paper.

"The one addressed to Halifax demanding the withdrawal of all British armed forces in Ireland?" said Matthew.

"Yes, well it looks as though they weren't bluffing."

"No, I didn't think they were for one minute. But, I mean, what did they expect? They must have known the British Government would never have complied with such a threat."

"I think it was, in their eyes, legitimising a bombing campaign. When we didn't respond, yesterday the IRA started posting copies of another proclamation declaring war on Britain. I've got a copy of it here."

He handed a piece of paper to Matthew who immediately started to read it.

"Hmm, let me see." Matthew read from the note. "It says here, they're calling on all Irishmen, both at home and 'in Exile', whatever that means, to give their utmost support to compel the withdrawal of the British from the island of Ireland so that a free Irish Republic could be established."

"Yes, and that could cause problems for us in America. The Germans will also be interested."

"Yes, indeed," affirmed Matthew.

"We need to deal with the immediate threat, Major.

They've started a bombing campaign. We've received several reports of explosions today, five in London and three in Manchester."

Matthew looked at the Colonel with a grave expression. "Hmm, I see. What's the impact? Any casualties?"

"Yes, one fatality in Manchester, and a great deal of damage."

"Do we have any more information?"

The Colonel looked down. "It seems they are going for the infrastructure; one went off at Hams Hall Power Station, two of the others at water mains supplying the power station. We're in contact with Special Branch, they're handling the investigation on the ground. We've been asked to provide intelligence and any other assistance. I've been speaking with the Home Office and, as a precaution, we've placed all power stations, gas works, telephone exchanges, oh, and the Droitwich transmitting station, under police protection. Patrols around the government buildings at Whitehall have been stepped up, and all ships from Ireland arriving at Holyhead, Fishguard and Liverpool are being closely monitored."

"What about the press?"

"Yes, they'll have a field day, but, if anything, it will be to our advantage. The campaign, if that's what it is, will be condemned. I can't see there being a great deal of sympathy for the perpetrators."

"No, that's true. What about these signatories?"

"Yes, the so called 'Army Council'; they are known to us. We believe it was written by Joseph McGarrity."

"What, the head of Clan na Gael?"

"Yes, the very same. He's still based in America, as far as we know, but does have influence in Ireland."

"What about Dublin?"

"We've been in touch with them, and they say they have no knowledge about this campaign; came as quite a shock, apparently."

"So, what do you want me to do?"

"I want you to coordinate all our intelligence activities to support the police investigations."

"Yes, Colonel."

"Do you have the resources?"

"I'll need to evaluate that."

"Yes, well let me know tomorrow. If you need more personnel, just say."

It was two-thirty a.m. before Matthew arrived back at the house. Both children, James and Dorothy were asleep.

It was six forty-five, and Matthew had been up for half an hour preparing breakfast for the family, in Grace's absence.

Twenty-year-old James Keating was in his second year at University in London studying Economics. Dorothy, three years younger, was in her final year at the prestigious (and expensive) St Paul's Girls School in Hammersmith. She took after her mother in her interest in social causes and was a member of the debating society and a senior prefect. A future in politics was on the cards.

It was unusual for the three of them to be seated together around the breakfast table, but with Grace still in Yorkshire, Matthew had taken over duties. They would leave together by seven-thirty to their respective destinations.

By any measure, James was a good-looking young man. He took after his father with thick dark hair, his 'five o'clock shadow' defining his jaw and lower face. His eyes were deep blue. Unsurprisingly, he had become the subject of attention from his female student colleagues.

He looked up from his breakfast and addressed his father.

"We heard about the bombings yesterday; it was on the wireless. Is that why you came back early?"

"I can't really talk about it James, but let's say I'm going to be busy for the next few weeks."

"But with all the problems with Hitler, I can't understand why the Irish would want to cause problems."

He took another slice of toast and looked at his father expecting a reply.

"It's complicated, James, and I don't have time to discuss it now, but we will, I promise."

James looked at his father. "Yes, I'll be interested." He paused. "There is something I want to ask, Dad. We've discussed my joining the RAF."

"Yes, James, after your studies."

"That's not until June, and they're looking for trainee pilots now."

"Where did you hear this?"

"At college, someone visited the University on Friday, an RAF officer, and spoke to the Vice Chancellor. There was a notice on the notice board. I want to apply."

"What about your studies?"

"I think protecting the country is more important than getting a degree. Everybody's saying that war will come, and it will take at least six months training."

"Let's talk about this when your mother gets back."

"When will that be?"

"Sometime this afternoon. We can discuss it over dinner this evening."

Matthew was back in his office by eight-thirty and was immediately called into a meeting with his boss, Colonel Monkton.

Colonel Stuart Monkton was an impressive character

29

with a distinguished record in the First World War, serving in Ypres as a lieutenant before joining Military intelligence, where he worked alongside Matthew. Monkton was well-regarded, and widely tipped to take over from the current head of the Secret Intelligence Service.

Matthew knocked on the Colonel's door and was immediately ushered in.

"Ah, Major, take a seat, I need to bring you up to date."

Matthew sat opposite the colonel and leaned forward to listen to the update.

"There've been more explosions, three around Birmingham. There was also an attempt to bring down a pylon over the Manchester Ship Canal. Fortunately, it failed to detonate. It looks like infrastructure again. I've been speaking to the Home Office and we're stepping up security on possible targets as a precaution. So that's all power stations, gas works, telephone exchanges, as well as the Droitwich transmitting station, and, as I said last night, we've reinforced police patrols around the government buildings in Whitehall. That's as well as the extra inspections on all ships from Ireland arriving at Holyhead, Fishguard and Liverpool."

"Have we made any arrests?"

"Yes, they've arrested seven men in Manchester in connection with the attempted bombing up there and are expected to make more as we get more intelligence. They've also managed to recover a considerable amount of bomb-making equipment."

"That's good news. I'll speak to Manchester and get the details; see if any of the names are known to us."

By the end of the day further bombings were reported in London including one outside a branch of Williams Deacons Bank which also damaged a gas main.

It was another long day and Matthew arrived home around seven o'clock. Grace was there to greet him as he entered the house.

Matthew and Grace still lived in their government-supplied house in Hereford Street, Acton, which had been their home for nearly twenty-three years.

"How was your journey, darling? Did you manage to travel back with Agnes?" asked Matthew as he kissed her warmly.

He placed his umbrella in the stand in the hall, next to the coat-hooks where several mackintoshes and coats were hanging. He placed his trilby hat on the vacant one which was always saved for Matthew's head apparel.

Grace continued. "Yes, luckily, we were able to get a compartment together, so it was just Agnes, Alistair, Gwen, and me; so, the journey passed quite quickly; it was nice to spend some time with them. It was cold though."

"What time did you get home?"

"It was about half-four. I decided to take a taxi from Kings Cross; the Tube was so busy. How was your day? I've been reading about the bombs."

"Yes, it's been busy. It looks like some long days ahead."

"Hi Dad," shouted James, who was in the living room listening to the radio.

Matthew walked in and acknowledged his son. Dorothy was seated at the dining table engrossed in some textbooks.

"Hello Dorothy, how's the studying?"

"I've a lot of homework; exams in two weeks."

"Yes, of course, well, we won't disturb you."

"Come into the kitchen; I've something to show you," said Grace, and they left the room. James tagged behind, giving up on his radio programme; he had matters to discuss.

There were four packages on the kitchen table. Matthew

looked at them.

"Are they what I think they are?" said Matthew.

"Gas masks, according to the label; they've been distributing them today. There are instructions on how to use them inside, according to the man from the council. He had a van full of them. Do you really think we're going to need them?" asked Grace.

"Let's hope not; they're only a precaution," replied Matthew.

"An expensive one if they're going to supply everyone in the country."

"Well, that's the intention, well not everyone exactly, those living in large conurbations will get one. There's an order for about thirty-five million, I understand." He picked up one of the boxes and examined the contents. "We need to keep these somewhere safe until we get further instructions," said Matthew.

"Dad, can we talk about the RAF?"

"Let your father get changed and have something to eat; he's had a long day," interjected Grace. She turned to Matthew. "I've made you something to eat; it'll be ready for you when you come down."

A few minutes later, Grace and James were at the kitchen table while Matthew ate his dinner, allowing Dorothy to continue her studies.

James was anxious to raise the topic of the RAF.

"I've made some egg custard for dessert," said Grace.

"Excellent," replied Matthew.

As Grace was spooning a portion into a bowl, Matthew picked up a napkin and wiped his mouth.

"Darling, James has been asking about joining the RAF; what do you think?" asked Grace.

"Yes, I know he asked me earlier; I said we would discuss

it as a family. For my part, I would prefer him to wait until he's finished his studies," said Matthew.

"Yes, I was thinking the same, but then I remembered when I joined the FANY's. I was desperate to do my bit, and I was the same age as James. Arthur had already joined the army by then."

"Yes and look what it did to him. Also, war is not a foregone conclusion. Chamberlain and Halifax are working hard to secure a workable peace," said Matthew.

"Hmm, the trip to Italy wasn't a resounding success, according to the newspaper," replied Grace.

"Yes, true."

"But, Dad, you said it was inevitable," interjected James.

Matthew looked at his son with a grave expression. "Yes, I do think there is a strong possibility."

"Well, according to the officer that visited college, they're desperate to start training pilots now," countered James.

Grace placed the bowl of egg custard in front of Matthew and handed him a spoon.

James continued passionately. "I can return to my studies later, in the future; my tutor told me they would keep a place open for anyone who signs up."

"It could be very dangerous," said Grace, looking at James with concern.

"No more dangerous than driving ambulances in a battle zone," countered James, referring to Grace's wartime activities.

Grace looked at Matthew.

"Hmm... Well, if you're determined to do this, James, then I won't stand in your way," said Grace.

Matthew finished another mouthful of egg custard.

"Very well, you have my blessing. What happens now?"

"Thanks Dad, I'll speak to my tutor tomorrow and get

an application form. There'll be a selection process to go through."

Earlier, in Blossom Cottage, Mildred was tidying up after her guests. Her radio, which had become a source of companionship, played music in the background as she carried out her chores. Nine-thirty, a bright, crispy day; the early morning frost was already melting. The cottage seemed empty with the family now dispersed back to their lives.

There was a knock on the door. Mildred wondered who it might be; she received few visitors these days. A smiley face greeted her.

"Oh, hello, Ethel, come in; it's not your usual day."

"No, Mam suggested you might need some help with your guests leaving an' that."

"Oh, that's very thoughtful of her... of you both. I was just going to start the washing."

"Oh, leave that to me; I'll see to it."

"I've stripped the beds; the sheets are in the scullery. Would you like a drink before you start?"

"Yes, why not, thank you. Oh, I've brought your paper."

Ethel rummaged in her hessian carrier bag and pulled out a neatly folded edition of The Times, Mildred's newspaper of choice since 1914, when it was recommended to her by her solicitor.

At the back of the cottage, the scullery had been converted into the washroom with a sink, mangle and 'copper'. The copper resembled a large cylindrical barrel with an element in the bottom to heat the water. The clothes would be placed inside with some soap suds, then rinsed before going through the mangle to get rid of some of the water. In warmer weather the clothes would be hung on the washing line outside, but today it would be hung on a clotheshorse in front of the fire to dry.

The two women sat down with their drinks. Ethel took after her mother, down to earth, and never afraid to express her views. Daisy Jessop had been Mildred's housekeeper while she lived at Springfield Hall, and was more a friend than an employee, but with Mildred's change of circumstances and her change of house, there was little need for a full-time home help. Ethel had agreed to take over on a part-time basis.

"I do enjoy a cup of coffee," said Mildred, taking her first sip.

"Yes, although I don't know when we'll be able to get anymore, Mam says it's getting harder to come by and quite expensive now. She only has a couple of jars left in the store. We still have some Camp Coffee, that seems to be gaining in popularity," said Ethel.

"I'm sure it is; although I do prefer the real thing," replied Mildred,

"How was the funeral?"

Mildred looked down. "It was very sad, but I think Arthur is in a better place now. He was a troubled soul for such a long time after the war; it changed him completely. I don't know how Ivy coped sometimes. Arthur was not an easy person to live with. He was so lucky to have her."

"At least you had your family to support you."

"Yes, I don't know how I would have managed. I do miss Agnes and Grace."

"How are they? Is Agnes going to be singing again?"

"I don't think so. She gets plenty of offers she was telling me, but she's not done much since she made the phonograph records; that must be over ten years ago. Gwen, their daughter's doing very well; already giving recitals, according to Alistair."

"Such a talented family... What about Grace?"

"She's well, thank you. Matthew, her husband, is something important in the military, all very hush-hush, so she's busy looking after the house and entertaining, she was saying."

They continued chatting about the funeral for a few minutes before Ethel excused herself to start on the washing.

23, Madison Close, Bloomsbury, London. Wednesday 18th January 1939.

Agnes was in the sitting room with her assistant, Mary Bushell, dealing with some administration regarding one of her houses.

Cameron Delaney, Agnes's former manager, had invested wisely and she was the landlord of eight, mostly terraced, houses in the area, which required upkeep and tenancy management, which was part of Mary's duties.

The telephone rang.

"I wonder who that is," said Agnes as she got up to answer it.

"Bloomsbury 4 8 2," said Agnes.

"Is that Agnes, Agnes Marsden?"

"Yes, who's calling?"

"Of course, let me explain, my name is Ephraim Solomon, my friends call me Solly."

"Yes, Mr Solomon, how can I help you?"

"I was an associate of your late manager, Cameron Delaney... The thing is, I have a business proposition for you which I'd like to discuss, if you would be so kind."

Agnes was straining her ears; he had quite a strong accent.

"What sort of proposition?"

"It's a singing engagement. Is it possible we could meet,

and I will explain everything."

"When were you thinking of?"

"Well, there's no time like the present; would you be free this lunchtime?"

Agnes looked at Mary.

"Yes, very well, where do you suggest?"

"I'm based in Soho; do you know the Hollybush?"

"Yes, of course."

"I can be there for twelve-thirty. I will cover your taxi fare."

"Twelve-thirty it is, Mr Solomon."

Agnes hung up.

"Who was that?" asked Mary.

"Someone called Solomon. He wants to meet me, an associate of Cameron's apparently. Says he has a singing engagement he wants to discuss."

"Couldn't he have told you over the telephone."

"He said he wanted to discuss it face-to-face this lunchtime at the Hollybush. Now that's something I don't want to pass by; the food's wonderful, not been for years."

"The Hollybush? I don't think I know it."

"It has fond memories for me. It's where I sang for the King, not this King, his father, George the Fifth."

"Really, I didn't know that."

"Yes, it was 1914, November/December time, if I remember rightly." Agnes started to daydream. "I was escorted by Lord Harford; although the restaurant wasn't called The Hollybush then. I can't remember what it was called."

"And you sang for the King? Goodness."

"Yes. He was dining upstairs, and I was summoned."

"How wonderful."

"It was something I will never forget... although I did

sing for him again, and the rest of the family, at the Palace, after the war."

"You didn't tell me."

"Well, it's something I don't like to brag about. They insist on discretion."

"What was it like... the Palace?"

"It was truly beautiful. It was a banquet, the first time."

"First time?"

"Yes, I was there twice more to perform for them. I have special memories of the occasions."

"I'm sure you have."

"They even gave me some mementos; there was no money involved."

"Oh, you must show me."

"Yes, they're in the attic. I'll get them out one day, remind me."

"What about this Lord you mentioned; what happened to him?"

"He asked me to marry him, but after I met Alistair, I sent back the ring he gave me."

"Oh, that must have been a difficult decision."

"No, not really, when I think about it, I was not cut out to be a Lady of the Manor. As it happened, he was badly wounded and blinded at Ypres. I had a letter from his mother to tell me. It was quite upsetting."

"Yes, I can imagine... Do you know what happened to him?"

"I heard he died in nineteen eighteen, just before the war ended. Like Arthur, he never recovered from his wounds."

Agnes left the house just after twelve o'clock for her lunchtime appointment, intrigued at the invitation. She was dressed warmly for the weather including her Mink coat.

The taxi pulled up outside the restaurant just after half-past. As the vehicle slowed to a stop, a man in a herring-bone three-piece suit approached the driver and paid the fare, then opened the back door for Agnes to get out.

The cab drove away, and the man introduced himself. They shook hands.

"Miss Marsden... Ephraim Solomon, at your service, pleased to meet you. Shall we go in?"

Agnes stopped for a moment and looked at the outside, remembering the occasion with the late Lord Harford. The building had received a considerable amount of attention; the frontage had been updated in keeping with the present fashion.

"Thank you Mr Solomon," responded Agnes as they went inside.

"Please call me Solly."

They were greeted by the Maître d. "Your usual table, Mr Solomon," said the man, resplendent in his dress suit.

"Thank you, Raymundo," acknowledged Solly, and they were escorted across the room to a corner table.

"May I take you coat, Madam?" enquired Raymundo, and relieved Agnes of her outer garment. Beneath, she was wearing a striking off-white/cream woollen dress, the height of fashion which had women at adjacent tables admiring. Agnes had lost none of her presence and knew how to dress for the occasion.

They took their seats. A waiter immediately appeared and started pouring water into crystal glasses. Agnes looked around.

"This place has changed since I was last here."

"How long ago was that?" enquired Solly as he took a sip of water.

"Oh, it was a long time ago, late 1914, a night I will never forget. I can't believe it's been nearly twenty-five years, goodness how time flies. It seems like only yesterday."

Solly didn't press for detail.

Another waiter appeared and handed the pair the luncheon menu.

"Would you like a drink with your meal?" asked Solly.

"I'll stay with water thank you," replied Agnes.

With drinks and food ordered, it was down to business. Agnes was weighing up her host. It was difficult to tell his age; he had a round face with glasses and had lost most of his hair which made him look a lot older than he probably was. He had a trimmed beard which gave him a rugged appearance. There was a small scar across his forehead.

"So, tell me about this proposition you have for me," said Agnes, getting straight to the point as befitting her Yorkshire heritage.

"Yes, of course, my dear, but before I do, I feel I need to introduce myself properly. I was a good friend of dear Cameron."

"Really? I don't recall him mentioning your name."

"No. it was after you had retired from public engagements. Cameron continued with his theatre productions until he left to return to Scotland. He never stopped talking about you, you know."

"Oh, that's most kind of you to say. He was a dear, dear friend; I owe him everything. I miss him a great deal."

"Yes, as do I... I have taken over much of his work. We co-produced several shows before his departure."

"So, you have me in mind for a part? Only I'm not really interested in returning to the stage at this moment."

"No, no, Cameron said that. It's something quite different. Do you know Robert Laing at all?"

"I don't think so, although his name sounds familiar.

Who is he?"

"He's a programme producer for the BBC."

"I see," said Agnes, now really intrigued.

Before they could continue, a waiter appeared with their lunch. They waited while the food was distributed.

"As I was saying, I received a call from Mr Laing. He's putting together a weekly variety show and was looking for artists. I mentioned your name straightaway."

"That's very kind."

"Oh, he was very interested; he'd heard about your work, but not seen you in person. He asked me to contact you to see if you would consider being a part of the programme. It won't be too onerous, once a week, I believe. They pay quite well, too." He smiled.

Agnes thought for a moment. "Yes, although I've never done any wireless."

"That won't be a problem... Would you like me to arrange a meeting?"

"Yes, very well."

"Excellent, excellent."

They finished their meal and ordered coffees.

"I was trying to place your accent," said Agnes. "It sounds German."

Solly looked down. He wiped his mouth with a napkin, then looked at Agnes; his expression had changed, one of sadness, deep sadness.

"I was born in Germany, yes, but my mother and father arranged for me and my sister to leave in 1933. My father had a jewellery business in Duisburg, where I also worked, but after Hitler came to power, being a Jew, our lives changed. Our business was confiscated, and we were forced to wear the Star of David. We were vilified. Our friends turned against us; we were forced to beg for food. Fortunately, my father had some contacts and he paid them to get me and my sister across the border into Belgium. He managed to hide some of his stock and used that. He also gave me and my sister some gold which we used to get to England."

Agnes listened intently. "How terrible. How old were you?"

"I was thirty-three, my sister, thirty. At the time, I was engaged to be married to a local girl who I loved dearly, but she was not Jewish. Marriages between Jews and non-Jews were banned in Germany, so we separated; in fact, she turned against us."

"I'm so sorry. What happened when you got to England?"

"There is a Jewish community in London, and we help each other. We were taken in by a family and I managed to get a job in the theatre as a stagehand. Gradually, I gained more experience and met Cameron who treated me like a son. I shall never forget his kindness. If it wasn't for him, I'm not sure what I would have done. With Cameron's encouragement, I became an agent and co-producer, doing exactly what he was doing."

Agnes was taking in the information. "Are you married, Solly?"

"Yes, to a nice Jewish girl, Miriam." He smiled. "We have a daughter, just two years old."

"That's lovely, what's her name?"

"Ruth."

"And what about your sister?"

"She has a stall in the market in Camden, selling clothes. She employs three people now."

"She's doing well?"

"Yes, very well. She has her own house."

"What about your parents?"

His expression changed. "I have not heard from them for

a long time. Things for Jews are really bad in Germany. They have started deporting some to concentration camps. There <u>is</u> a neighbour, who is not a Jew, who used to be able to send messages, but I've not heard from him in three months."

"Oh, I'm so sorry."

He shrugged his shoulders and extended the palms of his hands. "It is life; I should not burden you with these stories."

"No, please continue; I have not heard of these things."

"No, the British Newspapers, they do not like to report them. It's not what English people want to read about at their breakfast table." His face a picture of resignation.

"Have you heard of *Kristallnacht?*"

"No, I can't say that I have."

"In English it means the Night of the Broken Glass. It was last November; it seemed the whole of the population turned against the Jews. The neighbour I mentioned wrote to me and told me about it. The Nazis, police, and Hitler's henchmen started attacking Jews. They smashed thousands of businesses, burned down over three hundred synagogues. Over ninety Jews were killed. Then there were the deportations - over thirty thousand the neighbour said."

"Oh, dear Lord, but why hasn't anyone done anything about it?"

He shrugged his shoulders again. "They are frightened of upsetting Hitler. They say it is a German problem."

"I don't know what to say," said Agnes.

"We have managed to get some more children out, the *Kindertransport* programme. Do you know it?"

"No," replied Agnes.

"So far around ten thousand children have been taken in by Britain."

"Well, at least we're doing something."

"Yes, but it is merely a drop in the ocean... But enough of

Alan Reynolds

this, I have detained you enough already. Are you happy to let Mr Laing have your telephone number?"

"Why, of course."

"In which case, I will call him this afternoon."

Solly called the waiter for the bill and the pair left the restaurant. Agnes had a lot on her mind.

Outside, it had started to rain, that cold rain that permeates the soul. Agnes and Solly waited in the doorway for a taxi. After five minutes, one appeared and Solly stepped out and flagged it down.

He opened the door and gave the driver a half-crown. Agnes gave the cabbie her address. "That should cover it."

"Thanks, Guv, that's very generous," responded the driver.

"Thank you, Solly. I'll be in touch."

Solly waved as the taxi drove away. Agnes pulled her coat around her; reflecting on her appointment. It had been very enlightening on many levels.

44

Chapter Four

Later that afternoon, Agnes was in the lounge discussing her meeting with Solly with her assistant, Mary, when the telephone rang.

"I'll get it," said Mary.

She left the room into the hall where the telephone was on a high table close to the front door.

"Bloomsbury 4 8 2," she answered as she picked up the heavy black receiver. She listened to the voice, then called Agnes. "It's someone from the BBC."

Mary passed the phone.

"Agnes Marsden speaking."

"Oh, hello, Miss Marsden, Robert Laing, Head of Light Entertainment, BBC, I understand from Mr Solomon that you might be available to perform at one of our forthcoming productions."

His voice sounded as though it was emanating from the radio; rich, with perfect diction, in an accent that would always be associated with the BBC.

"Yes, we discussed it this lunchtime. Can you give me more details?"

"Yes, of course, but why don't you join me here at Broadcasting House, say tomorrow morning, and I can tell you what we have in mind. I can show you the studios and you could also do a test."

"An audition, you mean?"

"Not exactly, I've been listening to some of your gramophone recordings, you have an excellent voice, but performing on radio is very different to working on the stage. Some artists are not suited to radio."

"Yes, I understand... What time?"

"Shall we say eleven o'clock?"

Alistair arrived home just after five o'clock. It was only five stops from Shepherd's Bush Tube station, which was close to his school, to West Acton, a ten-minute walk away from their home in Hereford Street.

"Hello dear, how was your day?" said Alistair, as he took off his coat. Agnes went into the hall to welcome him. They kissed warmly.

"Oh, it's been very interesting. I've so much to tell you. We can talk about it over dinner. How was your day?"

"It's been busy with exams coming up, plenty of assessments to do. There are some excellent musicians. I've been talking to the principle about putting on a concert at the end of term."

"What a good idea."

An hour later, they had been joined by daughter Gwen, and were having dinner. Agnes described her meeting with Solly Solomon.

"The conditions in Germany for the Jewish community sound dreadful. They are being persecuted and no-one does anything about it," said Agnes.

"Yes, I was talking to Matthew about it at the funeral. It seems Hitler has carte blanche to do whatever he wants."

"But why the Jews, that's what I can't understand?"

"Hitler blames them for all the problems in Germany for some reason."

"But that's no excuse for the treatment they are going through. Poor Solly's family, goodness knows what's happened to them. Imagine if that was our family."

"Yes, I completely agree, but there is very little we can do."

"It's all very sad."

"So, what was the meeting about?"

"Solly has offered me some work with the BBC."

"You're going to be on the wireless?" said Gwen, looking up from her hotpot.

Agnes looked at her. "Possibly, I had a phone call from someone at the BBC and they want me to go for a meeting tomorrow at Broadcasting House."

"Oh, how exciting," said Alistair. "How do you feel about it?"

"I'm not sure," replied Agnes, having finished her meal. "Cameron mentioned it in the past a few times, but that was before the wireless was as popular as it is now. At the time, I was cutting back on performances, just doing the gramophone records."

"Do you know what you will be doing?"

"Solly said it was a new weekly variety programme. They are looking for acts to fill the shows, but I'll know more tomorrow; I'm meeting the Head of Light Entertainment."

The following day, Agnes was dressed in one of her favourite dresses. There was a beep from outside as the taxi pulled up. Alistair was at work and Gwen at school; Agnes had given her assistant the day off as she would be out for most of it.

It was a bright winter's day and Agnes was wearing her mink coat and a silk scarf to ward off the chill. She was carrying her handbag and a leather briefcase containing her music. She left the house and approached the taxi.

"Broadcasting House, please," she said assertively, as she got into the back.

As the taxi made its way through the streets of West London, Agnes noticed the change in the skyline. Barrage Balloons were increasing in number and formed a strange umbrella over the capital. Agnes stared at the nearest silvery construction glimmering in the sunshine. Part of her felt comforted that there was some thought being given to protecting the public. The more sinister question, however, was why were they necessary? The threat of war appeared to be growing.

The taxi pulled up outside the famous building. Agnes paid the fare and stopped for a moment to look up at the rather austere frontage with its statue of Prospero and Ariel, and clock tower above. The top of the wireless mast was just visible from street level. She went inside and walked to the reception desk wondering how many famous people had crossed that threshold.

In keeping with the rest of the building, the atrium was magnificent with marble flooring and walls. Art deco-inspired lighting set in columns enclosed the space. To the left of the desk a recess with an enormous bunch of flowers.

The receptionist looked up in expectation.

"Agnes Marsden to see Robert Laing."

"Please take a seat," said the lady in a voice that mirrored the producer's.

There were several leather-covered benches against the adjoining wall. Agnes sat down and admired the interior design.

It was ten minutes before a tall, slim man in dark grey suit walked towards her from one of the side doors. He would be in his mid-forties and walked with the stride of a guardsman.

He walked up to Agnes and extended his hand. "Agnes Marsden...? Robert Laing, we spoke on the telephone." That smooth, eloquent voice.

Agnes stood up and shook hands. "Yes, indeed, pleased to meet you."

"Yes, you too. Please follow me."

The Broadcasting House on Portman Square was unique in that it had been specifically constructed as a broadcasting centre. There was an inner core which stretched the nine floors dedicated to production, totally soundproofed from outside noise. It included a concert hall and some smaller studios. Only a small part was dedicated to television which was still in its infancy.

"I have reserved Studio 8a; there's an accompanist standing by."

Agnes followed the man through the set of doors where he had entered the reception area. There was a long corridor ahead.

"This is the studio tower block," he explained, and they reached the lifts. He pressed the call button.

"The lift only goes to the seventh floor; we'll need walk the rest of the way."

Agnes was trying to take it all in. It was the very essence of art deco, with design pieces everywhere.

They entered the lift and Laing pressed the button. Lifts were installed in most of the large hotels and Agnes was familiar with them, but it was still an exhilarating experience as they rose quickly to the seventh floor.

They turned left out of the lift and walked along a short corridor and a wide flight of stairs. They were spaced at three feet intervals giving a gentle ascent. Agnes noticed a vase-like object as they approached a set of double doors.

"What's that?" enquired Agnes as they passed.

Laing smiled. "Ah that's an unspillable cigarette ash container. It's made from bronze."

"It's beautiful. I've not seen anything like that before."

They continued through the doors and reached the studio. Agnes surveyed the scene.

It was a large area with tubular steel-framed settees

covered in striped coral pink brocade around the perimeter. The floor was covered with cork tiles of various colours to absorb the sound. There was an area circled to indicate the positioning of an orchestra or band, behind that, a conductor's rostrum. The doors were painted bright green with polished aluminium fittings.

There was a grand piano in the corner and a man in a dress suit and dickie-bow tie leaning against it.

"Let me introduce you to Mart Hazelwood. He's the resident pianist for our concert orchestra."

They walked over to the man and the three shook hands. Laing turned to the musician.

"Let me introduce you to Agnes Marsden."

"Yes, I'm familiar with your work, Miss Marsden, a pleasure to meet you."

"Thank you, Mr Hazelwood."

"It's Mart, please call me Mart."

"Thank you, Mart."

Agnes was weighing up the pianist. Up close, he was younger than he first appeared, probably the same age as Agnes.

"Have you a thought of what you would like to sing?"

"I have brought a selection; I wasn't sure what would be appropriate. I particularly like that song from Porgy and Bess, 'Summertime', but I have many songs from my music tours."

"'Summertime' would be most satisfactory," interjected Laing. "Let's try that and see how it sounds. I just need to speak to the engineer."

Agnes handed over the music to the pianist. It was a song that she had sung with Alistair many times at their home. She took off her coat and placed it on the piano.

"I'll see to that for you," said Mart, and he picked it up

and took it to a series of hooks by the entrance door. There was just a raincoat hanging up and the pianist placed it next to it.

"Lovely coat, Miss Marsden," said the pianist as he walked back to the piano. Agnes acknowledged with a smile.

A few moments later, Laing appeared with a young man dressed in suit but minus a jacket which had been replaced by a pair of drab, ochre-coloured overalls.

There was a large, oblong-shaped microphone on a boom stand which the engineer manoeuvred into the correct position.

"Stand on the mark," ordered the technician. There was a yellow square on the floor just behind them.

Agnes complied.

Laing was supervising the exercise. He pointed to a light on the wall just next to the door where the engineer had entered.

"When you see that light turn red; that's your signal to start... Good luck."

Agnes composed herself, as Laing made himself comfortable on one of the settees.

Agnes cleared her throat, then looked at Laing. "Have you a glass of water, please?"

"Of course, one moment."

Laing left the room and returned a few minutes later with a glass and handed it to Agnes. She took a long sip and placed the glass on the piano.

"I'm ready," she said, looking at Laing.

The red light shone, and the pianist nodded at Agnes. After an eight-bar introduction, Agnes hit the note. Laing smiled.

Three minutes later, Agnes finished and looked at the producer.

"That was magnificent, Agnes, your reputation is well-founded. Let's go into the control room and listen to the play back."

They walked through the set of doors that the engineer had entered earlier. The engineer was waiting.

"How was it?" asked Laing.

"Listen for yourself," said the technician, and pressed a button on his consol. Agnes's voice echoed around the control room.

He had managed to capture Agnes's voice perfectly. There were smiles all around.

"Do you want me to sing anymore?" asked Agnes.

"No, that won't be necessary; that was excellent. Let's go down to my office and I'll talk you through what we have in mind."

Matthew Keating was in his office reading the latest intercepts. The good news was that, following the previous day's bombings, fourteen arrests had been made in connection with the attacks; seven in Manchester and seven in London. Eight hundred-weight barrels of potassium chlorate, a large quantity of powdered charcoal, and forty sticks of gelignite were also uncovered. The suspects were being interrogated in secret locations to deter any rescue attempt.

His telephone rang. "Yes, sir, right away," answered Matthew, and he made his way to his boss's office.

"Sit down, Major. Have you read the latest on the IRA?"

"Yes, encouraging news."

"Quite... Actually, I have a job for you. I want you to go to Dublin and meet with our agent there, Eoghan Fleming. Do you know him?"

"Only by reputation."

"Hmm, yes, an excellent agent, his reputation is well-deserved. Served in the Spanish Civil War, joined us last year. He was born in Waterford; his parents are Irish; he's been undercover for six months and has managed to join the IRA."

"That's brave of him."

"Yes it is."

"What's my brief?"

"We need to improve communications; at the moment it's very hit and miss. I want you to take a wireless with you. We've been reliant on telephone calls, and they are just not secure enough for what he's doing. If he's spotted using a public phone box there's every chance it could blow his cover."

"Yes, I can understand that but, out of interest, why can't we just send it via the Embassy as usual?"

"Hmm, it's simple; he doesn't trust the Embassy. Also, he says he has some information that he didn't want to discuss over the telephone which is why I suggested a meet."

"When do you need me to go?"

"As soon as possible, in the light of events; this will have to take priority."

"I'll get my secretary to sort out the travel arrangements and leave tomorrow. Did you discuss where to meet?"

"He's calling me back later. Let me know where you'll be staying, and he'll contact you at your hotel. He didn't want to discuss it over the phone. You'll need to be vigilant, Matthew; it could be dangerous. You must take every precaution."

"Yes, I do have a suitable cover in place."

"Excellent, in which case, let's meet again at four o'clock. In the meantime, let me know when you expect to arrive in Dublin."

By mid-afternoon, Matthew's travel arrangements had been made. He would catch the eight-thirty Irish Mail train from Euston, which would arrive in Holyhead at just after two o'clock. The train co-ordinated with the departing ferry for Kingstown, Dublin, at three o'clock, arriving around six-thirty. He would take a taxi to his hotel, The Clarence, on the banks of the River Liffey.

Matthew passed on the itinerary to Colonel Monkton to relay to the agent.

The following morning, he was at Euston station just after eight o'clock to catch his train. He was wearing a business suit, trilby, and carrying a small suitcase and what looked like a hamper; it appeared heavy. He hadn't been able to tell Grace where he was going, merely saying he would be back in a couple of days. Grace was used to his occasional trips abroad 'on business' but was still anxious until he returned. She had no idea of Matthew's true mission; she might have been more anxious than usual.

He reached the platform and watched as the first three carriages were being loaded with mail by a team of men from rows of trolleys. Post office personnel would be sorting the letters and parcels for most of the journey.

He walked down the train and found the first-class compartment, took his seat, and waited patiently for departure.

The journey to Holyhead was pleasant enough; Matthew's first-class ticket provided a modicum of comfort. There was a twenty-minute stop at Chester just after midday, to enable the engine to take on water and allow passengers to stretch their legs and find some refreshment. The station cafeteria was doing a roaring trade. Matthew was able to buy some sandwiches and a cup of tea.

The train pulled into Holyhead station just after two o'clock. Matthew collected his luggage from the overhead rack and made his way onto the platform. As he exited the compartment, opposite, he could see the side of a boat.

The station was enclosed with a canopy roof which retained the smoke from the engine making it grimy and claustrophobic. The platform was soon packed with people from all walks of life waiting embarkation.

There was a lot of jostling as the passengers queued for the gangplanks which would take them on board. Matthew looked around at his fellow travellers. He noticed a number of nuns grouped together chatting animatedly in Gaelic. There were many navvies, returning from working on building sites in the North West taking money home for their families; and of course, fellow businessmen. Like on all his business trips, he rarely fraternised; not a question of standoffishness, merely a need for discretion. He wanted to be as anonymous as possible; his life may depend on it.

There was one gangplank reserved for post office personnel who started ferrying sacks of mail onboard the ferry in relays, rather like soldier ants.

He eventually boarded and made his way below deck to find somewhere comfortable to spend the journey. His two pieces of luggage would not leave his side.

Matthew was on deck as the MV Hibernia eased its way into Kingstown harbour or, more correctly, Dún Laoghaire, to give it its local Gaelic name. It was just after six-thirty, dark and cold; a brisk wind rocked the ferry as it made its way to the berth. As he surveyed the lights of the approaching town, Matthew had a strange feeling. This was not a friendly environment. With the present political climate, there were many with anti-British sentiments.

There was a bump as the boat reached its docking point, throwing one or two unwary people to the floor. Stevedores secured the boat to the capstans. The area was illuminated by lampposts which led from the dock to the arrival gates.

He eventually made his way down to one of the gang planks and exited the ferry.

Although the Irish Republic was an independent country; it was still part of the British Empire and customs checks were somewhat dilatory; there were no passport checks. Matthew was waived through with no more than a nod by the waiting official.

Matthew followed the signs to the line of taxis to make the journey to his hotel.

He reached the next cab in line and announced his destination. "Clarence Hotel, please."

There was confirmation, and that was the last of any discourse. There was no attempt by the driver to make conversation, and Matthew would never initiate any.

It was around six miles to the hotel, through the streets of Dublin. Matthew viewed the anonymous streets; pavements were deserted. Very few people were out on this winter's evening. Around half an hour later, the taxi pulled up outside the Clarence Hotel.

As he got out of the taxi, Mathhew looked up. It was a large, brick-built building overlooking the river. The frontage was lit up with two large wall lights, creating shadows, giving it an eerie feel. The entrance was via a set of revolving doors. There was a sign, 'The Clarence Hotel', painted above it in gold lettering.

It was eight o'clock as he registered in his alias as Matthew Wood. He was allocated a room and a bellboy with a luggage trolly hovered to take his two suitcases. They made the journey to the fourth floor and along the corridor to his room. The lad opened the door and carefully placed Matthew's luggage next to the wardrobe. Matthew tipped him a six-pence and he left the room.

Matthew placed his raincoat and hat in the wardrobe and looked around the room; it would serve his purpose. His first priority was to get something to eat.

Not all hotels had internal telephone systems, but The Clarence did. He was about to call reception to make a reservation in the restaurant when the phone rang.

"Mr Wood, I have a message for you at reception."

"I'll be right down."

Matthew left his room and took the lift to the ground floor, then walked to reception.

"Matthew Wood, I believe you have a message for me, room 428."

The receptionist checked the pigeonhole and presented Matthew with a sealed envelope addressed in handwriting to Matthew Wood.

He retrieved the message and took a seat in the atrium.

'*Matthew, hope you had a good journey, I will meet you in the breakfast room at eight-thirty tomorrow morning.*'

Back in London, mid-afternoon, Grace was relaxing, reading a letter which had arrived earlier from her dear friend, Hetty, her closest companion during her time working as an ambulance driver for the First-aid Nursing Yeomanry, colloquially know as 'Fannies'.

They had kept in touch after the war, albeit infrequently. Throughout the war, they had been through some terrifying experiences together, ferrying injured soldiers from the trenches to the hospital where they were based in Calais. Grace was always pleased to hear from her.

Hetty continued working for the Fannies until 1918 with

distinguished service and was awarded medals, both British and Belgian, in acknowledgement of the role she had played in supporting the troops.

After the war, she returned to her native Kent and the small village of Selling where her mother had a rented cottage. Her father had been the local vicar until his untimely death and Hetty, her mother, and brother moved from the vicarage to the church-owned cottage. Hetty's brother was a gifted mathematician and after the war, earned a scholarship to Cambridge.

During the summer of 1919, Hetty spent most of her time helping on one of the local hop-farms owned by Duncan Crouch, a traditional family-run farm that had been in the Crouch family for several generations. He was a widower, having lost his wife to tuberculosis in 1917 and, during the course of that summer, Hetty became a frequent visitor to the house, helping on the farm and looking after Duncan's five-year-old daughter, Chloe.

Duncan was almost twenty years older than Hetty, but she enjoyed his company and when he asked her to marry him, without too much conviction it should be said, she didn't hesitate in accepting his proposal.

Over the years, the farm dominated Hetty's life, and she immersed herself in every part of the business. By 1939, with her husband now in his late sixties, she had taken over the day-to-day running with support from her stepdaughter, Chloe. Duncan and Hetty had not been blessed with children, but she doted on her stepdaughter, and they made a great team.

Grace read the latest news, with interest, then the final paragraph.

'Before I sign off, old thing, I have a request. I need to visit my solicitor in town shortly and would dearly wish that

we could meet as I have some news I need to impart which is not appropriate in a letter. Please say you will be available. I will call you from the village telephone box on Monday 23rd to confirm my travel arrangements. Much love, Hetty.'

Saturday January 21st, The Clarence Hotel, Dublin. Matthew walked through reception to the breakfast room carrying the 'hamper'.

He scanned the restaurant, looking for his contact. Matthew was dressed formally in his suit, maintaining his cover as a businessman; he assumed his contact would similarly be apparelled.

He noticed a smart-looking man eating on his own in the corner of the room, well away from other diners. He looked at Matthew and nodded.

Matthew walked across the breakfast room which, at this time on a weekend, was sparsely populated. The man stood up and offered his hand.

"Eoghan Fleming."

"Matthew Wood, please to meet you."

They shook hands and took their seats. Matthew put the hamper under the table.

"Nice to meet you too. How was the journey yesterday?" enquired Fleming.

"Uneventful, I'm pleased to say."

"Is that the package I've been expecting?"

"Yes, it is. The office has asked that you make a test transmission tonight at six o'clock. I believe you are familiar with this model. They will be expecting you."

"Aye, that I can. How are things in London? I hear they've started putting up barrage balloons; a strange state of affairs, so it is."

"The Government think it will give the population a

signal that we are prepared if the worst comes to the worst, while Chamberlain and Halifax try to work out a route to peace."

"You think that's likely?"

"Honestly? No, I don't. The intelligence assessment suggests Hitler will invade the rest of Czechoslovakia within the next two months, and then, I believe, he'll turn his attention to Poland."

Matthew looked at his new acquaintance. He was barely in his early thirties if that. He appeared sharp, with fair hair and blue eyes, which were alert and attentive. He was clearly a good listener, an important attribute for an agent. He was intelligent in his questioning and assessed responses before replying. His Irish brogue was soft and understated. Matthew was impressed.

"Aye, I can see that, and so can the boyos round here." He leaned forward. "The Republican sympathisers see this as an opportunity."

"Yes, I'm sure they do, but the general feeling in London is, the activity on the mainland is more about raising the profile of the IRA. They can't seriously believe they can wage this so-called war and win, surely?"

"Some are misguided enough to believe it can bring about a united Ireland, so they do. The targets are infrastructure, but I suppose you've worked that out."

"Yes, it was a pretty obvious target. Needless to say, security has been increased."

"I would expect nothing less."

A waitress walked to their table and took their breakfast order. Her name badge said 'Móirín'.

She left the pair and Matthew noticed Fleming looking around the room. There was no-one in close proximity. Fleming reached inside his jacket and pulled out an A5 envelope and discretely slid it across the table to Matthew.

"This is what you came for. You must guard it with your life and don't get caught with it on your person, whatever you do. It will likely get both of us killed."

Matthew put it inside his jacket, and leaned forward, his voice just above a whisper.

"Don't worry, it will be quite safe. 'C' mentioned you managed to get yourself recruited. How did you achieve that?"

"Well, it's not so difficult if you know the right places. There are a few bars where they tend to congregate."

"Yes, but there must be some vetting process, surely. They'll be on the lookout for infiltrators, especially at the moment."

"Aye, that's true enough. I got to know one or two of the lads and offered to get involved with some posters and leaflets, and that was that. I've been to a few meetings, which I've detailed in the envelope, names, places."

Matthew looked at him sternly. "The big concern in London is any German interest."

"Aye, I'm aware of that possibility, and it has been discussed, so it has, but I don't have any evidence just yet."

A door opened on the far side of the room and Móirín approached holding two plates of food. A napkin on each hand protected her fingers from the hot plates. She reached the table then served the pair with their breakfast and returned to the kitchen.

They started to eat.

Eoghan resumed the conversation. "One thing I should mention; there are a few names on there of active members on the mainland. If you decide to arrest them, don't do it all at once; it will be obvious there's a leak. If you take them one by one, they will assume one of those arrested has talked."

"Yes, of course, I'll see to it."

Móirín returned to the kitchen. The chef was at the oven holding a frying pan cooking more eggs.

She went up to him and whispered. "There're are a couple of gents in the breakfast room; at least, one of them's a Brit; the other might be Irish."

"Show me," said the chef and he went to the port-hole shaped window in the access door to the restaurant. He peered through and scanned the room.

"In the corner," said Móirín.

"Yes, I can see them," said the chef.

"What do you want to do?" asked the waitress.

"Can you look after these eggs?" He left the frying pan he was holding. "I need to make a phone call."

A few minutes later, he returned to the kitchen.

"What's the craic?" asked Móirín.

"They're going to send a taxi."

Matthew and the agent finished their breakfast.

"So, what are you going to do today?" asked Eoghan.

"I hadn't thought. It's my first time in Dublin; I may take in an art gallery or museum."

"Well, if you take my advice, you'll go back to your room, read the newspaper, and then head for Dunlearie."

"Dunlearie...? Is that how it's pronounced?"

"Aye... there's another Irish Mail boat leaving at two o'clock; make sure yer on it. The sooner yer out of here, the better."

Matthew looked at Eoghan with a quizzical look. "As bad as that?"

"Aye, so it is."

He looked around the restaurant; it was empty.

"Right, I'll be off."

Eoghan stood up and shook Matthew's hand.

"Thanks for everything, Eoghan. I'll take your advice. I'll get my things together and get a taxi. We'll keep in touch."

"Aye, that we will. Have a safe journey back."

Eoghan picked up the hamper and left the restaurant. Móirín was watching from the kitchen porthole.

"One of them's leaving; I think it's the Irishman."

"They won't have got the taxi ready yet. They'll wait for the Brit; he's our main target," said the chef.

"I wonder what the meeting was all about," said Móirín.

"Well, if the boyos catch the Brit, I think they'll find out. They can be very persuasive."

"Aye, to be sure," said Móirín.

Matthew got up and left the restaurant with the agent's words ringing in his ear. On reflection, he had been naïve but, of course, Eoghan was right. He took the lift to his room and retrieved his suitcase from the wardrobe. It had a false bottom and Matthew secreted the agent's envelope before sealing it and packing his clothes.

He checked his watch, nine thirty-four, plenty of time to get to the ferry. He would feel safer there.

Outside the front of the hotel, there was a line of three taxis. An Austin 16 turned the corner from an adjoining side street and parked in front of the leading car. There followed an altercation with the driver from the cabbie who had been waiting at the head of the line for a fare for some time. The driver from the Austin got out and walked up to the man. There appeared to be an understanding as the cabbie put up his hands in acknowledgement. Money had changed hands.

Ten minutes later, Matthew appeared, wearing his customary raincoat, trilby hat, shiny black shoes, and three-piece suit. He was carrying his luggage. He couldn't have looked more English if he had been carrying a placard.

It was a cold and dreary morning.

He looked at the line of cars. The driver of the recently arrived taxi got out and approached him.

"You'll be wanting a taxi, so you will. Let me take this for yas."

"Yes, thank you, the ferry port at Dunlearie."

"I'll just put this in the back," said the cab driver. "Take a seat, why don't yas?"

He opened the door to the seats behind the driver and took Matthew's suitcase. The cabbie opened the boot, stowed the luggage, then closed the back door.

Straightaway, Matthew noticed something strange. The handles in both rear car doors had been removed, just the spindles were visible on both sides. It meant they could only be opened from the outside.

The driver got in; the engine was already running, and the taxi pulled away.

The Clarence Hotel is on Wellington Quay, in the Temple Bar area of the city, south of the river. The taxi headed west with the Liffey on the right-hand side, looking brown and unappealing as the car travelled parallel to it.

Matthew knew they would need to go south to the ferry port. Instead, the taxi turned right and crossed the Gratton Bridge, heading north.

Something wasn't right. He leaned forward.

"I say, driver, we're going the wrong way," announced Matthew.

"No, to be sure, this is a better way," replied the driver.

Chapter Five

Matthew wasn't convinced. He thought quickly and leaned forward again.

"I need to go back to the hotel. I think I've left something behind."

"Sorry, that won't be possible, so it won't. Sit back and make yerself comfortable. We're just going to take a little drive. There's some people who would like to meet yas."

The message was clear. Matthew was considering his options; he wasn't sure if there were any.

He looked out of the car window trying to look for possible landmarks. The city sprawl gradually gave way to more open spaces. They passed All Hallows College on the right, then Gaeltacht Park on the left, still heading north. Then, it was mostly fields and woods; they had left the city and were in bleak countryside.

Earlier, about a hundred yards from the hotel entrance, another anonymous car was parked, the driver observing through a pair of binoculars. He saw Matthew exit the hotel and being ushered into the taxi. Something didn't look right.

Eoghan got out of the car and wound the starting handle. The black Hillman Minx roared into life. This was the same model that had won the Monte Carlo Rally the previous year and as quick as any saloon car on the road.

Eoghan ducked down as the taxi passed the stationary Hillman. He got into the driver's seat and pulled away in pursuit of the rather modest Austin. Keeping a suitable distance, it soon became clear that the destination was not going to be the ferry terminal.

He was quite familiar with the roads of Dublin and

realised straightaway that the 'taxi' was heading north, possibly to the border. There were numerous farms in the area that would be a suitable destination for a kidnapped Brit; especially one as important as Matthew Wood/Keating.

They were on the Dublin to Drogheda road, one that Eoghan had used on many occasions. Although a main route towards the border, road traffic was relatively light, car ownership was the province of the wealthy. It was predominantly commercial traffic that frequented the roads.

Eoghan had been following the taxi for about twenty-five minutes and was trying to formulate a rescue plan. There was a small delivery van between him and the Austin, which on the one hand would obscure his visibility, but it was slow moving and the Austin was starting to pull away.

They had reached a long straight stretch of road just before the small town of Ballough. Right and left were just fields, and the area was flat and featureless. Suddenly, the Austin turned right. Luckily, Eoghan had seen it.

It was more a farm track than a made road, maybe wide enough for one and a half vehicles. Eoghan followed, recognising any action would have to happen soon before they reached the assumed farmhouse. Eoghan floored the Hillman and was soon right behind the Austin. The verges were low which enable him to pull alongside and then in front.

The driver had not seen him until the last minute, but Matthew had, and leaned forward and grabbed the man around the neck and pulled him upwards. The cabbie let go of the steering wheel and started flaying his arms trying to release Matthew's grip. The Austin swung left and right, out of control. Eoghan could see what was happening and nudged the Austin sideways into an adjoining field where it ground to a stop.

Eoghan pulled up and ran to the Austin where the driver and Matthew were still grappling. He opened the taxi door, removed a revolver from his back pocket and shot the driver in the head. Blood sprayed everywhere. The man stopped moving.

"Right, Matthew, we need to get yas away. Grab yer stuff and let's get out of here before the boyos find out what's happened."

Matthew was on full alert, adrenaline levels off the scale. He wiped blood off his face with his pocket handkerchief and exited the car, then retrieved his suitcase.

"What about the body?" asked Matthew as he got into the Hillman.

"We don't have time to bother about that; we need to get you to that ferry. There'll be people looking for yas."

Matthew retrieved his suitcase, put it on the back seat, and joined Eoghan in the front of the Hillman. Eoghan turned it around and headed back to the main road.

The carriageway was deserted as he turned left towards the city. He hoped he hadn't been spotted.

"Thank you for your timely intervention," said Matthew as he started to calm down. "How did you know?"

The Hillman was now making sixty miles an hour but would soon be caught up in the city traffic.

"I wasn't taking any chances; I wanted to see yer safely away. I recognised the car; I've seen it before. It belongs to one of the lads, Seamus O'Leary. Sure, it was him who was driving. It's not the first time they've kidnapped a Brit. None of them have ended well."

"I'm very grateful."

"Well, let's get you safely to the ferry, then yer can thank me. Once they discover the body, things could start moving quickly."

They reached the city and crossed the Liffey, continuing south. Matthew was only now beginning to come to terms with what had happened. He checked his raincoat; there were spatters of blood down the right-hand sleeve but not immediately noticeable.

"I've got blood all over my raincoat; I'll need somewhere to change."

Eoghan looked across. "Aye, yer shirt collar looks like yer cut yerself shaving, so it does. You'll need to change when yer get the chance."

Eoghan turned the Hillman into a side street. "I've got an idea."

He pulled to a stop. "Take off yer coat; you can have mine."

Eoghan was wearing a topcoat and casual jacket which looked as though it had seen better days.

They made the switch. "You'll need to ditch the trilby, too; yer can have my cap."

As exchanges go, it was heavily weighted in Eoghan's favour, but it made sense. It had at least toned-down Matthew's 'Englishness'.

It was twenty minutes later as they approached the port at Dunlearie.

"I'll drop yer at the passenger gate; yer should be safe enough. Then I need to disappear for a while, but I'll call tonight." He looked around to make sure no-one was in earshot. "Whatever yer do, don't visit the pub over the road; that's a favourite meeting place for the boyos." He nodded in the direction of The Red Lion; a 'spit and sawdust' establishment directly opposite the entrance.

"Thank you for everything; I owe you my life. I won't be back in time to pick up your call this evening, but I'll be in tomorrow."

"Aye, well yer keep yerself safe, and make sure yer keep a watchful eye out; yer not out the woods yet. They'll probably work out you'll be heading for the boat."

"Yes, will do."

Matthew exited the car and collected his suitcase from the boot, waved to the agent, and headed into the crowded terminal. He stopped for a moment and watched Eoghan's car turn and accelerate away.

The large clock in the departure hall said eleven twenty-five. Although embarkation would not be for another hour and a half, it was already busy.

He looked around his fellow passengers. With his cap and coat, his new disguise made him look like a race-horse trainer. He didn't stand out sufficiently for people to take notice.

There was a kiosk selling sandwiches and tea which had attracted a lengthy queue. He would need something for the boat. He joined the line and raised his collar of his coat to hide the bloodstains on his shirt.

Ten minutes later, he was in the corner of the departure lounge waiting for boarding, keeping a watchful eye for anything that might pose danger.

Eventually, passengers were called to embark, and Matthew breathed a sigh of relief. He reached one of the gangplanks and slowly climbed on board the MV Munster. As he reached the top he looked back and could see three men towards the back of the gangplank queues; they appeared to be jostling other passengers, checking their faces. He quickly went inside.

It was one o'clock and there was an hour to go before the ship was due to sail. Matthew had no idea whether any of the three men had been allowed on board, but he couldn't rule it out.

Just before two o'clock, there were shouts and a loud blast from the boat's foghorn as the gangplanks were removed and the ferry slowly left the dock.

Matthew went up on deck and watched as the harbour slowly retreated from view. There was no sign of activity.

The journey was stressful. Matthew could not be certain whether any of the men, presumably looking for him, were on board, and he remained on full alert. At least his new disguise made him less conspicuous.

It was with some relief as the boat entered the Holyhead berth, and Matthew made his way to the exit points. There was a bump as the boat reached the dock and within minutes, the gangplanks were being lowered. Again, the mail train was waiting, and men were quickly moving sacks of letters and parcels from the ferry to the waiting train, passing them down a long chain.

Matthew walked down the wooden walkways to the dockside and headed for the waiting train. The platform was crowded with passengers. He quickly found the First-Class compartment which was serviced by a corridor with a toilet at the end. Despite disapproving looks from his fellow travellers, he found a seat and made himself comfortable for the journey to London with a sigh of relief. He couldn't help thinking about Eoghan and his bravery.

It was eleven-thirty as Matthew felt the train engine slow as it entered Euston. There was a final hiss of steam as it came to a stop at the buffers. Matthew picked up his suitcase and left the compartment.

He felt drained after the trauma in Dublin and, although

he had tried to sleep on the train, it proved impossible. He took one of the waiting taxis and arrived home just after midnight, there was a welcoming light shining behind the front door.

He took his keys from his pocket and entered. He took off his coat that the Dublin agent had given him and hung it on one of the coat hooks along with the cap. The jacket reeked of smoke.

"Hello darling."

A soothing voice came from the sitting room, quickly followed by Grace's appearance. They were quickly engulfed in a long hug.

"Come into the sitting room, the fire's lit; it's warmer, and you can tell me all about it. Would you like a drink?"

"Yes, please, dear, I think I'll have a large Scotch."

Matthew took off his shoes and followed Grace into the sitting room where she was standing at the open bureau pouring a glass of whiskey from the drinks cabinet.

The heavy curtains and Art Deco table lights created a homely atmosphere; one which Matthew thought at one stage he would never see again.

Grace handed Matthew his drink which he consumed in one go.

"As bad as that?" said Grace.

"Yes, it was."

He sat down on the settee and Grace joined him and held his hand.

"Do you want to talk about it?"

"I can't unfortunately." He placed his head in his hands and breathed deeply.

"Is that a new coat I saw?"

"Yes, it belongs to the man I went to meet in Dublin; we had to do a swap."

"I think you came off second in that deal," she said and smiled.

"I think you could be right."

Grace looked at him more closely. "What's that on your shirt... and your neck? It looks like blood. Are you hurt?"

"No, no, I'll go and wash as soon as I've finished this," said Matthew lifting up his glass.

"Are you sure you don't want to talk about it?"

"I can't darling, I'm sorry, but I'm fine. There's nothing to worry about."

The following morning, not far away in Bloomsbury, Agnes had just come off the telephone with the BBC Producer. Her face beamed as she turned to Mary, her assistant.

"They want me to go for rehearsals on Thursday with the broadcast on Friday," she exclaimed. "I must tell Mam; she'll be so thrilled. I'll telephone her later."

Around eleven o'clock, there was a knock on the front door. Mary went to open it.

"There's a gentleman to see you," said Mary as she returned to the sitting room. A smart looking man was following her.

"Solly! What a wonderful surprise, please come in. I was going to telephone you later; I have some news. Would you like a drink?"

He was wearing a raincoat. He took off his Trilby hat and started fiddling with the rim, a nervous habit. "A tea would be most welcome, thank you."

Mary was dispatched to the kitchen. "Please take off your coat and take a seat... How are you?"

Solly removed his mackintosh and folded it. Agnes stood up, took it from him and put it over the back of one of the chairs with his hat on top. "I'll get Mary to see to that in a moment."

Agnes returned to her seat directly opposite Solly.

"So, what brings you here this morning?"

"Well, I, too, have some news and given our conversation the other day, I wanted to share it with you."

Just then, Mary arrived with the tea, milk, and cups and saucers on a tray.

"Can you see to Solly's coat, please?" asked Agnes, as Mary put the tray down onto a coffee table.

Mary picked up Solly's coat and Trilby and left the room. Agnes started to pour the tea.

"So, what's the news?" she asked.

"No, no, you go first. Is it about your meeting with Robert Laing?"

"Yes, it is. He telephoned me earlier, and he wants me for rehearsals on Thursday for the programme on Friday."

"Oh, that is good news. I did speak to Robert, and he was saying how very impressed he was with your singing."

"Oh, that's very kind."

Agnes took a sip of tea. "So, your news?"

Solly looked over the top of his teacup. "I told you about my parents back in Germany."

"Yes you did, so sad."

"Well, this morning I had a letter from an old neighbour in Germany." Solly took out a grubby envelope from his jacket pocket and showed it to Agnes. "It's in German but I can translate it for you."

Solly opened the envelop and removed the letter. The writing was in pencil and very faint; Solly squinted to read it.

"He says that my parents are now in Düsseldorf; Duisburg was too dangerous. He says they are hiding in a basement of a house owned by a... er... sympathiser. He says it's very dangerous... er... the police are rounding up all the Jews they can find and sending them away. Anyone found sheltering them... are, it says here, arrested with their families." Solly looked up at Agnes, his faced etched with sorrow.

"What can you do?" asked Agnes.

"I don't know. I've been talking to people in the Jewish community here. There are many families in the same situation. We are trying to find ways of getting them across the border into Belgium."

"How long ago was the letter written?"

"It was two weeks ago, even getting letters out now is difficult, but at least I know they are alive."

"I don't know what to say, Solly. What are you going to do?"

"I've been talking to a group of people in the community. They have formed a committee to try to get as many out of Germany as they can. Many of them are like me and have relatives trapped. We are going to start raising money to pay for transportation... and possibly bribes, if that's what it takes."

"Well, if I can help in any way, please let me know."

"That is most kind, Agnes."

Solly finished his tea and he made to get up.

"Did you know Hitler has just issued an order forbidding any Jew from practicing as chemists, veterinarians and dentists? It was in the newspaper."

"Why on earth would he do that? Surely they need those."

"Who knows what goes through the mind of that madman. Anyway, I've taken enough of your time. I just wanted to give you the news."

"Thank you for calling and don't forget, if there's anything I can do to help, just let me know."

Agnes walked Solly to the front door. "Thank you, and for the tea," said Solly, and put on his coat and hat. "I will be listening on Friday... I wish you good luck."

"Thank you Solly, and don't forget what I said."

"No, that's very kind."

Solly walked out into the cold wet day leaving Agnes with numerous thoughts.

"What do you think you can do?" asked Mary, who was clearing away the teacups.

"I don't know but I will speak to Alistair tonight."

The following day, despite it being a Sunday, by seven-forty-five, Matthew was exiting St James's Park Underground Station. It was quiet; the usual weekday bustle was gone, replaced by a comfortable melee of mostly early-morning tourists. He needed the walk to refresh his senses. The weather was cool, but bright. Unsurprisingly, he had not slept well and felt heady.

He arrived at Broadway Buildings just after eight o'clock, dressed in a fresh shirt, his usual suit, a replacement raincoat, and his spare trilby hat. He showed his pass to the receptionist and made his way downstairs to the basement offices where the secret service teams worked.

He entered the outer office which was, as usual, alive with activity. The incessant sound of women toiling away on typewriters, raised the voice levels of conversation to just below a shout. Smoke hung in the air from the numerous cigarettes that had already been consumed.

Matthew entered his office, took off his coat and hat, and started to empty the contents of his briefcase.

He was quickly joined by his secretary.

"How was your trip?" she asked in a voice considered 'posh' by those from Matthew's heritage. She put a pile of correspondence and cypher decrypts on his desk.

"Eventful, thank you Janet," replied Matthew.

"Colonel Monkton has asked to see you as soon as you arrived," said the secretary. "We weren't sure whether you would be in or not this morning. We've received a message from 'Night Wing'; he called last night."

"That's good to know," replied Matthew, looking at her.

A few minutes later, Matthew was seated in front of his immediate superior drinking tea from China cups.

"So, an eventful journey, I heard?" asked the Director.

"Somewhat," euphemised Matthew. "But we did manage to complete the transaction." Matthew handed over the envelope supplied by the Dublin agent. "I understand Night Wing made contact last evening."

"Yes, he said that you had been compromised but had made an escape."

"Hmm, yes, but for his intervention, the situation could have ended differently. He has put himself in grave danger."

"Yes, it would seem so. I did offer to pull him out, but he insisted he would stay... Is that the envelope?"

"Yes," said Matthew and handed it over to the Colonel. "He did say that we should be careful in releasing the names to the police. If we were to arrest everyone named, then it would be obvious that there had been a leak."

"Yes, I agree entirely, but several arrests have already been made, so I can't see it being an issue. I suggest we study the names and I'll speak to the Head of Special Branch."

"Excellent... What's the latest? Have there been any more bombings?"

"No, but yesterday the police found an unexploded package of gelignite and an alarm clock timer attached to an electricity pylon, in Lancashire somewhere. It seemed the alarm clock had stopped, and the bomb didn't detonate."

"Well, that's some good news."

"Yes it is." The commander leaned forward with an earnest expression. "Matthew, I want you to keep tabs on Night Wing; his position sounds precarious. Don't hesitate to pull him out if things get a bit sticky."

"Yes, of course... There's still the question of possible Germany involvement in this whole business; it's something that really concerns me. Unfortunately, there's no hard evidence, which in itself is frustrating. Night Wing said it is something that had been discussed within IRA hierarchy. I'm not sure if he'll be able to get any further information, given the recent course of events. I do have people working on it."

"Yes, that concerns me too, especially if they are the ones providing the weapons and explosives."

Friday, 27th January.

Agnes arrived at Broadcasting House at three-thirty, carrying her performance-wear in a special cloth cover, to start final rehearsals and recording of her first radio broadcast.

After her earlier audition, she noticed that her voice had felt tight, having not sung for a while, and was concerned it would affect her performance. She called Robert Laing, and, at his suggestion, she had spent a session with the BBC's voice coach on Wednesday. It had been a revelation. Agnes had never had any formal training. As she told the coach, she just sang. After singing a couple of songs, she was given different exercises which would help her breathing.

There was a sadness in the country following the capsizing of the St Ives lifeboat which had taken her eight crew. The newspapers and radio news broadcasts were full of the tragedy; it put life into some sort of perspective.

Alan Reynolds

Agnes was determined to try to change the atmosphere and had chosen some upbeat tunes.

She felt nervous as she reached the Concert Hall. The run-through the previous day had gone well, and the producer was effusive in his praise for Agnes. Today felt different; there was a tense atmosphere. Robert Laing was anxiously rushing around checking every detail. Cigarette smoke hung in the air as musicians calmed themselves with a nicotine hit while they tuned up in the main auditorium. One or two had resorted to hip flasks.

This would be a 'live' transmission; there were no recording facilities, in front of an invited audience of around five hundred people, chosen at random from the thousands of letters that had been received by the BBC asking for tickets.

The broadcast was going out at seven-thirty when millions of radios across the country would be tuned in to listen to the new variety show, which had been regularly promoted on other programmes.

The transmission would run for an hour and include comedians, a ventriloquist, and singers, plus popular tunes of the day played by the BBC Concert Orchestra.

The BBC Concert Hall takes up three floors of Broadcasting House and, in keeping with the remainder of the building, was adorned with art deco furnishings. The whole of the flooring, including the orchestra area was carpeted to ensure the acoustics were not significantly altered by the number of people in the audience. To accommodate them, they would be seated in two tiers - 'stalls' and 'balcony'. Lighting hung from metal gantries suspended from the ceiling, while an array of microphones were positioned around the orchestra. Three large ones were at the front to be used by the performers.

After a final run-through, Agnes returned to the 'green

room', where the artists could relax while waiting their turn to perform. Again, it was heavy with cigarette smoke as the performers helped themselves to various sandwiches, snacks, and drinks that had been provided for them. She noticed someone in a business suit who seemed to be carrying a small child; it looked very strange. Then she twigged; it was the ventriloquist. He noticed her looking in his direction and walked towards Agnes.

"Hello, you must be Agnes, we didn't get chance to meet properly at rehearsal. Let me introduce you to Maisy Day."

Suddenly, Agnes found herself engaging with the cute-looking dummy. Harry Took, the ventriloquist, was a seasoned pro and had been on radio many times. They were interrupted by one of the producer's assistants who introduced herself as Judith.

Judith was a jaunty character and spoke in the same tones as her boss. It seemed to be a requirement to work at the BBC.

"Agnes? Follow me, I'll show you to your dressing room. Someone will be down to do your makeup," said Judith.

She led Agnes down a short corridor which had rooms down each side. One or two had names which Agnes recognised straight away. These would belong to the compere, and the headline act who was one of the country's top comedians. The next one also had a name attached. Agnes couldn't believe her eyes. 'Agnes Marsden', it said.

Agnes was ushered inside, and they were quickly joined by a makeup artist. Agnes was reminded of the early days on her concert tours, but it had been a while since she had had so much attention.

Twenty minutes later, Agnes was ready, dressed in one of her 'glamorous' frocks which she had had especially made for her. She was led back to the green room by the makeup artist. The compere was chatting animatedly with Robert Laing, the producer; it didn't appear a friendly exchange. Tensions were high. The orchestra were in one corner, dressed in evening suits and bow ties. The large clock on the wall indicated ten minutes to go; the red light next to it was unlit.

There was a man talking to one of the assistants who Agnes recognised, and she approached him. He turned and his face beamed a smile. "Solly, what are you doing here?" asked Agnes.

"I came to give you some support. I thought you might want a friendly face on your first radio broadcast."

"Oh, that is sweet of you, yes, thank you."

The room was a buzz of conversation as the artists and musicians congregated together waiting anxiously for the call.

With ten minutes to go, the stage manager announced the orchestra to take their places and the room was soon emptied of half its occupants.

Solly continued to chat to Agnes as the musicians had a final tune-up. There was an air of expectancy and hum of chatter from the audience who were now seated, and the doors closed. The stage manager stood in front of the lead microphone and called for quiet as the clock on the wall indicated two minutes. An announcer was stood at a rostrum in the wings studying a sheet of paper. He was mouthing words as if rehearsing.

The clock ticked by; the second hand moving inexorably around the dial.

One minute.

The stage manager started counting down and switched on the red light.

"Three, two, one."

He pointed to Mart Hazelwood who immediately started conducting the orchestra for the introductory music. The announcer did his voice over.

"Welcome to the BBC Variety Show; an hour of light entertainment presented by your genial host... Arthur Bosworth."

It was the poshest of 'posh' voices.

The orchestra played a bouncy introductory tune as the flamboyantly dressed host entered the stage to rapturous applause, encouraged enthusiastically by the stage manager conducting the audience.

Back in Blossom Cottage, Mildred, Ivy, and her daughter, Daisy, were huddled around the radio waiting for Agnes. They were anxious as they listened to the various entertainers. Eventually, Agnes's name was called and there was enthusiastic applause as she took to the stage. With time limited, her performance was restricted to two songs. She started with her present favourite, the one she had done in the audition, 'Summertime'.

Tears streaked down Mildred's face as daughter Agnes's voice echoed around the room.

"Oh, Mam, she sounds so good," said Daisy to Ivy, as Agnes finished her first number.

"I wish Arthur could be here to hear her," said Ivy.

You could hear a pin drop as Agnes introduced her next song.

"Doesn't she sound posh?" said Ivy. They laughed.

Back at the BBC, Agnes finished her two songs and there was a standing ovation as she left the stage.

The flamboyant host returned to the microphone and thanked Agnes for her 'superb performance' before telling a couple of stories and announcing the finale, the popular comedian, Jack Denny.

In the green room, there were celebratory hugs from the performers as the announcer read out the final credits and the red light was extinguished.

"You were magnificent, Agnes," enthused Solly.

"Thank you, Solly," she replied.

Agnes was soon surrounded by other performers.

When the hubbub had subsided, Solly took Agnes to one side. "Agnes, I wanted to take up your offer of help, if you would be so kind."

"Yes, of course, anything I can do."

"I have in mind a concert to raise money; maybe your husband would also be available."

"Yes, that sounds a splendid idea."

"I will call round next week, and we can discuss it further; I can see you're busy at the moment."

The production assistant was hovering waiting to speak to Agnes.

"Yes, of course, telephone me first, and I will make sure I'm available."

Solly walked away allowing Judith to escort Agnes back to the dressing room to change.

A few minutes later, there was a knock on her door. Agnes was removing her makeup and Judith answered.

"Come in, Mr Laing, Agnes has nearly finished."

The producer entered. "Sorry to disturb you, Agnes. I just wanted to say 'well done' on your performance tonight; the audience response has been extremely positive. I wanted to ask if you will be available for more shows. I have in mind you could be our resident singer. What do you think? We are thinking of asking listeners to write in requesting songs for you to sing."

Agnes looked at Laing via the mirror.

"I'm lost for words, Robert; that would be a wonderful idea."

"Excellent, I will get my secretary to telephone you and confirm some dates. I would also like to arrange a feature in The Radio Times by way of advertisement, if you would be so kind."

"Yes, that would be most acceptable."

"Excellent," he repeated. "I'll arrange a photographer and interviewer for early next week."

It was gone ten o'clock before Agnes arrived home, her head still reeling from what had happened. The talk of a regular spot on the show was beyond her wildest dreams and she was finding it difficult to take in. She couldn't wait to tell the family.

Alistair and Gwen were waiting for her as the taxi pulled up outside the house. Alistair, having heard the cab arrive outside, opened the door for her to save her searching her handbag for her keys.

"Hello, darling," he said, as he ushered her inside.

They kissed.

She hung her dress on one of the coat pegs. Gwen joined her father. "Mam, you were so good."

"Thank you, did it sound alright?" said Agnes, as she followed the family into the sitting room.

"Oh, yes, perfect," replied Alistair. "Let me get you a drink and you can tell us all about it. The telephone hasn't stopped ringing. Grace sends her love; she said she'll call you tomorrow."

Alistair went to the bureau and poured a small measure of brandy and a similar amount of whiskey in two cut glasses.

"Oh, I need this," said Agnes, as he handed her the

brandy. "I don't know where to start."

Chapter Six

The following day, Saturday, back in Keighley there was only one topic of conversation in the bakery.

"Did tha hear our Auntie Aggie on t'radio?" asked William, as he brought the first batch of loaves into the shop ready for stacking.

"Oh aye, she were so good, our Mam had tears in her eyes," said Doris Tanner, one of the two regular assistants.

"Of course, tha Mam used to know Aunt Aggie," replied William.

"Aye, she used to call in when she lived at the Hall before she went to London. In fact, I took over from her in the shop when she started her first tour. I were only just turned fifteen," said Ruth, taking the basket of bread from William. She turned to Doris. "It were just me and tha Mam serving in t'shop back then."

"Aye, it were before I was born, but I knew she were a singer," said Doris.

"Aye, she were very popular, touring all over country doing recruitment concerts, then she went abroad to entertain the troops in France. Then she stopped and went to be a nurse. I admired her so much," said Ruth. She turned to William. "Have tha spoken to your grandma?"

"Nay, but me Mam and Daisy were at Blossom Cottage with her last night to listen to it," replied William.

"I wonder what tha Da would have made of it," said Ruth, who had worked for Arthur for almost twenty years.

"Aye, 'appen he wouldn't have been too impressed. I never heard him say owt about Aunt Aggie's singing, but I'm sure inside he would have been proud."

William returned to the bakery carrying the empty breadbasket ready to start the next batch.

Around eleven o'clock, William was back in the shop carrying another supply of freshly baked bread. There was a small queue, and both Doris and Ruth were serving. William started to replenish the shelves. As he was about to return to the bakery, he was aware of one of the customers waiting to be served; she appeared to be staring at him. He returned the gaze and her eyes dropped straightaway with a demure smile, as if she had been caught doing something inappropriate.

She reached the counter. "What can I get you?" asked Ruth.

The girl looked at her. "A large loaf, please."

Her gaze returned to William, who had deferred his return to the back and was fiddling around with a pile of paper bags. He looked at her and something happened.

William had never shown a great deal of interest in girls; he had always been too busy, and with a five o'clock start most mornings, socialising had been near impossible.

He was stricken. It was something he had never experienced before.

He smiled at her, unsure of what else to do. The smile was reciprocated. The loaf was served, and the girl turned and appeared reluctant to leave the queue, but the next customer barged in front. William lost sight of her as she left the shop. He leaned across to Ruth.

"Who was that girl you just served? Do you know her name?"

"Aye, it's Marjorie Sykes, she works at Fosters, you know, on the High Street, the clothes shop."

"Aye, I know it."

"I noticed her looking at you. I think you have an admirer there."

"You think so?" asked William.

"William, you're hopeless," Ruth said and laughed. She turned and started serving again.

William was feeling strange and found it difficult to concentrate on his baking, something not lost on his brother who was mixing another batch of dough.

"Are tha alright, Will? Tha seems in a dream."

"Aye, aye, 'appen I'm well enough. How's that mix coming on?"

"It'll be ready for t'oven in a couple of minutes."

Lunchtime arrived and William suddenly found himself needing a new shirt. A visit to Fosters was required.

"Are you coming up to parlour for tha dinner?" asked Robert. The shop closed at one o'clock for the lunch hour.

"Nay, 'appen I'll take a walk and clear my head. I'll be back shortly."

William left the shop and walked up James Street. Most of the shops closed for lunch and proprietors were pushing back their awnings. He was glad of his overcoat; there was a brisk north-easterly wind and bitter cold. The thick cloud cover indicated rain was due. In the distance the noise of industry gave an ambient backdrop to the day.

He crossed the High Street and walked along to the next junction. Fosters Clothes emporium was on the corner. It was part of a national chain with branches in most large towns. He reached the store and realised straightaway it would be closed. He walked up to the door and peered through the glass. He was about to turn away when a figure appeared, which made him jump. It was Marjorie.

The door bolt was unlocked, and the door opened.

"Were you wanting to buy something?"

William was trying to compose himself. "Aye... I did, but forgot tha were closed."

"Aye, till two o'clock. Tha should call back then."

Aye. 'appen I will," said William, looking disappointed.

He turned to walk away.

"You could accompany me to the tea shop, if you had a mind."

He stopped in his tracks.

"Why... er... aye, I'd like that; it would be my pleasure."

"Wait while I get my coat."

Five minutes later she reappeared in a raincoat and scarf. One of her colleagues locked the door behind her.

William was blowing into his hands to warm them.

He looked at her. The feeling he had had in the shop suddenly returned. He momentarily seemed to have lost the power of speech.

He quickly recovered. "The tea shop, tha said?"

"Aye, I often go there at dinner time."

"The Corner Café, tha mean?"

"Aye, me Mam still calls it the tea shop."

"Ha, aye, I remember that... Martha's Tea Shop; it mut be ten year since."

They crossed the High Street and headed towards Rotten Row where many solicitors and accountants had their offices, including Drummond Peacock, who still looked after Mildred's affairs.

The park in front of the offices was a shadow of its former self, a few trees with a paved way leading to James Street opposite the bakery where once families would picnic. Not that there would be anyone stopping for lunch outdoors today; it was bitterly cold. The few pedestrians that were traversing the park were dressed warmly for the weather.

Martha's Tea Shop was on the corner; it was the place where Agnes's first boyfriend, Norman, had proposed to her, a proposal that Agnes declined. The café had changed owners when Martha died in 1929 and became The Corner

Café.

They reached the eatery and William held the door open for Marjorie to enter.

Saturday lunchtime and it was busy. William looked around. The café had retained some of its old charm, but the new owners had modernised it. It was still a popular venue, particularly at this time of day.

With the number of customers, the windows had steamed up and the view to the outside street was obscured. There was a buzz of chatter and a blue layer of cigarette smoke hanging across the room.

There were two other people waiting by the doorway, but within a few minutes, William and Marjorie had been allocated a table.

"What would tha like?" asked William, as the waitress came to their table and handed them two menus.

"Just a cup of tea and a tea cake please," said Marjorie.

"Aye, I'll have the same," said William to the waitress.

She left them to process their order.

There was an embarrassed silence, neither knowing quite what to say. It was William who opened the conversation.

"How long have you worked for Fosters, then?"

"Four years, since I left school. My Mam knows the manager... What about you? How long have you been making bread?"

"Well, I used to help my Da at weekends when I were still at school. It's been in the family for over a hundred years, the bakery."

"Aye, I've been in a few times; my Mam shops there too. I was sorry to hear of your Da's passing."

William looked down. "Aye, ta, mind you he'd not been hisself for a while." He looked back at Marjorie. "I must keep an eye out for tha Mam; although I don't see many customers, I'm usually in the back making t'bread."

"Ha, aye, that makes it difficult." She smiled.

"I did notice you this morning, though," said William.

"Aye, you did, and what did you think?"

William didn't know what to say. "I thought tha looked nice," was the best he could do.

"I thought how handsome you looked in your baker's overalls."

"Ha, really? I've got flour in my hair too. It stays there for ages."

Marjorie laughed; it helped relax the atmosphere.

The waitress returned with a tray containing two cups, saucers, tea pot, sugar bowl, and milk jug.

"Your tea cakes won't be a minute; sugar's on the table," she said as she handed out the teacups.

Marjorie held up the milk jug. "Milk...?" she asked.

"Aye, ta."

"I always put milk in first; I think it tastes better," said Marjorie, as she poured a drop in each cup before pouring the tea. "Do you take sugar?" she added, lifting the bowl of sugar lumps and picking up the tongues.

"Aye, just one, please," said William. Marjorie dropped a cube into the bottom of the cup.

The waitress returned with the tea cakes. There was a knob of butter on the side of each plate.

William started to spread his butter on his tea cake, a luxury his mother could have only dreamed of when she was growing up above the butcher's shop.

"Do you like the pictures, William?"

"Pictures? Aye, but I've not been for a while. I'm usually too busy, and I do have an early start most mornings."

"'Stolen Life' is on at the Picture House with Michael Redgrave. I've heard it's very good. One of the customers was talking about it this morning. I would love to see it..." She paused. "But I couldn't go on my own; it wouldn't be right."

"Nay, I can see that."

He picked up his cup of tea and took a sip. Marjorie sighed; she couldn't understand why he hadn't taken the hint. She tried the bolder approach.

She looked him in the eyes.

"You could take me... If you had a mind."

William had taken a large sip of tea and was in danger of choking.

"Aye, 'appen I can. It's Sunday tomorrow, I don't have to work."

"What about church?"

"I don't usually go to church. Sunday is the only day I have to clean the shop and bakery."

"I can help... if you like. Clean, I mean," said Marjorie, enthusiastically. "I can skip church; I'd be happy to help."

"Aye, that would be grand, if tha's not busy or owt. Robert and Daisy usually chip in but we can always use more hands... that's my brother and sister," added William, seeing Marjorie hadn't connected. He was still feeling nervous. "What time does t'picture start?"

"I don't know," said Marjorie, taking a sip of tea.

"Nay, me neither. Wait, I'll ask t'waitress, she might know."

William attracted the attention of the girl, and she walked over to them.

"Do tha know what time the pictures start tonight?" asked William.

"The Picture House?" asked the waitress.

"Aye," replied William.

"Wait, there's a copy of The News by the till. I'll go and

check."

She left the pair and Marjorie smiled at William. He was starting to relax in her company.

They finished their tea cakes as the waitress returned. "It's seven-thirty start and the main picture, eight-thirty. Are you going to see 'Stolen Life'?" asked the waitress.

"Aye," said Marjorie.

"Oh, I went with my friend on Thursday; it's very good. I enjoyed it."

Marjorie and William continued chatting until William looked at the clock. Time had passed all too quickly. "It's five-to-two, I need to get back to open the shop."

"Aye, me too. Thank you for lunch; it was lovely." William looked down; he was blushing.

"I'll walk tha back to t'shop," said William. He settled the bill, and the pair left the café.

They reached the clothes emporium and said their goodbyes just as one of the other assistants unlocked the front entrance door to the shop.

"Did tha want to buy owt?" said Marjorie.

"It'll do another time. 'Appen I best get back," said William. "Where shall us meet tha?"

"Outside the Picture House, seven-fifteen... in case there's a queue," replied Marjorie.

"Aye, I'll be there."

William watched as Marjorie went inside. He turned and walked across the park to the bakery as if he was floating on air.

His concentration levels had dropped considerably as the afternoon dragged. Like most shops, it was an early finish on a Saturday and by four o'clock, he was outside the bakery pushing back the awning with the pole.

He could feel an excitement as he started clearing

everything away.

"Are you alright, William?" asked Robert, noticing his brother's strange behaviour. He seemed to be singing to himself.

"Aye, ta," replied William with a grin.

By five o'clock, William was walking up the stairs to the parlour. He had been shopping and had a paper bag under his arm which he appeared to be hiding. Ivy came out of the kitchen to greet him.

"Hello, Will, how was your day?" she asked, cleaning her hands with a tea towel. "It was busy when I went to the butcher's."

"Aye, Daisy said she were busy an'all."

"I've prepared tea, if you want to change... What's that you've got there? Have you been shopping?"

"Just some razor blades," he replied sheepishly. "Not much tea for me, 'appen I've no appetite."

Ivy went up to William and put her hand to his forehead to check his temperature. "I hope you're not sickening for something."

"Nay, Mam, I'm alright... I'm going to have a bath; going to the pictures tonight."

"The pictures?" queried Ivy.

"Aye." William looked down, slightly embarrassed.

"Who with? You've not said owt."

They were interrupted by Robert and Daisy who had entered the parlour having completed their tasks for the day. This gave William the chance to escape further interrogation and he walked through to his bedroom.

Ivy greeted them. "Tea won't be long; Will's having a bath. He's going to the pictures tonight."

"Ah, that explains it. 'Appen he's got a lady friend, I

reckon. He's been acting very strange s'afternoon," said Robert.

Ivy's face lit up. "Really? Oh, I do hope so... I must see if he needs his shirt ironed."

Robert and Daisy went to their rooms to change. William was in the bath.

The upstairs flat above the bakery had gone through significant changes since Mildred's day when she had brought up five children in a two-bedroomed apartment. In 1914 there was no electricity or water, and cooking was done on a large, black, cast-iron range. Bathing would be an old tin bath in front of the fire.

Ivy had been residing at Springfield Hall, at Mildred's insistence, during her pregnancy with William, while Arthur was in France. He returned from the trenches just before the birth. He was a different person, having lost his best pals and suffering serious injuries. He recuperated from his wounds while staying at the Hall, but once recovered, returned to his regiment only to succumb to Black Water Fever while serving in Egypt. Each time, Ivy nursed him back to health. It was a difficult time.

Unfit to serve, Arthur was invalided from the army.

He resented his mother's inherited wealth, and insisted they move back to James Street to resume baking. Ivy only agreed to go with him on condition that changes were made.

As a result, the apartment now had three bedrooms, bathroom, electricity, running water, and a kitchen with a gas oven.

William shared his bedroom with his brother, something they had grown used to.

He walked into the bedroom with a towel wrapped around his waist.

"I reckon tha's got a lady friend," said Robert, who was also changing. "Not known you have a bath on a Saturday afore; it's always Sundays."

"So, what if I have?" replied William."

"Really!" exclaimed Robert. "What's her name?"

William finished drying himself and started to dress in his best shirt and trousers.

"It's nobody tha knows," replied William indignantly.

"Go on, tell us, what's her name?"

"Marjorie," replied William in an attempt to escape further interrogation.

"Where did tha meet her?"

"In t'shop; she were a customer."

"Well, tha certainly kept that quiet."

"I only met her this morning."

"And tha's taking her to t'pictures already. Tha must've made an impression."

"Aye, 'appen I must have... Have tha seen my braces?"

"In top drawer."

Robert watched as William went to the set of drawers where they kept their clothes. He rummaged around for a moment. "I can't find them," said William.

Robert joined him and moved some of his undergarments. He soon found the missing items and held them up.

"Tha can't see for looking. 'Appen tha head's all over the place."

"Aye, that's right enough."

William started to fasten his braces to his trousers but his stubby fingers, which were never the most dexterous, were having difficulty with the buttons.

"Here, let me; t'film'll have finished by the time you've done it."

Robert started to button up William's braces. He stopped

and looked at his brother.

"Are tha wearing perfume?"

"Nay, course not, just some men's grooming lotion from t'chemist."

Robert saw the bottle on the dressing table.

"Well, it is an improvement on tha usual smell," replied Robert and started to laugh.

William ignored the jibe and finished his dressing, managing to do up his tie without further help from his brother.

He searched again in the drawer and found his best flat cap, the one he would use for special occasions. The last time he wore it was at his father's funeral.

William returned to the parlour to be greeted by whistles from his sister.

"My, our Will, tha does look smart," she said as he sat down at the table.

Ivy returned from the kitchen carrying a plate of sandwiches.

"So, who is this young lady?" asked Ivy as she started pouring the tea.

"Marjorie," interrupted Robert before William could answer.

"Do I know her?" asked Ivy.

"Nay, Mam, I wouldn't think so. She works in t'clothes shop on High Street."

"Foster's?" asked Ivy.

"Aye," said William nibbling at a sandwich.

"I must make a purchase on Monday, see if I can see her."

Daisy's ears pricked up. "Marjorie...? Marjorie Sykes?"

"Aye," said William.

"She used to go to my school. I didn't know her that well,

but she were very bright. Could have gone on to Grammar School, they reckon, but her mam said she had to get a job."

"Aye? Is that right?" said William. "She's offered to help clean tomorrow in shop."

"Has she now? She must be keen on you," replied Ivy.

"Aye, and me an'all."

"So how long have you been seeing her?"

"He only met her today," interrupted Robert again.

Ivy looked at William and frowned. "Today! Well, I hope you know what you are doing."

"Aye, Mam, I do."

He finished his sandwich and drank his cup of tea. "'Appen I've had enough."

"Are you sure?" asked Ivy. "You'll be hungry later."

"Aye, ta, can't eat owt more."

He looked at the clock on the mantlepiece; it was quarter to seven. "I think I better get going."

"What time are you meeting her?" asked Ivy.

"Quarter-past," replied William.

"Tha'll catch tha death of cold in this weather," proffered Daisy, as she tucked in to her third sandwich.

"Nay, I'll be fine," said William and left the table.

He returned a few minutes later wearing his topcoat and flat cap.

"Do you want to take a scarf, just in case?" said Ivy, who started fussing with William's coat, trying to brush out some creases.

"Nay, I'll be reet," replied William.

Ivy went to her purse which was on the table and took out a two-shilling piece. "Here, take this for the pictures," she said and gave it to him. He looked at it in his hand.

"Oh, ta, Mam."

"Go on, enjoy yourself," she added and watched as

William left the flat.

It was only a ten-minute brisk walk to the cinema; he was a good ten minutes early.

A queue had already started to line up and he decided to join it. He would keep a careful eye out for Marjorie.

It was nearly twenty-five-past seven and the doors were opened; the queue had started to move. William was in a quandary. He had almost reached the cinema door when he spotted her running across the road, looking anxiously at the queue.

"Marjorie!" he shouted, oblivious to others in the line. He waved to attract her attention and she walked quickly to him.

"Oh, I am so sorry I'm late; trolley were delayed. I were getting really worried."

"That's alright," he beamed. "Just glad you're here."

"Me too," she replied and joined him side by side. Without another thought, she reached for his hand and curled hers in his. William's heart skipped a beat. He squeezed it gently.

"My hands are cold, sorry."

"Need to warm them up then," she said and smiled.

They walked through the entrance and into the foyer; the box office was doing a roaring trade. He reached the cashier.

"Two please... stalls," William said, anxiously.

"Back row's all gone, dear," said the cashier looking at him, then Marjorie, and smiled. William looked embarrassed.

"Er, anywhere will do," he replied, and looked at Marjorie nervously.

"Next row, dear. How's that?"

"Aye, ta."

"That'll be one and eight please."

William handed over the two-shilling piece and she gave

him the fourpence change.

He took the tickets and headed towards the auditorium; Marjorie having now linked arms.

The lights were down, and they peered into the gloom The supporting feature had started. An usherette was waiting with a torch and led them to their seats.

The row was almost full and the man on the end stood up to let them pass. The usherette shone her torch to two empty seats about a third of the way in. Each customer had to stand as they shuffled towards the seats. They made their apologies as they passed.

William waited for Marjorie and then pushed down the retractable seat next to her. He exhaled and started to relax for the first time. The cinema was dotted with the orange glow of cigarettes; a blue haze hung across the auditorium, The beam from the projector seemed to swirl around in the air as it caught the smoke.

The support film was a comedy featuring The Three Stooges and soon they were joining the rest of the audience in fits of laughter. Marjorie was leaning close to William and holding his hand. Every now and then she would give it a gentle squeeze.

William responded; it was like a secret message.

The support film finished, and the Pathé News started. It showed events in Germany, and the new barrage balloons in London. William thought they looked very strange but didn't really connect with the significance; London was a world away.

The lights went up and the usherette was now at the front of the theatre with an assortment of ice creams on a tray.

"Would tha like an ice cream?" asked William.

"Aye, I have a mind to; I feel hungry," replied Marjorie.

"Aye, me an'all."

William ran the gauntlet of the customers who had to stand again to let him pass. There was a small queue, but just as the lights dimmed for the main feature, William was taking his seat and handing Marjorie her choc ice.

"Thank you," she whispered.

By nine-twenty the film had finished, and the audience were desperately trying to leave the stalls before the National Anthem started playing, when it was customary to stand to attention. William and Marjorie had reached the end of their row when the anthem began.

They dutifully paid homage to the Monarch before making their way into the foyer.

"How's tha getting home?" asked William.

"I'll catch trolley; it's not far... Ingrow."

"I'll walk tha to the stop."

"Aye, I'd like that."

They turned left and walked along the road towards the trolleybus stop with over a hundred other people. It was a cold night and the frost glistened like mini stars in the pavement.

They reached the stop at the top of James Street and sat on the bench in the bus shelter. Several other picture-goers were also waiting. Marjorie cuddled up to William.

"I've had a really good time, William... the best ever."

"Aye, me an'all."

Suddenly, they were kissing. Neither would recall who instigated it. It just seemed to happen. There were looks from the other waiting passengers, but the pair were oblivious to them.

Within a few minutes the trolleybus arrived; its lights giving a welcoming glow.

"I'll see you tomorrow about eleven o'clock," said Marjorie, as she got up to get on the trolleybus.

"Aye, that'll be grand."

All too soon, the bus had pulled away. The thought of seeing Marjorie again tomorrow, gave him a warm feeling as he walked back to the bakery.

Monday, 30th January, London.

Agnes was discussing the radio show and fending off numerous telephone calls from friends. They were all effusive in their praise for her.

There were however other thoughts running through her mind, something she had discussed with her husband at length. The plight of the Jewish community had become a regular topic of conversation following her meetings with Solly. The concert to raise money that he had suggested was the obvious choice. She would discuss it further with Solly.

Around ten o'clock there was a knock on the door. Mary, Agnes's assistant, had just arrived and went to answer it. She returned to the lounge carrying a cardboard box.

Agnes looked up from the table where she was writing a letter. "What's that?" she asked.

"I don't know. The cabbie said it was from the BBC."

Agnes was intrigued. Mary put the box on the table and helped Agnes open it. She couldn't believe her eyes.

"Goodness, what are we going to do with all these?" said Mary.

Agnes swished the contents around. "There must be hundreds in there."

The box was the morning delivery of letters addressed to Agnes care of the BBC following her performance on Friday. It was just like the old days when she and Céline Arneaux, her French assistant, would answer fan mail well into the night.

"Well, I would like to read as many as I can. What I

used to do with Céline when I used to tour was, she would read them and decide which ones to reply; some were just mischievous," she said and laughed.

"She was your assistant in the war?"

"Yes, she was with me for three years."

"What happened to her? Did you keep in touch?"

"We did for a while. She returned to Paris after the war, but, you know how it is, you lose touch. She's probably married to some count or politician or such. She was quite a strong character. Her father was a writer, if I remember correctly."

"Oh, that's a pity, not keeping in touch, I mean. Well, I can certainly do that for you."

"Thank you, that would be a great help. I suppose we'll be getting some more. I must ask Robert and see what other artists do."

A little later, Agnes received a telephone call.

"Hello, Agnes, Robert Laing, BBC. I'm just confirming arrangements for your Radio Times session. Are you available tomorrow?"

"Why, yes, Robert. What time?"

"Shall we say ten o'clock. I have an interviewer and photographer on standby. Oh, and one of our wardrobe mistresses will help you choose suitable costumes for the photographs. The editor wants to put you on the cover of this week's magazine."

"On the cover... oh my."

"Yes, I sent you the fan letters we received over the weekend this morning. The response has been outstanding. We can discuss future dates while you are here."

"Yes, I've received them... thank you, Robert."

They concluded the call and Agnes turned to Mary."

"He wants me to be on the cover of this week's Radio

Times."

"Oh, that's wonderful. You're going to need more staff at this rate."

"Ha, you could be right. I can't wait to tell Alistair."

There was another visitor later that morning. Mary went to answer the polite knock.

She returned to the room with Solly Solomon behind her,

"Solly, how wonderful to see you. How are you?"

Agnes looked at him; he appeared careworn and anxious. He was stood there in his raincoat holding his trilby hat in his hand and playing nervously with the rim.

"Mustn't complain, Agnes; there are people far worse off."

"Yes, that's true. Would you like a drink?"

"Yes please, a cup of tea, if you would be so kind."

"I'll make it," said Mary.

"I'll have one too," said Agnes. She turned to her visitor. "Please take off your coat and sit down. What brings you here this morning? It's good to see you."

"I had a call from Robert Laing this morning... about future dates. He seems to think I am your agent and it got me thinking. With the radio work you are doing, I could be of service."

"That is a coincidence; it is something Alistair and I have been discussing recently. I was going to ask if you wouldn't mind representing me. I've had a box of letters arrive this morning from the BBC and Mary and I have started to go through them. There are lots of requests to perform at fetes and various other functions for charity. Frankly, I don't have time to deal with them all."

"I would be delighted to help, and I can take the letters off your hands. I have a small team now, and I'll make them available to answer the letters on your behalf. I can deal with the performance requests at the same time. I won't arrange any work without your permission. It's the agreement I have with my other clients, and it seems to work. It means you can do as much or as little as you want. We will look after your diary and make all the arrangements, travel, hotels and so on."

"Oh, that would be excellent, although I am not sure how much theatre work I will do at the moment; I still have my family to consider, and the radio could keep me busy from what Mr Laing was saying."

"Yes, he is keen to sign you up for a series. That's something we can discuss, and of course, I will ensure you are properly compensated."

"Thank you... You will want a commission too, Solly?"

"Ahem, yes, my usual fee is twenty percent, the same as Cameron."

"Yes, that's correct. Yes, that will be quite acceptable."

Mary appeared with the tea and poured out two cups.

"There is another matter I would like to discuss with you," said Solly as he raised his cup to his lips and blew across the surface of his tea.

Chapter Seven

Agnes picked up her cup and subliminally mirrored Solly's movements.

"Go on," said Agnes.

"I wanted to let you know I'm arranging to go to Germany to see if I can get my parents out."

"Oh, is that wise? How will you do that?"

"I'm not sure it is, but it's necessary. Things are getting worse there right now."

"Yes, I can understand. It's a topic we've been discussing, Alistair and I. We would like to help if we can. We thought about your idea of putting on a concert to help raise money."

"Unfortunately, there isn't time. I had a letter from Germany this morning. It's the reason I need to do something."

He pulled out the letter from his pocket. The address was scribbled in pencil and the envelope soiled. He opened it.

"It's in German." He squinted at the writing as he made the translation. "My parents are still in Düsseldorf, but the letter says the police are going from house to house checking documents..." Solly looked up from the letter. "I fear it will only be a matter of time before they are found out."

"Hmm, yes, I can see... Do you know where they are?"

"Well, I have an address, but I don't know Düsseldorf at all."

"What about passports and things?"

"I'm hoping that won't be a problem; we're working on it. We have a contact at the British Embassy in Brussels who's been helping escaping Jews with travel documents."

Agnes thought for a moment. "Hmm, well I do know someone who might be able to help with advice."

"Really?"

"Yes, let me make some enquiries and I'll let you know tomorrow."

"That will be most kind, thank you."

Matthew was at his desk in his office in the bowels of Broadway Buildings. The Irish problem was still high on the agenda as the bombing campaign continued. The IRA and its activities were a police responsibility, and they were beginning to get the upper hand as more arrests were made, together with the discovery of quantities of explosive materials. With each arrest came more information and, with different police forces working on the bombings, the secret service was acting as collator. This gave them a better idea of the 'big picture'.

The names that the Irish agent had provided had been passed to the investigating officers and had helped in identifying possible activists. However, the lack of border controls in both the UK and Eire was making the tracking of potential threats more difficult, despite Special Branch having officers at all ports, notably Holyhead, through which the bulk of the traffic passed.

The most pressing question was what, if any, was the involvement of Germany in the bombing campaign. The Secret Service were aware of contact between the German authorities and the IRA. as early as 1937, but up-to-date intelligence was sketchy at best. Reports were beginning to be received indicating that the Germans were supplying funds and possibly arms and explosives to the IRA. Among these reports was one involving a certain Franz Fromme who was suspected of being a German agent and had recently visited Ireland. However, frustratingly, there was no evidence to suggest that he was directly involved in the bombing campaign.

That evening, Matthew was back home with Grace finishing dinner when they had a visitor. Grace got up from the table and went to open the door.

"Agnes, how lovely to see you, come in." Grace led Agnes into the sitting room.

"I hope I'm not disturbing you. I need to discuss something with Matthew, and I didn't want to talk about it over the telephone," said Agnes.

"No, of course not. Come in, we've just finished dinner; would you like a drink?"

"No, not for me, thank you. I won't keep you long. I've asked the cabbie to return in an hour."

Matthew entered the room from the kitchen. "Hello Agnes, I thought I could hear your voice. How are you? I heard all about your radio show. Congratulations. Unfortunately, I was working and missed it."

He leaned forward and kissed Agnes on the cheek.

"Thank you. I'm well, thank you. Actually, it's you I wanted to see, Matthew."

"Oh? I'm intrigued."

The pair sat down.

"Where are the children?" asked Agnes, looking around the room.

"Both out," replied Grace. "James is meeting some of his university friends. Dorothy's gone to the pictures. They won't be late."

"Are they well?"

"Yes, they're fine thank you," replied Grace. "James is off to Cranwell tomorrow."

"Cranwell?"

"Yes, he's applied to join the RAF. He's attending a

selection board," replied Matthew.

"Oh, really? How exciting. How do you feel about that?"

"Well, neither of us are particularly keen, but we can't stand in his way. He's old enough now to make his own decisions."

"Yes, I suppose he is. It's funny having watched him grow up, I can't believe he's almost twenty-one now," replied Agnes.

She turned to Matthew. "I need your advice, Matthew. Grace may have mentioned I have someone who has been acting as an agent for me - Solly Solomon."

"Yes, Grace has mentioned him."

"Well, he's Jewish; he escaped to London in 1933. Unfortunately, his parents were unable to leave and now they're hiding somewhere in Düsseldorf, and he wants to go and rescue them."

"Hmm, well that's not going to be easy."

"No, Solly was telling me about the clamp downs on Jewish people; it sounds dreadful."

"Yes, it is... So how can I help?"

"I thought you might have some advice. Solly says they have someone in Belgium who can supply their travel documents, but I wondered if there's anything else they need to think about."

"Hmm, travelling with forged documents? It's very dangerous. Assuming they can get the passports and visas, there are rigorous checks now at the ports. If they are found with forged papers, they will be deported, which means they will be returned to Belgium and effectively be stateless. I assume they are of German nationality."

"Well, I'm not entirely sure, but I suppose so, yes."

"The likelihood is they will end up back in Germany in that case, and in the present climate, arrested."

"Oh, goodness."

"I'm afraid so. But why have you decided to get involved?"

"Solly's been very good to me. It was him who arranged the BBC audition. But it's more than that; it's the injustice. I don't know why the government isn't doing more."

"Hmm, yes, the Government is being strict on immigration, particularly Jews. They're frightened of a stampede."

"But still, a bit of humanity is all that's needed."

"Unfortunately, there's not a lot of support for helping Jews in the country; indifference, one of my colleagues called it."

"I think we should be doing all we can to help them."

"That's not a view shared at the moment, I'm sorry to say. I think Chamberlain has enough on his plate trying to prevent a war."

"Do you think there will be a war?" asked Agnes.

"Hmm, certainly can't rule it out if Hitler's not stopped. But it seems that appeasement is the only Government policy at the moment. They won't do anything to upset him."

"But what about the Jewish communities?"

"Not a priority, as I said."

Agnes looked pained. "That can't be right," she responded animatedly.

"No, I agree, but it's a fact of life."

"I despair with what's happening to this world. I thought things would improve after the war, but it seems no one has learned anything."

"Yes, you could be right."

Grace intervened. "Come on you two, let's stop talking about depressing things. When are you next on the radio?"

Agnes refocussed. "A week on Friday, I think. I'm seeing

the producer tomorrow. They're arranging an interview and some pictures for the Radio Times."

"So, you'll be in the Radio Times?" said Matthew.

"On the cover, apparently," replied Agnes.

"Oh, that's wonderful. Mind, you'll get no peace," said Grace.

"Ha, yes, it's already happening. We had a box of letters delivered this morning from the BBC from Friday's broadcast. It's going to take ages to read them all."

"You're going to need more staff," said Grace.

"Well, Solly has said his team will look after the letters for me." Agnes noticed the clock on the mantelpiece.

"Anyway, I'd better go, the cabbie will be here shortly." She looked at her brother-in-law. "Thank you, Matthew, for your time. I'll call Solly tomorrow and tell him what you said."

Monday at the bakery and William hadn't stopped whistling, much to the annoyance of Robert.

"Eh up our William, 'appen tha's in a good mood."

"Aye, seeing Marjorie at dinner time. Going t'café."

"Aye, I thought as much. I tell you what; she's not afraid of hard work, that one. She were here till five o'clock yesterday. I think our Mam were impressed an'all."

"Aye, she said as much."

Robert took another batch of bread from the oven. William handed him the basket.

The shelves in the bakery were replenished and that wonderful smell of newly baked bread filled the shop.

The bakery was busy but there were less of the queues that had blighted the town before the war. Ruth and Doris were keeping the line moving.

By one o'clock, the customer activity was light, although

there was a demand for sandwiches which had proved popular at lunchtime. William had changed his shirt ready for his meeting with Marjorie.

Ruth glanced up as William went to lock the door for the hour's closure, dressed in his overcoat; his hair slicked down as was the modern trend.

"Eh up, tha looks fine, William. Young Marjorie will be impressed, I'm sure" said Ruth.

"Ta," replied William and left the bakery.

It was a short walk to the café where Marjorie was already waiting. It was a bitterly cold day; the temperature still hadn't reached above freezing. Marjorie was blowing into her hands to keep them warm and moving her feet from side-to-side.

She beamed a smile as William approached.

"Ah do, our Marjorie," said William and grabbed her hand. "Hope I've not kept tha waiting. Tha should have gone inside; tha hands are freezing."

"Nay, I wanted to watch you walk up the path."

"Really? I must say tha looks a treat, Marjorie," said William and bent down to kiss her. He was a good six inches taller than her.

"Actually, I've only just got here."

"How was your morning?" asked William as he opened the door to the café.

"It were grand. I couldn't stop thinking of you."

"Aye, me an'all. Me Mam were reet impressed with tha yesterday."

She looked up at him as they waited to be seated. There were several vacant tables. "It were nothing. I enjoyed myself. Better than going to church, any road."

A waitress approached. "Table for two?"

"Aye, ta," replied William.

They were escorted to a corner table and they both took off their overcoats and gave them to the waitress.

"Not so busy today," remarked Marjorie, looking around the café.

"Aye, probably the weather; it's been freezing in t'shed."

"Aye, tha could be right. I hope you wrap up warm."

"'Appen once oven's lit, it's not so bad."

The waitress returned and took their order. "Two teas and two toasted teacakes, please," said William, taking charge of things.

Marjorie smiled. "Tha remembered."

"Aye, how could I forget."

She reached across the table and took William's hand. There was a comfortable silence, just eye-contact.

"So, how was tha morning?" asked William after a few moments.

"Quiet, only had three customers. Mind you, Monday's are not usually very busy. What about you, have you been busy?"

"Aye, Monday is always busy, after t'weekend; people run out of bread."

They were interrupted by the waitress with their orders.

"Our Mam's been gossiping with our grandma; 'appen she wants to see tha for tea this weekend, if tha's free. What do tha think?" asked William.

"Aye, I'd like that. It'll have to be Sunday; I work on Saturday."

"Aye, 'appen we can take a trolley after we've done cleaning. She lives up in Oxenhope... Sorry, I didn't mean you should help with the cleaning, I didn't mean that."

"It's fine; I'll be happy to help. It means we can spend some time together."

"Aye true enough."

Marjorie continued. "Me Mam were asking after tha an'all. 'Appen she would like to be introduced to tha. I were thinking we could meet after work and have tea. What do tha think?"

"Aye, what about tomorrow? Mam'll have tea prepared for tonight."

"Aye, alright, I'll ask my Mam tonight."

Tuesday, 31st January.

Agnes was up early; it was going to be a busy day.

It had been a restless night, and she was feeling, and looking, weary. She had been thinking about Solly's situation and thinking of ways to help. She would meet him at lunchtime at the BBC Club after her meeting and interview.

She was looking forward to the photo session with some excitement; appearing on the cover of the Radio Times was indeed a great honour. The resurrection of her singing career had come out of the blue and had to thank Solly for that.

Agnes caught a taxi to Broadcasting House and, after a short wait, was greeted in reception by Robert Laing, the producer. They shook hands.

"Lovely to see you again Agnes, and might I say, how wonderful you look."

"Thank you, Robert, that's very kind."

"If you'd like to follow me. I've allocated the photographic studio for your session this morning; it's on the fifth floor."

He led the way along the corridor to the lifts and pressed the button. Agnes was still not used to the sensation, but it was better than climbing the five floors on foot. There was no conversation as the elevator moved smoothly to the chosen floor. Agnes gazed up at the floor indicator as the lift ascended.

The doors opened and, as with her previous visit, she was amazed at the opulent furnishings. She followed the producer along a short corridor and past the music library; there was a sign on the door indicating its presence.

"Probably got some of your recordings in there," said Laing. They reached another door with a small metal label - 'Studio 8b', it said. "Here we are."

He opened the door, and a man, probably in his mid-thirties, was setting up some lighting equipment. He was dressed casually with no tie, which was quite unusual for someone in a professional capacity.

"Agnes, can I introduce you to Hector Bailey, he's one of the best photographers in London."

The man turned and looked at Agnes. "Oh, take no notice of him, my dear, Robert's always the flatterer, aren't you, my love?"

Agnes was fascinated by her new acquaintance. He reminded her of her good friend Marmaduke Hersey, the set designer from the touring shows. She suddenly wondered what had happened to him.

"Pleased to meet you, Hector."

"No, no, no, my dear, I cannot abide the name. I can't think what mama was thinking about when she gave me such a moniker. Just Bailey will do."

"I'll leave you to it," interjected the producer with a smile. "I've set up the interview with one of our resident newsreaders. I'll get Bailey to take you; he knows where to go. I'll check in on you before you leave; we need to discuss future appearances."

Agnes turned to her host. "Thank you, Robert."

"My, you are honoured. He usually insists on being called Mr Laing," observed the photographer.

"Oh, I hope he doesn't think I'm being disrespectful. It's

what he told me to call him."

"No, no, no, I think he must have taken a shine to you. Mind you, you wouldn't be the first. He has a bit of a reputation, you know... Right, let me have a look at you."

Agnes stood for a moment while the photographer eyed her up and down. He put his hand to her cheek and moved her head to the left, then, to the right. Just then, a younger man entered with two large cameras.

"Oh, this is Tarquin De La Tour, my assistant. I should call him the Honourable Tarquin, more correctly, his mother is a Countess or something."

"A Duchess, as you well know, Bailey. You are always such a tease."

"Please to meet you, Tarquin... Is it alright to call you Tarquin?"

"By all means, my dear; it's what my friends call me."

"Tarquin will finish setting up the lighting while we discuss what you should wear. Robert wanted something tasteful but alluring, so he said. I have no idea what he means."

"Hmm, I think I have a good idea," responded Agnes with a smile. "Has he provided any costumes?"

The photographer went to a cupboard against the side wall. There were two wooden knobs and he pulled them apart to open it. It was full of dresses of every description.

"I'm sure there's something here that would suit, my dear. Help yourself. There's a screen over there where you can try on." He pointed to the said item in the corner of the room. "There's a makeup artist due shortly; she'll help you."

Agnes was browsing the various costumes when the door opened and a girl in her twenties walked in. Again, she was dressed casually, wearing trousers, which was most unusual. She was carrying a small valise.

Bailey was busy setting up his equipment and positioning a backdrop.

"Are you Agnes Marsden?" enquired the girl.

Agnes turned from the costumes. "Yes," she replied, and held out her hand in greeting.

"I'm Sophie; they've asked me to do your makeup." She responded to the greeting. It was a gentle handshake.

"Thank you... Bailey has asked me to choose a costume, but I have to say, I'm finding it difficult. Tasteful but alluring is what Robert wants, apparently."

"Robert Laing...? Ha, he'd have you naked given half the chance. Don't worry, I know exactly what you need. By the way, I heard you on the radio last week. I thought you were excellent."

"Thank you," replied Agnes.

Sophie skimmed though the dresses with an expert eye; then stopped. Agnes was watching with interest.

"This one, I think; try it on and let's see."

Fashions had changed significantly during the decade. In 1930, dresses would be long, calf-length; by 1939, they would fall just below the knee. The garment Sophie had chosen was the height of fashion. It was less 'dressy' than a ball gown of the period, chic and classy, something a sophisticated woman would wear to an informal lunch. It had a low neckline but nothing like the one's Agnes was used to wearing on stage.

"What do you think? I'm sure it's from one of the Paris collections."

"It looks wonderful, but I don't have any shoes to match."

"That shouldn't be a problem, there're are lots under here."

Underneath the hanging dresses there were three sets of drawers and Sophie pulled the first one open to reveal a number of fashionable shoes.

"The wardrobe department use this as well, but I'm sure we can find something suitable to match."

After a few minutes, Agnes had tried on the outfit and some suitable shoes. The photographer had taken an active interest.

"Yes, my dear, you look absolutely divine. I do have an image in mind which I think will match your singing. I'll get Tarquin to find a suitable backdrop while Sophie does your makeup."

"Over here, Agnes," said Sophie, and led her to a chair in front of a mirror, illuminated by four small light bulbs on each side.

Sophie placed her bag on an adjoining table and opened it.

"Right, let's see what we can do."

Twenty minutes later, Agnes's weary visage had been transformed.

Agnes examined herself in the mirror. "I can't believe it; you are a miracle worker, Sophie."

The photographer heard the remark and came over to check.

"My, that is beautiful, my dear. Yes, Sophie is an expert aren't you, dear. Works with all the stars, she does."

"Really?" said Agnes.

"Oh, it's nothing, they are just like ordinary people, just with more money. Some of them can be completely horrid."

"I don't know why people can be so rude."

"Oh, I could tell you a few stories, I could."

Bailey clapped his hands dramatically. "Right, if everybody's ready, let's take some pictures."

After half an hour, and many photographs, Bailey called

time.

"Thank you Agnes, my dear; I think that will do. We will get them printed this afternoon, and I will let the Radio Times people have the copy we decide. I'm sure Robert will want a say in it."

"Thank you, it has been quite an experience, very different to the photographic sessions I've had before. Mind you, I was a lot younger then." She smiled.

"Yes, camera equipment has improved greatly since the twenties. Come on, let me take you down to the studio for the interview."

Agnes said farewell and thanks to Tarquin and Sophie and followed Bailey out of the room.

The BBC Club is an institution which was established right at the start of the formation of the BBC. It was a place where 'stars' and celebrities could mix without being subjected to the constant intrusion by fans or by-standers.

An hour later, Agnes walked into the Club with Alison Jeffries, the BBC announcer who had just conducted the interview with her for the Radio Times.

"I'll sort out membership for you, Agnes. It's a great place to come and gossip. There are many here whose voices are known, but not their faces."

"Yes, I can imagine. Thank you, Alison, that's very kind."

The pair signed the visitors' book. Agnes looked around and could see Solly in the corner. He noticed Agnes and waved.

Alison said her goodbyes and Agnes walked across the bar to join Solly. They shook hands. They spoke as they sat down.

"I see you managed to get an introduction; I was going to do that for you."

"Oh, that's very kind. It's all new to me. Alison offered to bring me down when I told her I was meeting someone."

"Alison Jeffries?"

"Yes."

"Oh, she's excellent. Have you heard her broadcasts?"

"No, I can't say I have."

"You must make a point of it; I'm sure you will enjoy it. 'These you have loved', and 'The melody is there', are particularly good. I'm surprised she hasn't invited you to perform. I can speak to her producer if you like."

"Oh, that's very kind, Solly, but I think I have enough on my plate at the moment. I'm meeting Robert Laing after lunch. He wants to discuss his plans for the show."

"That's excellent... How did the session with the photographer go?"

"Ha, that was interesting. The photographer's name was Bailey."

"Hector Bailey?"

"Yes, but he was quite adamant I called him Bailey."

"Is that so? Well, he has an excellent reputation; it seems you have been well looked after."

"Yes, everyone has been very kind."

A waiter, dressed in a white jacket, arrived and took a drinks order.

"Is there any news about your parents?" asked Agnes in a whisper.

"No, not since yesterday."

"Well, I spoke to my contact; the person I mentioned yesterday, and he says it could be very dangerous."

"Yes, of course, I know that," replied Solly, not sharply.

"Well, he was saying, because they're not issuing visas to Jews, they're scrutinising passports and visas more thoroughly. He says that if they're discovered with forged papers your parents would be deported and could end up back in Germany."

Solly put his head in his hands in frustration. "I don't know if I will ever see my parents again."

Agnes stretched her hand across the table and held Solly's. "Yes, you will; yes, you will. What about the community here? You said they were going to help."

"Yes, they've agreed to pay for the train tickets and for the documents."

"Do you know who the person is who's supplying the passports? Can they be trusted?" Agnes clarified.

"It's someone in the Embassy in Brussels; he's Jewish. He's helped several people get out, so I've heard. Then there's a different contact in Eindhoven who's been able to help get refugees out of Germany."

"What about if I came with you?" Agnes spoke before thinking.

"You...!?"

"Yes, would it help? Maybe we could say you were my manager and we've been looking at possible venues to put on a concert tour. My passport still says I'm a singer."

"How will that help my parents?" He looked forlornly at Agnes.

"I don't know; we would have to work something out."

"I wouldn't want to put you in any danger."

"I can't see how it would, but I would need to speak to Alistair... I don't know, maybe he could come up with ideas. I'm sure he's performed in Belgium in the past."

The suggestion had lifted Solly's mood.

"Let's meet here again tomorrow. I need to see Robert Laing in a few minutes, and I don't want to be late."

"Yes, yes, thank you. I'll speak to some of my friends and see if they can come up with suggestions."

Earlier that morning, Matthew Keating was back at his desk in the basement of the Secret Intelligent Services H.Q.

Since his discussion with Agnes, he had taken more than a passing interest with what was happening in Germany and was reviewing a speech that Hitler had made at the Reichstag the previous day. It did not make good reading, especially if you were of Jewish extraction. The prediction Hitler made that "the annihilation of the Jewish race in Europe" would ensue if another world war were to occur was chillingly prescient.

Agnes had arrived home following her trip to the BBC. She was in her bedroom, changing, and contemplating her day. She noticed the silver napkin ring that had been presented to her by the late King George V, still in pride of place on her dressing table in a presentation case she had had made. She would never forget that night. She thought about Lord Harford, her escort that evening and, briefly, her fiancé. He had been another casualty of the war; she felt sad at the memory.

Her singing career had brought her fame and considerable wealth, something she never took for granted. She often reminisced about her time in France serving as a ward assistant in the Officer's hospital in Wimereux, where she had met and looked after Alistair. The struggles of others resonated with her, and the fate of Solly's parents was on her mind.

Just then, she heard the front door open. "Hello, anyone at home?"

It was Alistair and Gwendoline.

Agnes left the bedroom and went downstairs to greet the family.

"Hello, you two, how was your day?"

Gwendoline was taking off her coat; it was still bitterly cold outside.

"It was good thanks; got a lot of homework to do. My exams are only three weeks away. I'll go and make a start before dinner."

"Hello darling," said Alistair. He leaned to her and kissed her as a husband would do. "How was your day?"

"Interesting, I'll tell you more over dinner."

By six-thirty, the three were at the dining table. With Agnes out for much of the day, Mary had cooked the evening meal and it had been just a case of heating it in the oven.

"So, your interesting day?" said Alistair.

"I don't know where to start."

"How did you get on with the Radio Times interview?"

"Oh, that went very well. One of the presenters interviewed me."

"And the photography?"

"Ha, yes, the photographer's name was Bailey, the best in London according to Robert. He was very good, if a little dramatic." Agnes laughed.

"And what about more broadcasts?"

"Well, it seems I have a fan in Robert; he wants me to do a weekly request spot on the variety show. His idea is, he will invite listeners to write in and request songs for me to sing."

"What a wonderful idea."

"Yes, although there will be rehearsal time, so it's going to keep me busy."

"Yes, I can see."

"Then I met Solly for lunch in the BBC Club."

"How was that?"

"I'll tell you later."

Gwendoline had finished her meal and excused herself to continue her homework.

"So, what's the news about Solly and his family?" asked Alistair, who had also now finished his meal.

Agnes looked around to make sure Gwen was not in earshot.

"It's pretty bad, and he's going out of his mind with worry."

"Yes, I can imagine."

"He's planning to travel to Germany to try to get them away. He was saying that the Jewish community have contacts at the Embassy in Belgium who can get documents, visas, passports, and so on."

"Hmm, that could be dangerous."

"Yes, and of course, if they're discovered at the border with false passports, the likelihood is they will get deported back to Germany. Solly was saying the Germans are rounding up Jews and sending them to special camps."

Alistair looked at Agnes with an air of concern.

"I want to help in some way," said Agnes.

"Yes, of course. What about the concert we discussed?"

"No time. I suggested that, but things are changing by the day, and he wants to go as soon as possible... The thing is... I've offered to go with him."

Alistair looked at Agnes with surprise.

"But, surely, you can't be serious; it will be too dangerous."

"Nonsense, I could say I was arranging a concert tour or something, if I was asked."

"I don't like it, Agnes, if I'm truthful."

"No, I knew you would be concerned, but I was thinking I could be a help at the border on the way back. I could say they are part of my staff, helping with the tour."

"It's a bit thin."

"Well, I may think of a better plan while we're out there."

"Do you want me to come as well? I'd feel happier."

"No, dear, you're busy with exams; I'll be quite alright on my own."

A few streets away, Grace was preparing the evening meal when Matthew arrived. She left the kitchen and went to greet him.

"Hello darling, how was your day?" she said and kissed him fondly.

Matthew took off his overcoat and hung it on a vacant coat hook beside the door.

"Oh, the usual, I need to get back after dinner, unfortunately."

"Really? You work too hard, Matthew."

"Yes, unfortunately, it's the nature of the work. Intelligence issues don't stop at five o'clock."

"Ha, and don't I know it!"

Matthew followed Grace back to the kitchen. "I wonder how James got on; have you heard anything?"

"No, nothing, I thought he might have telephoned," replied Grace.

"He might not have had the opportunity; I'm sure he would have done so otherwise."

"Where is Cranwell?" asked Grace.

"Lincolnshire, I think. His train went to Sleaford; there's a branch line to the college, apparently. He showed me his selection instructions."

"He won't be back till late, I don't expect. He'll have had a long day. I do hope he will be alright. I did give him some money for a taxi in case he was late," said Grace.

"I'm sure he will be; he's very resourceful. I think they

will have him like a shot."

"I'm still unsure of him joining the RAF; it could be terribly dangerous if there is a war," said Grace.

"Yes, I'm sure, but then any fighting's going to be dangerous. Mark my words, if there is a war, it will be nothing like the last one."

Grace looked at Matthew with concern. "What do you mean?"

"I mean, I think it's going to involve everyone."

"Oh, I do hope it doesn't' come to that."

Chapter Eight

Monday February 6th, 1939.

Grace looked out of the window. It was a milder morning, and the winter sunshine was emitting some unseasonal warmth. Snowdrops in the front garden were adding colour and the daffodil flowers would soon be emerging from their green casing.

She was looking forward to seeing Hetty again. It had been at least five years; she was trying to remember. Hetty said she would be arriving around lunchtime.

By two o'clock, Grace was beginning to get worried. Hetty was a stickler for punctuality; it had been a standing joke during the war. Just then, the telephone rang; it was from a call box. The sound of coins dropping into the bowels of the apparatus could be heard.

"Hello... Grace? It's Hetty."

"Hello, Hetty, how are you? I was beginning to get a bit worried."

"Yes, it's why I'm ringing." There was the sound of money being fed into the pay phone. "There's been some problem on the Underground. Someone said it was a bomb."

"Are you alright?"

"Yes, I'm fine, old thing; it'll take more than these Irish clowns to frighten me. I'm trying to get a taxi, but the queues are frightfully horrid, so I don't know how long I will be."

"Oh, you poor thing. Well, thanks for letting me know. There'll be a nice pot of tea waiting for you when you get here."

"I think a large gin and tonic might be a better option."

"Ha, I can arrange one of those too."

It was gone three o'clock when the cheery sound of the front doorbell alerted Grace to a caller. She wiped her hands on a tea towel and left the kitchen.

"Hello, Hetty, you made it then? Come in."

"Oh, it's been a nightmare," said Hetty as she followed Grace into the house. "And London looks so different now with the barrage balloons, very strange."

"Yes, although, I think we've got used to them now."

Grace closed the front door, turned, and gave Hetty a hug; then looked at her oldest friend. Her face was careworn lined, her hair now quite grey, and she was wearing a very old-fashioned hat; one her mother would have worn. But, somehow, it was typically Hetty.

"It's so lovely to see you again. Let me take your coat and suitcase. I'll show you your room when you've had a chance to unwind. Would you like some tea?"

"Yes, that would be wonderful, thank you."

Hetty made herself comfortable on the settee while Grace went to get the drinks.

"Would you like something to eat?" Grace shouted from the kitchen.

"I managed to get a sandwich at the station, thanks," replied Hetty, as she looked around the room.

Grace returned with a tray containing a teapot, cups, and a milk jug. She placed them on the coffee table in front of the settee and returned to the kitchen.

She returned carrying a plate with four biscuits.

"Here, these will keep you going. McVitie's Royal Scots, I do love these."

Grace put the plate on the table next to the tea tray and started to pour the tea.

"Oh, thank you, me too... And how's Matthew?" said Hetty, helping herself to a biscuit.

"Hmm, he's always so busy; I don't see enough of him. I don't know what time he'll be back. He called earlier and said there had been some trouble on the Underground."

"Ha, yes, it must be the same thing. They've stopped all the trains, a bomb apparently."

"Oh dear, I do hope nobody was hurt."

"Yes, me too." Hetty took a sip of tea. "It's so good to see you again, old thing, and I have to say, I love this room. It's so homely."

"Thank you, it's lovely to see you too. You said you had something to tell me. I'm intrigued."

Hetty dipped the biscuit into her tea and took a bite. "I think these taste so much better when they've been dipped in tea, don't you?"

"Oh definitely, I'll join you. It's just like old times. Do you remember those biscuits we used to get in France? Dipping them in tea was the only way you could eat them without doing serious damage to your teeth." Grace laughed at the thought.

"Ha, ha, yes, I do. I think that's where I must have got the habit."

Grace followed suit and dipped her McVitie's in her tea, cupping her hand underneath it to catch any drips before biting the soggy biscuit.

Hetty looked at Grace with a serious expression.

"Well, the reason I'm in London is I have an appointment with the solicitor tomorrow at ten o'clock. We've decided to sell the farm."

Grace looked at Hetty with some surprise. "Really? But you always led me to believe in your letters that you enjoyed faming."

"I do, but hop farming is such hard work and the returns aren't as good as they once were."

"What about your stepdaughter? Chloe is it?"

"Yes... Duncan and I had a long discussion a couple of weeks ago, just before I called. The thing is." Hetty looked down. "He's not got long to live."

"Oh, Hetty, I'm so sorry..." There was a silence as Grace digested the information. "I don't know what to say. What is it?"

"It's cancer, I'm afraid. It's in his lungs. Doctors think it might be the hops. His father died with it too."

"But he's not that old is he?"

"He's sixty-nine."

"Nevertheless, that's not really that old."

"No, it isn't; I was hoping to have more time with him. We have always been very happy, despite the age gap."

Hetty finished her tea and Grace started to refill the cup without asking.

"Thanks," said Hetty and picked up another biscuit.

"So, what are you going to do?"

"Well, Duncan's keen to get things in order before... you know..." She sipped her tea in reflection. "We're thinking of moving to Tunbridge Wells, which isn't far. I think it will be easier to get around. The farm is quite cut off and we're always reliant on the car, or on occasions, the tractor."

"What will Chloe do?"

"She's a bright girl; she's talking about getting a job in the city."

"As a secretary, you mean?"

"I think she's got her sights on something better, but it's difficult for women to break through, as you know."

"Yes, indeed. Well, if there's anything I can do, you just have to say; I do have a few connections. In fact, I'll ask Matthew; they are always on the lookout for good people."

"Oh, that's so kind. I'll mention it to Chloe. She's looking after her father at the moment. It's reasonably quiet on the farm; we don't start stringing till next month."

"Stringing?"

"Oh, yes, it's one of the most important parts of the season. It's when we create the framework for the hops to climb." Grace took another sip of tea.

"Yes, I've seen pictures... Please go on; it's so interesting. I know nothing about hop farming."

"Well, as I said, it's hard work. The stringing is all done by hand. We use a long pole; we call it a 'monkey', and we thread the string from the peg in the ground up to the hooks on the top wirework, that's the best part of twenty feet. Each farm has their own way of doing it, but Crouch Farm has used the same method for three generations, so we stick with that."

"How long does it take?"

"About a month. Then we have to start threading the hops in April. We have casual workers to help, and they stay with us until the crop's harvested."

Grace looked at her long-time friend with admiration. When they worked together on the ambulances, Hetty was always a bit scatty, but hearing her speak, she had changed into an accomplished businesswoman.

"That really is fascinating. Do you know, I always thought you would end up marrying a vicar, for some reason."

"Like my father, you mean?"

"Oh yes, that's probably the association."

"I have no regrets at all. It would have been nice to have had children of our own, but it wasn't to be. Still, Chloe has been like a daughter; I couldn't have wished for better."

Hetty looked down as a wave of sadness took over. A tear rolled down her cheek.

Grace moved to Hetty and put her arm around her. "I'll

always be here for you, Hetty. I mean, I owe you my life. It was your quick thinking that saved me when the ambulance went over."

Hetty looked up. "Ha yes, what an absolute beast she was... Betty, I mean."

"Yes that's for sure, and it was God's own effort to get her started."

Hetty smiled at the recollection. "Do you still think about those days at Lamarck?"

"Oh, yes, often, so much suffering."

"Yes, that's true. I can't believe why anyone would want to go through that again."

"Well, if Herr Hitler is not stopped, it could happen."

Hetty was calmer now and Grace moved back to her seat.

"You think there <u>will</u> be a war?" asked Hetty.

"Matthew seems to think so."

Secret Intelligence Service HQ, Broadway Buildings. Mid-afternoon.

Matthew was studying the reports from officers who had attended the scenes of the latest IRA. atrocities. Both Tottenham Court Road and Leicester Square Underground stations had been targeted resulting in seven casualties including two severely injured, one of which was the Tottenham Court Road station foreman. Newsreels would later claim it was the work of 'politicians of the underworld', a euphemism for the IRA.

Underground services had been suspended for a short period of time, but the police were keen to minimise disruption as far as possible to negate the impact of the bombing and not allowing any propaganda for the terrorists.

The internal telephone rang; it was Colonel Monkton, his commander, requesting a meeting.

Matthew reached Monkton's office and knocked on the door. He was invited in.

"Sit down, Major. What do you think of the latest activity by the terrorists?"

"Hmm, well, it seems they've upped their game, although the Underground was always a likely target. The police have increased patrols on all the stations. We are making progress though. The latest arrests may yield more information."

"Yes, well let's hope so... Actually, that's not the reason I wanted to talk to you."

The Commander shuffled some papers on his desk and picked up the top copy.

"What do you know about Siemens Schukert?"

"The communications company?"

"Yes."

"Hmm, I can see where this is going... German, right?"

"Yes, I've had a memo from the Home Office, and, not to put too fine a point on it; they are worried. It seems their engineers are roaming about the country, unchecked."

"Well, that's part of their job. I'm not sure what we can do about that."

"You know the factories?"

"Of course, one's in Acton, just up the road from where we live. The other's in Ealing." Matthew was deep in thought. "Have there been any reports of suspected espionage?"

"No, but they've done some assessments on German businesses in the UK, and Siemens was at the top of their list as 'at risk.'"

"Yes, given the nature of their work, that makes sense. What do they want us to do?"

"We need to keep a close eye on them; I want us to get an agent inside both their factories. Will that be possible?" said the Commander.

"Hmm, it won't be easy; they'll almost certainly need engineering or radio communications experience."

"We do have radio engineers here."

"Hmm, yes, but I can't really spare them. We're up to our eyes in traffic at the moment."

The Commander looked at Matthew. "I think we need to be pro-active here, Major. If necessary we may need to recruit. Can you give this some urgency?"

"Yes, of course."

"Oh, before you go, just to let you know, we're moving D section to a new facility up in Buckinghamshire. It'll free up more space."

"Oh, right, thanks for letting me know. Where is it, this place?"

The Colonel picked up another piece of paper and scanned it. "Bletchley Park, some large mansion near Leighton Buzzard, apparently. It's going to be an important site; kitted out with transmitters and receivers. It's likely we'll be sending the cypher team over there in the summer."

"Is there anything you need me to do?"

"No, not for the moment. Let me know how you get on with Siemens."

Earlier, Agnes was in the BBC club waiting for Solly. He'd arranged to meet her for lunch to discuss travel arrangements to the Continent. She saw him arrive and leave his coat and umbrella with the maître d' at the door. He looked stressed as he strode over to her table.

"I'm sorry I'm late, there's been some problem on the Underground; it was difficult to get a taxi."

"Don't worry; yes, I had heard. The cabbie was full of it; something to do with a bomb."

"Oh, is that what it was? I hope no one was hurt. The

Irish again, I suppose."

"I don't know, but I expect it will be in the newspapers tomorrow."

A waiter arrived and took their order; sandwiches and coffee.

"I'll get these," said Solly.

"Thank you," replied Agnes.

She lowered her voice, although, with the hubbub of conversation in the room, the chances of being overheard was negligible. "So, do you have any more news?"

"Yes, I've spent some time at Bloomsbury House and spoke to the Jewish Refugees Committee there. There are several members who have managed to get families from Germany to England. Unfortunately, it's expensive and dangerous."

"I'm happy to contribute," said Agnes.

"Oh, that's very kind, but they've agreed to fund the trip and I have some details of trains, too... Are you still interested in accompanying me?"

"Yes, most definitely, I can certainly pay for my own transport. So, when do you want to go?"

"As soon as possible, later this week if I can."

"It will have to be after Friday; I have my broadcast to do."

"Yes, of course. Saturday then?"

"Yes, can you arrange everything by then?"

"I should be able to. I have someone who's going to get in touch with the contact at the British Embassy in Brussels."

"About the passports?"

"Yes, I had some old photos I let them have. They said they will get them to Brussels. I just hope they'll be satisfactory. They are many years old."

Solly bowed his head again but was shaken out of his

sadness as the waiter returned with their order. Solly fiddled in his jacket pocket and retrieved some coins.

"Keep the change," said Solly and the waiter acknowledged with a discreet bow of the head.

Agnes took a sip of tea. "What about getting in and out of Germany?"

"I don't think getting in will be a problem. According to those that have been before, the easiest route is to go via Holland. There's a train direct to Düsseldorf from Eindhoven; it's relatively straightforward." He looked down. "But getting back is something I worry about. There are crossing points into Belgium and Holland, but I need to speak to people to find out more detail. I'm not sure I want to risk going through a border control."

"Yes, I can understand, although I'm hoping I can help in that regard. I have had several invitations to appear in Germany in the past. Maybe I can take advantage of that."

"We would need to come up with a good story."

"Of course, but we have some time. I'll speak to my contact again and ask him."

They continued their discussion without coming up with a cohesive plan. There were more questions to consider. They agreed to meet again on Wednesday when Agnes had a rehearsal.

Tuesday February 7th, 1939.

Iveagh Market, Dublin, is split into a dry market, facing Francis Street, and a wet market in the rear, facing John Dillon Street. The dry market sold clothes, while the wet market sold fish, fruit and vegetables. An adjoining building housed laundry, disinfecting, and delousing facilities, a place Eoghan Flemming had used on a number of occasions.

It was mid-morning. Eoghan looked around his meagre

dwelling, one room with a bed, sink, table, two chairs, and a couple of cupboards. The toilet facilities and wash basin were down the hall, shared with two other occupants who also had rooms along the corridor.

His radio equipment was still in the suitcase under the bed; he had sent nightly messages to London, although there had not been a great deal to report; just the occasional snippet supplied by the corner shop owner with whom he had struck up a friendship.

He had not ventured far from his bedsit since Matthew's visit, only leaving when needing to buy provisions from the said corner shop, but a new shirt and trousers were required. The ones he was sporting were showing signs of wear. He had burned the soiled clothes which had resulted from his dispatch of the IRA driver, in an old oil drum in the back yard. However, with only a limited wardrobe, he needed to replenish. He believed it was now safe for a trip to the market.

He left the run-down terraced property and wandered up Francis Street; it was a cold and miserable February day. His raincoat, which formally belonged to Matthew, was keeping the chill out. The bloodstains had been carefully sponged away with soap and water. He still had Matthew's Trilby hanging behind the door; fortunately, he had a spare flat cap.

He passed the button factory on the left and the hosiery factory on the right, chimneys belched out smoke adding to the grey afternoon. Inside workers toiled in sweatshop conditions.

The entrance to the market was a grand affair, with ornate brick arches providing the frontage, the antithesis to what lay inside. Eoghan looked around before entering.

It was busy; there was a distinctive aroma of clothing and fish with the smell of sweat added in, not all that pleasant but something a visitor would soon get used to. Stalls were set in neat rows, but the whole ambience was what would be termed 'shabby' and in need of refurbishment.

The clothing area was busy with vendors attending stalls, their wares displayed on wooden tables in front of them. He was studying a selection of shirts with a genial proprietor giving him suggestions from the back of the stall. He had become engrossed in his purchase and had not spotted a possible threat.

James, 'Jimmy', Kelly was also in the marketplace, a prominent Nationalist and a local brigade commander in the IRA. He was a butcher by trade, and reputation. Eoghan had met him on several occasions at meetings and was only too aware of his predisposition towards violence. He was in an adjacent aisle and spotted Eoghan at the shirt stall.

He walked up behind Eoghan, who was still engrossed in his purchase.

"Ah, so is this where yer've been hiding yerself, Eoghan, me lad? Yer name was mentioned just the other night. Some of the boys were saying it seems we've not seen anything of yers since poor Seamus was murdered... and him with a wife and two kiddies."

Eoghan looked round with a start, cursing himself for not being more alert. He tried to compose himself.

"Well, hello Jimmy. Aye sure enough, I've been in bed laid up with the flu, so I have. It's my first time out for a week or more. I wouldn't get too close; I might still be contagious."

"Aye, is that right? Well, I'll take my chances. If I can interrupt yer shopping for a while, we'd like to have a word."

"Aye, Jimmy, just let me pay for this."

It was a delaying tactic; he recognised he could be in trouble. He handed the vendor two-pound notes and waited for change, trying to work out a possible escape.

Jimmy was close and had his hand in his jacket pocket. Eoghan felt something hard press into his back, a gun barrel, unmistakably.

"Now yer wouldn't be wanting to tinking of running, not with all these people about."

"Why would I want to run, Jimmy? There's no need for the gun, there isn't. I was tinking of coming down to the pub later, now I'm feeling a bit better."

"Well, it looks as though, I've saved yer a trip then... Walk."

"Aye, sure, but where do yer want us to go?"

"We'll go down to the pub; sure, some of the boys will be there."

Eoghan knew where Jimmy meant. It would mean going through the 'wet' section and out onto John Dillon Street. Jimmy started to push Eoghan who was deliberately walking slowly. The fruit and veg stalls were busy with customers. The stench of fish was overpowering as they passed the iced boxes of haddock, plaice, cod, and numerous other species that were on sale. Vendors were using hand-held portable scales to weigh their produce for the waiting customers.

They reached the back exit of the market; Jimmy was right behind Eoghan; the occasional prod with the gun barrel reminded Eoghan of his presence.

They waited at the pavement for a car to pass. It was followed by a bus about thirty yards behind. Eoghan waited; then, at the very last minute, sprinted in front of it before Jimmy could react.

There was a frantic sound of the horn and the squeal of brakes. A car was approaching in the opposite direction. Eoghan again dashed across in front of it, causing the vehicle to stop abruptly; there were more gestures of annoyance from the driver. People on the pavement stared.

In front of Eoghan was an arch and alleyway; he sped down the narrow path. It opened out into the back yards of terraced houses on either side. The footpath was partly paved, partly cinder, making running hazardous. He hadn't yet looked behind him.

Jimmy cursed as the stationary bus blocked his path. He ran around the obstacle and looked left and right. A delivery van passed in the opposite direction before Jimmy could cross the road. There was no sign of Eoghan. He stopped to get his bearings then noticed the alleyway.

By the time Jimmy approached the entrance, Eoghan had reached the next road, Back Lane, and turned right. He was starting to formulate a plan. He needed to get back to his bedsit, which he believed was secure, then he would decide on his next move. He would need to leave Ireland; his use to British Intelligent had been compromised.

He stopped running as it would draw attention to himself, but speed-walked towards Nicholas Street, another busy thoroughfare. He could see the ruins of St Nicholas Church to his left. He turned right which would eventually lead to his flat.

Then, he had a stroke of luck; he noticed a taxi approaching. Eoghan was stood on the corner of Bride Road, not far from the old baths; he stepped into the road and flagged down the vehicle.

The cab crossed the road and the driver leaned over. "Where do you want to be going?"

"The Garda Siochana station, Guiness Street."

"Aye, get in."

Eoghan opened the cab door and sat in the back seat. He was sweating profusely. The taxi pulled away and headed down Patrick Street and passed St Patrick's Park.

It was only about a mile to the destination, but Eoghan was on high alert. He was not out of the woods yet by any means. The police station was on the corner with the junction of Kevin Street, still about a quarter of a mile from his bedsit. He didn't know if he could trust the taxi driver and wasn't about to give away his address.

The cab pulled up outside the police station and Eoghan paid the fare plus tip. There had been no attempt at conversation. He watched as the taxi pulled away and crossed the road. Ten minutes later he was back at his bedsit.

He needed to call London.

Meanwhile, back in Bloomsbury, it was late afternoon; Agnes telephoned her sister.

"Hello Grace, I wondered if Matthew was available this evening; I could do with some advice again."

"Yes, of course, and you're in luck, he's just arrived, although he may need to go back later, something to do with these wretched problems on the underground."

"Oh, as long as it's not inconvenient."

"No, of course not, and I have a surprise for you. You remember my friend Hetty, from Fannies?"

"Yes, of course."

"Well, she's staying with us overnight. I'm sure she will be thrilled to meet you."

"That would be marvellous. As long as I'm not intruding."

"No, silly. What time will you be here?"

"About seven? If I can get a taxi."

"See you at seven."

It was another winter's evening, not as cold as January, and thoughts of spring gave a sense of optimism. Agnes alighted the taxi outside Grace's house and paid the driver.

There was a warm greeting between the sisters. Matthew was also present; he'd taken time out from his work to meet Agnes but thought he might have to return later.

"Would you like a drink?" asked Grace as Agnes took off her coat.

"Yes please, a cup of tea would be nice."

Agnes noticed someone seated on the settee. She got up. "Hello, I'm Hetty."

Agnes leaned and gave her a cheek kiss, then recognition. "Hello Hetty, yes of course. It's so good to meet you again after all these years. The last time was at the concert in St Omer, if I remember rightly. Grace was always telling stories of your exploits with the ambulances."

"Ha, yes, there are many to be told, and congratulations on your singing. We love your new radio show."

"Thank you," replied Agnes. "That's very kind."

Grace left the pair chatting and went to make the drink. Just then Matthew came in from the kitchen and welcomed Agnes with a cheek kiss.

"Thank you so much, Matthew, for sparing the time. I'm sorry to disturb you again; I know you are very busy."

"I'm glad to be of service; what would you like to know?"

Agnes looked at Hetty. "Please excuse my rudeness, Hetty, I just need a quick word with Matthew in private."

"We can use the dining room," said Matthew.

"Yes, of course," said Hetty.

Matthew and Agnes left the lounge and went into the adjacent room.

Agnes quickly explained the reason for her visit. "I've decided to go with Solly to help get his parents to England. I've got an idea which might help."

Agnes reached into her handbag and pulled out three letters. They were on headed notepaper from an opera house in Berlin asking if she could sing at a special concert. They were dated 1935.

"I have these letters; they are dated nineteen thirty-five. I declined the offer at that time as I'd stopped performing. I was wondering if they could be adapted in some way to suggest they had been sent last month."

Matthew examined the letters. "I don't see why not. What's you plan?"

"It's only an idea in case we were stopped for any reason. I had in mind that I could say that Solly's parents were part of my staff. I thought I could use the letters as confirmation."

"Hmm, and what if they check?"

"It's only in case we get stopped. I can't believe anyone would check them. They are in German; I had to get them translated."

"Do you have the translations?"

"Yes." Agnes burrowed back into her handbag, pulled out the three transcripts, and handed them to Matthew. He examined them. "These are not dated, so that won't be a problem."

"Solly is worried about crossing the border from Germany and whether they might be stopped and questioned. He was talking about finding a crossing point without border controls, given the present situation."

Matthew looked at Agnes with serious expression.

"You could do that, but there are logistical issues to consider. How will you get to the border? Do you have a local contact? I should add that if you get caught crossing the border at an unmanned checkpoint, then questions will definitely be asked, and the border is patrolled."

"Hmm, I see what you mean."

"I think you should go to the busiest crossing point you can find. Unless you give them any reason, you should get through without difficulty."

"Yes, thank you, that makes sense. Can I leave the letters with you? I'll need them back before the weekend."

"Yes, I'll make sure."

Agnes and Matthew retuned to the lounge where a tray with tea pot and cups were waiting.

"Sorry about that," said Agnes as they sat down. Grace poured the tea.

Hetty was keen to hear about Agnes's radio appearances. "I saw you on the cover of The Radio Times. You looked very glamourous."

"Thank you, there was a lot of makeup." Agnes laughed; the others joined in.

They continued their convivial discourse for another half an hour before Agnes asked if she could call a taxi.

After Agnes had left, Hetty and Grace were in the kitchen when the telephone rang. Matthew answered. He listened to the caller.

"Yes Colonel, I'll be there in forty-five minutes."

It had gone nine o'clock when Matthew arrived at Headquarters. The cypher room was busy as he walked through to his office and deposited his coat, hat, and umbrella in his wardrobe. Then he quickly made his way to the Colonel's office.

"Ah, Major, come in. Would you like something to warm you up?"

"Yes, why not."

The Colonel went to the cupboard and retrieved a bottle of scotch and two glasses.

"Sorry to pull you in, Matthew, but I couldn't speak over the phone. It's Night Wing."

"Nothing's happened, I hope."

"Hmm, it seems he's been compromised. We received a message a couple of hours ago; we need to get him out."

"What's his plan?"

"That's the problem; the ports are going to be watched. He's going to go to his mother's. She's got a farm out in County Sligo somewhere. He's going to sit tight and let the heat die down, then try to slip across the border to the north, then out through Belfast. They don't know him up there."

"What about his mother's place? Is it safe?"

"It's certainly safer than Dublin."

"True."

"I just wanted you to be aware of the situation. I'll let you know if we get any more information... The other thing I wanted to discuss with you is today's bombings. I've had the Home Office on asking what we're doing to catch the perpetrators. There was a debate in Parliament today; they're looking for answers. We need to stay on top of this. The newspapers will be full of it tomorrow."

"I've been in touch with Chief Superintendent Philips, Special Branch, at Scotland Yard; they're hopeful of making early arrests."

"Hmm, let's hope so; the headline in The Times doesn't help."

"No that's true. I spoke to the RUC in Belfast, apparently the plans to blow up Buckingham Palace were found in one of their raids. They don't know who leaked it to the press. The police have upped their security around all the Royal residencies, including Windsor."

There were considerable challenges facing Matthew and his team.

Chapter Nine

Hereford Street, Acton, Tuesday February 7th, 10 a.m.

Hetty had already left for her appointment in town with the solicitor, promising an early return. Grace had not had chance to speak to Matthew about possible employment opportunities for Chloe. Given everything that was going on, she didn't feel it appropriate, but would ask him that evening.

A letter arrived addressed to James Keating. He was still in bed, a study day. Grace shouted up the stairs.

"James there's a letter for you; I think it's from the RAF."

There was a bump, then an urgent sound of footsteps. James descended the stairs in his pyjamas two at a time. Grace handed him the letter. There was a silence as James ripped open the envelope and digested the content.

"I'm in; I'm in. I've been selected," he squealed in delight.

Grace had mixed feelings, but she was happy for him; it was his dream, and she wouldn't stand in his way.

"You'd better call your father; he'll want to know."

"Yes, I'll call him after breakfast."

"When will you need to go? Does it say?"

"No, it says 'joining instructions to follow'."

James Street, Keighley. Tuesday morning back at the bakery, it was hectic as preparation for the morning's service was well underway. The first batch of bread had already been baked and was on the shelves waiting for opening time. Daisy was making a tray of scones in the oven.

William seemed in a pensive mood which didn't go

unnoticed by his brother.

"Eh up, Will, 'appen tha's got summat on tha mind."

William looked up from the mixing vat. "Aye, 'appen I have."

"Go on then, what's tha mithering about?"

"It's Marjorie."

"Aye, I guessed it might be. She's not fed up with tha already?"

"Nay, nay, nowt like that, opposite, if anything."

"Well, what's tha mithering about then?"

"I want to ask her to marry me, but what if she says no?"

"Tha's daft, she's desperate to get wed, I reckon. Why don't tha speak to Mam; she's a woman. She knows about these things."

"Aye, 'appen I'll do that. I'll pop up when I've finished mix. Can you see to the baking?"

"Aye, I'll see to it."

An hour later, William had taken a break and ascended the stairs to the parlour. Ivy was in the kitchen and heard someone enter the flat. She went to investigate.

"William, what are you doing up here at this time?"

"I wanted to ask tha advice."

"Of course, nothing wrong is there? Would you like a drink?"

"Aye, go on, ta, 'appen I'm parched."

William sat down and started tapping the table nervously. A few minutes later Ivy returned with a cup of tea on a saucer.

"So, go on what's on your mind?" Ivy sat opposite him.

"It's Marjorie."

"Oh aye, you've not had words, have you?"

"No, nowt like that, I want to ask her to marry me."

Ivy's face lit up. "But that's wonderful. She'll make you a good wife."

"Aye, but what if she's says no?"

"She'll not turn you down; you mark my words. I reckon she's struck on you."

"Tha think so?"

"Aye, I do. Have you thought about a ring?"

"Aye, I was going to ask her first, then we can go and choose a ring from Peplows. No point in buying a ring if she says no. 'Appen they won't take it back for a refund."

Ivy looked at William, His hands were shaking so much, most of his tea was spilling into his saucer.

"William, Marjorie will be daft to turn you down, and I'm positive she won't. You're just like your Da; he never had no confidence before the war."

Ivy looked down for a moment in sadness at the memory. William was deep in thought.

"Aye, 'appen tha's right."

"When are you going to ask her?"

"I'm meeting her at the café at dinner time."

William felt much better for his heart to heart with his mother and went back to work invigorated.

Time passed slowly, but eventually, one o'clock arrived, and Robert agreed to close the shop and retract the awning.

William quickly went upstairs and washed his face and brushed the flour dust out of his hair. He picked up his jacket and cap and headed out of the flat and down into the bakery. As he reached the front door, Robert and Daisy were waiting.

"Good luck, Will," said Robert.

"Let us know how tha gets on," added Daisy.

William crossed James Street, still busy with traffic. A trolley bus stopped and disgorged three passengers before moving on.

It was a better morning, bright but cloudy and several

degrees warmer than previous days. As he crossed the park, clumps of crocuses were in full bloom under the trees, not that William would have noticed; the nerves had returned.

Marjorie was stood outside the café waiting for him and waved as he approached. Although younger than William, she was more mature and looked older than her years. Her dark hair was tied in a bun, as was the fashion, and wore a scarf and topcoat.

"Ah do, Marjorie," said William. "Tha looks smashing; I hope tha's not been waiting long."

"No, just got here. How was your morning?"

"Aye, not bad, ta."

William pushed open the door and waited while Marjorie entered.

They were ushered to a seat by the window; it had become their regular position. The waitress handed them a menu as they sat down. Marjorie unbuttoned her coat and draped it over the back of her chair. She was wearing a cardigan over a blouse.

"Usual is it?" asked the waitress.

William looked at Marjorie and replied. "Aye, ta."

The waitress took back the menus and headed to the kitchen.

Marjorie sensed something wasn't right; William seemed anxious and was fiddling with the sleeve of his jacket.

"Are you alright, William?"

"Aye, 'appen I just need toilet."

He got up and headed for the washroom on the other side of the café.

Marjorie looked around at the other customers. It was busy with only a couple of free tables which were being prepared for the next occupants. People were queuing at the door. The room was full of cigarette smoke.

William reappeared and walked back to the table. He hadn't bothered with a topcoat, just his usual jacket.

The tea cakes and pot of tea had been delivered but Marjorie had waited before starting. William sat down and she poured the tea.

"Come on William, what's the matter? You're not usually like this."

"Aye, aye, sorry, I've had summat on my mind."

It was Marjorie's turn to look worried.

"Nay, nay, don't fret none... The thing is... I want us to get married; what do tha say?"

Marjorie was about to take a sip of tea and had to replace her cup.

"Oh, thank goodness, I though you wanted to call everything off."

"Nay, nay, I love tha more than I can say, and I want us to get wed. What do tha reckon?"

She reached forward and held his hands. She could feel them trembling.

"William Marsden, that would make me the happiest girl in the world."

William breathed a huge sigh of relief.

"I've not brought tha a ring. I thought we could go to Peplows after work and choose. What do tha think?"

"Aye, I think it's a lovely idea. I'll ask the manager if I can leave at four."

"Aye, I can meet you outside the store... You won't have to leave your job or owt... Now we're engaged, I mean?"

"No, but after we're wed I might, company policy. I'll have to speak to the manager."

"Well, 'appen I can support tha. Tha could even work in t'bakery. There's always plenty of work."

"Yes, I'm sure... I feel so happy, William. I can't wait to

tell me mam."

"I hope she won't object."

"No, not at all, she thought you were a very nice boy when you came to tea."

"Aye, I were on my best behaviour." He laughed, but mostly one of relief.

William returned to the bakery and told his mother before returning to the shop.

"We should have a party to celebrate," said Daisy.

Later, William and Marjorie went to the jewellers and chose a ring, one very happy couple.

Hereford Street, Acton. Matthew returned home after another stressful day. The pressure was mounting to catch the perpetrators of the Underground bombings, and, although it was a police operation, intelligence was vital in supporting the investigation. He had spent most of the afternoon at New Scotland Yard briefing Special Branch police officers on the latest information. There had been no contact with Night Wing, which was also a concern, but there was little they could do about it.

Grace welcomed him warmly as he took off his coat and placed his trilby on the hook.

It was seven o'clock and Matthew had been in the office for twelve hours without a break. Then there was the call out the previous evening which had kept him at headquarters till midnight.

"You must be exhausted, darling, would you like a drink?"

"Yes, dear, I think a large Scotch would hit the spot. I don't think I'll get called out again tonight."

Grace joined Matthew for the evening meal and the

atmosphere relaxed. The radio was on, playing light music in the background.

"Oh, I meant to mention, Hetty was talking about her stepdaughter. She's looking for a job in the City and I wondered if there was any openings in your department."

"Can she type?"

"I'm not sure, but Hetty was saying she's very bright."

Matthew wiped his mouth with a napkin; he was thinking.

"Actually, there may be an opening. We're always on the lookout for wireless operators."

"Oh, I'm sure she would love that. What do you want me to do?"

"I'll write it down. Viginia Tennison, she looks after the recruits; I'll have a word with her make sure, what was her name?"

"Chloe."

"Chloe, gets an interview."

"Thank you."

Matthew yawned. "I think I'm going to have an early night and try to catch up on some sleep."

"I'll finish the dishes and read for a while. I won't disturb you," replied Grace.

Saturday, 11th February. 8 a.m.

Agnes was fussing about with her suitcase, making sure she had everything she needed. This time she had to pack lighter than when going on tour; she had no-one to carry her bags.

"What time's the taxi coming?" asked Alistair.

"Eight o'clock; should be here any time." Agnes went to the window and looked out anxiously.

Gwen was stood next to her father. "There's a car just pulled up outside."

Agnes went to the front door, while Alistair carried her suitcase and valise.

"Bye, Mum, stay safe," said Gwen.

"What time's your train?" asked Alistair as they walked to the taxi.

"Five to ten," replied Agnes, as the taxi driver took the cases and opened the boot.

"You should be in good time."

Alistair hugged Agnes. "Look after yourself. Don't do anything dangerous. I love you, darling."

"I love you too," said Agnes, and got into the back of the cab.

She had applied more makeup than usual and was wearing her mink coat and a hat that was the height of fashion from one of London's top milliners. Normally, she would not dress so ostentatiously, in order to avoid attracting attention, but this morning she had decided to play the part of the famous singer. She thought it might help the mission,

The streets of London were busy with Saturday morning traffic as they headed for the station. She looked skywards; she still hadn't got use to the barrage balloons which were creating a spectral canopy over the city. She reflected on her radio performance the previous evening. Robert Lang was once again effusive with praise. Since her appearance on the Radio Times cover, fan mail had increased significantly. Fortunately, the letters had been passed on to Solly's team who would deal with them.

They arrived at Liverpool Street station just after nine o'clock, in good time for the train. The taxi was able to drive through the grand entrance and up to the platforms before stopping. Agnes could see Solly at the head of the line of taxis. He was wearing a smart topcoat and trilby hat with a small suitcase next to him.

The cabbie opened the rear door for her. Agnes got out while he went to the boot to retrieve the luggage. She opened her purse and gave the driver his fare plus tip. He then produced a pencil and a piece of paper from his pocket.

"Can I have your autograph, Miss Agnes. I'm a big fan."

"Of course," she replied and duly signed. The cabbie was grinning from ear to ear as he drove away.

She picked up her luggage and walked up the platform to meet Solly.

"Hello Agnes," said Solly, as she reached him. "May I say how glamorous you look. It seems you have a fan; I saw you signing his piece of paper."

"Yes, thank you, it seems so," replied Agnes, and they walked into the main station concourse.

"Do you want me to get a porter?"

"No, thank you, I can manage."

Several engines were steamed up along the various platforms waiting to leave; smoke billowed into the station's glass canopy. Hundreds of people were milling about. The noise of conversations and general hubbub gave it a special atmosphere. From here people would leave to fulfil dreams.

"We have some time to wait; would you like to get a drink before we leave?"

"That's an excellent idea."

There was a large newspaper stall at the back of the concourse; the refreshment room was next to it.

"Would you like a magazine for the journey?" asked Solly.

"As long as it's not the Radio Times," joked Agnes.

"I have my copy at home; I want to frame it... the cover I mean."

"I'm sure Robert can get one of the original photographs."

"Oh, now that's a thought."

Solly queued and eventually bought two newspapers and a magazine for Agnes, before making their way into the refreshment room.

It was stuffy from smoke, and busy, but they managed to find a seat, and Solly went to the counter and bought two teas. Agnes could feel she was being stared at, and smiled at one or two people who had clearly recognised her. She was becoming a topic of conversation.

Agnes had signed more autographs before they finished their refreshments and headed for their train.

"Platform six, the boat train," said Solly, as they looked for the platform.

Five minutes later, they were making themselves comfortable in a first-class compartment.

Solly lifted the suitcases onto the luggage rack above them. For the moment they had the compartment to themselves.

Agnes took off her coat, and it, too, was stowed overhead. She was wearing a green, long-sleeved dress with high shoulder pads, all the rage according to the fashion magazines.

"Have you got everything?" asked Agnes.

"Well, I think so. I just hope our contact will be at Eindhoven with the passports. If not then we're stuck."

"Have you spoken to him?"

"No, it's all been arranged through the Jewish Refugee Committee."

"I've got the letters I mentioned. I've been able to get the date changed," said Agnes.

"Hmm. well let's hope we won't need them."

He looked through the window at an adjacent platform. A train had pulled in and passengers were getting out.

"This takes me back, you know... This is where we met the

children arriving as part of the *Kindertransport* programme."

"Yes, you mentioned that. Do you still have any involvement with them?"

"No, they've all been distributed around the country now, although there are some, of course, in London."

The compartment door opened, and a distinguished-looking man entered the carriage. He was sporting a grey moustache and carried a briefcase. He nodded at Agnes and Solly before taking his seat and opened a newspaper.

It took the express train just under an hour and fifty minutes to cover the sixty-four miles to Harwich Quay Station. The fellow passenger got up as the train slowed to a stop, nodded to Agnes and Solly, then left the carriage. His presence had prevented any further discussion about their 'mission' during the journey.

"Oh look, the sea," said Agnes as she looked out of the window. There was no platform on the right-hand side, just some painted railings, then the water. The tide was out and the beach, such as it was, was just a mixture of stones and debris, mixed with oil.

Solly retrieved the suitcases and Agnes's coat from the overhead rack, and they left the compartment to exit the train.

It was almost midday, as they walked through the station and joined the other passengers at the departure gate, both wearing their outer garments and carrying their luggage. In front of them, the TS Prague waited at the dock ready to receive her customers.

"It's busy," said Agnes as she observed the bustling crowd waiting to embark. One or two looked in their direction at the 'glamourous' couple.

"Yes, I think we should try to find somewhere to get some

food. I've no idea what catering facilities are available. We have plenty of time."

"Good idea," replied Agnes.

At two o'clock there was a huge blast of the steamer's whistle, and the gangplanks were withdrawn. Agnes and Solly were below decks in the saloon as the ship started to ease away from the quayside. The smoke-filled room was crowded as fellow passengers jostled for seats.

It was the first time Agnes had taken a boat trip since her return from France twenty-four years earlier. Then, it was a nerve-wracking experience with the danger of mines and German submarines. At least they had been spared that worry this time. Nevertheless, other challenges lay ahead.

It was a seven-hour journey. Agnes passed the time reading her magazine while Solly attempted one of the crossword puzzles in his newspaper.

It was dark as the steamer edged slowly along the quayside in Holland.

The gangplanks were attached to the boat with ropes and passengers started to walk across into the arrival area. The sea was quite choppy, and the boat was rising and falling with the waves making the narrow 'bridge' to the dock treacherous.

Agnes and Solly carried their suitcases across and waited in turn at the customs barrier. Solly appeared anxious but within twenty minutes, and without much formality, their passports had been stamped and they officially entered Holland.

There were signs in Dutch and English directing passengers to the exit and trains. The quay station was similar to Harwich, in as much that trains were able to meet the ferries at the dock side.

The pair followed the signs through an arch where a train was waiting; passengers were queuing to get on.

"These run every half an hour into Rotterdam, according to someone I was speaking to at the centre."

"Thank goodness, I can't wait to get to the hotel."

"Yes, it's been a long day."

Sunday morning, Agnes was applying the last of her makeup before joining Solly for breakfast. She had slept well but still felt tired from the previous day's journey.

The hotel was only five minutes' walk from the Rotterdam Delftsche Poort station, where they had arrived. The room was comfortable for an overnight stay but not particularly large, dominated by the bed. The décor was faded and yellow from cigarette smoke. Agnes had stayed in worse.

Solly was already seated in the dining room when Agnes entered. She was wearing another fashionable outfit, in keeping with her 'celebrity' status. It was all part of the mission.

"Good morning, Agnes," said Solly, as she approached and sat down. "Hope you slept well."

"I did, thank you, Solly."

She looked at him. She noticed he was losing his hair, and his face was lined; he looked older than his thirty-nine years.

He continued. "I've been going over our itinerary; our train to Eindhoven leaves at ten-thirty; we should be there for midday. We'll need to take a taxi; it's a different station from where we arrived. Maas, according to my notes."

Solly was reading his bits of paper which had all the information for the journey.

"What time is your contact arriving?"

"He's intending driving up from Brussels, according to his letter. It's not too far, around seventy miles. He said he would meet us at the station in Eindhoven around two o'clock." Solly was holding another piece of paper and reading from it.

"What's his name?"

"Ernst Jacob."

"Do you know what he looks like?"

"No, but he says he'll be wearing a light raincoat and trilby hat."

"Hmm, not sure if that's going to narrow it down too much. It's what everyone seems to be wearing."

Solly looked up and smiled as a waiter came to take their order.

By nine-thirty, they had vacated the hotel. There were several taxis waiting outside and Solly approached the first one.

"Maas Station, please."

The cabbie thought for a moment before heading off.

A few minutes later, they were making their way through the streets of Rotterdam. There was no conversation; Agnes just looked out of the window at the unfamiliar surroundings. She had been transported back to another time when she was in a foreign country.

Tramlines snaked towards the station and the route was busy with tramcars. As the cab reached the destination, Agnes could see the two large glass canopies which were landmarks in the city.

The taxi entered the forecourt, the noise of the tyres rumbled as it drove over the brick-paved station forecourt. It pulled up outside the main entrance and the pair got out.

It was a cloudy, cool morning with a brisk wind and

Agnes was wearing her fur coat and the same hat. She had only brought one with her as they tended to squash in the suitcase. The driver retrieved their luggage from the boot.

Solly reached in his jacket pocket. He had exchanged fifty pounds into Dutch Guilders in London which he hoped would cover expenses while in Holland.

"This is impressive," she observed, looking up at the station façade.

"Yes, it's the oldest station in Rotterdam, apparently.

As a major transport hub, inside it was busy, not like Liverpool Street but, nevertheless, it meant a queue at the ticket kiosk. Agnes looked after the luggage as Solly waited in line.

There was just time to grab a coffee and a pastry before boarding the train.

The carriages were similar to the ones they had travelled in from Liverpool Street but there was no first-class compartment or toilet facilities.

The other passengers in the compartment were Dutch and they seemed to be chatting the whole journey. Agnes looked out of the window for most of the time. Solly was reading his folder of letters, preparing for the final leg of the journey.

It was just under two hours when the train pulled into the station at Eindhoven, enabling Agnes and Solly to leave the train and stretch their legs. The platform was busy with departing passengers but instead of heading to the exit, the pair made their way to the cafeteria where they could have something to eat.

"Well, so far, so good," said Solly as he carried a tray of coffee cups and sandwiches to one of the vacant tables.

"What time did you say your contact will arrive?" asked Agnes as Solly took his seat.

"Around two o'clock, he said. We can wait outside the entrance for him."

"Are you alright, you seem anxious," observed Agnes, as she took a sip of coffee.

"Yes, it's the next part I'm dreading. I'm just hoping my parents have received the letter I sent them."

"You sent it to their friend?"

"Yes, he said he doesn't live too far away from where they are staying."

"Well, there's not much more we can do for the moment."

"No, you're right. How are the sandwiches?"

Agnes looked at the chunky bread filled with a wedge of cheese.

"They're quite tasty. I don't know about you, but I was quite hungry."

At one-thirty, Solly got up from the table.

"I think I'll go and get our tickets and wait for Ernst outside in case he's early. There's no need for you to join me; you can look after the luggage and stay warm."

"Very well, I might come out for some fresh air in a few minutes; it's so stuffy in here." Agnes could smell cigarettes on her precious coat.

Agnes ordered another coffee and waited.

The large clock on the cafeteria wall said one fifty-five. Agnes was about to leave when she saw two gentlemen walking towards her. It was Solly, accompanied by a man wearing a light-coloured raincoat and trilby. Solly appeared to be grinning happily.

"Agnes, this is Ernst Jacob."

The man doffed his trilby and shook hands. "Miss Marsden, it's an honour to meet you.. My mother lives in London and was thrilled when I told her I was meeting you."

"That's very kind."

"I should also say the community owes you a big debt in supporting Solly like this."

"I felt I had to do something when Solly explained what was happening in Germany."

Solly went to get more refreshments, leaving Agnes and Ernst to continue their conversation.

"How was your journey?" asked Agnes.

"It was uneventful, I'm glad to say. It's not that far, just about a hundred kilometres."

"I know Solly has been so worried about his parents, and how grateful he is of your help," added Agnes.

The diplomat continued. "Well, being half-Jewish myself, I have an affinity with those caught up in Germany. It really is quite bad there... I should add, the Embassy is not directly involved; it's against Government policy, but the Ambassador is happy for me to provide assistance from time to time, or, should I say, he looks the other way." He smiled.

Agnes was weighing him up. Urbane, about the same age as her, mid-forties, probably, dark eyes and hair, but not typically Jewish-looking. He was immaculately dressed in a lounge suit, white shirt and red-patterned tie under his opened raincoat. He also had a white handkerchief in his top pocket.

"What's the latest over there?" asked Agnes.

"Since *Kristallnacht* there has been unbelievable hardship for the Jews. They are forced to wear the Star of David, they can't own businesses, many have had their property confiscated, and many have been deported. Officially, there are no restrictions on Jews leaving Germany; the big problem is no country will take them. For all its good intentions, the British Government are doing nothing to help, and are, if anything, discouraging immigrants. They say they are protecting British jobs."

"What about Solly's parents?"

"Hmm, if you can get them out of Germany, the passports should get them into England."

Solly arrived with more drinks.

"Have you eaten, Ernst? They serve food here."

"I will get something shortly. What time is your train?"

"Three o'clock."

"Oh, in that case I'll get something after you've gone. There are one or two things we should discuss."

"Yes, of course, I have a few questions."

"Oh, before I forget, these are your parents' passports."

While Solly distributed the drinks and sat down, Ernst reached into his inside pocket and produced two new documents. Solly received them and started flicking through the pages.

"Oh, I see you managed with the photographs I sent."

"Yes, there's a photographer we use who can clean them up; I am sure they will pass scrutiny."

"I certainly hope so; their lives may depend on it."

"Quite," said Ernst.

"We were discussing how best to cross the border back into Holland from Germany," said Agnes. "I have a friend who works for the Home Office who suggested we use one of the normal routes."

"Yes, he's right, the busier the better. I assume you'll cross the border at Veno."

Agnes looked at Solly for confirmation.

"Yes," interjected Solly, "Then onto Mönchengladbach."

"Then that's the route I would choose to return. As long as your parents are not on any watch list, they should be safe."

"But what's this we heard about rounding up Jews and

deporting them to camps?"

Ernst looked down. "Yes, we have heard some dreadful tales. But your parents have British passports now. Oh, we changed their name from Solomon to Spencer; it's less Jewish. They will have to remember that when they cross the border."

"But they don't speak English. Won't that look strange having a British passport and not speaking the language?"

"Hmm, yes, I had assumed they could speak English."

"Well, they know a little, but they were born in Germany; they've never been out of the country."

"Then you'll have to stay close to them."

The three continued chatting, with the diplomat providing more advice, before the time had come for Agnes and Solly to catch their train for the final leg of the journey.

Agnes and Solly shook hands with Ernst and left the saloon. Ernst headed for the service counter to order some food.

The train was waiting at the platform. A railway official in a uniform was walking up and down the train. Solly approached him and showed him the tickets. He said something in Dutch and Solly shrugged his shoulders in misapprehension.

The man gestured to the pair and walked to one of the carriages and pointed.

"Here," he said in English.

Solly answered in German.

The official picked up Agnes's luggage. "You come," he said and smiled.

He opened the carriage door and carried Agnes's suitcase to the appropriate compartment. Solly followed.

Again, it was a similar carriage to the one they travelled to Harwich but was soon crowded. They made themselves comfortable and Solly took out the passports from his pocket and started nervously flicking through them again.

"I just had a terrible thought," said Solly.

"What's that?"

"The entry stamp... into Germany. If they were part of your staff, as we said, they would have one. They're going to know they are fakes."

He turned over the last page. "Oh, thank goodness... he remembered." Solly visibly breathed a sigh of relief, seeing the appropriate mark.

There was a whistle, a lurch, then slowly the train chugged its way out of the station. Next stop Venlo, then across the border.

Chapter Ten

Monday morning, Düsseldorf, Agnes opened the hotel curtains. She blinked as the daylight bathed the room. It was a bright day, although the sun had yet to make an appearance. In the distance she could see the top of the Oberkassel Bridge, the famous landmark crossing of the Rhine.

Düsseldorf wasn't what she was expecting; although she hadn't had any real preconceptions, just those painted by the newspapers which seemed to imply that all German cities were ugly.

Wide thoroughfares lined with trees, beautiful architecture, the Hauptbahnhof Central Station, where they had arrived, was the very essence of Art Deco with its distinctive clock tower. There were surprisingly few Swastikas; most were on Government buildings and one draped over the station facia.

The arrival into Germany proved to be as smooth as Ernst had said. After the stop at Venlo, there was a further stop at the border where German Customs officials, accompanied by armed guards, walked down the train checking documents. Solly was making mental notes for the return. Their passports were examined then stamped with no more than a cursory attention by the official.

Their chosen accommodation, The Eisen Hotel, was behind the station on *Eisen Strasse,* a ten-minute walk. It had been recommended by a former resident who was now part of the Jewish Refugee Council in London. They hadn't made any reservations, but the hotel was not busy, and two rooms were readily available.

It was a comfortable room with a large double bed; it compared favourably with hotels Agnes had stayed in before.

She went into the ensuite bathroom and started running a bath. Her hair and clothes smelt like an ashtray after being cooped up with smokers for much of the previous day.

Just after nine o'clock, she descended the three floors and entered the breakfast room. It was quiet with only two other tables occupied. They seemed like business-types, judging by their apparel. Solly was chatting to one of the waiters in German. He got up from his seat when he saw Agnes approach.

"How was your night?" he asked as she took her place at the table, assisted by the waiter.

He handed her a menu and spoke to Agnes in German. She looked at Solly for translation.

"It's alright, I've ordered the traditional breakfast and tea." He spoke to the waiter again and he left, seemingly satisfied with the instructions.

"Thank you, yes, I slept well. I think I was exhausted from all the travel yesterday."

Solly took a drink from a glass of water on the table. "I was asking the waiter how far *Bürger Strasse* was."

"Is it far?"

He poured Agnes a glass of water. "He doesn't know. We need to take a taxi; although I don't believe it's that far. I've just been reading the latest letter I received from my parents' friends again."

"What are their names, the people we are going to see?" Agnes took a sip of water.

"Martens... Horst and Ursula."

"Have you met them before?"

"No, as I said, they're friends of my parents. I think they must have met them after my sister, and I left. As I said, we lived in Duisburg when I was growing up. I've not been to Düsseldorf before."

They finished breakfast and went back to their respective rooms to collect their luggage. Solly was settling the bill at the reception desk when Agnes walked down the stairs followed by a porter carrying her suitcases.

Again, Agnes was wearing her mink coat, fashionable hat, and a lot of makeup. The receptionist looked up, did a double-take, and smiled.

She gave the porter two fifty Pfennig pieces, about half a crown in English money. He looked delighted.

The porter spoke to Solly who turned to Agnes. "He wants to know if we want a taxi."

Solly answered, and the porter led the pair to the entrance, once again carrying Agnes's luggage.

There was one taxi parked outside the hotel. The driver was inside reading a newspaper. He looked up and rolled down the window as they approached the car.

Solly leaned forward. *"Bitte Burgerstrasse."*

The porter opened the door for Agnes to get in, then stowed the suitcases in the boot.

The sun had risen; it was a bright early-spring morning. Agnes watched the city pass by; it looked very similar to London, trams, people bustling about their business. It was difficult to rationalise that these were the same people who were causing so much suffering to their fellow citizens.

They passed the *Jan Wellen* statue in front of the City Hall, another magnificent building.

The driver spoke to Solly. "He says it's just a short distance, just off *Frieden Strasse*, which we're coming to now."

The taxi made a turn. Agnes noticed three shops on the corner with their awnings raised; it could have been the bakery back in Keighley.

Solly checked his letter and leaned forward. *"Bitte*

Vierundfünfzig."

Solly turned to Agnes. "Number fifty-four," he translated.

The taxi slowed as it checked the numbers then stopped about halfway down just behind a black Opel Saloon.

"We're here," said Solly.

The driver retrieved the suitcases while Solly reached for his wallet and took out some notes. There were more discussions in German and the cabbie got in and drove away.

Agnes and Solly looked around examining their surroundings. It was a leafy avenue, not unlike where Grace and Matthew lived in London; the houses were not dissimilar.

Solly straightened his hat, walked up the short path to the front door, then knocked anxiously; Agnes followed, carrying her suitcases.

Moments later the door opened, and a man appeared wearing a cardigan over a shirt and suit trousers.

His eyes lit up and he talked excitedly in German. Solly replied and the pair hugged fondly. They were ushered in where a woman was standing in the hallway. Again, more introductions. Solly introduced Agnes, who also became the subject of an affectionate hug.

"Come in, I am Ursula" said the woman in English, with a strong German accent. After breaking away from the embrace, the pair were led into a sitting room. The suitcases were left in the hall.

"Please to meet you, Ursula. I'm sorry, I don't speak German," said Agnes, as she removed her coat and handed it to the woman. Ursula smiled and looked at it admiringly.

"*Ein wunderbarer Mantel...* er, a nice coat."

"Thank you," said Agnes.

There was more excited conversation and the offer of drinks. Solly was translating for Agnes. He explained that

Agnes was a singer and was helping him in securing his parents escape to England.

The coffee was served in a tall coffee pot; there was no offer of milk or sugar.

Horst spoke quickly, as if to emphasise the urgency of the situation. Solly turned to Agnes.

"Horst says my parents have been moved again, but they are safe and are expecting us. He says the Germans took away all Jewish passports in January and replaced them with something called a '*Kennkarten*' which contain their fingerprints. He doesn't think my parents have been issued with one as they've been in hiding since *Kristallnacht*. If they get stopped without one, questions will be asked. I've explained about the new passports."

Ursula looked at Agnes. "You are a... er, singer in England. On the... er, radio?" She pronounced it 'raddio'.

"Yes," replied Agnes.

Ursula spoke to Solly in German.

"Ursula says how glamorous you look," he translated.

"Thank you, *Danke*," replied Agnes, who had reached the limit of her German.

They finished their coffees and there was more discussion. Solly turned to Agnes.

"Horst is going to drive us to where my parents are and then to the station."

"That's very kind of him," replied Agnes.

There were fond farewells and expressions of gratitude with Ursula, as Horst led the pair to the Opel which was parked outside. He opened the boot and secured their luggage. Then inserted the starting handle into the front of the car and swung it. The engine putted into life. Horst got in and released the handbrake.

The pair waved to Ursula as the car pulled away. Solly and Horst continued to talk in German.

Fifteen minutes later, the Opel pulled up outside a large property on *Ehren Strasse*. The area was more urban and close to the *Marien Hospital*.

Horst left the car running and got out.

"*Bleib hier,*" he said.

Solly turned to Agnes. He wants us to stay here.

They watched as Horst knocked on the door. It opened and he was ushered inside.

A few minutes later, a couple in their late-fifties emerged from the house carrying a suitcase each. They were dressed warmly in overcoats and scarves.

Solly looked excitedly. "It's them! It's them!"

He got out of the car and ran towards them. They embraced, as the emotions of six years' absence came to the surface. All three were in tears.

"*Wir müssen schnell gehen,*" said Horst, telling them they needed to leave quickly. He was scanning the street for any unusual cars.

Horst was trying to negotiate the suitcases into the boot, but there was insufficient room for all of them. Solly took his father's luggage and carried it to the passenger seat. He got in and Horst manoeuvre it onto Solly's lap, then shut the lid to the boot.

Solly's parents were in the back with Agnes. There were quick introductions.

Horst looked around again, and, satisfied there were no police vehicles in the vicinity, headed to the station.

The concourse was busy as the Opel pulled up outside the station entrance. The time on the tall clock tower said eleven forty-five. The presense of the large Swastika flag, hanging by ropes from the roof above the entrance had Solly's parents on edge. It had become an emblem of menace.

Everyone alighted and retrieved their suitcases. There were more emotional moments as Solly's parents embraced Horst, before the four headed into the station.

"What time is the train?" asked Agnes as they walked towards the ticket office.

"There's one at twelve-thirty," replied Solly.

There was a queue waiting for tickets. Agnes looked around the busy station concourse. She counted at least twenty armed military police patrolling the area in their khaki uniforms and black kepis-style hats. They looked intimidating. She noticed other men in ill-fitting suits, stood at strategic points at the platform gates. They were all smoking, and appeared to be scrutinising the waiting passengers as they made their way to their trains. Every now and then, they would stop a passenger and examine their documents. She noticed one couple being marched away. Agnes had no idea who they were.

Solly's parents were holding each other closely, still very much afraid. The three waited away from the line, while Solly bought the tickets to Eindhoven.

With their travel documents duly purchased, the four headed to the waiting room. Agnes looked around; there seemed to be eyes everywhere. The police presence was causing a great deal of stress.

Solly got up. "I'll get us something for the journey," he said, and headed to the buffet bar.

"Do you speak English?" asked Agnes. "I am Agnes."

"Yes... a little, I am Benjamin, this is Gerda. Thank you for helping us."

"Oh, I have not done anything."

"Oh, but you have... we are ...er, grateful. You are a singer, I think?" replied Benjamin.

"Yes, that's right."

There was an uneasy silence. Agnes looked at the couple; they seemed careworn and incredibly thin. They had not eaten well for several months. Benjamin was like an older version of Solly. He was wearing a trilby hat, but it appeared he was bald or balding at least. His visible hair was grey. He did have a prominent nose which did, of course, mark him out as a Jew. It was a trait which Germans were asked to be on the lookout for. Gerda was also wearing a hat, her face, lined. She looked as though she was desperately in need of sleep.

Despite regulations, they were not wearing the Star of David, which, in itself, would lead to arrest if it was discovered they were Jews. Solly explained later that they had burned their clothes with the embriodered emblem.

Agnes smiled at Gerda not really know what to say.

Solly returned with a paper bag containing sandwiches and pastries.

"We need to board the train," said Solly, then spoke in German.

He turned to Agnes. "I've explained to them about the new rules regarding Jewish names. Jews are not allowed to use their original surnames and must use the name either Israel or Sarah."

"Why?"

"It's something the German Government have thought up to identify Jews."

"But that's dreadful," said Agnes.

"Oh, there are worse things, I promise."

Solly handed his parents their new British passports and explained their new names.

The couple were shaking, and Agnes was worried that their demeanour would give them away.

"Solly, please ask your parents to relax; they could give themselves away."

"Yes, you're right."

Solly spoke again to his parents, but it seemed to make little difference.

The group headed towards their departure gate where a ticket inspector was waiting, holding a manifest of some kind. He was flanked by two armed guards in military uniform.

"Let me go first," said Agnes. She opened her handbag and retrieved the letters.

She approached the ticket inspector.

"*Tickets, Reisepass, bitte.*" Agnes handed her ticket and passport. The man examined them and looked at Agnes. He spoke in German.

"I'm sorry, I don't understand. I don't speak German," she said in the 'poshest' voice she could manage.

Solly intervened and there were looks at Agnes.

"Show him the letters." Agnes opened the first letter and handed it to the ticket inspector.

He read it. "*Du bist ein Sänger?*" he asked. Solly translated.

"A singer? Yes, from London, these are my staff." Solly translated again.

"*Sehr gut,*" said the man and stamped the four tickets.

The two guards blocked their path momentarily, looked at the group with suspicion, but moved to one side, allowing them to pass.

There was no conversation as they walked up the platform, just relief; although they were not out of the woods yet.

They boarded the train and found their seats. Fortunately, they had a compartment to themselves.

Solly put the suitcases on the overhead rack and sat

down. He was holding the bag of food. His parents were seated opposite him and Agnes.

Agnes turned to Solly. "What did you say to the ticket inspector?"

"I told him you were a famous singer on the radio in England. I think he was impressed."

Gerda lay back in the seat and closed her eyes. Tears streamed down her face. She spoke to Solly in German; there was anger and worry in the tone.

"What did she say?" asked Agnes.

"She doesn't think she can go through with it. She says she wants to go back and take her chances."

Benjamin appeared to berate his wife.

Agnes leaned forward and took Gerda's hand. "Gerda, you must leave; they will kill you if you stay here."

Agnes's voice was soothing, and Gerda started to relax.

The train started moving, and Agnes looked out of the window. She could see more armed soldiers along the platform, as if providing a guard of honour. Solly handed around the food.

The smoke from the engine wafted past the carriage window as it picked up speed and left the urban scrawl behind. It was clear Solly's parents were still extremely anxious. Agnes had tried to engage with them with Solly's help in translation, but with little effect.

After another nerve-wracking stop at Mönchengladbach, the train continued towards the border. Benjamin and Gerda were holding onto each other, their faces etched with worry, unable to speak.

"Solly, we must get them to relax," said Agnes. "Ask them to take their coats off; they look like they are ready to leave."

Solly spoke to them in German and the pair stood up and took off their outer garments. Benjamin was wearing a suit, Gerda, a dress, which, on closer inspection, was stained and looked well-used.

Agnes had an idea. "Solly can you get my suitcase for me?"

Solly complied, and Agnes took Gerda's hand and left the compartment carrying her valise.

Solly looked at Benjamin and shrugged his shoulders.

Ten minutes later, the pair returned. Gerda was wearing one of Agnes's dresses and makeup.

Solly looked at his mother, unable to take in the transformation.

"I need my staff looking their best," said Agnes, and smiled. Solly translated. Benjamin replied.

"He says he hasn't seen her looking as good since their wedding day." They all laughed.

A few minutes later, the train started to slow down. Gerda looked at Benjamin and put her hand over her mouth in fear.

Agnes took her hand. "Don't worry, keep smiling, you will be alright." Solly translated and Gerda grimaced a smile.

The train pulled to a stop. There was a platform with armed guards stood in line. Swastikas were everywhere, with various notices in German. Behind the platform stood a building resembling a Bavarian cottage. It was dark when they had crossed the previous evening and hadn't noticed it. Several men appeared from its entrance and headed for different points on the train. They could hear doors opening and slamming shut. They were getting louder. The shadow of a man appeared before the door to the compartment opened. In walked an official in the uniform of a customs inspector. An armed soldier stood behind him.

"*Papiere*," snapped the man officiously.

Agnes had taken charge of the passports and handed them to him. She smiled. Benjamim and Gerda were at least looking more relaxed.

As the man looked at the group in turn, Gerda smiled nervously.

The man took one more look at the passports. Then handed them back and left the compartment.

Solly looked at his parents and put his finger to his mouth. "Shh," he whispered.

They could hear the hissing of steam from the engine. Time passed too slowly. Through the window, guards patrolled the platform. There was a kerfuffle of some sort.

Agnes watched as a man and woman in overcoats and carrying suitcases were being manhandled by armed soldiers towards the building. There was a lot of shoving and pushing. The woman appeared to be holding her hands to them as if in prayer, begging, beseeching. The man was shouting at the soldier who was restraining them.

Agnes watched as an officer in a black uniform with an 'SS' insignia approached the couple.

She saw the soldier speak to the officer. "*Juden,*" he appeared to say.

The officer took out his Luger and shot them both in the head. Agnes gasped.

Solly's parents hadn't witnessed the incident; they were looking the other way but had heard the shots.

They looked at each other; Benjamin hugged his wife. Agnes could see the bodies being dragged away, leaving a trail of blood on the platform. Another soldier picked up the suitcases.

There was the piercing shriek of the train's whistle, which made Agnes jump. Then movement.

Agnes looked at Solly and smiled but was still trying to process what she had just witnessed. The train moved slowly passed a manned machine gun post. Then notices in Dutch, some trees, then flat countryside.

"We're through," she said. Solly translated.

He embraced his parents in turn. Gerda had tears flowing down her face, she leant forward and hugged Agnes. "Thank you, thank you."

The landscape passed by; the light was beginning to fade as clouds rolled in. Agnes explained to Solly what she had witnessed.

"It is what I said; people have no idea what's happening."

The train stopped at Venlo for the engine to take on water which allowed them to buy some more food and stretch their legs. The relief of all concern was palpable.

It was another three hours before the train eventually pulled into Eindhoven station. It was hard emotionally. Solly's parents were still trying to come to terms with what had happened and there were, naturally, concerns for what the future might hold. Much of the journey was spent in silence; there would be time for celebration later.

Solly retrieved the luggage from the overhead racks and the four left the train.

They needed to buy new tickets for the journey to Rotterdam. Fortunately, the trains were running every hour; the next one would be at five o'clock according to the chalk-script noticeboard adjacent to the ticket office.

"There's a train at five o'clock," said Solly having read the notice. "That gives us half an hour. We should be in Rotterdam for six-thirty."

"Do you know the times of the boat?"

"I'm sure there's an overnight sailing, but we can check

when we get to the port. If not, it will mean a hotel in Rotterdam."

"Oh, I hope so; I just want to get home," said Agnes.

The rest of the journey was long and tedious. The four tried to nap as the train ate up the miles.

Eventually, they arrived in Rotterdam where they had to take a short taxi drive to Delftsche Poort station, which would connect them to the quay. On arrival, they took the opportunity to buy a coffee and sandwiches. Solly made an enquiry at the ticket office.

He returned with a smile on his face. "Good news, there's a boat leaving at ten o'clock. We have plenty of time."

Harwich Harbour. 5 a.m.

The party were in the First-Class section waiting for the ship to dock. Despite the comparative comfort of reclining seats, sleeping had been difficult, a mixture of exhaustion and anxiety. The saloon was smoky and claustrophobic, plus it was a choppy crossing which did nothing to aid a restful night.

Their ship, the T.S. Vienna, had a shop and cafeteria onboard, and they had been able to acquire some sandwiches and tea as an early breakfast.

Throughout the journey, conversation had been muted, partly due to Solly's parents' lack of English, but also the pair were still trying to come to terms with their situation. They whispered to each other from time to time to check on their respective well-being. They would tell their story in time.

It was still dark, but, through the large windows, the lights of the town were visible. Agnes watched as they grew closer. A few minutes later there was a bump as the boat reached the quayside.

One more hurdle for the group to negotiate.

Agnes had again applied some makeup for Gerda and made the men shave. "I don't want my staff looking like tramps," she joked. Solly translated.

At least they looked the part, as they made their way to the gangplanks.

As First-Class passengers, they were allowed off ahead of the rest, and a mariner supervised the departure like a mother hen. The saloon was less than a quarter full, but nevertheless there were over a hundred passengers to process.

A steward in a white jacket approached Agnes and shepherded the group to the gangplank. He ordered a waiting porter to assist with a wooden trolley.

They followed the steward down the ramp and handed over their luggage which was duly loaded by the porter.

The steward turned to Agnes. "It's Agnes Marsden, isn't it?"

"Yes," replied Agnes, rather surprised.

"I thought it was; I recognised you from the Radio Times. I do hope you've enjoyed your crossing with us today, Miss Marsden." He leaned forward and whispered. "My wife is a big fan; I can't wait to tell her I've met you."

"That's very kind, thank you." She turned to Solly. "Have you got one of the photographs to hand?"

"Yes, I think so," replied Solly, and he rummaged around in his wallet and produced a post-card size publicity photo of Agness from her BBC sessions.

There was a queue building, but Agnes took a pen from her handbag and signed the photo with a dedication to the steward's wife.

He was speechless.

Agnes sensed an opportunity. "I don't suppose we can

speed things up, do you? Since my Radio Times appearance, I do tend to get recognised and it's sometimes quite a chore signing autographs."

"Of course, Miss Marsden, follow me; we do have a VIP passageway. Have you got your passports?"

"Yes," said Agnes and handed over the documents. She pointed to Solly. "This is my manager, and these two are my assistants. We've been arranging appearances on the Continent."

The group complied and followed the steward towards the Customs Hall. He rummaged in his pocket for a set of keys and opened a door next to the entrance. He held open the door while the porter pushed the luggage trolley through and down a corridor. The group tagged on behind. They were at the back of the customs facility.

They reached a window with a sliding frame. The steward knocked and an officer pulled it open.

"This is Agnes Marsden and party returning from Holland." He presented their passports to the customs official.

He took little more than a cursory glance, then handed them back to the steward.

"The trains are just through there, Miss Marsden." He pointed to a door with the word 'EXIT' stencilled on it.

"Just follow the porter; he will ensure you get to your seat."

"I need to purchase tickets," said Solly.

"Of course, you'll see the ticket office on the right-hand side."

"Thank you," said Agnes to the steward.

"My pleasure, have a safe onward journey, and thank you for the photograph."

The steward spoke to the porter and the group followed

him out of the Customs Hall and to the ticket office.

The early train was due to leave at six o'clock to allow passengers time to pass through customs. Within a few minutes the four were making themselves comfortable in the first-class compartment. Solly had tipped the porter appropriately.

There was a loud shriek of the whistle and then movement.

"Next stop, London," said Solly, and Gerda started to cry.

As Agnes's train was pulling into Liverpool Street Station, in another part of London, Matthew was at his desk studying the reports of the latest IRA bombing campaign. He had been in the office since six a.m.

There had been a further attack the previous Thursday when two bombs exploded at Kings Cross Underground Station. Luckily, no one was hurt, and the police were confident of swift arrests.

Interestingly, there were movements in Ireland on the political front, almost certainly prompted by the British Government.

Matthew read the report in the Times.

'*Two Bills giving the Government of Ireland extraordinary powers were introduced in the Dáil yesterday. The first of these, called the Treason Act, imposes the death penalty for persons guilty of treason as defined in the Irish Constitution. This penalty is to apply whether the act was committed within or outside the boundaries of the State. Its aim is to curtail IRA activity both within the Irish state and the United Kingdom. The second measure, called the Offences against the State Act, makes it possible for citizens to be interned without trial, and confers elaborate powers of search, arrest, and detention upon the police. It declares seditious any suggestion in a newspaper or magazine that the elected*

Government of Ireland was not the lawful government.'

Matthew wondered whether it would actually deter the bombing campaign, as was intended, or just embolden the perpetrators; only time would tell.

The same newspaper continued to play down the effect the bombing campaign was having on the wider community in the UK. As it reported:

'The signatories of the ridiculous ultimatum (the declaration of war) to Great Britain are men of no account. Nobody in this country would have taken them seriously, but for the recent outrages in Great Britain. As a political force in Éire, the IRA simply does not count.'

There was a knock on the door.

"Come in."

The door opened and a woman in her late-thirties/early-forties appeared, dressed immaculately, her fair hair neatly pinned in a fashionable 'rag curl'.

"Hello Virginia, what can I do for you?"

"Sorry to disturb you, sir. I have received a request for employment from a Chloe Crouch; I understand she is an acquaintance of yours."

Matthew thought for a moment. "Ah, Chloe, yes, actually, she's the stepdaughter of one of my wife's closest friend. I gave her your name and suggested she wrote to you. A bright girl by all accounts."

"I see, well, I've invited her in for an interview at two o'clock."

"Excellent, do please let me know how she gets on."

"Yes, of course. Do you want to see her?"

"Actually, that's not a bad idea. I've not met her. If she's as bright as they say, I thought she could train as a radio operator. We are going to need more of those."

"Yes, indeed, sir. I'll bring her over after I've interviewed her."

Three o'clock, Matthew had been in meetings again with police chiefs but was now back at his desk. There was a knock on his door. It was Virginia Tennison, the head of the women's section. She was called in.

"I have Miss Crouch for you, sir."

"Ah, yes, come in Chloe."

"I'll leave you to it," said Tennison, and left the room.

"Have a seat. Would you like a cup of tea, coffee?"

"No, thank you."

Chloe sat down opposite Matthew. He had no idea what to expect. Working on a hop farm had conjured up an image far removed from the person seated in front of him.

Dark hair, tied back in curls, below a small, unfussy hat, giving her a sophisticated appearance, she had high cheek bones and a complexion that had benefitted from working outdoors. She was dressed in a coat which was unbuttoned revealing a white blouse and brown pleated skirt which fell just below the knees.

"So, Chloe, how did you get on with Miss Tennison?"

"Very well, sir; she explained everything, very interesting."

"Do you think you would like working here?"

"Yes, I do, as long as it's interesting. I don't want to be stuck behind a typewriter all day."

"How do you feel about being a wireless operator? It's hard work, long hours, but very rewarding."

"Yes, I could do that."

"Do you speak any languages?"

"No, only English."

"That's a pity, we're desperate for German speakers. Still there are plenty of other opportunities." Matthew leaned forward. "So, tell me a bit about yourself. You work on a hop farm I understand?"

"I run it, actually... since my father became ill. My stepmother helps too."

"Hetty?"

"Yes."

Her voice was clear and not defined by an accent, slightly rural if anything.

"It must be hard work."

"Yes, it is, but very rewarding. Unfortunately, the financial returns are not as good as they were, which is why we're selling the farm."

"Yes, Grace mentioned that."

"It makes sense. Daddy can't do anything, unfortunately."

"I'm sorry to hear that. What about looking after him? Who's going to do that?"

"Hetty, most of the time, until the farm's sold anyway. Someone has to keep it going."

They continued chatting for another half an hour before Matthew called time.

"I'll have a chat with Miss Tennant and write to you shortly... Oh, when can you start, by the way, if you were successful, I mean?"

"Straight away, we have someone who can take over the management of the farm if necessary."

"Thank you, any questions?"

"No, I don't think so."

Chloe got up and left the room.

Matthew picked up his internal phone and called the head of the woman's section. Ten minutes later, she arrived carrying a cup of tea that Matthew had requested.

"Thanks," said Matthew, taking the drink. Have a seat."
He took a sip of tea, "So, Miss Tennison, what do you think?"

"She's a bright girl, alright. I think she'll fit in very well here."

"A wireless operator?"

"Yes, I don't think she's cut out for typing."

"No, she mentioned that."

"I think there are several roles she could do," said Tennison.

"I agree. I'm happy for you to write to her and offer her a wireless operator role and we can see how she develops."

Chapter Eleven

Sunday 26th February 1939.

It had been a mild and relatively dry month compared with the record rainfall in January, the second wettest of the century.

It was a pleasant afternoon, and the sun was making a welcome appearance. Mildred was tending the front garden, picking out a few early weeds and dead heading some of the Hydrangeas which bordered the lawn. Years ago, the area would contain enough vegetables to last the winter but was now completely grassed. She noticed the lawn was showing signs of life and a cut was going to be necessary in a couple of weeks. She would need to contact Jed Dewhurst's son, Donald, who had taken over the gardening business from his father after Jed had retired in 1937. She made a mental note.

Just then, the front gate opened, and two figures walked through. Mildred shielded her eyes to see who was calling; she wasn't expecting anyone. Then recognised the visitors.

"Freddie... and Jean, what a wonderful surprise."

Mildred walked towards them.

"Hello, Aunt Mildred, sorry to call unannounced, but we were just passing, so we thought we would call in and say hello," said Freddie.

Mildred noticed Freddie was using a walking stick. Despite the relatively mild afternoon, they were both wearing coats, Freddie, his usual flat cap, Jean, a scarf.

"I'm so glad you did. I've been doing a few chores in the garden, making the most of this clement weather. It's given me an excuse to take a break and have a cup of tea... How are you both?" enquired Mildred, as she opened the front door and ushered the pair into the house. Freddie took off his cap.

"We're well, thank you," replied Jean.

"And young Arthur?"

"He's well."

"Growing up, I don't doubt. How old is he now?"

"Sixteen, he's gone out with some friends."

"My, my, how the time flies... I won't be a moment; make yourself at home." Mildred left the lounge while Freddie and Jean settled on the sofa.

Freddie had lost a leg in 1915, and his thoughts of leading a normal life had disappeared. After the war, like many veterans, he had suffered with mental health issues, particularly depression. He would stay in his room for hours, despite the loving care given to him by his mother, Kitty. Meeting Jean had turned his life around.

On his return to fitness, Mildred had employed him in his old job as a gardener at Springfield Hall, helping Jed Dewhurst. As his confidence returned, Freddie started doing gardening work elsewhere; there was not always enough work to keep two gardeners occupied at the Hall.

Margaret Longmore was one of Mildred's friends in the Oakworth Christian Welfare Association, and at one afternoon at one of their regular meetings, mentioned to Mildred that she was looking for a gardener. Mildred immediately recommended Freddie, who was duly hired.

Mrs Longmore lived with her husband, an accountant, in Keighley, and they owned a large house in the nearby village of Oldfield. The couple had an eighteen-year-old daughter, Jean, who was just finishing her schooling.

During the summer holiday, Jean would regularly take refreshments to the new gardener and a friendship grew from there. The pair started seeing each other and the rest, as they say, is history.

Freddie was still living at Blossom Cottage with his mother, and after they got married, Jean moved in. After Kitty's death, they sold the property to Mildred.

"I've brought some homemade scones in case you were hungry. Ethel brought a batch over on Friday," said Mildred, as she entered the lounge with a tea tray. She placed it on the table, then went back into the kitchen.

"Thank you," said Jean.

Mildred returned with another tray containing a plate with half a dozen scones, jam and butter.

Mildred was fond of Jean; she had been exactly what Freddie needed. She was a homely sort, quite studious, like her father, but with the pragmatism of her mother. She also spoke 'well', without the harshness of the local dialect.

"How is young Arthur getting on at school?" asked Mildred as she poured the tea.

Freddie and Jean had named their son after Freddie's stepbrother, who had saved him from no-man's land back in 1915.

"He's doing well, thank you. He's talking about joining the navy when he's old enough."

"What do you think about that?"

"If that's what he wants; then I'm happy," said Jean.

"What about you, Freddie, what do you think?"

"Aye, same, if it's what he wants; as long as it's not the army. I wouldn't wish that on anyone. Soldiers are just cannon-fodder to my mind."

"What if there's a war?" asked Mildred.

Freddie looked at Jean.

"Do you think there's going to be one?" asked Jean, with an expression of concern.

"Matthew says it's quite probable."

Freddie looked down. "'Appen folk have got short

memories. Who in their right mind would want to go through all that again...?"

He went quiet, a trait he had developed since he came back from the trenches over twenty years earlier; it was his way of dealing with things. Jean recognised the signs.

"These scones are delicious," said Jean, changing the subject.

"Thank you," said Mildred. "How is work, Freddie? Have you plenty on?"

"Aye, can't complain."

"And your mother, Jean, how is she?"

"She's well enough. Although, she's finding it difficult managing the house since father died; she's talking about moving to a smaller one."

"Yes, I can understand that. I was faced with that same dilemma, as you know... Would you like me to speak to her? I've not been in touch for some time; not since we disbanded the Association."

"Actually, that might be helpful. I know she thinks highly of your opinion, and she did enjoy her time with the group."

"I'll do that directly," replied Mildred.

"There is something we would like to discuss while we're here," said Jean. "Come on, Freddie, say something."

Freddie sat up and took a drink of tea, then helped himself to a scone.

"Aye, I'm thinking of giving up gardening," he said, and took a bite of his snack.

"Really, after all this time? What will you do?" said Mildred, with an expression of surprise.

"I'm not sure; I can turn my hand to most things."

"What's brought this on?"

"The weather... I don't think I can go through another winter."

"But this one has been mild, so far."

"Aye, but it was the rain in January. I wasn't able to work for three weeks."

"Are you short of money?"

"Nay, it's nowt like that, 'appen we do alright. Jean's very good at managing money." He looked at her and smiled.

"That was my father, that was, always instilled financial discipline," said Jean.

"Of course, he was an accountant."

"Tell Mildred about your leg," said Jean.

"Aye, I were about to... It's the cold and damp. It affects my leg, or at least what they left me with. Where I fit my false leg; it gets very sore," said Freddie.

"It's right enough, Mildred. I've seen him in tears with the pain."

"Oh, Freddie, I'm so sorry. I noticed you were using your stick."

"Aye, it helps if I'm walking a distance."

"Do you want to see someone? I'll be happy to pay for a specialist to look at it for you."

"Nay, they can't do owt, but thank you."

"He went to the doctor in January, and they just gave him some cream, didn't do any good," interjected Jean.

"Let me find someone who can treat you properly."

"It's better at the moment, now the weather's faired, but I do want to do something different. I've been a gardener all my life."

"And a very good one, too," said Mildred. "Have you got anything in mind?"

"Not really. I were thinking about one of the mills."

"Do you want me to ask William? I'm sure they would find something for you in the bakery. I know they are always very busy."

"Aye, alright, thank you, Auntie Mildred."

Mildred was in effect Freddie's step-mum, but he always referred to her as Auntie Mildred.

"Did you hear William's gone and got himself engaged?" said Mildred.

"Yes, we had a letter from Ivy to tell us," said Jean.

"They came to visit last Sunday. I have to say, she's a delightful girl. Marjorie, she's called."

"When's the wedding?" asked Jean.

"Later this year, August/September time, so they said."

An hour later, the couple said their farewells. Mildred promised to make enquiries regarding possible job opportunities for Freddie.

Molly Taylor was busy in her studio working on her latest designs. In the adjacent 'shed', ten girls were working away on sewing machines bringing them to life. It was far removed from her early days learning her drapery skills at Blossom Cottage.

Of the four Marsden girls, Molly was the one who closest resembled her mother in her later years. Facial expressions, hairstyle, pragmatism, were all traits passed down from Mildred. Her embroidery skills came from her maternal grandmother.

Molly's husband, John, was an impressive character, having inherited many of the features of his father. Tall in stature, almost six feet, always dressed in a three-piece suit and neat haircut with fashionable moustache, he cut a dashing figure. He was a year older than Molly having just reached his fortieth year,

He looked after the business side and, when he wasn't out meeting customers, he would be in the shed supervising the work. The present order book was reasonable full. In fact, such was the demand, the biggest problem was keeping up with orders, and getting suitable quality cloth.

The couple had acquired the trappings of success, a nice house in a desirable location, a van which was used to ferry them from home to work and garments to local customers. It was all a far cry from Molly's humble beginnings back in the bakery in Keighley. Molly always had a creative side and was selling embroideries at just fourteen when she went to work as an apprentice with Kitty in her studio in Blossom Cottage. Molly and John had been blessed with a son, Daniel, now fourteen, and at a private school in Bradford.

John's father was a successful wool merchant before he retired but was still actively involved in various associations linked to the wool trade, including President of the Master Wool Guild. He had contributed both financially and with business advice. He recognised the potential of Molly's talent and suggested they 'scaled up'. With his help, they bought a small factory unit on the outskirts of Bradford. It was part of a former wool mill which, like many in the area, had closed.

It had taken a lot of hard work but, ten years on, they were reaping the rewards.

It was late afternoon and Molly was finishing up when John rushed into the studio.

"I need to go across to my parents; Mam's just called; my father's had a fall."

"Oh, dear Lord, how is he?"

"I don't know; Mam's called the doctor."

"Then you must go directly. I was just finishing. Do you want to take the van? I can call a cabbie."

"Yes, I don't know how long this is going to take."

"Telephone me at home when you have some news."

David and Lauren Taylor lived in a large house in Allerton, just ten miles away. John arrived minutes after the doctor.

He opened the front door, and his mother was in the hall being comforted by the medic.

She turned and looked at John with tears in her eyes.

"What's happened?" he asked.

"He's gone, John. He's gone."

"Gone...? But... he was fine yesterday. What happened?" he repeated.

"I found him on the floor in the study; I thought he'd just fallen. I managed to sit him up and called the doctor, then you. I was sat with him, he was breathing, but then he just took a deep breath and just stopped."

John went over and comforted his mother. He turned to the doctor. "What do we need to do?"

"I'll examine him, but it looks like a heart attack. If I can confirm that, I can issue a death certificate straightaway, and you can call an undertaker. I can recommend one if necessary."

"Yes, thank you," said John, still trying to take everything in.

"How old was he?" asked the doctor, who was rummaging around in his bag.

"Sixty-seven said John.

The doctor walked back to the study where John's father was still lay.

"What will we do? What will we do?" asked his mother.

"Don't worry, Mother, we'll manage," replied John.

Molly had arrived home when she received John's

telephone call advising her of his father's passing. There would be much to do.

Monday, 27th February.

It had been over a fortnight since Agnes's return from Germany. It was an experience that would never leave her, having seen at first hand the brutality of life for a proportion of the population.

She had made another two appearances on the variety radio show and now had her own regular spot, 'Agnes Marsden sings for you', where listeners were requesting songs for her to sing. Robert Lang, the producer was delighted.

For Solly, Agnes's popularity had been a mixed blessing. He was inundated with requests for her to perform and had now employed three full time staff to deal with the correspondence.

Agnes was in her sitting room with Mary, her assistant, discussing her diary when there was a knock on the door.

Mary went to answer and moments later a familiar figure appeared.

"Solly, how lovely to see you. Would you like a drink?"

"A coffee, please, yes."

"I'll see to it," said Mary. "Would you like one?"

"Yes, please, and have one yourself; you can join us."

Mary left them and Solly took off his coat and hat.

"How are your parents?"

"They are well, thank you, still staying with me at the moment. We're looking for somewhere for them to live more permanently."

"What about residency? Have you managed to sort that out?"

"I have someone at the Jewish Refugee Centre who's working on that, but he says it shouldn't be a problem."

"What about money?"

"Well, they will have enough for a while. They managed to smuggle out the rest of their jewellery in their clothing."

"Really? I didn't know that."

"No, neither did I, until we arrived back It was the reason they were reluctant to take off their coats. My father didn't want to cause us additional worry, he said." Agnes smiled.

"That's considerate of him... You know I still can't get the sight of that poor couple out of my mind, the ones that were shot at the border; it's something I'll never forget as long as I live. I told Matthew about it... my brother-in-law, the one who works for the Home Office. He said he was going to pass the information on."

"I don't see what good it will do, unfortunately. It seems the Government are intent on pursuing this appeasement agenda. Still, it's right that the message gets out."

Mary returned with the drinks. Solly took a cup and saucer from the tray.

"The reason I called, I wanted to know what your thoughts were on taking on more singing engagements, only I'm getting so many requests." said Solly.

"Hmm, at the moment, I want to just do the radio work. I don't think I'll have time for anything else."

"No, that's what I thought. I've spoken to Robert about the variety show. He's very pleased, by the way; it's one of the most popular shows on the radio. There's an audience of over six million. You should see the letters we're getting. There are gifts too; I'll bring them round next time I call."

"Goodness, that's pleasing to know," said Agnes.

"Robert was saying that the current series is due to finish in the spring, and then they'll look at it returning in the autumn for a winter season. They are already planning a Christmas special."

"Christmas...? Already?"

"Yes, they take a lot of arranging, apparently; booking artists, musicians and so on."

"Yes, I can imagine. So how many shows will that be before it closes?"

"Another six or seven. So, I wanted to plan what's next. I've had several offers for you to do a tour, as I said, but I know you are not keen on travelling."

"That's true. I did that a long time ago when I was younger," she laughed. "Do you know I miss those times. I had this friend called Gloria, a juggler. Used to get me into all kinds of trouble."

"Really? I won't ask."

"Ha, yes, we used to lead poor Cameron a merry dance, bless him... I wonder what happened to her. She was such good fun." She took another sip of coffee and started to daydream for a moment.

Solly brought her back to earth. "Well, I did think a tour would not be welcomed, however, there is another offer on the table which you may want to consider, a season here in London at one of the theatres. How does that sound?"

"Yes, now that's possible, if you can find out more details."

"Yes, of course, I'll speak to the promoter."

There was a break in conversation Agnes picked up her coffee and took a sip.

"How are your parents coping with the language?" asked Agnes.

"Hmm, that is an issue. I'm trying to teach them but, at the moment, they would find it difficult to manage on their own."

"You mentioned trying to find somewhere for them to live?"

"Yes, I'm happy for them to stay with me for as long as they want, but it's not ideal."

"Well, I do have a tenant leaving one of my houses, shortly; they've just given notice. The agent's looking for someone to move in. Would you like me to talk to them?"

"Oh, that would be wonderful, yes."

"It's not very grand, but there are plenty of shops nearby. Why don't I take you there after we've finished our coffees. I can call a taxi."

"Yes, I have no other plans this morning; I was just going to do some shopping."

Matthew Keating was in his office having just returned from another meeting at New Scotland Yard. There was a knock on the door.

"Come," he shouted.

His secretary opened the door.

"Sir, I have Night Wing on the telephone."

"Put him through, Janet, put him through."

The secretary left and moments later Matthew's telephone rang. He picked up the receiver.

"Keating."

"It's Eoghan."

"Eoghan, how are you? Or should I say, where are you?"

"I'm at Stranraer; arrived from Larne half an hour ago."

"Oh, that is good news. What are your plans?"

"I want to get to London, but I have a problem; I don't have any money."

"Can you get to a bank?"

"I don't know; I'm still at the quay."

"I can transfer some money by telegraph, if you can find a bank."

"Aye, I'll do that. I'll call you when I find one."

"What name are you using? They'll need identification."

"Ryan Harris."

Agent Eoghan Flannagan's escape had not been straightforward.

After his close call in Dublin, he returned to his bedsit and collected his clothes and transmitter. He needed to leave in a hurry but, before venturing out, he decided to change his appearance. He had a false beard which he had used before but not in a 'real world' situation. His hands were shaking as he made the necessary adjustments, ensuring it was secure, then applied his 'prop' glasses. Finally, he donned his overcoat and Matthew's trilby hat.

He looked more like a businessman, which he hoped would be enough. He checked the mirror and was satisfied that his identity had been camouflaged sufficiently to fool most people. It would certainly confuse anyone who didn't know him.

He left the bedsit and stopped at the local store for some provisions, carrying his two suitcases. The proprietor hadn't recognised him which gave him confidence.

Having thought through the situation, his best route out would be by train. He was working on the belief that it would take time to mobilise resources to cover all escape routes.

He decided not to take a taxi, despite a mile walk to Westland Row where the trains left for Sligo. It was now mid-afternoon, a chilly day, and he had raised the lapels of his overcoat to keep warm. By the time he had reached his destination, however, he was sweating. He remained vigilant; danger was everywhere.

Westland Row was a famous street in Dublin, where the prisoners from the 1917 uprising were released. The station also appears in works by James Joyce. It was elevated with a bridge crossing the road below. Eoghan entered the station via the steps to the concourse and ticket office.

There were three trains a day to Sligo; the next, due to leave at four o'clock, according to the notice board. Thirty-five minutes to wait.

Eoghan purchased his ticket and then, not wishing to get himself cornered in a waiting room, stood out of sight behind one of the stanchions that supported the roof. Minutes later, the train pulled in. He picked up his two suitcases and walked up the platform. There was a final glance at the concourse before climbing aboard.

He found a seat and secured his luggage; for the moment he kept his coat and hat on; the train was cold. He exhaled loudly. There was a loud shriek of the train's whistle and gradually the train started moving, then picked up speed.

He was looking out of the window and noticed three men enter the station. The lead one of the three was pointing and the group split up. Eoghan moved away from the window. He could see the three men looking at the departing train in frustration.

Two and a half hours later, the train pulled into MacDiarmada Station, Sligo.

This time, he did take a taxi; it was five miles to his mother's home.

Mary Flannagan's cottage was on the banks of Lough Gill, a small holding containing some livestock and chickens. With a farmhand to help, she made just enough to eke out a living, although Eoghan would regularly help out financially if things got tight.

Mary was used to his comings and goings; he had called unannounced many times before, but, as he entered the cottage, she detected something wasn't right.

"Eoghan, what on earth have yer done with yerself? I nearly didn't recognise yer. What's with the beard?"

There were warm hugs.

"It's along story, Mam," he replied.

"Well, yer better sit yerself down. I'll go and make us some tea and yer can tell me all about it."

He looked at his mother, her hair now white, eyes lined with crow's feet. She had all the looks of a farmer's wife, or more correctly, widow of five years. She left him and went into the kitchen.

The cottage was a typical rural dwelling with little frills. Beams ran the ceiling indicated its age. The furnishings were no more than functional and quite worn. The old sideboard dominated the room decked with faded black and white photographs. There was a roaring fire in the hearth.

Eoghan made himself comfortable on the settee, his suitcase and radio were by his side.

A few minutes later, Mary returned with the tea.

"Are you in trouble, Eoghan?" asked his mother as they sat at the table drinking tea,

"Aye, I need to stay for a while and then I'll head north."

"So, what will you do in the north?"

"I'll take a ferry, so I will."

"So, when will you leave?"

"A week or two."

"So, I better make use of yer, while yer here, then."

"Aye, I'll earn my keep." He smiled.

It was ten days later when the agent headed north. His mother's farmhand, Padraig, had agreed to take him across the border as far as Enniskillen, a forty-mile journey, in his small lorry.

There were no issues in crossing the border; as part of the

Common Travel Area, there were no customs checks.

Unfortunately, Padraig turned out to be less than sociable, and complained about everything for the whole journey. Eoghan was glad when they reached the bus station in Enniskillen.

He thanked Padraig for the lift and gave him an Irish pound note, more than a day's wages. It was the first time Eoghan had seen him smile since they left Sligo.

There are no trains from Enniskillen to Belfast, but a regular bus service. The roads were not conducive to any sort of speed and the eighty-mile journey had taken nearly three hours, including a brief refreshment stop in Dungannon.

There were less than twelve people travelling on the bus. Eoghan felt fairly safe but would remain vigilant. His false beard had been replaced by a real one, or as close to one that two weeks of growth would allow. He was still wearing Matthew's raincoat but with a flat cap, more in keeping with his surroundings.

Once in Belfast, he found a bed and breakfast for the night. He would undertake the final leg of the journey to Larne the following morning. He would sail on the ten o'clock ferry.

Following his telephone call with Matthew, Eoghan found a bank and was eventually able to obtain some money, sufficient for the long journey south.

Wednesday, 1st March.

Mildred was in her sitting room reading the newspaper. It was Ethel's non-workday; she would return on Friday to help with the washing.

Daisy Jessop had taken over the running of the village store in Oakworth after her husband, Oswald, had died in

1934. Their daughter, Ethel, when not working for Mildred, also helped in the store, and on Wednesdays would take the van to the wholesaler's to buy stock.

Mildred's attention was drawn to an article about new corrugated shelters, known as Anderson shelters. They were being distributed in the Islington area of London. She found it alarming and would discuss it with Grace on their next telephone call; maybe Matthew knew something. Why would they need air raid shelters?

There was the sound of a vehicle pulling up outside, followed a few minutes later by a knock on the door. Mildred put down her newspaper and went to answer it.

"Molly, what a lovely surprise! Come in... Would you like a drink?"

"Hello Mam, aye, that would be nice, thank you."

Molly was wearing a coat; it was a chilly morning and there was no heater in the van.

"Let me take your coat; the kettle's on," said Mildred, returning from the kitchen.

Molly took off her topcoat and passed it to Mildred. Molly had on her work smock underneath.

"I can't stay long; we're rushed off our feet at the moment; I just wanted to let you know about the funeral arrangements."

"Oh, yes, so sad, how's Lauren coping?"

"I don't think it's hit her properly yet. Oh, she asked me to thank you for the flowers."

"That's alright, dear. I'll just go and make the tea."

A few minutes later, Mildred returned with the drinks.

"How are things at work? You said you were busy."

"Yes, thank goodness; we've just had some cloth arrive at last. It's been the devil's own job getting the right quality. I don't know what we'll do if we can't get the fabric. It's a real worry." Molly took a sip of tea.

"Oh, is there a reason?" asked Mildred.

"It's a national issue, according to my normal suppliers. They just can't get hold of the fabric I need."

"You must tell me if I can help at all."

"Thanks, Mam... Actually, John's talking about taking over some of his father's old clients."

"You mean as a Wool Merchant?"

"Yes, but I don't know how he'll manage it... and the shed; although it was much quieter until the cloth arrived and we could get on with the outstanding orders. Daniel's too young just yet to get involved; we're keen for him to take his matriculation exams."

"You want him to go to university?"

"Yes, he's doing well at school and his headmaster seems to think he's bright enough. He's talking about studying law."

"Oh, I do hope so; it will be hard work, mind."

"I don't think that worries him. Mind you, it depends on what happens."

"How do you mean?"

"Whether there's going to be a war or not."

"Hmm, that's true. Have you read the newspapers this morning?"

"No, I haven't had the time."

Mildred picked up her copy of The Times and flicked through the pages. There was a photograph of a street in Islington with several lorries. Men were handing out corrugated sheets, which had been constructed in an arch shape.

"What are they?" asked Molly, with a degree of interest.

"Anderson Shelters, it says. They've been distributing them in London."

"But why?"

"Hmm, they're air raid shelters. You're supposed to put them in the back garden and cover them with earth. It will stop a bomb apparently. I believe someone thinks there's going to be a war; that's what it looks like. Why else would they start supplying them? It's such a worry. I don't think I could go through all that again, not after the last one. I had Arthur in the trenches, Grace driving ambulances, and Agnes working in a hospital in France. I lived from day-to-day expecting a telegram at any moment."

Mildred looked down in sadness, then sipped her tea.

"Yes, I remember; it seems a world away."

"Well, it killed our Arthur, that's for sure; he was never the same man when he came back... Anyway, enough of that; you mentioned the funeral."

"Yes, next Wednesday at St Giles' Church, two o'clock. Lauren is putting on some food back at the house afterwards."

"Oh, that's kind of her." Mildred took another sip of tea. "Actually, I've just thought of something; what you were saying about John and his job... Freddie and Jean called round the other day."

"Oh, how are they?"

"They're all fine thanks, but Freddie mentioned he's thinking about giving up gardening. He's finding the cold and damp a problem... with his leg. He was talking about going into one of the mills. I suggested he could work in the bakery; I know William would employ him. What about him?"

"Hmm, do you know, that's not a bad idea. He used to help Kitty with the books and of course he knows the business."

"Yes, that's what I thought."

"I'll telephone him tonight and see what he says."

"Excellent, excellent."

After a further catch up, Molly left. Mildred picked up her newspaper and continued reading.

23, Hereford Street, Acton. It was almost seven o'clock. Grace was in the kitchen, finishing the dishes. Her daughter Gwen was drying up. Matthew had been called back to the Secret Service Headquarters. The radio was on in the background.

The telephone rang. Grace went to answer it.

"Hello, old thing... It's Hetty."

"Oh, hello, Hetty. It's lovely to hear from you. How are you?"

"Duncan died this afternoon."

"Oh, dear God, no. I'm so sorry. Is there anything I can do?"

"No, thank you, that's very kind."

"But what happened? You were talking about a year or so when I saw you."

"Yes, that's what we were told. Unfortunately, he was taken ill the day before yesterday; he caught pneumonia. Of course, his body was so weak it couldn't cope."

"Oh. I'm so sorry. Look, if there's anything I can do, you only have to ask... How's Chloe?"

"She's been very stoic about it, but I know she's hurting. Did you hear she's got a job with the Secret Service?"

"Yes, Matthew told me. That's some good news, at least."

"Yes, she's really looking forward to starting."

"What about the farm?"

"We've already put it up for sale two weeks ago. The agent says there's someone interested. Hopefully, we can move things quickly. We just have to sort out Duncan's affairs now. I've spoken to the solicitor this afternoon. I'll need to come into town to discuss matters later this week. I'll let you know."

"Yes, we can meet up, or you can stay here if you want."

"I'll call tomorrow and confirm; I can't think properly at the moment."

"No, I can understand that. Take care, sending you all our best wishes."

"Thank you."

Grace put down the phone and stood for a moment deep in thought.

Chapter Twelve

Grace was at home reading the newspaper, although her concentration levels were variable. She was distracted about thoughts of her time with Hetty; her former colleague's recent bereavement was on her mind. After all that she had given to others, she deserved some happiness. It was so sad it had been taken away from her prematurely.

Time was passing quickly; it was now over two weeks into March. Like many people, thoughts of war had taken over, after the false dawn of Chamberlain's Munich 'peace in our time' speech. The newspapers did nothing to dispel these concerns; bomb shelters, barrage balloons, and news of rearmament, belay any thoughts of appeasement.

Her attention was drawn to an advertisement, not a large one; she nearly missed it. It was more an appeal. 'London Ambulance Service seek ambulance drivers', together with a contact address and telephone number.

With James about to join the RAF, Dorothy studying for her exams, and Matthew working all hours, days were starting to drag. She would discuss it later with Matthew.

It was a Thursday and Matthew was in his office studying the latest reports concerning the IRA bombing campaign. Although arrests were being made, the bombings continued. The pressure from the Government on the police and Secret Service to put an end to it was strong, requiring weekly updates to the Home Secretary, Sir Samuel Hoare. Matthew had a plan that he had discussed with the Commander; it was potentially dangerous. He had arranged to meet Eoghan Flanagan, aka Ryan Harris, for lunch.

At just after twelve-thirty, Matthew left Broadway

Buildings dressed in his suit and trilby hat, covered by a topcoat. As he exited, he looked up at the sky, a dull uninspiring day. He still hadn't got used to the grey canopy that seemed to envelope the city; barrage balloons had become a part of life for many Londoners, but whether they generated comfort and security, or fear, was a moot point.

The Old Star pub was just along Broadway, on the opposite side of the road, on the corner of Queen Anne's Gate. It was a non-descript hostelry on three floors, the ground floor had two large windows on each side of the corner. An awning was pulled down on the Broadway frontage, ostensibly to shield it from the sun, a little optimistic in today's weather. Matthew waited for a gap in the traffic; Broadway was a well-used thoroughfare, then crossed the road.

Matthew walked thirty yards down St Anne's Gate to the pub entrance and went inside. He was greeted by the usual miasma of smoke and beer fumes. The bar was busy. He turned to the left of the serving counter and headed down a flight of concrete stairs to the basement where he had arranged to meet the agent.

It was a drab room with fifteen or so tables scattered around the floor with accompanying chairs. He looked around the room. Only half the covers were occupied with a mix of clientele, but with a distinct lack of trilby hats. One or two looked up from their conversations at the new arrival. Matthew felt like an interloper.

He spotted Eoghan in the corner, staring into a pint of Guinness. Matthew approached the table; the agent looked up. There was a nod of the head in acknowledgement. Eoghan stood up and the pair shook hands. The agent looked different to how Matthew remembered him. He had dyed his hair, and dispensed with his beard, but was sporting a thin moustache, one made fashionable by movie stars like Clark

Gable. With his flat cap, he would not have looked out of place in the more down-market drinking holes of London.

"Have a seat; I'll get us a beer. What're yer having?" said Eoghan.

"Just a half of best," replied Matthew, and took a seat.

He removed his topcoat revealing his suit, crisp white shirt, and red-patterned tie. He couldn't help but feel conspicuous, although the initial curiosity seemed to have passed. Everyone was back to their conversations.

The usual blue fog was being reflected in the wall lights; there was no natural illumination. The décor was faded, and tobacco stained.

A few minutes later Eoghan returned with the beer and presented it to Matthew.

"Thanks," said Matthew and took a sip.

Eoghan sat opposite but leaning forward and spoke just above a whisper.

"So, how are tings upstairs?" It was his name for Broadway House.

"Oh, you know plenty of challenges," replied Matthew and smiled. "How are the new digs?"

"Aye, I've slept in worse, so I have, but I can't remember when." He smiled.

"Bad as that?"

"Aye, anyhow they'll do for the moment... But I suppose this is not a social meeting."

Matthew took another sip of beer.

"Hmm, not exactly, no, but it is good to see you again. I shan't forget what you did for me."

"Comes with the job," said Eoghan, dismissively.

Matthew paused. "I have a proposal for you. Well, I say proposal... It's more a request really."

"Go on," said Eoghan, as he wiped away some Guinness

froth with the back of his hand.

"We would like you to infiltrate an IRA cell here, in London."

"Aye, I thought you might, now I'm here."

"Do you think that's possible?"

"Aye, it might be. I know where some of them drink. I've been keeping an eye out; they're not hard to spot."

"Kentish Town?"

"Aye, sure, that's where most of 'em live, and The Rose and Crown is where they drink. Actually, it's not far from my digs. I've frequented it myself. They keep a good Guiness, so they do."

"Do you need anything from me?"

"Aye, any local intelligence."

"We don't have a great deal, which is why we need someone on the inside. We know there's a large Irish community in Kentish Town, so it makes sense there will be sympathisers there. Whether any of the bombers are based there, we don't know; we have no intelligence on that. It's what I'm hoping you can find out."

"What about communication?"

"Do you still have your radio?"

"Yes, although it has taken a battering. I'm not sure if it still works."

"Hmm, you have my direct telephone number, haven't you?"

"Aye, so I have."

"Well, you can use that for any information, or in emergencies... I know, why don't we meet again here in say, three or four days' time?" He looked at his watch. "Today's the 16th, what about Monday, same time?"

"Aye, sure, I'll be here."

It was late afternoon. Earlier, Matthew had apprised the Commander of his conversation with the agent and was back in his office when the telephone rang.

"Keating," he said, picking up the receiver. "Yes, right away,"

He left his desk and made his way back to the Commander's office and knocked on the door.

"Come in, Major, take a seat."

Colonel Monkton was seated holding a piece of paper displaying a stern expression. Matthew detected straightaway this was not good news.

"Just had a message from one of our agents in Prague... The Germans have just invaded."

"What!?" exclaimed Matthew.

"Yes, although of course, it was something we expected."

"Yes, that's true. What's the Government's response?"

"Still waiting to hear. According to our agent, Hitler met up with President Hacha yesterday and threatened to bomb Prague unless he allowed German troops to enter Czech borders. We can only assume he agreed. It seems this morning the German Army marched into Bohemia and Moravia unopposed. Hitler's actually in Prague. Apparently, he's announced, 'Czechoslovakia has ceased to exist'. As we speak, the Germans are taking over all their factories, including the Skoda works, and of course there're the minerals - coal, steel. I'm sure that was what Hitler was after."

"What about the army?"

"It's been stood down."

"So, the German's will have access to all their weaponry."

"Yes, we can presume so; I can't believe they would have destroyed it."

"Hmm, that sounds rather uncompromising."

"Yes, and very worrying. What's next?"

"My guess it will be Poland."

"Yes, I think you may well be right. I've been trying to speak to the Foreign Office, but they're tied up at the moment."

"Hmm, I wonder why?" said Matthew with a hint of sarcasm. "It's certainly blown Chamberlain's appeasement policy out of the water."

"Yes, that's true; so much for Hitler being a man we can do business with."

"Yes it's certainly left Chamberlain looking foolish."

Thursday afternoon, and in Keighley, thoughts of possible conflicts had largely become no more than occasional conversation pieces.

At the bakery, William seemed to be always smiling. Robert had remarked how he had changed. This was true; the daily meeting with Marjorie at the café had become a permanent fixture. Thoughts and talk were firmly focused on the wedding, but tonight was going to be special. They had arranged to go to the pictures again. It was a film his customers were all talking about - 'Stagecoach', starring John Wayne.

William, like most young men, enjoyed Westerns; they were pure escapism. They took him out of his workaday world and transported him to some mystical place far away, vast open spaces, dusty deserts, huge cacti, strange-shaped mountains, and Red Indians. They always seemed to be depicted as the 'baddies'; they were savages after all. William had no reason to doubt this. It was war by proxy. Then there were the real villains – the bank robbers; and the local sheriff, who always seemed to look immaculate, white horse, a pearl-handled revolver. Then, the gun fights, where gunslingers, with amazing skill, were able to shoot the revolver from his opponent's hand without further injury. There was no blood; the bad guys just fell in a heap on the dusty street before being dragged to the undertakers.

William's favourite cowboy was Roy Rodgers. He had seen the film 'Billy the Kid Returns' three times the previous year.

"What time are you going tonight?" asked Robert as they were cleaning down, after another busy day.

"I'm meeting Marjorie at seven o'clock at the trolley stop."

"Do you want me to start the baking tomorrow, if you're going to be late?"

"Aye, thanks, although I shouldn't be too late. Last trolley's quarter-to-eleven."

William was waiting at the bus stop just opposite the park. It was the same stop that his father and grandmother would have used in a different time. Only the trolleybuses had changed, no longer an open-top deck, but comfortable seats, and better reliability.

It was a chilly night, but dry and he was wearing his topcoat over his three-piece suit.

He watched the vehicle approach; it seemed crowded; several people were standing. He waited at the entrance as the trolleybus stopped and the doors opened. There was an outflow of people, including several couples, who also seemed to be heading for the cinema. He stood to one side to allow the exiting passengers to get by.

William spotted Marjorie who waved. William reciprocated.

"Ah do," said William as she got off and they kissed fondly.

"Hello William, how was your day?"

"Aye, not bad thanks, hectic."

"Aye, we were quite busy this afternoon."

They turned and walked towards the cinema arm-in-arm. They could see it in the distance, it's neon sign beckoning a welcome to its customers who appeared to be approaching from all directions.

"It looks like it's going to be a full house," said William, quickening his stride. "We need to get a place in the queue. I'm glad we decided to meet earlier."

William was right. The queue stretched the full length of the cinema.

"I hope we can get in," said Marjorie.

"Aye, should do; they've not opened t'doors yet."

They joined the back of the line and within minutes, it stretched behind them and around the corner. He reached for his pocket-watch in his waistcoat pocket, the one he had inherited from his father, and checked the time.

"They'll be opening doors, in a minute."

The queue started moving and Marjorie grabbed William's arm and pulled him closer.

She leaned to his ear and whispered. "What time do you finish on Saturday?"

William turned and looked at her. "We close at three."

"Mam's going over to see Aunt Aggie in Bradford. She won't be back until late. You could come over; we'll have the house to ourselves. What do you think?"

"Aye, 'appen I'd like that."

"Aye, me too. I can cook us some tea if you like."

"Aye, that'll be grand."

They reached the foyer which was heaving with customers waiting to buy ice cream and other confectionery. William followed the queue to the ticket office.

"Two rear stalls, please," he said when it was his turn.

"One and eight," said the woman behind the glass screen.

William handed over a two-shilling piece. She pressed something mechanical, and two tickets spewed from a machine at the side and landed in front of the woman. There were small piles of four pennies in a row, and the woman moved the nearest to the opening together with the tickets.

"Next," shouted the woman, indicating the transaction was completed.

Marjorie returned from the confectionery stall with two bars of Rowntree's Aero chocolate that she knew William liked. She handed one to him.

"Be careful it doesn't melt," she said and smiled.

They walked into the auditorium; the lights were still on. They found their seats, two rows from the back, and made themselves comfortable. They had both taken off their coats and placed them on their laps.

Five minutes later, the faders gradually turned the theatre to darkness and the projector started. The whirring sound above them was audible from their seats but not intrusively. Many in the audience were already smoking, the blue smoke in the theatre swirling in the beam of light illuminating the screen.

There was a gradual hush as the opening feature started, 'A Day at The Zoo', a seven-minute Merry Melodies cartoon in colour. It had everyone laughing.

People were still coming in and, every now and then, the door opened with an annoying shaft of light. The usherette used a torch to direct people to their seats.

William and Marjorie were holding hands as the Pathé News feature started. It was full of jingoistic content, extolling the readiness of Britain and her allies in the event of war.

There was a visit of the King and Queen to Short Brother's, the aeroplane manufacturers, where they watched the maiden flight of the latest sea plane. There was a description and demonstration of the new gas masks for babies. But the main focus was the visit of the French President, Albert Lebrun, and his wife. The message was the strength of the 'Entente Cordiale', with scenes of the British and French navies, the largest in the world; combined they would be more than a match for any adversary, came the earnest commentary. There were scenes of new armaments and planes. Britain was spending a quarter of a million pounds every day on new aircraft, according to the narrator in his 'plummy' voice. There were scenes of marching soldiers with references to 'Tommy Atkins', the cheery British private, described as 'guardians and arbiters of peace'.

The newsreel finished, somewhat incongruously, with a short clip on the graduation ceremony of cadets at the Argentina Military School in Buenos Aries.

With no television, newsreels played a vital role in spreading Government propaganda. William felt a mixture of pride and sense of safety knowing their security was in good hands.

There was an intermission before the main feature film. The lights went up and two usherettes appeared on each side of the auditorium with trays of ice cream.

"Would you like an ice cream?" asked William.

"Still got my chocolate bar... but you have one," said Marjorie.

"I've still got mine too," said William.

He removed it from his pocket and peeled back the wrapper.

"It's gone soft," he said, and Marjorie laughed.

"We can't have that, can we?" she said and smiled, mischievously.

She took a bite of her chocolate bar. "Do you think there will be a war, William?"

"I don't know, but 'appen we'll be a match for anyone that tries it on, especially with France on our side."

"Aye, let's hope you're right."

The lights went down again, and it was time for the main feature. 'Stagecoach' was John Wayne's debut film, where he played the Ringo Kid. It would become one of the most popular films of 1939.

Friday, March 17th.

Agnes had finished breakfast and was in her kitchen reading the newspaper. Her assistant, Mary had just arrived and was making some coffee.

Agnes was not one to regularly scan the obituary column, but she suddenly noticed a name she knew.

"Oh no," she exclaimed.

"What's the matter?" enquired Mary, looking up from the sink.

"Gloria's died."

"Gloria?"

"Gloria Davidson, she was my best friend when we were touring. She was a juggler, a very good one too."

"How old was she?"

"Sixty-seven... I didn't realise she was that old."

"Is there any more information?"

"No, it just says she died after a short illness. The funeral's next Tuesday; I would like to go. How is my diary looking?"

Mary went to her bag and pulled out a small notebook where Agnes's itinerary was maintained.

"You're free at the moment."

"Can you hold it for me, the afternoon, at least. It's at two o'clock."

"Where is it?"

"Balham Methodist Church, it says... Where's Balham?"

"South of the river, near Clapham, I think."

"I'll need a taxi... It's a shame we never kept in touch; she was such good fun. Mind you, she was a bad influence. It's where I got my taste for brandy. She used to give me her magic powder sometimes too. It helped me get over the tiredness."

"White powder?"

"Hmm, yes. It wasn't until I was telling Alistair about it, years later, that I found out what it was."

"Heroin?"

"Yes, it must have been. Fortunately, I didn't use it very often; I was so innocent in those days. I had no idea about drugs."

"Gloria had such a zest for life... and would chase anything in trousers. Ha, she was always trying to catch an officer, someone who could set her up for life, she said. I know Cameron was fond of her, not in that way, but he would always include her in his variety shows."

"I wonder what happened."

"Yes, maybe I'll find out next week."

Agnes reminisced for a while with a tinge of sadness, and a little guilt at not keeping in touch with her old friend.

Back in Bradford, Thursday morning was also busy for Molly. The previous day was John's father's funeral and, unsurprisingly, she had missed work. There was plenty of catching up to do. John was at his parent's house helping his mother clear his father's possessions and clothes.

Molly did, however, have a visitor booked in at eleven

o'clock.

Just before the allotted time, there was a knock on her studio door, one of the seamstresses.

"Mr Bluet is here," said the girl.

Molly got up from her desk and went to greet her visitor.

"Freddie, lovely to see you, sorry we've had to delay our meeting, but what with the funeral and everything..." she tailed off. "Anyway, take a seat. How's Jean?"

"Aye, she's grand ta. I was sorry to hear about John's Da," replied Freddie, and limped to the only spare seat in the room with the aid of his walking stick.

"Thank you," replied Molly with a fond smile.

With time always a factor in Molly's busy world, she got straight to the point. Freddie thought she reminded him of Mildred who always appeared to be abrupt in conversation, but it was just her way.

"Have you had a chance to consider the proposal we discussed over the telephone?"

"Aye, I have. I'd like to work with tha."

"Good, good, when can you start?"

"As soon as you want. I've cancelled all my gardening work."

"What about Monday?"

"Aye 'appen I can."

"Good, good. Let me show you around. It will give you an idea of what we do here... You used to do Kitty's books for her didn't you?"

"Aye, I did."

"Do you think you could look after ours? I'm in danger of sinking in paperwork. I need to concentrate on getting designs out; we're getting behind with orders."

"Aye, I don't see why not. It's been a while, though."

"I'm sure you'll soon pick it up."

"Aye, I'm sure I will."

Molly took Freddie into the 'shed' and introduced him to the girls. A weight had been lifted from her shoulders.

Friday, 17th March.

Grace was looking out of the window, waiting for her visitor. Hetty had telephoned to say she would be calling after her solicitor's meeting, late morning probably.

It was just gone one o'clock when a taxi pulled up and Hetty got out. Grace opened the front door to receive her guest.

"Hello, old thing," said Hetty as she approached,

There was a fond embrace and Grace ushered her in.

"How are things?" asked Grace as Hetty took off her coat.

"Oh, you know..."

"Let me get you a drink and you can tell me how you got on at the solicitor's?"

Grace returned a few minutes later with a plate of sandwiches and a pot of tea.

"I made you a snack; I didn't know if you had the chance to eat anything."

"Thanks, that's good of you," replied Hetty.

She took a bite of her sandwich.

"It's cheese, I remembered you liked it," said Grace.

"Oh yes, thanks. Do you remember the cheeses we used to get in France?"

"Oh yes, goodness, quite strong, if I remember."

"We used to live on it for a while."

"Yes, that's true... So, how did you get on?"

"Well, everything's moving satisfactorily, according to Mr Bainbridge; he's been our solicitor for a long time, nice man."

"What are you going to do about accommodation?"

"I'm not sure at the moment. We've had an offer for the farm from one of the local breweries; they want to put a tenant in."

"I see, I didn't know they were into farming."

"Neither did I, but Mr Bainbridge said they're looking to build a portfolio. They have made a generous offer. He thinks we should accept."

"How do you feel about it?"

"To be perfectly honest, I don't want the bother. The sooner everything is sorted, the better."

"Yes, I can understand. What about Chloe?"

"Well, she's suggested we buy a place together. Duncan has left us well-provided for."

"Have you any idea where?"

"Well, now Chloe is working in London, it will need to be somewhere she can commute from. I don't want to move into London, though."

"No, it's not for everyone, especially having lived in the country for so long."

"Yes, that's true. I think Tunbridge Wells would be nice. It was where Duncan and I were intending to live."

"I've heard it's nice, I've not been myself."

"Chloe and I drove out there on Tuesday to have a look round... These sandwiches are nice."

"Thank you, would you like some more? Agnes gave me a lovely jar of chutney."

"It's delicious; I think I will, thank you."

"I don't think she made it; probably Mary's mum."

"Mary?"

"Yes, it's Agnes's assistant."

"She has an assistant?"

"Ha, yes, full time, and a manager. She was saying she may need to employ someone else to help."

"Oh, that's wonderful. She's doing so well. I always listen to her Variety Show; I never miss it. We kept the Radio Times with her picture on the cover too. You must be very proud of her."

"Yes, I am. Do you know she's just returned from Germany?"

"Really? A singing engagement?"

"No." Grace leant forward and lowered her voice as though someone might be eavesdropping. "Between you and me, she was helping someone escape."

"Escape?" Hetty stopped eating, giving Grace her full attention.

"It was her manager's parents; they're Jewish. Agnes was saying how badly they're being treated over there; it's dreadful."

"Why, did she say that?"

"It's Hitler; he has this hatred for Jews, apparently."

"Hmm, I don't like him one bit. Do you think there 'll be a war."

"Mmm, Matthew was talking about it last night. With this Czechoslovakia business, he says it's highly likely."

"Oh dear, I don't think I could face all that again."

"No, I know what you mean... Actually, there is something I wanted to mention. I saw an advertisement in the newspaper; they're looking for volunteer ambulance drivers."

"Really? Where?"

"In London, the London Ambulance Service."

"Are you thinking of applying?"

"I already have. Now James and Dorothy are pretty well off my hands, and with Matthew working all hours, it does get boring at times... Why don't you apply, Hetty? It would be like old times again."

"Hmm, I'll give it some thought. I'll need to get everything sorted before I can commit myself to something like that."

"Yes, I understand, but it might be just what you need."

"I'll certainly think about it," said Hetty and took another sip of tea.

There was a silence as Hetty contemplated the discussion.

"You were going to give me details of the funeral," said Grace, changing the subject.

"Oh, what? Oh...Yes, it's next Tuesday at St Mary The Virgin Church, in Selling, two o'clock. I went to see the vicar earlier in the week and it's all arranged."

"Is there a station in Selling."

"Yes, it's at the top of the village; it's not far to the church. You'll need to change at Faversham."

"I'll find out the train times," said Grace.

It was eight o'clock and dark outside. Matthew was still in his office, listening to the radio. He didn't normally have it on during the day; it was only used when there was an important broadcast. This evening was a case in point. He had been joined by Janet Bryant, his secretary, who had also stayed late.

Neville Chamberlain, the British Prime Minister was giving a speech while on a visit to Birmingham in response to the German invasion of Czechoslovakia. It was something Matthew wanted to listen to as it could have a direct bearing on his work.

The Prime Minister spoke in grave tones; his voice reflecting the severity of the situation.

'I had intended tonight to talk to you upon a variety of subjects, upon trade and employment, upon social service, and upon finance. But the tremendous events which have been taking place this week in Europe have thrown everything else

into the background, and I feel that what you, and those who are not in this hall but are listening to me, will want to hear is some indication of the views of His Majesty's Government as to the nature and the implications of those events.'

Some of the press had commented, unfairly in his eyes, that the situation in Czechoslovakia was as a direct result of his Munich agreement with Hitler. He refuted that strongly. He described his 'disappointment and indignation', that the hopes of the Munich Agreement had been so 'wantonly shattered'.

It was a speech that virtually confined the policy of appeasement to history, although Chamberlain was careful not to say that directly; he still held out hope of avoiding war. Unfortunately, it was clear that Hitler's word could not be trusted, and Great Britain would need to react.

He spoke for over twenty minutes and, when he had finished, Matthew looked at Janet and shook his head.

"What does it mean?" asked Janet.

"I think we've just moved one step closer to war."

It was ten o'clock before he returned home. Grace welcomed him warmly and poured him a large shot of whiskey.

"I thought you might need this. Have you eaten?"

"Yes, I managed to get something at the office; the canteen was serving late. Did you hear Chamberlain's speech?"

"Yes, I did; it doesn't sound very optimistic. What's Hitler up to, that's what I don't understand? He's got what he wanted."

Matthew took off his jacket and sat down, then took a large mouthful of whiskey.

"Hmm, I don't think anyone knows what Hitler does want; not sure he knows himself, but I don't think his territorial ambitions have been exhausted yet."

"What do you mean?"

"Well, Poland is clearly vulnerable; that's the big concern. It wouldn't surprise me if Chamberlain makes that the line in the sand."

About the same time, Secret Service agent, Eoghan Flemming, now using the name of Ryan Harris, was at the bar in the Rose and Crown, Kentish Town. It was his third visit, and fairly quiet for a Friday night. A scattering of customers around the room spending their hard-earned money; most were drinking Guiness. There was no one at the bar, and the agent had been chatting to the landlord, not to gather information, but to pass the time.

He finished his Guiness and immediately mine host was to him.

"Would you like another, Ryan?"

"Aye, sure yer can put another in there, so yer can, then I'm off to my bed."

Just then a group of men walked in. They were dressed in work attire and looked like they had come from a building sight.

"What about yer, Patrick," said the first one, a scruffy man about thirty years of age.

They approached the bar and man number one eyed Ryan with suspicion. Ryan glanced around but quickly returned to his stout.

"Usual, Finn?" enquired the barman.

"Aye, and whatever yer having," replied the scruffy one.

Ryan noticed white paint splattered on his trousers. He had piercing blue eyes and thick, wavy dark hair which was also speckled with paint.

"Yer late tonight; working overtime?" asked the landlord, making conversation.

"Aye, been working over at Phelan's; it's a big job, so it is."

The landlord dispensed three pints of Guiness and then poured three measures of Paddy's Irish Whiskey. The three men picked up the whiskeys and downed them in one go. Then, they took their drinks and walked to the corner of the room to a spare table. They were soon in deep conversation, leaning forward and talking in no more than whispers.

Patrick, the landlord, was back to cleaning glasses, vigorously applying a tea towel.

Ryan looked around at the men who were oblivious to his interest.

"Do you think yer man there would get us a job?" said Ryan to the landlord.

"Who Finn?"

"Aye."

"I don't know. Why don't you ask him?"

"I don't want to disturb him."

"Don't yer worry about that... Finn," he called over to the men. "Have yer got a minute?"

Finn turned to the enquiry, got up, and walked towards the bar.

"Yer man here's looking for a bit of work," said the landlord with a nod of his head.

Chapter Thirteen

Finn eyed Ryan up and down. "So, what is it yer after?"

"I can turn my hands to most tings. I'm up fer a bit of decorating, so I am... Ryan, Ryan Harris."

The agent offered his hand to shake. Finn reciprocated. "Finlan Connor... So, what brings yer to London, Ryan?"

"Well, it seems me and the Garda Síochána did not see eye-to-eye."

"Aye, is that so? Should I be enquiring why that is?" Finn was weighing up his new acquaintance.

"Well, I did a bit of fetchin' and carryin', so I did, across the border. It earned me a bit of money."

"Where was this?"

"Sligo."

"So, yer from the South?"

"Aye, that I am. It seems the police were taking a bit of interest in the feller I was delivering for, so I decided I'd try me luck here and earn some proper money without the stress."

"Aye, I see that... Look, why don't yer come over and join us. Bring yer drink with yer."

Ryan picked up his Guinness and followed Finn to the table in the corner where his two colleagues were seated.

"Lads, this is Ryan, says he wants some work... This is Aidan, and the pretty one here is Niall."

Ryan shook hands with the men in turn.

Both would be in their late twenties. Niall was short and swarthy, hair trimmed, short at the sides, his face scarred, his nose crooked, as though he had spent some time in a boxing ring. There seemed to be a natural stoop.

Aidan was very different, tall, slim, sandy-coloured hair

beginning to recede. Both, like Finn were wearing work overalls spattered with paint.

"So, what is it yer do, Ryan?" asked Niall, before a long slug of Guinness.

"Worked on me mam's farm. If you can call ten cows, six pigs, and a dozen chickens a farm."

"Ran into a bit of a problem with the Garda Síochána, so he was saying." said Finn to his associates.

"Aye, true enough," said Ryan.

"And what was it yer were fetching and carrying?" asked Finn, who was looking closely at Ryan for any signs of lying.

"Now, why would I know that? Sure, they were wooden crates, so they were."

"And how often would yer be doing this."

"We used to cross the border on a Tuesday to the market in Belcoo. Mam's got an old Austin Seven Station Wagon, so she has."

"So how long were yer doing this fetching and carrying?"

"It would be a few months. Sure, this feller came up to me at the market one day and asked if I was interested in making some extra money. It was easy enough."

"What was his name, this feller?"

"He didn't say, and I didn't enquire. It pays not to ask too many questions." Finn looked at his associates and raised his eyebrows. Ryan had finished his Guinness.

"Aidan, why don't you get in another round before yer man calls time?"

Aidan picked up the glass and went to the bar.

While the barman was pouring the drinks, Aiden leaned over and whispered to him. "So, what's the craic with yer man over there? Do you think he's on the level?"

The barman looked up. "I don't know, to be honest. He's been coming in for a couple of weeks. Seems pleasant enough."

Back at the table, Niall took over the questioning. Ryan was well-rehearsed; he was expecting a certain amount of scrutiny.

"So where did the packages come from?"

There was a certain menace about the interrogator; Ryan was wary but spoke with confidence.

"I have no idea. I'd meet them outside Connolly's Bar on a Monday in the wagon. They'd transfer the package from their lorry and pay me and that was that."

"So, how long were you involved?" Niall repeated the question.

"It must be three months or thereabouts."

"When did yer know you were of interest to the police?"

"It was last month. I was outside the bar waiting for the next delivery as usual, when one of the lads came over and told us that there was going to be no more packages, and that I should disappear for a while."

"And yer don't know any of these lads names?"

"No, I didn't ask. It was the money, so it was; that was all I was interested in. Times are not easy. So, I tought I would try my luck over here."

"Aye, I can see that."

Aiden returned with the Guinness and handed one to Ryan.

"Tanks, Sláinte," said Ryan, and raised his glass. The others responded.

"So, yer say yer up fer a bit of decorating?"

"Aye, that I am."

"You know Phelan's, I take it?"

"Aye, I pass it most days."

"Can yer be there fer seven-thirty tomorrow?"

"Aye, that I can."

Just then, there was a loud clanging noise as the landlord rang the large silver bell at the end of the bar.

"Time, gentlemen, time," he called.

The four lads tipped back the remaining dregs of their drinks and got up.

"So, we'll see yer tomorrow, don't be late; there's a lot to do."

"Aye, I'll be there."

There was a builder's lorry parked outside the pub containing pots of paint and two ladders.

"Will yer be wanting a lift, Ryan? We can drop yer off."

"No, that's good of yers, but I tink the walk will do me good. It's not far."

"Aye, suit yerself."

Ryan waited as Finn went round to the front of the lorry and cranked the handle.

"See yers tomorrow," he shouted, and the truck pulled away.

The agent started walking in the opposite direction. He had a call to make.

Saturday, 18th March.

As Mathew walked to the office from the tube station, there seemed to be change in the atmosphere since the Prime Minister's broadcast; it was nothing to do with the gloomy weather. He noticed several lorries piled high with sandbags. Men were ferrying them to office building frontages and positioning them across the windows.

He was at his desk by eight-thirty and was drinking his first cup of tea of the day, when one of the operatives knocked on the door.

"Come," shouted Matthew.

The door opened. "Message from Night Wing, sir."

The messenger was in his early twenties and in military uniform.

"Yes, private."

"He called in last night from a telephone kiosk. Says he's contacted possible suspects. Won't make Monday's meeting but will call with further information when he can."

"Thank you, private."

The door closed leaving Matthew contemplating the information.

Saturday morning at the bakery, William was whistling as the bread mix was being readied for the oven. The thought of seeing Marjorie was at the forefront of his mind.

Saturday was the busiest day of the week and customers would be queuing at the door at eight o'clock; William and Robert would be on the go all morning. Daisy, in the cake shop, would also be rushed off her feet. She had employed two 'Saturday girls' to help her. The baker's would stay open at lunchtime, like most in James Street, but close at three o'clock. The afternoon custom was much lighter which gave them time to start clearing up. Robert was aware of William's meeting and had agreed to finish off for him.

At two-thirty, William went upstairs to the parlour. Ivy was in the kitchen and came out when she heard someone enter.

"Hello William, I've run your bath. What time's the trolley?"

"Quarter past three."

"Oh, good, you have plenty of time. It was good of Mrs Sykes to invite you to tea again."

"Yes, Mam."

William had decided not to say anything about Marjorie's mother not being present. Questions might be raised.

Ingrow was only about twenty minutes on the trolleybus. It was just outside the Keighley town border, and a separate community with several mills still providing employment for the locals. By five-past three, William was at the stop waiting for the bus to arrive. He had a strange feeling, one of excitement but also nervousness. This was the first occasion he and Marjorie had spent time properly alone together, and he was a little uncertain of what was expected.

The bus arrived and William waited while most of the passengers exited and went on their way. He decided to ride on the top deck and went upstairs. As they pulled away, he could see people walking through the park; the town was busy with shoppers.

As the bus reached Ingrow, he had already descended the stairs and was waiting by the driver as the bus pulled slowly to a stop.

It was only a short walk to the Sykes' residence, a modest terraced house just off the main road.

William reached the front door and knocked.

Marjorie opened the door and beamed a smile.

"Ah do, Marjorie," said William and took off his cap. Marjorie ushered him inside.

There was no hallway; the front door opened directly into the living room. There was a heavy curtain on a rail which pulled across to prevent droughts.

William stood for a moment nervously fingering his cap.

"Tha looks handsome William. Sit thaself down and I'll make us some tea."

"Ta," said William, and made himself comfortable while Marjorie went into the kitchen.

William was still tense and looked around the room. It was a place of order and tidiness; a three-piece suite, dining table, and sideboard, dominated the room. There was a coal fire blazing in the hearth; the settee faced it. On the corner of the sideboard there was a radio with brown curly wire disappearing behind to an obscured plug socket.

A few minutes later, Marjorie walked in carrying a tray with a tea pot, milk jug, and sugar bowl. She placed it on the dining table behind the settee, then returned to the kitchen to fetch the cups.

"How was the journey; was the trolley busy?"

"Aye, not bad, trolley weren't that full. How was work?"

"It were grand, ta. I had trouble concentrating."

"Aye, me an' all."

"They let me leave at two o'clock. I told them I had an important meeting."

"That's nice of them."

"Well, it were true." She looked at William and smiled. "Oh, I did have an interesting customer this morning; came in for a new suit."

William looked at Marjorie, waiting for more information.

"Aye, well 'appen he came to the right place then," said William, and chuckled, nervously.

"Ha, yes, the thing was, he only had one leg."

"Really?"

"Aye, it were my first time I've served someone with one leg. It were so sad. I reckon he lost in in the war."

"Aye 'appen there were lots of men that came back with bad injuries. My uncle lost his leg in t'war, Uncle Freddie. Well, he's a step uncle, really, his father was my grandfather."

"Oh, is that so?" Marjorie was curious. "What happened?"

"I don't know the full story, my grandma won't speak of it, but 'appen my Da saved Uncle Freddie from no-man's land; even got a medal, so me Mam says. Da would never speak of the war."

"Oh, that's awful... Wait a minute; did you say his name

was Freddie?"

"Aye, Uncle Freddie. Not seen him for a while, used to do t'garden for my grandma when she lived in t'big house."

"That was his name... Bluet, I think. I have to put the name and address on the receipt when it's an expensive item."

"Aye, that'll be him, Freddie Bluet."

"Well, what a coincidence," said Marjorie.

She could sense William was starting to relax.

"It's so nice to be on our own. I've made us some tea for later."

"Oh, aye? That's grand," replied William sipping his drink.

Marjorie went to the front window and drew the curtains together, then sat down next to William. The room was bathed in the flickering light from the fire. She took his teacup from him and placed the cup on the hearth.

She decided to take the lead. She leaned to William and started kissing him. The kissing became more intense. It was different from the kissing they had snatched in alleyways on the way back from the cinema.

She held William's hand and drew it to her bosom. She could feel his hands shaking as he gently started to caress Marjorie's breast over her cardigan.

"Would you like to go upstairs? It will be much more comfortable."

"Aye," he replied.

They left their teacups, half drunk, on the hearth, as Marjorie guided William through the door to the flight of stairs that led to the first floor.

It was almost seven o'clock before Marjorie and William returned to the sitting room. For both of them life had changed. There was a lot of fumbling and uncertainty, but eventually the relationship had been consummated.

The room was in darkness and Marjorie flicked the light switch. The two teacups were still on the hearth, stone cold with a dark film on top. Marjorie picked them up and went into the kitchen.

"I'll make us some fresh in a minute."

"I can't wait for us to be man and wife," said William, as he followed her into the kitchen.

"Aye, me and all," said Marjorie, and kissed William.

She went to the oven and turned it off. She had made a stew which had been simmering on a low heat for most of the afternoon.

23, Madison Close, Bloomsbury, London, Sunday morning.

Agnes had slept in, and Alistair was downstairs making breakfast. Their daughter, Gwen, was helping.

Alistair called upstairs. "Breakfast's ready."

Agnes placed a silk dressing gown over her nightdress and went downstairs.

"Thank you for making breakfast; it's a real treat."

"I've got some marking to do this morning," replied Alistair. "I wanted to make an early start."

"What are you doing today, Gwen?" asked Agnes.

"I'm meeting some of my friends later, there's a concert at the Royal Albert Hall."

"Ah, yes, Vivaldi," said Alistair. "You'll enjoy that. What time does it finish?"

"It's a matinee, so around five-ish, I expect."

"Oh, good, I'm not sure it's safe these days to be wandering around late at night."

"Don't worry, father, we'll be careful. There are eight of us."

"Do you have tickets?"

"Yes, Phoebe's father works nearby and collected them."

"I'll give you some money before you go."

"What about you, darling?" asked Alistair.

"Solly brought round some more letters yesterday he wanted me to read. Some of them are heartbreaking. I want to reply to some of them in person."

"Ah, yes, that one from that Scottish lady you showed me, the one who had just lost her husband. It was very moving. You touched her heart, she said... It's amazing the effect music can have on people when it's delivered so well."

"Thank you, darling." Agnes smiled at Alistair.

Later that morning, Agnes was catching up with the correspondence; it was Mary's day off, when there was a knock on the door.

Alistair was in his 'den' marking papers, and Gwen had left for her concert. Agnes went to answer.

She stopped and stared at the visitor. "'Allo, Agnes, 'ow are you?"

Agnes couldn't believe her eyes. "Céline...? I... I can't believe it."

"Oui, c'est moi."

"Come in, come in... Oh, it's so good to see you."

Agnes led her visitor into the sitting room. "Let me take your coat. I hope you can stay for a while; we have so much catching up to do."

"Er... oui, c'est vrai... it is true... I did not know if... er you would still live 'ere."

Alistair, having heard the French accent, broke off his work and came downstairs to investigate.

"Darling, it's Céline," said Agnes.

Alistair went up to the uninvited guest and kissed her on

both cheeks.

"It's wonderful to see you after all these years. Let me take your coat," said Alistair.

Céline was wearing a fashionable topcoat over a chic green dress, which could only have come from Paris. There was an elegance about her.

Agnes hugged her former assistant, then looked at her. "You look so well. You know, you haven't changed one bit."

"Ha, I think you are being, er, very kind."

"I'll make some coffee," said Alistair. "While you two catch up."

Céline sat down on the settee and made herself comfortable. She looked around the room. "It is, how you say? Just like I remember it... Er, you must excuse my English, I have not, er... *parctisé…*"

"Practised?" interjected Agnes.

Céline smiled. "Er, oui, that is it."

"Well, it's better than my French, ha. It's been a while since I've had to speak it. The last time you wrote to me, that was, let me think, nineteen-twenty-two, something like that. I did reply, but I didn't hear back so I assumed you had moved."

Céline was working out the translation. "Er, oui, zat is true. I left my apartment. I had met a dear man, Jean-Paul; he was my, er, *professeur* at my university."

"Yes, you said you had gone back to study."

"Oui... We got married and I moved in with him."

"But that's wonderful, how is he?"

"*Il mort.*"

"Oh, I am so sorry."

"*Merci,* thank you... It has been six years, but I have a nice apartment and money to live on."

"Do you have a job?"

"Oui, I am... er, a teacher."

"But that's wonderful. What do you teach?"

"Géographie, le histoire, er, art."

"That's wonderful... Alistair's still a teacher, music."

"Oui, I remember... zee piano?"

"Yes, that's right. He teaches at one of the music conservatoires here in London."

"Ah, bon."

"Our daughter plays very well too; she's also at one of the music schools," said Agnes.

"Yes, she's better than I was at her age," added Alistair, as he arrived back in the room with a tray.

Alistair distributed the cups. "I hope it's as you like it."

"Ah, oui. It will be *merveilleuse,*" said Céline, as she accepted one of the cups from Alistair. She continued. "And do you still sing, Agnes?"

"Yes, I sing on the radio, on a Friday night."

"Zee raddio, so you are still famous, I think."

"She gets plenty of letters," said Alistair, and laughed.

"Ha, oui, I remember zee letters, always from zee men, I think, very... er, *coquin.*"

"Yes, that's true, some were, hm, naughty, but not now; it's mostly old ladies." Agnes laughed. "So, what brings you to London?"

"I had to get away from Paris for a while; it is very bad zere at the moment. We have many, how you say? Er... *grèves.*"

"*Grèves*... I don't know this word," said Agnes. She turned to Alistair. "Do you know the word 'grèves', darling?"

"No, I don't think so."

Céline was thinking. "Oui, *les troubles industriels.*"

"Ah, yes, industrial unrest; she means 'strikes'," said Alistair.

"Oui, oui c'est ca, very bad, zee telephone, zee, er, gas, electricité. It is zee Communists, I 'ate zem for causing so much problem, and now we 'ave zee guerre, zee war."

"You think there's going to be a war?" asked Agnes, sipping from her coffee cup.

"Mais oui, zey 'ave, er, started digging zee, er, 'oles for zee people to hide from zee bombs."

"Oh, I didn't know it was so bad in France," said Agnes, looking at Alistair.

"Oui, *malheureusement*." Céline sipped her coffee.

"What will you do?"

"I do not know, but I don't want to stay in Paris. I 'ave friends in zee country I will, er, think about."

"You could always move to London."

Céline stopped drinking and thought for a moment.

"I 'ad not thought about London."

"But you enjoyed your time here."

"Mais oui, of course."

"And I'm sure we could find somewhere for you to live."

"Oui, oui, I will think about it; it is a big... er, décision."

"How long are you staying in London?"

"One, maybe two weeks."

"Oh, that's lovely; we must meet up for a shopping trip. Where are you staying?"

"It is not too far."

Monday, 20th March.

Eight o'clock, and Freddie was walking into the yard in front of Molly's premises. The tarmacked area was where delivery vehicles could turn and was surrounded by other small businesses which had set up in the former mill. There were weeds growing in the margins suggesting neglect.

He looked up at the five-story edifice, a grand building

of traditional Yorkshire stone, once housing a thriving wool business providing work for maybe a thousand people.

He looked smart in his new suit, a point not lost on Jean. "I think I've got me a new husband," she said, as Freddie left to catch the bus.

He felt nervous as he reached the doorway and, using his walking stick to help him negotiate the steep wooden staircase, walked up to the first floor where the seamstresses worked. Several women were beavering away on their sewing machines, and they looked up at the new arrival.

He acknowledged them with a nod of his head and headed towards Molly's studio-cum office.

"Hello Freddie. Come in, how was the journey?" said Molly, seeing Freddie at the door.

"Aye, it were fine, thanks just half an hour."

"Do you want to sit down? I'll go over what I'd like you to do. There's a desk in the corner which you can use. John's still at his parents' house helping his mother clear his father's things; he won't be needing it. There's a small kitchen which the girls use if you want a drink, but you'll have to bring your own milk and sugar." Molly laughed. "I'm sure they won't mind sharing for one day."

By lunchtime, Freddie was feeling more confident, but his head was in a daze at all the information Molly had given him. She had introduced him to the girls as the 'office manager' and would be their boss. They were trying to weigh him up. The girls were remarkably young, late teens, mainly.

He had commented on this.

"Yes, we're always needing new girls. Most tend to leave when they get married. It's something you'll need to think about. It does take time to train them. The most important thing is to make sure the garments are high quality. I can't afford any returns; it's my reputation at stake. You'll need to check the stitching on every item that leaves here." Freddie was looking unsure.

"Don't worry, I'll show you what to look for... One other thing, over the last few weeks we've been having problems getting the cloth we need; all our normal suppliers have had difficulties, so we need to keep an eye on any wastage. Unfortunately, it's meant price increases. We're having to pay more."

"Aye, I understand," said Feddie.

"I suggest we take a break for some lunch. Did you bring anything?"

"Aye, Jean made us some sandwiches. I wasn't sure what was going to be available."

"Ah, well, that's fine. I'll make us some tea, then."

Broadway Buildings, London, SIS H.Q. Later that afternoon, Matthew had just returned from another intelligence briefing with the Special Branch police at New Scotland Yard. With no new bombings for over a fortnight, it appeared, on the face of it, that the authorities were gaining the upper hand. Recent terrorist activity appeared to be concentrating on targets in the Midlands, and police were on high alert in the major cities in the area. They had made a number of arrests.

His door was open and there was brief knock followed by the presence of his boss, Colonel Monkton. Matthew went to stand.

"As you were, Major, I've just been speaking to the Foreign Office, thought you should know, we're receiving some reports of problems in Lithuania."

Matthew looked up and gestured for the Colonel to sit down. "Lithuania?"

"Yes, another ultimatum from Hitler. According to our sources, Von Ribbentrop has demanded they give up the Memel Territory, or they will bomb the capital."

"Hmm, so much for their 'no more territorial ambitions'... Actually, when you think about it we shouldn't be too surprised. It was part of Germany during the war. Any news from number ten?"

"They won't intervene; not over this, nor France... We are, though, getting reports of many of the Jewish population fleeing. Most seem to be heading for Poland. We haven't got an exact note of numbers, but it could be as high as seven thousand."

"Seven thousand? That's going to cause problems for Poland."

"Yes, it is, but the Foreign Office won't get involved," said Monkton. "Their view is we can't look after more Jews in Britain."

"Well, I know that's the official line," said Matthew.

"Yes, as far as the F.O. are concerned, they're someone else's problem... Any news from Night Wing?"

"No, not since the original message. I'm hoping he'll get in touch soon."

"Right, let me know if you hear from him."

"Yes, Colonel."

Ryan Harris had been working with Finlan Connor and his two associates for three days.

He'd arrived at the Phelan site Saturday morning, just before the seven-thirty deadline as arranged. He was still sporting his moustache which was now more defined. It was a large office complex on four floors, being renovated by a local building company who had sub-contracted Finn and his associates to look after the decorating, at least a month's work.

"Ah, yer here," said Finn, as Ryan walked into the yard where Finn, Aidan, and Niall were unloading the lorry.

"Niall had a shilling with me that yer wouldn't turn up, so he did."

Ryan looked at Niall. "I'm a man of my word."

Niall looked at Ryan. "Well, I'm glad to hear that." He rummaged in his trouser pocket and handed over a coin to Finn.

"Well, let's get on; we've a lot to do," said Finn, and grabbed two tins of paint from the lorry and headed towards the entrance. He turned to Ryan. "We'll make a start, bring the stuff off the wagon. We're on the third floor."

Ryan picked up one of the step ladders and a tin of paint and followed the lads inside.

After three more trips, Ryan had unloaded the gear from the lorry. The third floor was a bare suite of four offices, and an open space, all requiring decorating.

Ryan was allocated one of the suites. Finn approached him.

"Now, yer know how to paint, I take it?" said Finn.

"Aye," replied Ryan.

"Well, help yerself to emulsion – it's all the same colour, and a brush or two. Yer'll need a ladder. The ceilings are done, so don't go messing them up otherwise yer'll be doing 'em again, am I clear?"

"Aye, Finn, I know what to do."

Finn took his gear and went into the first office suite. He had brought an old duffle bag containing a pair of overalls and some sandwiches for later.

While changing into his overalls, he took a look out of the window. He was at the back of the building; it was an uninspiring sight, a derelict building and an underground railway line, dominated the scene.

After an hour, Finn walked in to undertake an inspection.

"Well, yer doing a grand job there, so you are." He smiled as he examined Ryan's handiwork with a tradesman's eye. "Why don't yer join us for breakfast."

Ryan wiped his hands with an old rag and left his paintbrush soaking in a jar of turpentine.

"Niall, Aidan," he called. "Let's get some breakfast."

They left the building and walked up the road to a small café. Several other tradesmen were using it from other parts of the development.

Ryan blinked as he walked in. It could have been the place where the term 'greasy spoon' originated. Heavy with tobacco smoke and an overwhelming smell of fried food, it was not somewhere conducive to a lengthy stay.

"What're yer having?" asked Finn. "I'll see to it; find a table."

There were only two available and the three sat down at the nearest while Finn went to the counter to order.

"Don't yer worry about this place," said Niall, seeing Ryan looking around. "Sure, the food is good, so it is."

"That's good to hear," replied Ryan.

Aidan took out a packet of cigarettes and handed one to Niall, then offered the pack to Ryan.

"No, ta, I don't." Niall raised his eyebrows disapprovingly.

Finn returned a few minutes later. "Four breakfasts, on their way," he said as he sat down.

He turned to Niall and Aidan. "Yer man here, knows his way around a paint brush, so he does." He turned to Ryan. "We may have some more work after this, if yer up for it."

"Aye, if it pays well, I'm up fer it."

"It'll be more than what yer've been used to, I'll tell yer that," said Finn and laughed.

By Monday, Ryan had been integrated into the team. He had even been invited to join them in the pub after work. There was the usual boyish banter which Ryan had joined in. Unfortunately, there had been no indication that they were involved in anything suspicious.

They were back at the 'greasy spoon' for lunch. There had been some whispering, Ryan had noticed, during the morning. As they were tucking into their lunch, Finn made an announcement.

"Ryan, how do yer feel to holding the fort for us tomorrow? Me and the lads have got another job to do."

"Aye, I can do that... What about the paint and ladders?"

"Niall will drop the stuff off for yers by seven o'clock. We've got a journey to do."

"I can come with yer if yer want. I don't mind a bit of travelling."

"Yer'll be doing me a favour by working here in case the owners turn up."

"Aye, fair enough. So, where are yer going on this job then?"

"That's not for you to worry about," said Finn with an expression that suggested the matter was closed.

"Sure, sorry for asking."

Later, Ryan, on his way back to his bedsit, called Matthew from a telephone kiosk.

Matthew was in his office when the call came through.

"Keating."

"It's Night Wing."

"Good to hear from you. How is the project?"

"It's going well. I've been working with three lads since Saturday. The leader is a Finlan Connor, his associates, Niall and Aidan. I don't have their surnames."

Matthew made a note of their names. "Anything else?"

The agent continued. "I don't know whether they have any political interest or not; they have not expressed any sentiments in my hearing, but today there was a development. They've asked me to manage on my own tomorrow. They said they have another job to do which involves travelling. It might be nothing, but it is definitely unusual. They have asked me to stay behind and continue with the job we're on."

"So, is there any way you can find out where they are going?"

"Well, I did ask them, but I was told to mind my business. I do have an idea."

"Go on."

"One of the lads is bringing the lorry to drop off the materials to the job tomorrow morning. I was thinking, if someone could be waiting for the lorry, they could follow them."

"Yes, I can arrange that," said Matthew, "Do you have details of the lorry?"

"Aye, it's a Leyland Badger, license plate number PAU 735."

"Thank you, that's excellent. What time are they arriving?"

"Seven o'clock, they said. It's Phelan's on Cromwell Road; yer can't miss it."

The agent hung up and Matthew dialled a number.

"New Scotland Yard," came the voice as the call connected.

"Chief Superintendent Travis, please... Major Keating."

Chapter Fourteen

Tuesday morning, Grace was putting the final touches to her makeup when there was a knock on the front door. She went downstairs to open it. It was the postman with a large envelope addressed to James Keating.

Grace accepted the package and called her son.

"James, there's a package for you."

Moments later, James had left his bedroom and joined Grace in the hall.

"That will be your joining instructions, I expect," said Grace, as she handed over the package to her son. "It's post-marked 'Cranwell.'"

Grace watched as James excitedly opened the envelope and started reading the narrative.

"Does it say when you have to start?"

"Yes, they say I need to report on 10th April," replied James, as he continued to read the accompanying letter.

"That's the day after Easter," said Grace. "When do you break up from school?"

"End of the month, 31st," he confirmed.

"That doesn't give us much time. You'll need to check what clothes you'll need."

"Yes, there's a list here."

James walked back upstairs, continuing reading through the instructions.

Grace, meanwhile, was almost ready for her trip to Kent. She read Hetty's instructions again and put the letter in her handbag. The taxi was due in five minutes.

Selling is a small community on the Kent Downs, a predominantly agricultural area with rolling hills. Grace's train pulled into the village station just before lunch. She left the carriage with just two other passengers and looked for the exit. The platform was dominated by the signal box and a wrought iron footbridge which crossed the tracks. There was a sign indicating she would need to cross it to exit the station.

It was a bright, but cloudy morning, temperature about average for the time of year. Grace was wearing a coat, and, as she crossed the bridge, she took in the scenery; there was a good view of the surrounding countryside from her vantage point. She noticed several oast houses dotted about with their distinctive shapes, which would receive hops from the neighbouring farms.

For a country station, the main building was a magnificent example of traditional railway architecture and appeared well-maintained; very different from the London terminus. Grace presented her ticket to the inspector at the gate. He punched a hole in it and gave it her back. She would need it for the return journey, he explained. She could see Hetty waiting outside, standing next to her car. She waved seeing Grace at the barrier.

"Hello, old thing," said Hetty as Grace approached, and the pair embraced. "How was the journey?"

"It was comfortable, thanks; no delays, I'm pleased to report. It's a beautiful part of the world; I can see why you like it here."

"Yes, we've been very happy... Jump in, I'll take you to the farm; it's not far. We'll have time for a spot of lunch before we go to the church."

They passed the primary school and the church before turning into a narrow lane. The hedgerows were high, but behind them the tops of the hop poles were visible, rows and rows.

"My goodness are all these yours?" asked Grace.

"Yes, we've been very busy with stringing this last week."

"Ah, yes, you mentioned that."

"Normally, Chloe and I would be involved but I've had to hire some help this year."

"Yes, I can understand."

They pulled into a gravel yard in front of a cottage which seemed to be dwarfed by an adjacent oast house.

Hetty pulled up to the front door and turned off the engine.

"We're here."

Grace got out and looked around. "Oh, what a beautiful place!"

The front door opened, and a young lady approached them.

"This is Chloe," announced Hetty, proudly.

"Hello Chloe, I'm Grace." The pair shook hands and then hugged.

"Hello and thank you for helping me get my job; your husband has been very kind," said Chloe.

"Oh, it was my pleasure."

"Come on inside," said Hetty. "I've made some sandwiches. You've not met my brother, Luke, have you? He's just arrived."

The cottage was white-walled with a red, terracotta roof, typical of the area.

Grace entered the small hallway, then through into a rustic sitting room. It had a very 'homely' feel and much in keeping with Hetty's personality, warm and welcoming. A fire blazed in the hearth. The furniture was functional - armchairs, a dining table, a sideboard with large wooden mantel clock in the middle. As with every house these days, there was also a radio to the left of the sideboard on a bespoke table, on the opposite side, a display of family photographs in frames.

"Grace, this is Luke."

She was introduced to an academic-looking man, medium height, in his forties, with receding hair, wearing glasses and an ill-fitting suit.

"Hello, Luke, I've heard a lot about you. Hetty would always read me your letters when we were in France."

They shook hands.

"Seems a long time ago now."

"Yes, it certainly was. What do you do now?"

"I'm at Cambridge; I lecture in Mathematics."

"Ha, Hetty always said you were the brainy one," said Grace and he smiled.

Hetty intervened. "Come on you too, sit down, I'll get the lunch. The cars will be here about quarter-to-two."

She disappeared into the kitchen. Chloe sat opposite Grace on the other armchair, with Luke on the settee."

"Do you have a family, Luke?"

"Yes, I have a boy and girl, both at boarding school. My wife also teaches."

"Oh, how lovely. Is she here, your wife?" asked Grace.

"No, she sent her apologies. Up to their eyes in exams at the moment," replied Luke.

Grace and turned to Chloe. "So, Chloe, how are you enjoying work?"

"It's early days, and I'm still getting used to the commuting, but the work is really interesting. You feel you're at the centre of things."

"Yes, I can imagine," said Grace. "And how are you bearing up? Hetty said you were close to your father."

"Yes, we were very close, and I really miss him, but I know he would want me to be strong. I'll be glad when today's over, though. I'm pleased Hetty's here; she's been like a mother to me."

"Yes, she is a very special person... When did you lose your mother?"

"I was only five when she died; I don't have many memories of her." Chloe looked down.

Just then, Hetty called from the kitchen. "Chloe, can you give me a hand?"

Chloe responded and, a couple of minutes later, returned, carrying some plates and teacups. Hetty followed with the sandwiches.

"Have you done anything more about the ambulances?" asked Hetty as they started eating.

"Still waiting for a reply; I've sent off a letter... What about you? Have you thought anymore about joining?"

"Yes, I have. I'll see how the move goes, but it is something to consider. I must admit it will be good to team up again. Just like old times."

Chloe was listening. "What was it like... in the war I mean?" she asked.

Grace looked at Hetty and Luke. "There were some terrible times, Chloe. Hetty and I were often in danger, but, I don't know about you, Hetty, I wouldn't have missed it for the world. There was a sense of... I don't know, it's difficult to explain... you were doing your bit, I suppose."

"Hetty doesn't talk about it at all," said Chloe.

Grace looked at Hetty. "Yes, I must admit, neither do I, not the detail anyway." Grace turned to Chloe. "She saved my life, you know?"

Hetty looked embarrassed. "I did no such thing."

"Oh, you did, when the ambulance tipped over."

"What happened?" asked Chloe.

"We were driving down this road in Belgium and the road gave way. The ambulance rolled and I was trapped. Hetty got me out."

"Well, it was the soldiers that lifted the ambulance; I just managed to pull you from underneath."

"Then what happened?" asked Chloe.

Hetty took over. "We managed to get Grace to a hospital; she was in a coma for three days."

"Oh, that's awful," said Chloe.

"Luckily, I made a full recovery, but I wouldn't be here now if it wasn't for Hetty," said Grace.

"You know, you should write about it; it would be an example to others," said Chloe.

"Hmm, you could be right; maybe one day," said Grace.

There was the sound of a vehicle pulling up outside the cottage.

"That will be the car; we better get going," said Hetty.

It was a sad afternoon. The church had been full of well-wishers which was an indication of the regard in which Hetty's husband was held. Tears were shed, although Hetty appeared very stoic, wanting to be strong for Chloe.

After the service, the coffin was carried out of the church just a few small steps to the churchyard where a freshly dug grave had been prepared. The presiding vicar said a few words, and the coffin was gently lowered in by the pall bearers.

As the mourners departed, Grace was standing next to Hetty as she shook hands with numerous villagers and distant relatives who had come to pay their respects. A few had been invited to return to the family cottage for refreshments.

"What time is your train?" asked Hetty, as they eventually walked back to the car.

"There's one at six o'clock. At least I'll miss the crush at Victoria. It's only an hour or so from Faversham."

"I'll run you to the station, make sure you get the train,"

said Hetty.

"Thank you," said Grace.

Meanwhile, back in London, Matthew received a telephone call from New Scotland Yard. He made a note of the details and left his office to report the news to the Commander.

He knocked and entered. The Commander looked up from a mountain of paperwork.

"Some news, Major?"

"Yes, sir. I've just had a telephone call from Chief Superintendent Travis, New Scotland Yard. It appears Night Wing maybe onto something. A team of plain-clothes Special Branch officers followed the builders' lorry this morning; they ended up at an address in Coventry. It seems they dropped off several wooden crates."

"Now, that is interesting. Do we know the contents of the crates?"

"No, for the moment they've decided to put the property under surveillance."

"What about the builder's lorry?"

"It returned to London. The police here will be keeping an eye on them."

It was six o'clock, Ryan had been finishing off the final coat of paint in one of the suites when he heard the sound of a lorry pulling into the yard. It was getting dark, and its lights illuminated the front of the building.

With no electricity, Ryan had been working with a hurricane lamp. It had been a productive day without the interruptions, and he was about to start packing up.

The door opened, and Finn and his two associates walked in. Finn looked around.

"Yer've done a fine job, so yer have. I tought yer would have been long gone by now."

"Wanted to finish the job, so I did. This floor's finished, I reckon."

"Well, I tink yer deserve a pint or two, we're just dropping off some stuff and then we're off to the pub; yer very welcome to join us, so yer are."

"Aye, I'll just finished clearing up."

"Aye, yer can leave the stuff; it'll be safe enough until the morning."

The men left, and Ryan washed off his brushes and wiped down his hands. The smell of turpentine hung in the air and would linger for days.

Ryan was about to enter the yard when he noticed Niall carrying a box from the lorry into another entrance of the office complex. It was an area in the block which was next to be renovated; building work had not yet started.

After a few minutes, Finn exited the same doorway, followed by the other two in urgent discussion. He locked the door. Ryan ducked back into the building and waited for them to get in the lorry. Ryan left the building and approached the truck. Finn saw him.

"Hop in," said Finn and the three squashed up to allow him to sit. Niall was driving.

"Sure, yer've done a great job today," said Finn as they left the yard.

"Tanks, so was the trip successful?"

"Aye, I tink yer can say it was," said Finn.

Five minutes later they pulled up outside the Rose and Crown and extracted themselves from the lorry.

"What're yer having?" said Finn as they entered the pub.

It was ten o'clock by the time they left the Rose and

Crown. The three lads drove off in the lorry while Ryan walked back to his bed sit, despite the offer of a lift.

His mind was firmly fixed on the earlier incident. He needed to find out what was in the other building.

First, he needed to get back to the bed-sit and collect some tools he would need.

It was almost midnight by the time he returned to the building site. The yard was surrounded by a chain-linked fence with a gate in the middle. It was clearly a temporary measure until the building work was completed, just to secure the site.

Ryan reached the gate. A train went by, rattling across a nearby bridge; a dog barked in the distance. He looked around, on high alert. There was no streetlight in the immediate vicinity and Ryan was in total darkness, or as much as the city surrounds would allow.

The padlock was a standard affair and easily opened by one of Ryan's skeleton keys. He passed though and closed the gate behind him, leaving the padlock unlocked in case he had to leave in a hurry. He crouch-walked to the door which he had seen the lads use earlier. He pulled out his torch from his pocket. It was a British Military standard issue; no more than a narrow, six-inch tube housing a battery with a small bulb at one end but would do the job.

He checked the door. It was an old-fashioned rim lock, probably the original Edwardian model.

Again, it proved no challenge to Ryan's lock-picking skills. Within moments, he was inside. He shone his torch around. The ground floor was strewn with rubble, plaster, bits of wood, old beams, and pieces of metal, but nothing of interest.

Having checked the ground floor, he ascended the stairs to the next level. It was similarly presented but there were a series of offices, similar to the building Ryan and the lads had been working on.

His torch made strange shadows as the beam swept the area. He entered the first suite and in the corner there were several wooden boxes stacked in two columns halfway to the ceiling. There were smaller boxes next to them.

The tops of the crates were nailed down, but it was easy enough to ease the lid off the nearest container with a screwdriver. Ryan couldn't believe his eyes – a case of hand grenades. He replaced the top and checked the next; rows of what looked like putty in tube-like shapes – plastic explosives.

He continued checking the containers - detonators, handguns. There was no doubt it was quite a significant stash.

He checked everything was how he had found it, then left the building. He needed to contact his handler.

The following day there was another funeral, Gloria Davidson, one time speciality act and one of Cameron Delaney's stable of artists. Agnes was in reflective mood as she got ready to attend the occasion. The concert tours had been a rite of passage for Agnes, and Gloria had been a significant influence and support at that time, not always in a good way. The relationship had, however, helped Agnes mature and cope with the pressures of performing. As she did so, she gained in confidence.

Gloria was an effervescent character, 'incorrigible' the eighteen-year-old Agnes called her, not a normal word for a baker's girl from Keighley, but she was, by now, mixing in different circles. As Agnes's fame grew, Gloria was there to help and guide her, particularly when it came to the attention of predatory males, of which there were many.

Gloria's passing had brought back so many memories. She thought of her first real relationship, not Norman, the solicitor's clerk, who had joined the army when Agnes turned down his proposal of marriage, but Lord Harford with whom she was briefly betrothed.

Both Lord Harford and Norman had sadly been killed in the conflict. She snapped out of her reminiscing; some memories were painful.

Agnes had chosen a special outfit for the occasion, dark colours with a small, black-netted hat, with fashionable shoes. She would also wear her mink coat; it was a cool day. Unsure of the venue, she had ordered a taxi to take her south of the river. It would take an hour, allowing for the traffic. the taxi firm had told her.

Balham in 1939 was a thriving community based around the High Road which was lined with shops. Agnes had never been to the town before but, coincidently, there was an article in the newspaper the previous day which had caught her eye. It concerned an incident that had happened in one of the buildings a few days earlier. According to the article, a fourteen-year-old boy had been found dead at the bottom of the lift shaft. Police were still investigating, it said.

The taxi drove through the suburb and reached the Methodist Church on Holly Grove. It was one-forty, and there were a few people waiting outside the church.

She paid the driver and arranged a pickup in two hours, which she thought would give her plenty of time.

With smoking generally frowned upon in church, several of the waiting mourners had taken the opportunity to light up. One of them spotted Agnes and walked towards her.

"It's Agnes Marsden, isn't it?" he said.

Agnes looked at him. Quite tall, well-dressed, and

wearing a trilby hat which he doffed courteously.

"Yes," replied Agnes.

"I'm Desmond Davidson, Gloria's brother. I am so glad to see you. We didn't have your address; I was hoping you would see the notice in the paper."

He held out his hand in greeting. Agness shook it warmly.

"Pleased to meet you, Desmond. I had no idea Gloria had a brother."

"No, I don't suppose she mentioned me; we were estranged for a long time."

"Oh, I'm sorry to hear that."

"It's alright; it's all in the past."

"Why were you estranged? If you don't mind me asking." The man took a long drag of his cigarette. The smoke drifted in the wind.

"I was only about fourteen. Gloria wanted to join a circus, she was just sixteen and already a good juggler. Our mother and father refused, but she went anyway. We were told we couldn't speak to her."

"We?"

"Yes, there were two older sisters, but they too have passed on."

"Oh, I'm so sorry. You know, Gloria never talked about her family."

"Hmm, I can imagine. I started making enquiries to see if I could find her about two years ago. Somehow, it felt wrong after all these years. Luckily, I managed to trace Gloria, last August, I think it was."

The man was joined by a woman of about the same age, mid/late fifties.

"This is my wife, Una. Una this is Agnes Marsden."

The woman shook hands. "It's so nice to meet you."

The man addressed Una. "I was just telling Agnes about

tracing Gloria."

"Oh, yes, it took quite a while. He became quite obsessive about it, didn't you, dear?"

"I suppose I did."

"So, how did you manage to find her?"

"As a last resort, I placed an advertisement in The London Evening Standard and a neighbour responded."

"It was quite a shock meeting her for the first time," continued Una. "She had a small bedsit just the other side of the High Road above a shop."

"Oh, I'm so sorry to hear. I wish I had known. I'd not heard from her since just after the war; she was on one of the tours. I think Cameron kept in touch for a while; that's the agent," said Agnes with an expression of sadness.

"Hmm, you probably wouldn't have recognised her. She was an alcoholic and in a bad way when we found her. We did manage to get her off the drink, but unfortunately, her liver failed, which is how she died."

"Oh, that is so sad. She was like an older sister to me. I owe her a great deal; she was my guardian angel."

"Yes, she did mention you many times. She heard you on the radio; she was so proud. We didn't believe her at first, but she had some old photographs which she said were taken in France."

"Oh yes, I think I remember that. Cameron arranged for some pictures to be taken to advertise the tour. I never knew what had become of them."

Agnes could feel tears beginning to fall down her cheek. She took out a handkerchief from her handbag and dabbed her cheek.

"Sorry about that," said Agnes, "I had no idea. I've thought of Gloria from time to time and wondered how she was but had no means of contacting her."

"Of course, please don't be concerned; it took us some time to find her, and I'm so glad we did. We were reconciled and I was there for her at the end."

"I'm pleased she had you," said Agnes.

"I think we should go in; the hearse will be here shortly," said Desmond.

The three walked towards the entrance. Several other mourners were milling about, one or two recognised Agnes and were immediately engaged in conversation.

Inside, there were less than twenty people taking up the first two rows of the church. Agnes was on the first row next to Desmond and Una.

As the coffin was brought in, Agnes was overwhelmed by sadness and guilt at not making more of an effort to locate her good friend. Maybe she could have helped her.

It was only a short service, and the hearse took Gloria's body to the graveyard in Tooting. She would be buried on her own.

Desmond was at the church entrance, thanking people for attending; most were neighbours and recent acquaintances, no one from the 'old days'.

They had soon disappeared to their own world, leaving Desmond, Una, and Agnes at the church steps.

"What are you doing now?" asked Desmond.

"I've ordered a taxi for four o'clock." He checked his watch.

"Oh, but that's over an hour. Why don't we go for a coffee? I would love to hear more about your time with Gloria."

"Yes, very well, that's a good idea," replied Agnes.

"We'll take the car. I can drop you back here in time for your taxi."

Later, as Agnes returned to her house in the taxi, she reflected on her afternoon.

They had managed to find a nice café on the High Road, and, during conversation, she learned more of the Davidson family. Desmond was the youngest, followed by Gloria; the two other sisters, now also deceased, were older. Desmond had joined a bank after school and was soon to retire as a manager at one of the local branches in Barnet, where he and Una now lived. They had three children who were all at grammar school.

Agnes was able to fill in some of the gaps from the tours, the recruitment tour, and the one to France being the most memorable. There were many amusing anecdotes which helped to lift the sad atmosphere.

Before leaving the café, Gloria and Una agreed to keep in touch and exchanged addresses and telephone numbers. They had promised to send the photographs that Gloria had kept.

Thursday, 23rd March.

Back at Phelan's building site, Ryan and the Connor gang had moved to the second floor which was laid out in a similar fashion to the first.

They were taking a mid-morning break when Finn approached Ryan.

"I've been chatting to the lads and was wondering if yer were up to another bit of fetching and carrying."

Ryan was on alert. "Aye, sure, if there's money in it."

"Aye, they'll be some money in it for yer."

"What'll I drive? I have no car."

"Don't yer worry yerself about that; I'll see to that."

"When do yer want us to start?"

"Tonight, six o'clock. Niall will bring round a van for

yers. There will be some packages in the back to take to an address in Islington he will give yer. It's not far, three miles maybe. Do yer tink yer can do that?"

"Aye, I don't see why not, and how much are yer paying?"

"I'll pay yer hourly rate plus a bonus when yer done. Let's call it five shillings."

This was double Ryan's normal hourly rate.

"Aye, that's a deal, so it is," said Ryan. "It'll be my round."

"Aye, so it will."

Ryan was relaxed about his new courier job; he had a pretty good idea about the nature of the cargo. After he had dropped it off, he would call in, and tell his handler the address. It would be another link in the chain.

It was gone six-thirty, an innocuous-looking Ford delivery van, the kind used for transporting parcels or produce, arrived in the yard. Ryan had heard it, moved to the window, and started painting the frame. It was starting to get dark, and he would not be easily visible from the yard.

He could see Niall and two other men walk to the other building where the stash of explosives and weaponry was hidden.

He was watching what was going on, when, suddenly, Finn walked into the room. Ryan nearly jumped out of his skin.

"Ryan, yer van's arrived, so yer see. It'll be ready for yer shortly. Yer can finish off now."

Ryan quickly composed himself. "Aye, I'll do that. Just finishing the window, then it's all done in here."

He went into the main office and started cleaning his brushes.

"Yer might want to take off yer overalls, sure yer'll stink

the van out, so yer will."

"Aye, I'll do that," replied Ryan.

Ryan washed up and went down to the yard. Niall was stood next to the van; there was no sign of the two lads that had delivered it.

Outside the complex, another innocuous car was parked next to a telephone kiosk in a side road with visual on the gate. It had seen the van arrive. One of the occupants got out of the car, darted into the call box, and quickly inserted coins into the slot. There was a brief conversation and the man returned to the car.

"What do they want us to do?" asked his colleague in the driver's seat.

"We are to follow the van when it leaves."

"What about surveillance?"

"They're sending another car; should be here in half an hour."

Ten minutes passed before the van left the yard. The unmarked police car slowly pulled out of the junction and accelerated to within twenty yards of the van. As they reached the main road, the traffic increased, and the pursuit car had to wait for several vehicles and a bus to pass before they could continue following.

"Can you see him?" asked the driver, who was now caught behind the bus and had to wait while passengers got off and on.

"No, I think we've lost him. Can you get by the bus?"

The driver pulled out and completed the manoeuvre. Both occupants were scanning the line of traffic in front of them and any side roads they passed.

"Damn, damn, damn," said the driver in frustration.

"We better call in," said the passenger.

"Let's give it a few minutes; we might spot him."

The road was straight, and the streetlights provided reasonable illumination. They passed a parade of shops.

"Wait, look, there, just past that church; a van's turning," said the passenger.

It was about two hundred yards away up a slight incline.

"You're right. Let's take a look."

There were a number of buses in the crawling traffic resulting in several minutes before they reached the church and made the turn. The driver continued to curse.

The road was less well-lit than the main drag, and it spawned several smaller side streets with rows of terraced houses.

"Damn, we're never going to find it down here," said the driver, looking left and right. "Do you know where we are?"

"Brook Street, Islington, according to the road sign."

"Well, if we see a kiosk, we'll phone in."

Ryan was oblivious to the following vehicle, concentrating on the road. Niall's directions were clear enough and he knew the route into Islington; as Finn had said, it was not far away.

He was making slow progress due the heavy traffic at this time of night, exacerbated by the numbers of buses which seemed to have a herding instinct.

He climbed the gentle rise in the road and could see the church towards the top. He wound down the window and stuck out his arm to indicate a right-hand turn. It had started to rain, adding to the gloom.

The receiving road was much darker and the headlights hardly sufficient to provide any meaningful illumination.

Third on the right, was his instructions, Cadwallader Street. He counted the turnings and saw the street sign.

He was holding a piece of paper in his hand trying to read it by the intermittent light of the streetlamps. He was squinting. About halfway along on the left, number fifty-six, it said.

All the houses looked the same, just a long row of terraced properties on both sides; many had their lights on. He slowed and looked across at the door numbers. Some were just chalked on the wall next to front door.

He counted down the doors until he reached number fifty-six. As he slowed to a stop, he noticed the curtain twitch. Then the front door opened.

A man in a worker's shirt and dungarees stood in the doorway. Ryan got out and walked towards him.

"You Ryan?" asked the man.

"Aye."

"Ronan O'Doyle, come inside; I'll get some of the lads to collect the stuff. Give us the keys."

Ryan was uneasy at the request; his sixth sense suggested caution.

"Well, that's very kind of yers, but I'll get back if it's all the same. I can catch a bus."

"No, no, yer don't want to be doing that in all this rain. Sure, there's a bottle or two waiting inside and the lads will be interested in meeting yer, so they will. Finlan speaks well of yer."

With little option, Ryan was ushered inside. There were five men seated around the room on chairs and a settee. It resembled a council meeting.

O'Doyle handed the keys to the nearest. "Ciarán, you and Cormac unload the stuff; take it round the back and be careful; we don't want any accidents."

There was an arch built into the terrace next to the front door with an alleyway, which serviced the back yards of the five properties to the left and right. The two lads left the house and started shifting the cargo down the alleyway and into the yard of number fifty-six, where it would be stored in an outhouse. Some boxes were heavy requiring both of the lads to carry one between them.

Meanwhile, inside, O'Doyle was introducing Ryan to the group. Ryan was trying to remember their names. There was a noise from the kitchen.

"Hey, Jimmy, bring in a bottle or two, will yer? There's someone here yer should meet."

The man entered from what was the kitchen holding two pint bottles of Guinness. He stopped and stared at Ryan.

"Well, sweet Jesus, if it isn't Eoghan Flemming. It's been a while, me lad, so it has."

Ryan's blood ran cold.

Chapter Fifteen

A little earlier, the two pursuing police officers, Baker and Johnson, were still trawling the rows of avenues behind the church. They eventually reached Cadwallader Street and noticed a van parked on the left-hand side.

"What's that, there?" said P.C. Baker, the passenger, sitting forward to get a better view.

"I'll drive by and take a look," responded Johnson.

"It's the van alright; we need to call in."

"There's a phone-box on the corner, I noticed. Have you got any change? I've only got a half-crown."

The driver rummaged in the breast pocket of his uniform and pulled out several pennies and handed them to his colleague.

They turned around and headed back towards the main road. Johnson parked close to the junction. It was still raining, and Baker had to make a dash for the telephone kiosk. It was illuminated, and the officer could see someone using the phone. He immediately opened the door and held out his warrant card.

"Police! Hang up the call and leave the kiosk," he said assertively.

It was an elderly man and the intrusion made him jump. He immediately complied. Baker lifted the receiver, dialled the number, and reached his superior.

"It's Baker, sir, we've been following the van from the Phelan's site as ordered. It's parked in a side street in Islington, Cadwallader Street, number fifty-six. What do you want us to do?"

"Can you maintain observation? I'll get back-up to you within the hour."

"Yes, sir," replied Baker. He hung up the phone and returned to the car.

"What do they want us to do?" asked Johnson as his partner got in.

"We're to maintain observation. They're sending back up."

Johnson reversed the car and headed back to Cadwallader Street. He parked on the opposite side of the road.

"Well, we'll just wait. Did you bring any sandwiches?" asked Johnson.

"No," replied Baker.

"Bugger, I'm starving."

It was over an hour before a police van turned the corner and pulled up behind the unmarked car. Baker got out and spoke to the driver, then returned to their vehicle.

"What's happening?" asked Johnson.

"They're going in, in five minutes."

Ten officers exited the back of the Black Maria and walked across the road; half went down the alleyway. One of the officers was holding a dog on a short leash which was straining to get into the action.

The lead officer banged on the door. "Police, open up!" he bellowed.

There was no reply, but they could hear a great deal of activity inside, urgent shouting, furniture being moved. One of the officers produced a long-handled sledgehammer and proceeded to hit the door. Bits of wood flew in all directions. Another officer kicked the flimsy barrier, and it gave way.

The five officers and the dog entered the building. Ronan O'Doyle was seated on the sofa. The dog started barking.

He looked up at the officer. "What's all this about? Yer

can't go round beating people's door down, so yer can't."

"Name," bellowed Sergeant Sanders, the officer in charge.

"Ronan, Ronan O'Doyle."

"Ronan O'Doyle, I'm arresting you on suspicion of involvement with terrorist activities. Hands behind your back... now!" shouted the sergeant.

One of the officers handcuffed O'Doyle.

Meanwhile, three of the gang were trying to make good their escape through the back. Two had been apprehended, the third was being chased by two officers. As they closed on their quarry, he turned and fired a gun at the pursuers. The first officer went down and the other stopped to aid his colleague..

Back inside, two further men had been handcuffed from upstairs and brought to the sitting room to join O'Doyle.

P.C.'s Johnson and Baker were outside keeping watch. Sergeant Sanders appeared at the broken door frame and looked around.

"All secure here, you two, go and phone for more back up and get an ambulance; there's an officer down.

The pair went back to their car, turned, and headed for the telephone kiosk.

Half an hour later, the house was a hive of activity. An ambulance had arrived and taken away the injured officer whose condition was described as 'stable'. Detectives had arrived to gather evidence. One of them was searching one of the bedrooms when he made a gruesome discovery. At the back of a built-in cupboard, hidden by a piece of old tarpaulin, was the half-naked body of a man. He had been badly beaten and there were cigarette burns and stab wounds on his torso.

Seven o'clock, Friday morning, Major Keating was already at his desk reading the latest reports. There had been more bombings in Coventry. Luckily, no-one was hurt. The perpetrators had targeted the GPO telephone network, and there was considerable damage affecting the local exchange. As far as the police could tell, it had not been perpetrated by the residents of the property visited by Finn and his gang. The address was still under surveillance. In light of the recent events, according to Matthew's notes, the house would be raided today.

His telephone rang; it was Chief Superintendent Travis from New Scotland Yard.

He listened to the message. It was the worse news.

He hung up, put his head in his hands, and walked to Monkton's office.

"Some dreadful news, sir," he announced, as he walked into the room. "Just been speaking to Travis from Scotland Yard. They raided a house in Islington last night and found a body. They're pretty certain it's Night Wing."

"Oh, dear Lord," said Monkton, his face etched with concern.

"They've asked me to go and identify the body; it's in the morgue at the Yard waiting for the postmortem."

"Do we know what happened?"

"No, but they've arrested seven men; one escaped after shooting one of the officers. They found a cache of weapons and explosives in an outhouse. They're carrying out further raids today."

"I hope they nail the bastards," said Monkton.

"Hmm, yes, with a bit of luck they'll deport them back to Ireland to hang."

Friday evening, seven o'clock, Freddie had returned

from Molly's factory. His initial week had exceeded his expectations. It was his first experience of indoor labour, having spent the whole of his working life in the fresh air. Molly had commented favourably on how quickly Freddie had picked up everything. His initial anxieties had gone, and he was thoroughly enjoying his new responsibilities.

As he ate his dinner with wife, Jean, and son, Arthur junior, recounting his day, he spoke enthusiastically about the progress he had made. As Freddie talked, Jean was pleased for him; she had held reservations at his change of career.

There was a topic, however, Arthur was dying to raise. Whereas Freddie had taken after his mother, Kitty, Arthur Taylor was a Marsden in character and had inherited his grandfather's forthrightness. At an appropriate moment, he interrupted the conversation.

"It's my birthday next week."

Freddie was trying to work out the relevance. "Aye, don't worry, son, I'll get tha something."

"No, I want to join up - the navy."

Freddie stopped eating. "Aye, tha've said before, but I thought that would be after tha had finished thar schooling."

"Aye, but 'appen they want lads now. It were in t'paper; some of my school friends have already signed up."

"But why the navy?"

"'Appen I'll see places and not be stuck down holes waiting for bombs to drop on tha."

"Aye, that's true enough."

"Tha was in t'army, not much older than me, Da."

"Aye, that's true enough, and I wouldn't wish that on my worst enemy."

Arthur looked at his father. "Tha's never said owt about it. What were it like?"

Freddie put his knife and fork down and looked at Jean.

"Let's say this, if tha can imagine tha worst nightmare, it would still not come close."

"It were Uncle Arthur that saved tha... Mam told me."

Freddie looked at Jean again. "Aye, it's summat that's not easy to talk about."

"Your father still has nightmares," interjected Jean.

"Aye, 'appen he risked his life to pull me from no-man's land after I'd been wounded," continued Freddie. He looked down. "And now he's gone. 'Appen he were never the same man when he came back."

"I liked Uncle Arthur; he were a brave man."

"Aye, that he was," replied Freddie.

"And a good baker, an'all by all accounts."

"Aye..."

Freddie was deep in thought and had lost the thread of the conversation. Jean took over.

"But why do you want to join up now? Why not wait until your school finishes in June?"

"They say at school there's going to be a war soon. 'Appen they need us now; there's training to be had. I want to be ready..." He paused. "I'm no good at school anyhow; I'm not clever or owt."

"Don't say that; of course you are; just not academic, Arthur. You're practical and good with your hands; that stands for a lot, these days." Jean looked at Freddie. "Well, if you've made up your mind, I won't stand in your way. What do you say, Freddie?"

"Aye, if that's what tha want to do."

"Ta, Dad; I'll speak to my teacher tomorrow and find out what to do."

Friday night, Mildred was in her sitting room waiting

for her favourite radio programme to start. It was Agnes's Variety Show. She had company; she had invited William and Marjorie to tea.

After work at the bakery, William changed and caught the trolleybus to Oakworth. Marjorie was waiting at Ingrow and joined him on the top deck. William always preferred to travel upstairs; he could see the countryside more clearly.

They were given a warm welcome by Mildred when they arrived at Blossom Cottage. She and Ethel Jessop had made a meat pie which had taken most of the afternoon to prepare and cook. It was warming in the oven.

"Let me take your coats," said Mildred as the pair were ushered into the sitting room. "How was the journey?"

"Aye, not bad, Gran. It were quite busy when I left but most got off before we got here. We got two seats together." He turned and smiled at Marjorie.

"Would you like a cup of tea before dinner?"

"Aye, thank you?" said William.

"Yes please," said Marjorie.

A few minutes later, the three were sat around the fireside with their drinks chatting about fairly mundane matters. Mildred was always interested on how things were going at the bakery and was delighted on how William had turned it into such a success.

"I had a telephone call from Freda, yesterday," said Mildred.

"Oh, how is she?" asked William. "I've not seen her since Da's funeral."

"She's well, thank you, been appointed Headmistress of that large girls' school in Utley."

"Well, that's good news," replied William.

"Yes, she's been wanting something new for some time. She's been at Micklethwaite for, let me see, close on twenty years, must be. She was saying they have some of the Basque refugees there, at Utley."

"That's so sad what happened to them," said Marjorie. "I read about it in the News. Imagine having to leave your home and family. I don't suppose they could speak English."

"Certainly, not when they arrived," replied Mildred. "But they've been here two years, so I'm sure they will have learned by now. I must ask Freda once she gets settled."

Mildred did have another reason for inviting William and Marjorie.

"It's so kind of you to come all this way after a busy day."

"Thank you for inviting us," said Marjorie.

"Well, I wanted to discuss a wedding present with you."

William looked at Marjorie. "Thank you, that's very kind," said Marjorie.

"I've been to see my solicitor this morning, and I would like to give you a house, somewhere to live when you get married."

William was speechless. "Oh, but I don't know what to say," said Marjorie.

"Well, when I sold the Hall, there was some money left over after I'd bought Blossom Cottage, and my solicitor advised me to invest it in property. Very wise council, if I may say, after the Stock Market crash. I have a cottage in Aireworth Street which will be empty shortly; the tenants are moving out and I'd like to give it to you as a wedding present."

William was struggling for words. "Aye, that's grand, thank you very much, Gran." William looked at Marjorie; he wanted to hug her.

"It should be vacant next month which means you can spend some time decorating and making it homely for yourselves."

"Oh, I can't wait to tell my Mam," said Marjorie.

"I've already mentioned it to your mother, William. I asked her not to say anything until I had spoken to you both."

"Aye, she's not said owt," said William.

"Well, that's settled then. I'll let you know when you can start work on it. You will have to sign some papers at the solicitor's office too."

The pair were beyond excited.

"Let me go and attend to the dinner; it won't be long."

Later, William and Marjorie helped Mildred wash and dry the dishes; they would be in good time before Agnes's broadcast started.

"How long has Aunt Agnes been singing for?" asked William, as they settled down next to the radio.

"It's been a long time... I'll never forget her first audition. It was at the Hippodrome, in town. Agnes was so nervous, but she did have a lovely voice, and the agent liked her. Next thing we knew, she was in a touring party trying to recruit men for the war, top of the bill, no less." Mildred said with pride. "We went to see her in Bradford at the Alhambra theatre, which had only just opened. It was just me, Freddie's Mum, Kitty, and Freda... oh, and Molly, if I remember correctly. I think Grace was away, and your father was at a training camp somewhere waiting to go to France."

"That's a long time ago," said William.

"Yes, although she stopped singing for a while after she had Gwen, but now she's older, I think Agnes was happy to start again. I have to say, I didn't think she would be so popular, picture on the front page of the Radio Times. Who would have thought it?"

"Aye, Mam's bought a copy; she keeps it in the drawer in her bedroom," said William.

Just then the theme music to the Variety Show started and an announcer in a plummy accent, introduced the programme.

"*It's Friday Night and time for The Variety Show, starring your very own Agnes Marsden, who will be singing a selection of songs requested by you, the listeners...*" He continued to name the support cast of comedians and a male singer. William looked at Mildred and smiled.

Saturday Morning, seven a.m., Matthew had not had a day's break for over a fortnight and on a couple of occasions had used the sleeping quarters at the office. He was starting to feel the pressure. Grace had pleaded with him to take some rest; she was worried about him.

The news did not improve. In Germany, Hitler had made his expected grab for Memel and thirty-one navel warships had been stationed off the port in a show of strength; not that they were needed. The province was handed over without a fight as the rest of the world, including Britain and France, watched on.

Matthew was not looking forward to his morning's task, a visit to the morgue to identify the body of Night Wing, the agent who had almost certainly saved his life.

Later, he confirmed it was, in fact, the agent. It was a difficult time, and he couldn't help noticing the bruising to his face. He wondered about Eoghan's last moments with deep sadness. He also had a letter to write.

The only good news was that Finn and his cohorts had been arrested and numerous weapons and explosives had been found. There were also letters and papers relating to the 'S' plan.

Across the country, the sheer scale of the arrests meant

that Special Branch was being stretched which resulted in numerous secondments to boost resources.

It had been a tough day and Matthew's concentration levels had dropped, something his secretary noticed.

She brought him a cup of tea after lunch. "Sir, do you mind if I say something?"

Matthew looked up, his eyes bloodshot from yawning. "No, of course not."

"You really need to get some rest, sir. You'll be having a breakdown if you carry on like this, with respect."

"You sound like my wife."

"Well, she's right. I hope you don't mind me speaking my mind, sir."

Matthew rubbed his face with his hands, something he would not normally do in front of staff. He desperately needed to sleep.

"No, no, you're quite right, thank you."

Janet smiled. "Enjoy your tea, sir," she said, and left his office.

He thought about his secretary's remarks. He couldn't remember the last time he'd had a proper break. The death of the agent bothered him a great deal and he felt some responsibility; he did need to get away. He drank his tea and left his office.

He knocked on the Commander's door and was called in.

"Ah, Major, glad you stopped by, I wanted a word with you about Siemens... Where are we with that?"

"We've identified two agents who are presently being trained. They should be in place in two weeks or so."

"Good, good, I trust the company haven't got wind of this; we don't want to alert them."

"All very discreet, sir."

"Good, good. I've had the Home Office asking earlier. I told them we had everything in hand."

"Yes, sir, it is."

"How did you get on this morning at the morgue?"

"Hmm, yes, it was Night Wing alright; he seemed to have been badly beaten."

"Terrible business, terrible business; still, unfortunately, these things go with the job. They know the dangers when they sign up."

"True, sir. He's going to be difficult to replace. Finding sympathisers to the Unionist cause in the present climate is going to be a challenge."

"Yes, agreed. What about speaking to someone in the RUC? Do we have any contacts there?"

"Not directly, no."

"Pity... Well, I'm sure you have it all under control."

"Yes, sir... I do have a request, sir."

"Oh, what is it?"

"I'd like to take a spot of leave, just a few days... to recharge the old batteries, so to speak."

The Commander looked at him. "You're not ill are you, Major?"

"No, sir."

"Good, good. These are difficult times, and they're not going to get any easier, especially if we go to war."

"No, I agree, sir."

The Commander looked at Matthew. "Hmm, very well. How long will you need?"

"Just three days. I will make sure I can be reached by telephone in case there's anything urgent."

"Who's going to look after your desk in your absence?"

"Well, nobody, I'll catch up when I get back; it's only three days."

"Hmm, a lot can happen in three days. What about an assistant?"

"An assistant?"

"Yes, I think it would be helpful; someone to do some of the donkey work. I'm aware of the pressures we're all under at the moment. I'll authorise the resource."

Matthew thought for a moment. "Yes, I'll consider that, and thank you. Actually, I do have someone in mind."

"What's his name?"

"It's a 'she', sir."

The Commander looked at Matthew in a quizzical way. "Hmm, as long as you know what you're doing."

Matthew walked though into the main office where the noise of typewriters and conversation was intrusive to an onlooker. He spotted who he was looking for and went to her desk. She was listening to chatter on a radio receiver.

She noticed Matthew and pushed back her headphones. "Yes, sir."

"My office, when you can spare a minute?"

Matthew had picked up some reports and was reading them when there was a knock on the door a few minutes later.

"You wanted to see me, sir?"

"Yes, Chloe, take a seat. How are you settling in?"

"Well, it's a bit different from hop farming, that's for sure."

Matthew smiled. "Yes indeed... The reason I've asked you in for a chat is I need an assistant, and I'd like you to work for me. I need someone who can think on their feet and act on their own initiative. I believe you have shown you can do that. Your supervisor speaks highly of you."

"Thank you, sir, I don't know what to say."

"I think it's because most of the people here, girls certainly, have joined the department straight from school or university, whereas you have had to run a business and been able to handle responsibility."

"Thank you, sir."

"It will mean long hours and hard work."

"Yes, I understand. What about my other work?"

"Don't worry, I'll speak to your supervisor."

"When will you want me to start?"

"Well, I'm going to take a short break, so officially, when I get back, but I want you to filter any information for me. Just hold back essential briefings. I'll only be away for a few days. I'll go over it in detail later."

Chloe was speechless. "Yes, I'm sure I can do that."

"It will be on a one month's trial, then I'll make it permanent if everything works out."

"Thank you, sir," said Chloe and left the office.

Matthew needed to brief the supervisor.

He was home by seven o'clock, an early night by recent experience. He had so many things in his head but felt better with the thought of a few days away. He had been pleased with Chloe's response and his briefing. He had informed the Commander of his decision.

Grace welcomed him warmly. "How was your day, darling?" she said as he removed his raincoat and trilby in the hallway.

"I'm not sure where to start."

He walked into the sitting room and went to the whiskey decanter.

"Oh, one of those days," observed Grace.

"Yes, it was. How are James and Dotty?"

"They're both in their rooms; they've already eaten.

James can't wait to get to start with the RAF. He's hoping to be selected for pilot training."

"Yes, that sounds like James, the glamour job."

"Ha, yes... So, not a good day, then?"

"No, we lost one of our agents."

"Oh, I'm sorry."

"Yes, a good man, incredibly brave." He took a large slug of whiskey. "I do have some better news; I'm taking three days leave."

"Really, that's wonderful; I said you needed a break."

"Yes, you did, and you were right."

"When will you be off?"

"From tonight... After today, I needed to get away. I don't have to be back until Wednesday morning. Unless there's a major incident. They've let me have an assistant as well; the workloads are just overwhelming at the moment."

"Well, that's good."

"Yes, I've chosen Chloe."

"What, Hetty's Chloe?"

"Yes, she's made an impressive start to her career."

"Oh, Hetty will be so pleased... Let me dish up and you can tell me more. Dinner's ready."

A few minutes later, Grace had served the dinner, and the pair were at the dining table.

"I've been thinking about your break. We need to get out of London; you'll only go back in at the slightest excuse. I know what you're like."

"Ha, yes, that's true... What do you have in mind?"

"Well, you won't believe this, but I had a letter from Jane Garner this morning."

"What, Lady Jane?"

"Yes, not heard from her since the Christmas Card. It's

her sixtieth birthday on Monday and she's having a small party at the Manor. I was going to telephone her and give her our apologies, but now you have some time off, we can go up there. What do you think?"

"Sounds like a good idea."

"We can stay at Mam's; I know she won't mind. You can call in and see your sister, too. It's been a while."

"Yes, that's true."

"I'll telephone Mam after dinner, and Jane too; it will be lovely to see her again."

Sunday Morning, with arrangements made, Grace and Matthew were at St Pancras Station to catch the train to Bradford.

It was a four-hour journey, with frequent stops, but eventually they arrived at the terminus in Bradford. With Sunday service, the number of trains had been reduced and they decided to take a taxi to Oakworth to avoid a long wait.

"Oh, it's so nice to be back," said Grace, as the taxi pulled up outside Blossom Cottage.

The pair exited the cab and Matthew paid. Grace looked up at the sky and took deep breaths.

"I'd forgotten how peaceful it was up here. It almost feels like there's more air, you know."

"Yes, it does feel so different," said Matthew who was on luggage duty.

Grace reached the front door, but Mildred had already opened it having heard the vehicle pull up.

"Grace, dear, how lovely to see you," she said, and hugged her daughter. "And Matthew, looking as handsome as ever," she added, seeing her son-in-law. More affectionate hugs followed.

"Come in, come in, I expect you're hungry after that

journey. Did you manage to get anything to eat?"

"The train stopped at Leicester to take on water, and we managed to get some chocolate biscuits and a cup of tea at the station shop," said Matthew.

"Yes, they had Huntley and Palmers Tivoli biscuits, my favourite," added Grace.

"Well, there's a joint of pork in the oven, Ethel brought it round earlier. I called her and said you were coming. You've just missed her."

"Oh, how is she?"

"She's well, thank you; I don't know what I would do without her."

Mildred ushered the pair into the sitting room.

"Make yourself comfortable, I'll put the kettle on."

"I'll give you a hand," said Grace.

There was a long catch up over dinner - Hetty's husband's funeral, ambulance service, James' RAF enrolment, Dorothy's school progress. Mildred brought them up to date with William and Marjorie's betrothal, and life at the bakery.

"Have you seen anything of Agnes?" asked Mildred.

"Yes, we catch up quite often, though not so much recently since she started the radio show."

"Yes, I can understand. I had a lovely letter from her. I'm so pleased for her. We never miss her radio show. I listened to it with William and Marjorie on Friday."

"That's nice," said Grace. "What's she like, Marjorie."

"Marjorie? She's a delightful girl; just what William needs. They go so well together... Oh, I nearly forgot, sorry, my mind's not as keen as it was," added Mildred. "Lady Jane telephoned to ask if you would like to go riding tomorrow morning – both of you. I said you would let her know. She said something about sending a car."

"Oh, that's very kind of her; that sounds lovely. What do you think, darling?" asked Grace.

"Well, yes, although I haven't ridden for probably thirty years," replied Matthew, with a frown.

"Oh, I'm sure it will soon come back to you," said Grace and laughed.

"Yes, I suppose it will."

"I'll telephone Jane after we've eaten; if I can use your telephone," said Grace.

"Yes, of course," replied Mildred.

Later that afternoon, after the dishes had been washed and put away, Grace had spoken to Lady Jane and accepted her offer of going horse riding.

It was a beautiful early evening and Grace and Matthew decided to go for a walk.

"Oh, this is lovely," said Grace, as they walked up Main Street past the village store. "I don't think there's anything to beat England in the spring."

They turned left down the narrow road next to the store; it had memories for Grace, but a long time ago. There were no footpaths, just high hedgerows; the margins, decked with daffodils.

"I haven't been down here for a long time," said Grace. "It's not changed at all. Look you can see all across to Bradford from here," she said, as they reached a gap in the hedge and a style.

Matthew climbed over. "Come on let's explore."

"There are cows over there," said Grace, as she crossed into the field.

"They won't hurt us if we stay out of their way," said Matthew.

The walk was exactly what Matthew needed; he could

feel himself energised and invigorated.

"We should have brought a blanket," he teased, as they reached the end of the field.

"Ha, I think I'm getting a bit old for romping in a field," said Grace.

"Yes, you're probably right, and I don't think the cows would be amused," said Matthew.

By seven o'clock, they were back in the cottage; it had started to get dark.

"How was your walk?" enquired Mildred as they entered the cottage.

"Excellent, we went down Back Lane, by the store."

"Oh, I know where you mean; haven't been down there for years."

"It's so pretty; the hedges are full of daffodils and primroses."

"Yes, it's lovely this time of year, but I think we take it for granted when it's on your doorstep."

"Well, it certainly beats London; that's for sure," said Matthew.

The following morning, Grace and Matthew were downstairs in the kitchen. Mildred was already cooking breakfast.

"Do you have any Tribek Cereals by any chance?" asked Grace. "I'm quite partial to them."

"Not got any in," said Mildred. "But I'll call in at the store later and get some."

"I don't want you to go to any trouble," said Grace.

"It's no trouble; the walk will do me good."

"Actually, come to think of it, I need to go to the store; I want to get some flowers for Jane for her birthday."

"I'm not sure what Daisy'll have. They don't do much in the line of flowers," commented Mildred.

"We could always pick some daffodils," said Matthew.

"Ha, I'm sure the Manor will have enough daffodils," replied Grace.

Grace left Matthew helping Mildred with the post-breakfast clearing up, while she went across the road to the store. She returned twenty minutes later and walked into the kitchen carrying a bunch of spring flowers encased in paper, and a box of her cereals.

"It was all they had," said Grace, showing Mildred the flowers.

It was ten o'clock, Grace and Matthew were ready for their ride to Laycock. There was the sound of a car pulling up outside.

"It looks like he's here," said Matthew as he put on his coat.

"Bye," shouted Grace, as Matthew opened the door. Grace was carrying the bunch of flowers.

"Enjoy yourselves," said Mildred, as she came to the door to see them out.

"Oh, my," said Grace. "A Rolls Royce."

Matthew looked. "Yes, a Silver Wraith, beautiful cars."

The driver, dressed in a chauffer's uniform, got out and opened the back door for them to get in.

"This is a bit different," said Grace. "It used to be a pony and trap."

The chauffer heard the remark. "Aye, that be some years ago, when old Bartholomew were here."

He started the car and it purred away.

"Yes, that's right... What happened to Bartholomew?" asked Grace.

"Bartholomew? He's been dead must be ten years since," replied the chauffer.

"Oh, that's sad. He was a nice man."

"Aye, that he were, so they say. I never met him, mind; it were before I got here."

"How long have you been working for her ladyship?" asked Grace.

"Five years, it'll be."

They turned down the narrow lane and a familiar scene came into view. "Oh look, the cricket ground is still here," said Grace.

She suddenly remembered the time the pony and trap turned over, resulting in Bartholomew ending up with concussion. Hard to believe it was almost twenty-five years ago.

A few minutes later, Coltswood Manor came into view. Grace looked at it, bathed in the early spring sunshine.

"Oh, it's so good to be back," she said.

Chapter Sixteen

The limousine pulled onto the large, white-gravel forecourt in front of the main house. Her Ladyship was waiting at the front door, ready to greet her guests, two golden retrievers by her side. She was dressed in what would be termed 'country casuals', complete with an ochre-coloured cashmere scarf draped over her shoulder, the very essence of style and landed gentry.

The chauffer parked up and opened the door for Matthew and Grace to alight.

"Hello, Jane," said Grace, and hugged her host warmly, then handed her the flowers. "Happy birthday."

"Hello, Grace, that's lovely of you, thank you, I'll get them in water directly." Jane sniffed the blooms, then looked at Grace. "My, you do look well... Oh, and before I forget, thanks for your card; it arrived this morning." Jane turned and welcomed Matthew. "And Matthew, how lovely to see you, too; it's been such a long time."

"Hello, Jane, yes far too long." Matthew kissed Jane on both cheeks. "And many happy returns."

"Thank you, that's very kind... Oh, I see you've come prepared," said Jane, noticing Grace was wearing jodhpurs.

"Would you believe these are the same ones I wore the last time we went riding together."

"Really? That must be, what, twenty-five years ago."

"Yes, and they still fit." Grace laughed.

The dogs were sniffing round at the new arrivals before wandering off.

"What lovely dogs. How long have you had them?"

"About eighteen months. I decided to replace Bella and Sheba. After Sheba died, it left such a hole."

"Yes, I can imagine," replied Grace.

"Come in, come in, I'll get Helga to make us some coffee. I do think it goes well this time of day."

"Helga?" queried Grace.

"Yes, she's my new housekeeper, been here six months. She's from Heidelburg, part of an exchange programme I'm involved with... You remember Annie Young, my previous housekeeper? She retired last year. She had been with me since before the war."

"Yes, of course... Heidelberg, you say? That's in Germany," said Grace, with an unintended element of surprise.

"Yes, a beautiful city, I visited it in, let me see, nineteen thirty-one, it must be... Do you know it?"

"No, I've not been," replied Grace.

Jane ushered her guests through the large hall into the magnificent drawing room. Then, took the flowers to the kitchen. "Make yourself at home; I'll just get these in water."

The pair sat together on one of the large settees. Grace looked around as Jane returned.

"I love this room, Jane. It does have some good memories," said Grace.

"Yes, yes, FANY's... I think you were so brave, what you did. Do you still keep in touch with anyone from those days?"

"Well, funny you should say that. Hetty, my best friend back then, has just lost her husband. I was at the funeral last week."

"Oh, I'm sorry."

"Yes, it was very sad... What about Lieutenant Ashley-Smythe... Flora, the C/O? She was a friend of yours, I remember you saying."

"Oh, yes, she retired not long after the war. Lived in

Sussex until she died in... let me see, thirty-two, or thirty-three. She was made a Dame, you know."

"Really?"

"Yes, and she received the Croix de Guerre from the French, and another honour from the Belgian King. She was always attending ceremonies."

"I think that is so well-deserved. She was a hard taskmaster, but always fair. I respected her immensely... Actually, I've applied to drive ambulances again. There was an advertisement in the newspaper; the London Ambulance Service are looking for volunteers."

"Really? What on earth made you want to go through all that again?" said Jane.

"Well, with the children less demanding now and Matthew out most of the day, I have time on my hands, so I thought I could put it to good use."

"That's very admirable," said Jane.

Just then, a young woman, late teens/early twenties, 'student-looking', entered, dressed very smartly, with her blonde hair tied back in a bun.

"Ah, Helga, this is Grace and her husband, Matthew, I mentioned earlier. We'll be going riding shortly, and they'll be joining us for the dinner this evening."

"Hello," said Helga and bowed her head reverentially.

Grace and Matthew acknowledged.

"Can you make the coffee please, Helga? We'll take it in the sitting room."

"Yes, your Ladyship," responded Helga.

"Let's go through to next door; it's more conducive for coffee and discussion I find," said Lady Jane.

The three went through to the sitting room, which again Grace knew from previous visits.

"This is a beautiful room, Jane," said Matthew, looking

around at the chandeliers, paintings, and rare antiques.

There was a fire burning in the wood-panelled hearth surrounded by an exquisite three-piece suite. A number of birthday cards had been positioned on one of the occasional tables, next to a silver candelabra.

"Thank you, please take a seat. So, how are things at the Ministry?" asked Jane.

Matthew did not reveal he worked for the Secret Service and referred any enquiry about his employment as 'the Ministry'.

"Oh, very busy, as you can imagine."

"Yes, indeed... Do you think there will be a war?"

"Hmm, I get asked that a lot. Let's just say I think it's more likely following Hitler's move on Czechoslovakia. Even Chamberlain has admitted that the man can't be trusted."

"Oh, dear, it's such a worry, and all these refugees I keep hearing about, the Jews."

"Yes, it's a real problem, but, unfortunately, there's very little appetite to get involved, certainly as far as the Government is concerned."

Grace interjected. "Actually, my sister, Agnes has not long returned from Germany. She has a new agent who's Jewish, and his parents were trapped there, in Düsseldorf. They managed to get them out. She was saying how bad things were, the way they treat the Jews."

"Really? That's desperately sad," replied Jane. "I do so like her new Variety Programme; we never miss it. The staff listen to it as well. And her picture on the front cover of the Radio Times; she looked so glamourous, like a film star. You must be very proud."

"Yes, we all are," replied Grace, looking at Matthew.

Just then Helga entered the room pushing a trolley-tray

with a coffee pot, milk jug, and cups and saucers. There was a plate of biscuits on the shelf below,

"I have also ze biscuits," she said in a strong accent.

"Thank you, Helga."

"Is zere anything else zat you need?"

"No, that's all, thank you... Oh, you could ask the groom to start preparing the horses. We'll be there shortly."

"Yes, Your Ladyship," replied Helga, and left the room.

"Do you know anything about her background?" whispered Matthew, as he accepted a cup of coffee from Jane.

Jane looked at Matthew in a quizzical way. "Well, not a great deal."

"Has she expressed any political views at all?"

"Goodness, no, I've always kept well away from politics. Why do you ask?"

"Curiosity, really," replied Matthew. "These are dangerous times. Tell me more about the exchange programme you mentioned."

Grace was starting to feel embarrassed by Matthew's questioning.

"You think she might be a spy?" asked Jane.

"No, no, no, I'm sure not. Sorry, a force of habit, goes with the job I'm afraid," replied Matthew.

Jane looked at Matthew and smiled. "It's perfectly alright, I understand; you're quite correct to be inquisitive... The exchange programme has been going for about five years. It was designed to help foster a better understanding between our two countries. We send girls over to Germany, and they reciprocate. She's from a very good family, I'm reliably informed."

"Hmm, that's not always a good sign. Many high-ranking Nazis are from the upper classes."

"Yes, of course."

"Hey, let's change the subject," said Grace. "I want to know about your horses."

Matthew excused himself for the bathroom; Jane provided directions.

Grace leaned forward and in a low voice. "I must apologise for Matthew's behaviour; he never switches off, which is why it was so good to be able to get away."

"Oh, think nothing of it; he's right, though. I'd given no thought to the possibility of spying. I think we take everything for granted." For a moment, she was in deep thought, drinking her coffee.

They continued chatting while they finished their coffees, then headed to the stables.

"Do you remember Peter, the groom?" said Jane, as they approached the paddock.

"Yes, of course."

"He now looks after the stables completely, been with me for over twenty-five years. Unfortunately, I had to cut back on staff; it's just him and the groom. I've sold several horses, too; I just have the three now."

"Yes, I can understand; there have been a lot of changes since the financial crash."

"Oh, yes, I don't mind telling you, they were difficult times, but, luckily, we came through it."

Half an hour later, the three were out on the moors. Both Jane and Grace were sporting jodhpurs; Matthew didn't own any riding gear so was in his casual trousers and leather calf-boots. All three were wearing jackets and the traditional cork riding helmets. Matthew hadn't ridden since he was in his teens, but with some practice, was soon trotting gently alongside Grace and Jane.

It was a bright morning, the hedgerows along the bridlepath were a ray of colour, primroses, daffodils, and some late-flowering snowdrops in sheltered spots. The three were taking in the spectacular views, just a gentle meander.

Suddenly, a dog ran from an adjacent field and started barking at the horses. They immediately became agitated, and Jane and Grace had to use all their skills to stay mounted.

Matthew, with his lack of experience, was not so lucky, and was tipped to the ground; his horse galloped away. The dog disappeared.

Both Jane and Grace dismounted, left their horses and ran to Matthew.

"Matthew, Matthew are you alright?" asked Grace, as she reached her husband.

His helmet had been dislodged and was lying a few feet away.

"Is he alright?" asked Jane as she reached Grace.

"I don't know; he's unconscious; he must have hit his head." She examined him for any other injuries. "It looks like he's broken his arm too."

"I'll ride back to the house and get help," said Jane and remounted her horse.

Grace watched as she galloped into the distance.

Just then, there was a groaning noise.

"Matthew, Matthew, are you alright?"

"I... I... I think so." he tried to sit up. "Ow, my head."

He intuitively reached to touch the back of his head.

"Sit still, don't move, let me check you over."

Grace was remembering her medical training from her ambulance driving days, and carefully checked Matthew's limbs.

"It looks like you've broken your arm, and you could

possibly have a concussion. I think you may have hit your head. Luckily, your helmet seems to have taken most of the blow. Jane's gone for help. Don't try and move."

It was over half an hour before Grace could see a pony and trap approach; there was no way they could get a motor vehicle down the narrow bridleway.

Peter was holding the reins and whip, with Jane alongside.

"How is he?" asked Jane, as she dismounted from the carriage. "We've called for an ambulance."

Matthew was lucid, still sitting on the ground near where he fell. The ground was wet and cold, and Grace had taken off her coat for him to sit on.

"I think we've been very lucky; the helmet has saved him. His arm's broken, but I can't find any other injuries."

"I'll be fine," said Matthew, trying to get up, but immediately sat back down.

"Let Peter help," said Jane, and the stableman got down from the carriage, hooked his arm under Matthew's and got him to his feet.

Matthew was still very groggy and unable to stand unsupported.

"Can we get Matthew onto the trap, Grace, and I can bring in the horses?" said Jane.

Between them, they managed to get Matthew onboard.

"The ambulance should be at the house by the time we get back. I used that new 999, service. It seemed very efficient."

"Thank you, Jane."

Grace could see Matthew's horse chewing grass down the bridlepath about a hundred yards away. She walked along to it, calmed it down, then mounted up and joined Jane.

The ambulance was waiting outside the house for the

pony and trap. Helga was talking to one of the crew, as Peter guided the carriage alongside.

The Emergency Hospital Service was a new institution, set up in 1938, when war seemed a possible prospect. The crew were not medically trained except in basic life-saving procedures; their job was to get the patient to hospital as quickly as possible where proper treatment could be administered.

They helped Matthew from the trap and into the waiting vehicle. Grace dismounted and handed the reins to Peter. David, the new groom also attended, to check the horses.

Grace walked up to Her Ladyship. "Jane, I'll need to go with Matthew,"

"Yes, of course. Please let me know how you get on."

"Yes, I will... I'm so sorry for disrupting your birthday celebrations."

"Oh, think nothing of it; it was unfortunate, just one of those things The main thing is that Matthew's alright."

Away from the drama in Yorkshire, back in London, Agnes had received a package along with her usual raft of letters. Such was her fame, envelopes addressed to 'Agnes Marsden, London', were being delivered. Her assistant was already sorting them.

"Oh, look," said Agnes, emptying the contents onto the table. "It's the photographs which Gloria's brother promised. I must reply and thank him."

Agnes sat at the table with Mary and started looking at the pictures.

"Oh, they bring back so many memories," said Agnes. "I'd completely forgotten about them. Cameron was always arranging photographers to promote his tours."

"You look so young," said Mary, looking over Agnes's

shoulder at the grainy images.

"I was... I was only just nineteen when those were taken, and so naïve, looking back on it."

After a trip down memory lane, there was a knock on the door. Mary answered it. Solly appeared at the sitting room door.

Agnes got up to greet him.

"Hello, Solly, how are you?"

"I am well, thank you..."

"And your parents?"

"Yes, thank you. Actually, I wanted to let you know that they would like to move into the house you kindly arranged this weekend. I wanted to confirm with you."

"Yes, I'll let the agent know; he has the key. You'll need to call round and collect it."

"Yes, of course... I have some other news. I've been talking to a promoter, and he would like to put together a variety show, similar to the one on the radio, at one of the theatres. They want you to be the star of the show. The other performers will be guests - comedians, acrobats, and so on. They're going to call it 'The Agnes Marsden Variety Show'. I've spoken to Robert Laing at the BBC and he's more than happy. It will keep your profile in the public eye until the new series in the autumn."

"Well, that sounds wonderful; I don't know what to say... When do we start?"

"The promotor's looking for a suitable theatre, but he's hoping the end of May."

"Well, that will give time for rehearsal."

"Yes, it will; at the moment, he's also looking for musicians and possible acts. I'll arrange for you to meet with him over the next week or so."

Back at the Keighley bakery, around eleven o'clock, Phyllis, from the butcher's, knocked on the parlour door of the flat above the baker's shop and walked in. Ivy was in the kitchen and went to see who it was.

"Phyllis...? Is everything alright?"

"Nay, 'appen tha best come. Mam's had a fall."

"Oh no, how is she?"

"Lillian's called a doctor, but she's not too well; I think tha should come."

"Aye, I'll be right there."

Ivy took off her pinafore and grabbed her coat. Phyllis was waiting by the door.

The bakery was busy with customers as Ivy and Phyllis left the shop and walked the short distance up James Street to the butcher's.

Inside the shop, there was that familiar smell of sawdust and fresh meat as they walked in. The counter had been replaced with better lighting, and modern cash registers installed but otherwise, customers entering the shop in 1914 would barely notice the difference. Even some of the advertisements on the back wall had remained the same.

There were only two customers and Ernest and Lilliam were serving.

Phyllis opened the counter flap to allow them to enter behind the serving area and headed upstairs.

Gladys was at the door and let them into the parlour.

"How is she?" asked Phyllis.

She could see Violet lay on the settee and didn't appear to be moving.

"I don't rightly know," Gladys replied. "She seems to be asleep."

"What happened?" asked Ivy.

"I were just clearing breakfast things away when I heard

a noise from parlour. I were in kitchen. I think Mam had tried to get up from the table. I found her on the floor," said Gladys. "Phyllis and me got her onto the sofa. I called the doctor and he said he would be down directly. That would be forty minutes since."

It was another ten minutes before the medic arrived carrying his Gladstone bag. Violet was still unconscious.

"Can you explain what happened?" asked the doctor.

Gladys described the course of events.

The doctor walked over to Violet and took out his stethoscope and placed the end on her chest.

"Hmm... breathing's very shallow. We need to get her to the hospital."

"What do you think's wrong with her?" asked Ivy.

"I think it might be a stroke; she's very ill," replied the doctor. "Do you have a telephone?"

Phyllis put her hand to her mouth, an expression of despair.

"Yes, please help yourself; it's there," said Ivy, pointing to the sideboard.

The doctor dialled some numbers with his back to the girls and spoke quietly into the receiver, not wishing to alarm them.

It was twenty-minutes before the sound of a bell could be heard coming down James Street. Ivy looked out of the window.

"The ambulance is here," she shouted.

"I'll go and bring them up," said Phillis and left the parlour.

The doctor was taking Violet's pulse. His expression changed. He took out his stethoscope again., then looked at the girls and shook his head.

"She's gone, I'm sorry."

Ivy and Gladys looked on unable to grasp the situation.

"She's dead?" questioned Ivy.

"Yes, I'm afraid she is."

The ambulance crew arrived, led by Phyllis. Straightaway, she could see something wasn't right.

"What's wrong?" she asked.

"Mam's gone," replied Ivy.

"No, no." Phyllis went to run to the settee where Violet was laying but she was stopped by Ivy.

"There's nowt to be done. Mam's in a better place now."

At the butcher's shop, the remaining customers were served before Ernest closed the shop, leaving a note in the window explaining the circumstances.

News of Violet's passing soon spread. Ivy telephoned Mildred to let her know and naturally, she wanted to drop everything and travel into town to see if she could help; she was sure Grace and Matthew would understand. In the end, logic prevailed, and she remained at Blossom Cottage. Her guests were still at Lady Jane's, or more correctly, the local hospital.

It was mid-afternoon before Grace and Matthew arrived back at Blossom Cottage. Grace paid the taxi and helped Matthew to the front door. "I'm perfectly fine, darling," he complained.

Mildred opened the door and straightaway noticed Matthew's arm in a sling.

"Oh, dear Lord, what on earth's happened."

"I stupidly fell off my horse," replied Matthew, "Don't worry, it's nothing serious, just broke my wrist. I must have put my arms out to lessen the fall; I don't rightly remember."

"He hit his head, too," said Grace as they walked into the

cottage. "He's got a mild concussion and needs to rest."

"Yes, of course. Would you like a nice cup of tea?"

"Yes, please," they said together.

"I'll just let Jane know. I don't think we should go to the dinner party this evening; you need to rest," said Grace, looking at Matthew.

A few minutes later, Mildred presented the pair with their drinks.

"I do have some sad news... Violet Stonehouse has died."

Grace looked at Matthew. "Ivy's Mam, the butcher's," she clarified. "Oh, that's so sad. What happened?"

"I don't know the full story, but it seems she had a fall this morning and she died shortly after. The doctor seemed to think she'd had a stroke."

"Oh, that's dreadful. Please pass on our condolences when you see them."

"Yes, of course, I'll be going into town in the morning," replied Mildred.

Tuesday, 28th March.

Grace and Matthew returned to London following their eventful few days' break.

Thankfully, Matthew seemed non-the-worse following his mishap, apart from the sling and plaster cast on his wrist. It was a six-week healing process.

Lady Jane had been disappointed but understanding when Grace cancelled their dinner engagement. In the circumstances, they had decided to travel back to London first thing.

On their arrival back home, James and Dorothy were both at school, and the house was empty. It was lunchtime and Matthew was already feeling restless.

"I think I'll go into the office after lunch and see what's

going on,"

Grace looked at him sternly. "But the doctor told you to rest."

"Yes, I know, but I'll not be able to settle with everything that's going on."

Grace knew she was fighting a losing battle. "Very well, I'll go and make us some sandwiches."

She left Matthew and walked into the kitchen.

By two-thirty, Matthew was walking through the hubbub of the cypher room. He was wearing his raincoat and trilby with his left sleeve in the pocket to avoid it flapping around. His arm was still in a sling, underneath.

Conversations stopped as eyes followed him to his office, followed by whispers. His secretary was quickly to his room.

"We weren't expecting you back until tomorrow; what's happened, sir? Are you alright?"

She watched as he struggled with his topcoat. "Can I help?"

"No, I can manage, thank you, Janet. Just fell off a horse; broke my wrist, nothing to worry about."

"Do you need a hand with anything?"

"No, I'm sure I'll manage. Luckily, it was my left arm, so I can still write."

"Oh, that's good, just say if you need anything. Would you like a drink, sir?"

"Yes please, Janet, a coffee, thank you."

His coffee was brought in but by a different visitor.

"I've brought your coffee, sir. Sorry to hear about your arm."

Matthew looked up. "Oh, hello Chloe, thank you. Take a seat."

For the next twenty minutes, Chloe brought Matthew up to date with the help of a note pad she had been keeping. Matthew was impressed with her grasp of the facts and the authority with which she was able to communicate.

"Any news on the Night Wing investigation?" asked Matthew.

"Yes, sir... Scotland Yard confirmed that three men have been charged with Night Wing's murder. They're wanted for offences in Ireland and the police want to extradite them to Dublin to face trial... They are more likely to get the death penalty there."

"Yes, I can certainly agree with that; I'll speak to Travis and get the latest."

Matthew's telephone rang; he answered. "Yes, sir, I'll be there."

"Can we finish this later? The Commander wants me."

"Yes, of course," said Chloe.

"Thank you, and well done. That was very helpful."

Matthew was seated opposite the Commander who was eying up Matthew's sling.

"What's this I hear about you falling off a horse."

"Yes, sir, it's true."

"Hmm, how long will you be incapacitated?"

"It won't impede my work at all, just waiting for it to heal and they'll take off the cast, about six weeks apparently."

"Good, good... I have to say I <u>have</u> been impressed with your new assistant while you've been away, very efficient; you've made a damn good choice there, I think."

"Thank you," replied Matthew. This was praise indeed.

That was the limit of the 'small talk', the Commander got straight to the point.

"I suppose you've heard the latest from Spain?"

"Only what was in the newspaper; Franco's troops have surrounded Madrid."

"Actually, things have moved on; they've since entered Madrid and the Republicans have surrendered. Franco's assumed power."

"Hmm, another fascist government."

"Precisely. The Foreign Office are trying to assess what this might mean for peace in Europe. We certainly don't want the Spanish teaming up with Hitler and Mussolini."

"Is that likely?"

"Well, the Germans have certainly been supplying Franco with arms and tanks."

"I thought there was an embargo."

"Yes, there was the 'Non-Intervention Pact' which Germany signed, but Hitler, as usual, chose to ignore it... The general consensus is there's unlikely to be a formal military alliance. We think the Spanish people have had enough after three years of war. It's cost more than a million lives."

"Yes, I agree, that's the logical conclusion... Have we heard any response from Hitler?"

"No, not at this time, but, actually, he's been quite clever. With the rest of Europe looking at events in Spain; he's continued to re-arm."

Meanwhile, Grace was reading through the correspondence that had arrived in their absence. One letter was post-marked 'London City Hall'. She opened the envelope and read the contents. It was on headed notepaper.

'Dear Mrs Keating,

Thank you for replying to the recent advertisement in the newspapers for a voluntary position with the London Ambulance Service. We would like you to attend an interview on Wednesday 29ᵗʰ March 1939, at London County Hall, Westminster Bridge Road, London, at 11.15am.

Yours sincerely,

H.B. Nicholls, (Recruiting Officer).'

Grace had a copy of the newspaper which contained the advertisement and found the page again. A picture of an ambulance with its door open. 'You are wanted at this wheel,' it said, followed by the narrative;

'Volunteers who can drive a car are urgently required and one of the finest contributions a woman driver can make to National Service is to enrol for the work. Free training is given.'

She suddenly realised the commitment she was making and was starting to have feelings of self-doubt. She would discuss it again with Matthew on his return.

It was gone eight o'clock before Matthew arrived back home. Both children were out and there was just the sound of music coming from the radio in the sitting room.

"How did you manage at work... with your arm?" said Grace as she helped Matthew with his topcoat.

"Oh, I had a few comments, but I can write perfectly well. Janet helped me with my coat. Oh, I meant to tell you, young Chloe's settling in very well, even had praise from the Commander."

"Oh, I'm so pleased. I must tell Hetty when I next speak to her."

Grace had made a meal for Matthew and joined him at the dining table. She showed him the letter and explained her reservations.

"Why don't you go for the interview, see what they say, then you can make up your mind."

"Yes, I'll do that." It seemed a sensible suggestion.

Matthew was managing quite well one-handed, but the sling was a nuisance. "I think I'm going to ditch the sling, I don't need it anymore."

"What did the doctor say?"

"He just said to use it as long as I needed it."

The following day, Grace chose the Underground for her journey to County Hall, just a five-minute walk from Waterloo Station. It was not an area Grace knew well, and she couldn't believe how much it had changed since her war-time visits to the station. Bicycles were in abundance, as people avoided the delays caused by traffic congestion.

As she walked, signs of war preparation were everywhere, sandbags piled up against office windows, barrage balloons providing a grey, protective umbrella in the sky. It was a frightening prospect.

She arrived in good time, which was just as well, as it took ten minutes to find the recruitment office in the labyrinth of rooms.

There were several others, seated in a small waiting room on uncomfortable chairs. It was nearly midday before she was called in to see Mr Nicholls, who, on first appearance, seemed a dour, humourless man with a weaselly face.

However, as the interview progressed, Grace warmed to him. He took a keen interest in Grace's time with the First Aid Nursing Yeomanry and was impressed with the medals she had been awarded from the French and Belgium Governments. He was also keen to learn more about her later ambulance work with Endell Street Hospital.

"You are exactly the calibre of woman we're looking for. I wish there were more like you," he stated as he completed his questions. "When can you start?"

"Thank you," said Grace. "After Easter, towards the end of April. I would like to work three days a week to begin with if that's convenient. I do have a house to run."

Nicholls looked over his glasses, disapprovingly.

"Very well, if that's all you can manage."

"I may be able to increase my hours later."

"Hmm." He seemed to smile. "You live in Acton, I see. I may get you to report to the North Western Headquarters in Hampstead, that's in Lawn Road, depending on how many recruits we get. We're short of staff there, and it's reasonably close, but I will confirm by letter. There will be a period of training of around three months."

"Yes, thank you, I understand," replied Grace.

"I'll write to you over the next day or so to verify details and send you a contract."

Grace left County Hall with a mix of emotions. She had not worked since the end of the war and realised there would be challenges that lay ahead.

Back in the headquarters of the Secret Service, Matthew had dispensed with his sling and was more mobile as a result. He was in the Commander's office discussing the latest IRA situation when a messenger knocked and entered with a note.

The Commander took it from the officer and read it. He peered over the piece of paper at Matthew.

"Chamberlain has just announced he's doubling the Territorial Army."

Chapter Seventeen

Easter 1939 was an even more sombre time than usual, both for the Marsden family and the wider public. The spectre of war hung ever closer like the sword of Damocles, following Britain and France entering into a pact at the end of March, pledging to come to Poland's aid in the event of an invasion. Most commentators believed this would come sooner rather than later, despite this entente.

On the face of it the strategy had some logic. Would Hitler really risk taking on the combined forces of Great Britain and France, particularly with the size of their respective navies which were far superior to that of Germany? In the event, Hitler thought they were bluffing and continued to formulate secret invasion plans of Poland code named, *'Fall Weiss'*, or 'Case White' to be launched from September 1st onwards.

The day after the announcement, Hitler, while attending a ceremony, made a bellicose speech that included a response to Chamberlain's pledge of the previous day to support Poland, saying, *"If they* (the Western Allies) *expect the Germany of today to sit patiently by until the very last day while they create satellite States and set them against Germany, then they are mistaking the Germany of today for the Germany of before the war.'*

Early April saw the funeral of Violet, the once formidable figure of the Stonehouse family. The church was packed with mourners, Mildred, of course, and Ivy, the eldest surviving child, together with the rest of the Stonehouse family were in the front pews. The butcher's had closed for the morning. William and Marjorie were also present to pay their respects. Violet was later buried next to her son Wilfred, so tragically lost in the war.

Following the Bank Holiday, in the Keating household there was a mixture of excitement and anxiousness as James prepared to join the RAF.

He was instructed to report to RAF Training College at Cranwell in Lincolnshire where his initial training and assessment would take place. Matthew had offered to drive James to the college, but he insisted on taking the train. As James had pointed out, with Matthew's wrist still in a plaster cast, there were some doubts as to whether he would be able to drive. Grace had also offered, but James was adamant on taking the train.

Carrying two suitcases, on Tuesday morning, April 11th, James Keating took a taxi to Kings Cross Station where he would catch the train to Sleaford. There were emotional farewells from Grace and Dorothy; Matthew had already left for work.

In the headquarters of the Secret Service, Matthew was in the Commander's office catching up on agents reports that had come in over the Easter holiday.

"What's the Government's response on Italy's invasion of Albania?" asked Matthew.

The Commander stroked his chin in a sagely fashion.

"They've made no response at the moment. According to the Foreign Office, there could be the usual diplomatic complaint, but, aside from that, I can't see any military involvement. Britain has no economic or financial interests in Albania."

"Yes, there are certainly more pressing matters."

"Talking of pressing matters, any news on Siemens?"

"Yes, and no. I've asked Chloe to be the contact point

for our two agents; it will be good experience for her. So far there has been no indication of espionage, but it's early days."

"Good, good, well, keep me informed."

The Commander picked up a piece of paper from his desk and scan read it.

"I suppose you've seen the latest on the bombing campaign."

"Yes, Liverpool and Coventry."

"Yes, bad show, it seems, despite our best efforts, the terrorists are still able to hit our cities. The big question is, where are they getting their money and supplies?"

"Yes, and how are they getting it into the country."

"Hmm, yes, it's a pity about Night Wing; we could certainly use him now."

"Well, we can't rule out the Germans," responded Matthew.

"No, we can't... Wait, there was something." He rummaged through his 'in-tray' and retrieved a piece of paper.

"This came in a couple of days ago; it was forwarded to us by the Foreign Office."

He handed the report to Matthew who proceeded to read it.

"The Czech Consul...? What's his interest?"

"Good question. As you can imagine, there's a great deal of anti-German sentiment among those Czechs working or living abroad after the invasion. It could be why someone's passed on the information. Unfortunately, we can't verify the accuracy of communication. It's even possible it might have been planted."

"A German agent you mean?"

"It's not out of the question."

"Hmm, but it's saying here that there was a meeting between the German Minister in Ireland, three Nazi party members, and representatives of the IRA."

"Yes, as I understand it, the meeting was held at a hotel in Donegal which is owned by a German national. Apparently, it was set up through the German Embassy in London."

"How do we know this?"

"It seems a Czech waiter working at the hotel was on duty at the conference. He passed the information to the Czech Consul who passed it on to us."

"And we are sure the IRA were there?"

"No, we're not, and as I said, the Foreign Office are not convinced of its authenticity. It's doubtful the IRA would attend such an event; they would bound to be noticed... However, we can't rule it out," said Monkton.

"Is it worth one of the attachés at the British Embassy trying to make contact with this waiter?"

"Hmm, not sure it will do much good," said the Commander, with an expression of doubt.

"It's the only way we can confirm it; or at least get an impression of this fellow. If he _is_ genuine, he could be useful in the future," said Matthew.

"Very well, speak to Miles Jordan, he's the Foreign Office contact at the Embassy. Maybe they can check out the hotel and see if the conference took place at all."

"Yes, I know Miles from my Army days... I'll get onto it right away."

"Yes, we do need to keep an eye on Ireland. The Foreign Office are well aware of the consequences if we do go to war; Ireland could become problematical."

In 1939, external listening to telephone conversations was not common, as the equipment necessary to carry out eavesdropping activities was expensive and complicated to set up. Nevertheless, the Secret Service had taken delivery of a new scrambling device which had been invented by the GPO a year earlier. It had a distinctive green handset.

Matthew walked to the secure phone booth, little more than a broom cupboard, which housed the telephone, and called the British Embassy in Dublin.

The switchboard eventually located Matthew's contact and connected the call.

"Miles...? It's Matthew Keating." There was a short pause.

"Matthew...? Oh, hello, it's good to hear from you. It's been a while."

They exchanged greetings and caught up with small talk, then Matthew outlined his request, explaining the message they had received from the Czech Consul.

"The information originates from a Czech waiter called Tomáŝ Hácha, he works at the Drumbeg Hotel at a place called Inver. It's near Donegal."

"Tomáŝ Hácha... Yes, I've got that," replied the attaché. "What do you want me to do?"

"The F.O. are not convinced that he's on the level, and we need someone to give us an assessment. If he _is_ reliable, then he could be a valuable source of information. The hotel where he works is owned by a German national and it's not beyond the realms of possibility that it's being used as a meeting place between the Germans and the IRA. It's certainly remote enough. We need to know whether we can rely on the information he's provided."

Matthew concluded the call, with the promise of a speedy response.

In the British Embassy, Dublin, preparations were soon in motion for diplomat Miles Jordan to spend a couple of days fishing in Donegal. Reservation at the Drumbeg Hotel had been secured.

Two days later, a well-to-do businessman, in a smart suit, and sporting an 'Errol Flyn' moustache was checking in at reception of the Drumbeg Hotel, Inver, ten miles outside the town of Donegal. He had taken one of the Embassy cars for the trip, his fishing gear safely stowed in the boot.

The hotel was miles from anywhere, easy to see why it could have been chosen for a discreet meeting. It was in reality a large, white house with extensions to both sides and a conservatory with views of the surrounding countryside on the end. Behind the hotel, it was just a collection of small, craggy mounds before dropping down to the ocean.

Announcing himself as Joshua Schneider, company director, from Dublin, he explained to the receptionist he was there for a fishing trip on the nearby Eany River, renowned for its salmon and sea trout. He was happy to share this information; it might be the subject of gossip among the staff.

That evening, he was in the conservatory, which served as the restaurant, for his evening meal. He was shown to his seat next to the window by the maître d'.

He scanned the room, not large, around fifteen tables with accompanying seats. Tonight, there was only one other guest. Outside, it was pitch black, no twinkling lights, not a sign of any human presence.

"I will get a waiter to bring you the menu," said the front-of-house.

A man in his late twenties was summoned and approached the table in a waiter's uniform, carrying the evening choices. Straightaway, the diplomat was alerted to his Slavic appearance.

He could read his name badge, 'Tomas'. It had to be the Czech waiter he was looking for.

As the man described the available food, Miles was assessing him. His English was fair but with a strong accent, his demeanour seemed understated, not someone you would immediately be drawn to.

Miles ordered his food. "Where are you from?" he asked after completing his choice.

"Er, from Czechoslovakia."

"Really? You must be very worried at things in your home country."

He kept his vocabulary simple to aid the waiter's understanding.

"Yes, that is true, my parents are there still. It is a difficult time."

He looked down and made to leave but was stopped by a further question.

"So, how do you feel about the German's... the invasion?"

The waiter looked at him as he digested the question. He looked around making sure no-one was listening.

"I hate them," he spat. "Excuse me, I will take your order to the kitchen."

Before Miles could respond, he had left the table and was walking towards the door labelled 'kitchen'.

It was over twenty minutes before the waiter returned carrying a bowl of soup, Miles' first course.

He served the dish and was about to walk away. Miles needed to engage him further.

"How long have you been in Ireland?" The waiter stopped and turned to Miles.

"Three months," came the reply.

"So, you have not been home since the Germans invaded your country?"

"No."

"Have you had word from your family?"

"No." He looked down in sadness; he seemed uncomfortable with the question.

This time Miles looked around. "Tell me, do you get many Germans staying here?"

"Why do you want to know?"

"Oh, nothing just curious. The owner is German, I understand."

"Yes, that is true."

"I was thinking it must have been hard for you having to serve them."

"Yes, very difficult."

"I hope you spit in their soup." The diplomat mimicked the action.

The waiter laughed. "Ha, I had not thought, but it is good. Yes we had a... er, conference, is that the word?"

"Yes, it could be. Were you on duty when they were here?"

"I will return when you have finished," said Tomas, ignoring the question, allowing Miles to complete his first course.

The waiter returned ten minutes later, carrying a dinner plate, holding it with a napkin. Miles was sat with his arms folded, looking around the room. Seeing the waiter approach, he moved the empty soup dish to one side.

The waiter removed it and served the meal. He went to return to the kitchen but was stopped again by Miles.

"Before you go, I've been thinking; we have a lot in common, you and me. My name is Joshua; my parents are Jewish and are still in Germany. I have not heard from them in three months."

The waiter looked at him.

"What time do you finish? Maybe I could buy you a drink; we can talk some more," added the attaché.

"I am not sure. The people here will see me; they do not like us to talk to the guests." He looked around the dining room; it was just the two of them.

"Why is that a problem?"

"I do not know..." He thought for a moment. "Yes, alright, ten o'clock, I will be finished."

"I'll be in the bar; I'll wait for you."

Just after ten o'clock, the British Embassy diplomat was alone in the guest lounge. It was a small room, comfortable for pre-dinner drinks or after-meal cocktails, with three stools at the well-lit, and well-stocked bar. It was nicely decorated with four other tables placed around the back wall,

Miles was dressed casually, but smart, seated at the bar, ruminating over a pint of Guinness when the waiter walked in. The woman, who had been on reception when Miles checked in, was serving, and looked disapprovingly at Tomas as he stood anxiously next to him.

"A beer, please," said Miles, having received the preference from the waiter.

He was served, and Miles invited Tomas to join him in a quiet part of the room.

"It's a nice hotel; I've not been here before," said the attaché, trying to break the ice.

Tomas didn't acknowledge him but looked anxiously at the woman who appeared to be keeping a careful eye on the pair.

Miles leaned forward and spoke just above a whisper. "Look, I'll get straight to the point; I want to ask you a question," said Miles. He took a sip of his Guinness. "You told me you hated the Germans. I know people who would be very interested in finding out more about any activities of German guests who might visit here. They would be very generous for any assistance you could provide. Would you be interested?"

Tomas looked at the diplomat with an air of suspicion. "You want me to... er, spy?"

"No, no, no, just let me know when you get any more German visitors, and I will tell you what to do."

Miles reached into his pocket and pulled out a white banknote and passed it surreptitiously to the waiter. There was no-one else in the bar, the woman who had been serving, had returned to reception duties.

The waiter looked around and picked up the note, then smiled at Miles.

"Yes, I can do that... er, if it will help."

"Good, good... I'll give you a telephone number where you can reach me anytime."

He took another long swig of Guinness. "So, back to my question. Were there any Irishmen at the meeting with the Germans."

Miles, of course, knew the answer, but wanted to test the waiter and also find out more detail.

The waiter looked around, anxiously. "Yes, there were four men."

"Do you know who they were?"

"Not their names, but I did hear them say they were from Dublin."

"Anything else?"

"Yes, they were talking about money, and then later about guns. I heard one of the Irishmen ask about... he used a word I didn't understand."

"Shipment? By any chance."

"I don't know; it may be. I cannot remember."

"What about the Germans? Do you know their names?"

"Yes, one was a German minister, his name was, er, Stumpf, I think, and another was called, er, Wendall. I know this because we were told that an important German was coming, and we had to give special attention."

"Do you think you could find out their names? We would be very generous."

Miles pulled out another white 'fiver' and handed it to the waiter.

"Er... yes, I will try."

"Good, I'm going to be here for a couple of days. If you can find out before I leave, that would be terribly helpful."

"Yes, yes," replied the waiter.

Miles took another swig of Guinness, mulling over the information.

"Would you say the meeting between the Irish and Germans was friendly?"

"Yes, I think so. The Irish were later singing and telling the Germans the songs. They had drunk much beer." The waiter laughed.

Miles took out a notepad from his pocket, wrote his name down on a page and the number of the British Embassy in Dublin. He ripped it out and handed it to the waiter.

The bartender was back at her duties and had seen the exchange. She needed to make a telephone call.

Two days later, armed with more information, Miles Jordan headed back to Dublin.

Matthew was at his desk when the call from the Embassy came through.

There was a quick catch up, then Miles' assessment of the Czech waiter.

"I think the original information you received was

accurate. Robert Stumpf was definitely there, he's head of the German legation here in Dublin, together with the Consular Secretary, Wendall. There were two other legation staff."

"What about the IRA?"

"Now, this is where it gets interesting. He confirmed there were definitely four Irishmen at the conference. He heard the word 'guns' mentioned, so we certainly can't rule out that there was a discussion about providing weaponry."

"Hmm, yes... How reliable do you think he is?"

"Well, he's got no reason to lie, and I'm as positive as I can be that he's not working for the Germans. Frankly, I think he is genuine. He certainly seems bitter enough; his family are still in Prague."

"Thanks Miles, that's very helpful. How have you left it?"

"I've given him my telephone number, and he says he will call me if they get anymore German guests."

Matthew dropped the call and walked to the Commander's office to relay the information.

Monday, April 24th.

Grace was feeling anxious as she prepared for her first day at work for over twenty years. There had been a change of plan, and she had been asked to report to the Ealing Ambulance Station, which was even closer than Hampstead, as originally suggested, just a short bus-ride away. She was dressed in a smart blouse and skirt, with her hair layered in the latest fashion, she chose a maroon hat to match her coat.

She arrived at her destination around nine forty-five, in good time to start her shift.

She looked at the austere building. It consisted of a large garage, open at the front, which could hold up to twelve ambulances.

Grace looked inside and could see a recent volunteer cleaning one of the ambulances. She approached the woman.

"Hello, I'm Grace Keating; I'm due to start today. I need to report to Station Officer Smythe."

"Hello, yes dearie, it's at the back of the garage; you can't miss it." The woman pointed to the appropriate direction.

Grace thanked the woman and walked past the line of ambulances to the far end where there was a flight of stairs. A sign with an arrow indicating 'Station Officer' pointed upwards.

At the top of the stairs, there was a short corridor and just along was a door with the words 'Station Officer' stencilled on it.

Grace knocked.

"Come in," said an authoritative voice.

Grace opened the door. It was a small room with three dirty skylights at the back, letting in only a modicum of light. An older man was seated at a desk, dressed in uniform, and wearing glasses.

"Ah, you must be Mrs Keating."

His mouth was almost covered by a grey moustache, desperately in need of a trim. Ear-hair was also an issue.

He got up and offered a hand to Grace.

"Douglas Smythe, Station Officer, please take a seat."

Grace sat down and looked around.

The room was functional, with two metal cabinets on the right-hand side. Above them a poster, a copy of which had appeared in the newspapers for volunteer ambulance drivers. The flooring was linoleum over floorboards which seemed to amplify the conversation. There were two trays on either side of the desk which were overflowing with paper.

The officer picked up Grace's letter.

"I've read your letter with interest, Mrs Keating, very impressive. Two years with the FANY's working in France, medals from the Belgium and French Governments. Tell me, why do you want to volunteer now?"

He spoke in a distinct 'London' accent, but without the harsher tones of the East End.

"Well, as you can see, I have the experience, and with children grown up, I have the time to spare."

"Well, I am very glad to have you here. We have had many volunteers, as you no doubt have heard, but very few with your experience. You will of course need training up; the ambulances have improved since nineteen eighteen." He smiled. "What did you drive?"

"A Wolsley, sir."

"Oh, I remember those; dreadful things to drive."

Grace smiled at the recollection. "Yes, that's true."

"There will be some first-aid training to complete as well."

"Yes, I had assumed there would be. It has been a long time."

"You will notice many changes, but some things stay the same. Getting patients to hospital and early care, is the priority. It can save lives."

"Yes, of course."

"Let me show you around and I'll introduce you to one or two people, then we can start your training."

Grace got up from her chair and followed the officer out of the room.

Further along the corridor, there was another office area where the telephone was manned. There was a small switchboard with a woman, in her late forties, waiting for calls. She was knitting.

Smythe led Grace inside and introduced her to the

operator.

"This is Kathy, been here for ten years. Kathy, this is Grace. She's just joined us to start her training."

There were brief introductions.

He turned to Grace. "If we lose the line for any reason and need support, we have to send a messenger on foot. Luckily, that doesn't happen too often."

They left the 'switch', as it was known, then moved further down the corridor.

The officer opened the next door. Grace was immediately hit by the smell of fried food and sweat, not a pleasant concoction.

It was the main recreational room, and quite large, complete with a ping pong table. Two men were in the middle of a game. At the far end, there was a sink unit, and cooker, partitioned off from the rest of the area, with tables and seating, including four battered armchairs in desperate need of a re-cover. Grace noticed three women chatting away while they knitted.

"This is the rest room. There are tea-making facilities and a small kitchen. You'll find there's quite a bit of down time, depending, of course, on demand. You will need to bring your own food." He looked at Grace with a serious expression. "If there is a war, that is likely to change. It's why we want to make sure we have enough staff in the event of an emergency."

He walked to the end of the corridor and opened another door. There was another flight of stairs. Grace followed the officer to the top floor.

More rest rooms, two bathrooms, and another common room where staff provided their own chairs. Two rooms were reserved for sleeping. There were no beds but six mattresses, laid out so they wouldn't need to sleep on the bare wooden floor.

"We have a twenty-four-hour operation, so we provide sleeping facilities for those on call," he explained.

"Let's head back, and I'll introduce you to one of the drivers who can show you the ropes. If we get a shout while you're here, you can tag along as an observer."

The officer took Grace back to the 'garage' where all the ambulances were housed. They approached the woman that Grace had met when she first arrived.

"This is Queenie, one of our experienced drivers. I have suggested she can look after your ambulance training."

"Nice to meet you, Queenie; I'm Grace." The pair shook hands.

"I'll leave you in Queenie's capable hands. She'll find you a uniform."

The Station Officer left the two women and returned to his paperwork.

"Hello dearie, let me take you to the stores and fix you up with a uniform, then I'll show you around the ambulance. The boss says you were in the war."

"Yes, I was with the FANY's."

"Oh, you must tell me some of your stories. I bet you have so many."

"Ha, yes, just a few."

Monday, May 1st.

Agnes had finished her present contract with the BBC Radio programme and was rehearsing hard for her forthcoming theatre shows. She had persuaded the promoter to employ Alistair as musical director for the duration; it would give Agnes much needed support but also avoid long absences. He had taken a short sabbatical from his teaching duties.

The show was due to run at The Vaudeville Theatre from the beginning of June until the end of August, giving a few weeks rest until the radio show which was due to resume at the end of September for the winter season.

Agnes was delighted that Marie Lloyd's daughter, Matilda Courtney, known professionally as Marie Lloyd Jnr, had agreed to perform, and would end the first half, singing some of her mother's songs, and adding comedy. Agnes knew her, of course, through her friendship with her famous mother who had sadly passed away in nineteen twenty-two.

Mayday, considered in many countries to be the day of the workers and is celebrated as such. Back in Bradford, this would prove to be ironic.

Freddie was at his table in the sewing shed, holding the fort while Molly had an appointment. She didn't expand on the detail, Freddie assumed it would be with a possible supplier. Cloth, over recent weeks, had become very difficult to source, and the quality was not up to the usual standard.

Only two girls were working, the others had run out of cotton thread; Molly had assured them that new supplies would be delivered 'any day'. Some were knitting, others stood at the doorway talking.

Around midday, the girls that were not working quickly vacated the doorway and rushed to their machines. Freddie thought this strange until he saw Molly walk through. She was dressed in a smart outfit, jacket, blouse, skirt, and a hat – all her own designs.

Her head was down, and she made no eye contact with anyone. Freddie looked at the senior machinist and she raised her eyebrows.

Freddie followed Molly into her office/ cum atelier.

"Ah do, Molly, tha alreet?" he said, noticing tear stains

on her cheek.

"You better sit down, Freddie."

Molly took off her hat and jacket.

"I've just come back from the bank; it's bad news I'm afraid."

Freddie looked at her and frowned. "What do tha mean?"

"They need their money back. They say we're losing too much money."

"Nay, that can't be reet."

"It is Freddie. You know from the books that over recent months business has dropped, we've not been able to get enough orders. I've had to borrow money to pay the wages."

"Aye, but 'appen things'll pick up."

"But that's not the problem. It's cloth; we can't get any, certainly of the quality we need. So, even if we got more orders we can't fulfil them. According to the manager at the bank, many clothing businesses are having the same problem. I've spoken to Vivian Johnson, at Archways Fabrics; they are in the same situation."

"Aye, I can see that, so what'd to be done?"

"I've got no option; I have to close the business. I can't afford to pay the wages."

The blood drained from Freddie's face.

"Nay, tha can't do that."

"I've got no alternative. We've only got two invoices outstanding, and they won't be enough to pay the rent and wages. Mr Jenkins, the bank manager, was very understanding and has given us time to repay the debt at the bank, but without more orders, and the cloth to make them, we can't continue."

"What about Auntie Agnes, the singer? She must have plenty. Can't tha ask her?"

"I wouldn't dream of it, but in any case, it wouldn't help.

We're not making enough money and without cloth, we can't make clothes. It would be throwing good money after bad."

Molly put her head in her hands. She didn't want to cry in front of Freddie but was finding it difficult to hold back the tears.

"Have tha spoken to John?" asked Freddie.

"No, not yet, he's busy with his new job."

"So, what will tha do?"

"Well, in the war, your mam changed from making dresses to repairing them."

"Aye, I remember."

"That's what I intend to do. I'll have to sell the sewing machines and things I don't need and go back to working from home. It's what I used to do before we started the factory."

"What's tha going to say t'girls?"

"I'll tell them the truth. I'll pay them till Friday from my own money, and, of course, I'll pay you too, Freddie."

"Aye, 'appen us'll manage."

It had been one of the worse days of her life, certainly in business terms. Molly arrived home and John was in the kitchen.

"You're late, it's nearly eight o'clock; I was getting worried. Is everything alright?"

Molly went up to him and put her arms around his neck and started sobbing.

"Hey, hey, whatever's the matter, come and sit down and tell me what's happened."

Molly let go of her embrace and took off her jacket.

"Would you like a drink?"

"No, I'll be alright."

Molly composed herself and related the day.

"But I don't know what to say. Why didn't you tell me?"

"I wanted to make it work. I was too embarrassed if I'm honest. We just haven't been able to get the cloth."

"Yes, I know all about the shortages. One or two clients are talking about rationing if there's a war."

"Oh, I hope it won't come to that."

"So, what are you going to do?"

"I'm paying the girls and Freddie till Friday, then I'll close the factory. I've already spoken to the landlord. I've made arrangements with the bank, and they have given me time to clear the debt with them."

"Well, we can certainly manage that from father's inheritance."

"But I thought you didn't want to touch that. For a rainy day, you said."

"Well, as I see it, it's pouring down."

Molly smiled for the first time.

"Look, we will manage."

"But what about your job?"

"At the moment, there seems to be a good supply of wool; although the price has risen by over ten percent in the last month. Don't worry, we will manage."

"But what if there is another war?"

"Let's not think about that right now."

"Where's Daniel?"

"He's in his room doing homework. He's been asking about whether there will be a war too. They're all talking about it at school, apparently; having drills and things. Oh, there was a leaflet came today, being delivered to every household according to the postman this morning." He showed the document to Molly. "It's from the Canned Foods Advisory Bureau."

"Hmm, no wonder people are worried."

"Yes, but it does contain some useful information about how to store food."

"I'll read it later; I'll just go and see Daniel."

Chapter Eighteen

Friday, May 5th, 1939.

Matthew had just returned from another meeting with Special Branch at New Scotland Yard. His assistant, Chloe, was waiting for him.

He hung up his jacket in his wardrobe. His plaster cast was still making certain movements cumbersome, but he was now used to it; he was visiting the hospital later in the week to get it removed.

It was a warm Spring morning, and the office was comfortable without the need of overgarments.

"Hello, sir, how did the meeting go?"

"Very well, that trial in Birmingham has got everybody smiling. It looks like we're making a breakthrough; there's been no serious activity for over three weeks."

"Yes, I can imagine, although I don't think we should be counting our chickens just yet; this has just come through."

She handed him a sheet of paper.

"Damn, damn," said Matthew. "Has the Commander seen this?"

"No, he was engaged when I went round to show him."

"Hmm, leave it with me; I'll deal with it. Any news on Siemens?"

"Not of any interest, sir. I'm getting daily reports but there's no indication of any espionage activity. They are taking a special interest in the German staff there."

"Good, good. Keep me updated with any developments won't you?"

"Yes, of course, sir."

Matthew's telephone rang. Chloe left the room and shut the door.

"Keating," said Matthew as he lifted the handset.

"Matthew, it's Miles calling, from Dublin."

"Hello, Miles, good to hear from you. The Commander and I were only talking about you yesterday. Wondered if there had been any news from our Czech friend."

"Yes, that's why I'm phoning. I hadn't heard from him since my visit to the hotel, so I tried to call him earlier. It seems he's disappeared."

"Disappeared?"

"Yes, I spoke to the receptionist. I made up some story about a future visit. I asked them about Tomas, said he'd been particularly helpful on my stay and to pass on my thanks, and she said he had left."

"Left?"

"That's what she said. I tried pressing her for more information, but she just said he didn't report for work the day after my visit, and all his stuff had gone from his quarters."

"Do you think there's more to it?"

"I don't know. He was very scared of being seen with me at first, said something about not being allowed to talk to the guests. I mean, it's perfectly feasible he just upped and left, as the receptionist said, on the other hand, it's also possible he's been abducted. I have to say, I was not particularly enamoured with her. She was very curt, and I'm sure I heard her calling me a 'fecking Brit' to someone when I was checking out."

"Hmm, that's a pity; he could have been very useful. Thanks, anyway, Miles, please let me know if you hear anything."

"Yes, will do."

Matthew replaced the receiver and left his office holding the report that Chloe had delivered. He knocked on the

Commander's door and went in.

"Ah, Major, take a seat."

Matthew sat down in front of the Commander's desk.

"Glad you popped in, just been getting an update from the Foreign Office about German involvement in Ireland."

"Have there been developments?"

"Hmm, you could say that. They've had some reports that a German national by the name of... just a minute, it's here somewhere." He picked up a piece of paper. "Franz Fromme. They think he's been acting as a go-between for the IRA and the Germans. Now, we don't know the nature of this liaison, but we can't rule out the Germans have been supporting the terrorists with money and weapons. It's quite disturbing."

"Well, they're certainly getting them from somewhere. We've just had this come through."

Matthew handed the commander the report.

"What's this? Liverpool, Coventry... and in London."

"Yes, it appears tear gas bombs exploded in two cinemas in Liverpool, which is a new one."

"Says here fifteen injuries."

"Yes, sir. There were four bombs in the Coventry attack, and another two here, in London. There are no reports of casualties."

"Hmm, so much for getting on top of things."

"Yes, Special Branch were hoping the trial in Birmingham may have put a dent in their activities, but it seems not. They do have several suspects under surveillance, apparently, and they're hopeful we'll see more arrests shortly."

Grace was getting ready for her shift at the ambulance station. She was about to leave when several letters dropped onto the doormat. There was one from her mother, she recognised, and a couple of circulars, then one with a Lincolnshire postmark. She put it in her handbag to read on the bus.

As Grace made the short journey to Ealing on the top deck, she opened the letter from her son. It was the first she had received since his arrival at the college.

Dear Mum,

I'm sorry for the delay in writing, but since I got here they have been working us pretty hard. The accommodation is comfortable, and the food is good. There are two others sharing the dormitory; they are both from public schools, as are most of the new recruits. I do have some wonderful news, I have been accepted for pilot training and I will be posted to Brize Norton, which is near Oxford, next week to start training on single engine Harvards. I will write to you again when I have more news. Please send my love to Father and Dotty.

With love from James

Grace read it again and considered the message. She would discuss it with Matthew later.

Grace's training was going well. She had updated her first-aid training, which wasn't all that different from what she had received with the FANYs in 1914 and familiarised herself with the new Talbot ambulances. They were far easier to drive than 'Betty', the Wolsley that Grace and Hetty had used in France.

She was resplendent in her new uniform – a white apron with a red cross on the chest. She and Queenie were cleaning out one of the ambulances, when the alarm bell sounded. Moments later, one of the male volunteers came running across the garage and handed the 'chit' to Queenie.

"Your shout," he called.

"Thanks George." She took the slip of paper and started to read it. "Right Grace, you can take charge of the bell. I'll drive... Alexandria Road, I know it."

The pair got into the ambulance, and Queenie started the engine. The large silver bell on the front bumper of the Talbot, gleamed in the sunshine. It was electronically activated by a button inside the cab. Grace immediately started ringing it as they left the garage. A passing car immediately stopped to let the ambulance into the traffic.

They reached the destination in under seven minutes. It was a busy road junction. There was a horse-drawn coal wagon, on its side. The horse was still in its harness attached to the trailer thrashing about in shock trying to get up. The road was blocked with sacks of coal. Several people were milling around trying to help.

The driver had been thrown from the cart and was lying on the pavement. The lorry which had collided with it was parked just behind the stricken wagon.

Queenie immediately took charge. "I'll see to that man."

She pointed to the driver who was being attended by a pedestrian. He had blood pouring down the side of his face.

"I'll see if I can do anything for the horse," shouted Grace.

The horse was lay on its side with the poles and harness still in place. It had stopped moving. Grace could see its flanks moving up and down. Another pedestrian in a boiler suit approached.

"Is it dead?" asked the man.

"No, but I think its badly injured; it's also in shock. Can you undo the harness and get the poles off her? Did you see what happened?"

"Yes, the horse and cart came straight out of that road there. The lorry didn't stand a chance."

"Did you see it hit the horse?"

"No, it hit the side of the wagon and tipped it over. The driver was thrown clear, but I think he hit his head."

"What about the horse?"

"I think the weight pulled her over."

Suddenly the horse started trying to kick its legs again. Grace tried to calm it, gently stroking its head. Its eyes opened wide, a look of blind terror. It started to neigh frantically.

"Have you undone the harness?"

"Yes," replied the man.

"Can you help me see if we can help her up?"

Just then, a police car arrived. Two officers got out and one started to manage the traffic which was now starting to back up.

Grace shouted to the other. "Can you give me a hand here, officer?"

While the pedestrian removed the connecting pole which had been broken at its joint with the trailer, Grace continued to calm down the horse.

"Help me with the reins; she may try to bolt," instructed Grace.

The officer was on one side, Grace on the other and slowly, they tried helping the horse onto its feet, but it was immobile. Grace immediately checked its legs.

"I think the back one's broken. We need to call a vet," said Grace.

"I know where there's a veterinary surgery not five minutes away; I take my dog there," said the pedestrian.

"Can you see if you can get someone?" said Grace.

The man left hurriedly.

"We need to keep her calm," said Grace, who was

stroking the horses head and whispering to her.

Queenie had patched up the patient and walked over to Grace.

"What's the situation?"

"I think the horse has a broken leg; we're just waiting for a vet. Someone's gone to get one."

"Well, the driver needs to go to hospital; his head needs stitching, and I think he may have a skull fracture."

Grace was kneeling next to the horses head. "Can you manage? I'll need to stay with the horse."

"Very well, I'll get one of the officers to help me get him into the ambulance."

Minutes later, the cart driver was safely in the ambulance and heading to the local hospital with Queenie at the wheel.

It was another ten minutes before the pedestrian returned accompanied by another man in a brown suit carrying a Gladstone bag.

They reached Grace.

"Hello, I'm Henry Duncan, veterinary surgeon; can you tell me what happened?"

The eyewitness interjected and explained the course of events.

"I think, she's broken her back hind," said Grace, who was still stroking the horse's head.

The vet did a quick check. "Hmm, yes, you're right."

"Is there anything you can do?" asked Grace.

"No, unfortunately, she'll have to be put down." He rummaged around in his bag and pulled out a large syringe.

"You're familiar with horses?" asked the vet.

"Yes, I was with the First-aid Nurses Yeomanry, in the war,"

"Ah, a FANY, I think you girls did an amazing job."

"Thank you."

"Can you hold her steady? This won't take long; she may kick out."

It was over an hour before Grace returned to the Ambulance Station. Queenie was in the back of the ambulance. Grace joined her.

"How was the driver?"

"Not very well, he may have a fractured skull, but I think he'll recover. Where did you learn to look after horses?"

"It was with the Nursing Yeomanry. When I first joined, we had no motor ambulances; everything was horse-driven. I spent most of my time in the early days tending them."

"I'll let the other drivers know; it will be useful. We do get called out from time to time, to accidents like today, when horses are involved. It makes our lives a lot more difficult; they can be very unpredictable. I'll let the Officer know too; it will be good to have someone who knows what they are doing. How was it?"

"The horse?" Grace looked down. "Hmm, unfortunately it had broken its back leg. The vet had to put her down."

"Oh, that's so sad. The driver was asking about it; kept saying, 'how's me horse? How's me horse?'"

"Well, she was part of his livelihood, and working horses like that one are very expensive. I can understand."

Grace was overcome by a wave of sadness. Queenie could see she was upset.

"Come on, let's go and get a cup of tea; you'll feel better."

There was more sadness in Bradford.

Molly had said farewell to the seamstresses - one or two had worked for her since she first started the business, and Freddie, too, who had offered to help Molly clear everything, without payment. A lot of tears were shed as the 'girls' left the factory for the last time.

Since Monday, Molly had come to terms with what had happened. She visited Mildred on Tuesday evening to tell her the course of events. Mildred immediately offered to pay off any remaining debts. Molly, of course, refused but, with Mildred's insistence, she eventually relented and would be able to start her new garment altering service with a clean sheet.

Molly had kept the newest sewing machine, and the last of the thread and fabric; it was enough to make a start.

Freddie was devastated that his change of career had been so short. William had offered him a position at the bakery but for the moment, he had decided to see what other opportunities were on offer.

Friday, May 26th.

Ivy was in the parlour reading the newspaper. The headline was disturbing.

'Military Training Act given King's seal.'

She read the narrative.

According to the newspaper, all men between the ages of twenty and twenty-two were to be called up for a period of full-time military training before being transferred to the Reserve. It was Britain's first act of peacetime conscription and was intended to be temporary in nature, continuing for three years unless an Order in Council declared it was no longer necessary.

There were provisions for bone-fide conscientious objectors, who would be thoroughly vetted, and a number of exemptions, including coal miners and railway workers. Bakers were also exempt.

Men called up were to be known as 'militiamen' to distinguish them from the regular army. To emphasise this distinction, each man would be issued with a suit in addition to a uniform. The intention was for the first intake to undergo six months of basic training before being discharged into an active reserve. They would then be recalled for short training periods and attend annual camps.

Ivy considered the implications. She thought of Arthur and everything he had gone through. She was dreading having to repeat that experience. She recalled that bakers had been exempt in nineteen fourteen, but it hadn't stopped Arthur from being pressganged into service.

William took a break mid-morning. Ivy showed him the article.

"What does it mean, Mam?" he asked, digesting the information.

"They're calling up all lads aged twenty and twenty-one."

"Aye, I read that; 'appen I'm too old."

"Aye, and bakers are exempt anyway, but there're pals of yours and Daisy, that will have to go. I'm pretty sure Grace's eldest is twenty as well. Mind you, he's already joined the Airforce, according to your Gran."

"It seems like we're going to get another war," said William.

"Aye, it does."

"What'll happen to bakery if us can't get flour?"

"Your Da managed; there were all kinds of restrictions, mind. Some bakers were mixing their bread mix with potato flour. Tasted terrible."

"'Appen we can start buying extra yeast and salt in case things get short. We'll have to find somewhere to store it." He paused to think for a moment. "I know, we can use the old privy. Don't know about flour; I'll talk to Robert."

"Don't go making hasty decisions just yet. Mr Chamberlain is working hard for peace," said Ivy.

"Then why all this? And gas masks. I read they've even got air raid shelters in London."

"Aye, that's right enough; it's all very worrying... What about the wedding?" asked Ivy.

"What about the wedding?" replied William, with a look of surprise.

"Do you want to bring it forward? I mean, you've got your house nice."

"I don't know; Marjorie's in charge of all that. I'll have to ask her."

"Well, a lot can happen between now and September."

"Aye, that's true. I'll ask her tonight; we're going to the pictures."

"What are you going to see?"

"'The Face at The Window'. I heard some of the customers talking about it."

"What's it about?"

"It's got Todd Slaughter in it, a murder mystery."

"Oh, as if there's not enough misery in the world."

That evening, William and Marjorie were queuing outside the cinema. William needed to discuss the question of the wedding with Marjorie. He explained the circumstances.

"Mam were saying we should get wed sooner in case there's a war. What do tha think?"

"Why does she think that?"

"It were that news in paper about the call up; it got her thinking."

"Aye, I read that. But you wouldn't have to go; you're a baker."

"Aye, so were me Da the last time; he had to go."

"I can speak to me Mam and see what she says."

They reached the foyer and William paid for their

tickets. Inside, the usual layer of cigarette smoke filled the auditorium.

Before the main feature, the Pathé Newsreel played. Again, it was the regular up-beat, jingoistic fare, with the 'aristocratic-sounding' narrator espousing Britain's preparedness for any conflict. A brief clip of a new aircraft carrier being launched; the King and the rest of the Royal family at a scout jamboree joining in a sing song; 'like normal people' said the narrator. There was also footage of the Mayday parade in London, which took part in driving rain. It did little to 'dampen their spirits', according to the commentator. Thousands of workers marching with their banners declaring 'deep bomb-proof shelters for all, now!', some expressed anti-Government sentiments, others waving the Russian flag.

The newsreel continued.

In another part of the country, more traditional Mayday celebrations were taking place, a tranquil village green with its maypole. The cinema audience were treated to the scene of the arrival of the May queen on a pony and cart attended by a small entourage, watched by the rest of the local inhabitants. The 'queen' was duly crowned, and the rest of the village applauded. 'The spirit of merry England still lives', extolled the voice-over.

The audience took it all in.

The following day, Saturday, Matthew was back in his office; there were no weekend breaks. Mid-morning and he was going through the latest reports with his assistant.

His telephone rang.

"Keating... Hello Miles." He listened to the diplomat for a couple of minutes. "Oh, dear God, no. Thanks for letting me know. If you get any more information, can you get in touch?"

He dropped the call and ran his hands down his face.

"Problems?" asked Chloe.

"Yes, that was Miles Jordan, the diplomat from the British Embassy in Dublin. The police in Donegal have found a body washed up in the river. They believe it's the Czech waiter from the hotel. I need to let the Commander know."

Five minutes later, Matthew was with the Commander relaying the message about the demise of the waiter.

"Do we know how he died?" asked the Commander.

"No, Miles didn't have that information."

"Well, we can't rule out the IRA, which by itself gives credence to the information he provided. It does seem to confirm some link between the terrorists and the German legation."

"Yes, although, I'm not sure what we can do about it. What about the Garda Síochána?" asked Matthew.

"Do they know about our Czech friend?"

"I wouldn't think so; at least not any connection with MI6," replied Matthew.

"Have a word with Travis, see what liaison we have with them. It'll be interesting to see if they are investigating the death. I assume it's murder."

"Miles didn't say, but, yes, we assume it is."

There was a pause. "Would you like a drink? There's another matter I want to discuss with you."

"Yes, thanks, sir."

A few minutes later, a secretary arrived with a tray and China tea service.

As she poured the tea, Commander Monkton was looking through a pile of reports from his 'in-tray'.

"Can you close the door, Geraldine," said the Commander.

The secretary left the Commander's office. Monkton looked at Matthew.

"I've had some fresh information about our old friend Seán Russell."

"Oh, and what's the former head of the IRA up to now? He's still in the States, I take it?"

The Commander stroked his greying moustache. "Yes, over a month now, Special Branch have asked the 'G-men' to trail him; they've been getting regular reports."

"It's nice to know we can get cooperation from our friends in the FBI. So, what's he been up to?"

"Well, according to Special Branch, he's been making a number of speeches at rallies, drumming up support for the nationalist cause. As you can imagine, it's gone down well with the Irish American community over there. There's no doubt money is involved. My guess is, the IRA are getting more money from America than they are from Germany."

"Yes, you could be right. I don't know what, if anything, we can do about it, though."

"Hmm, true. For the time being, Special Branch are keeping tabs on Russell through the FBI. But there's something else. We've had a rather strange request."

"Really?" Matthew looked at the Commander expectantly.

"It seems De Valera is trying to discredit him."

"Why would the Irish Government do that?"

"Well, for a start, De Valera is no fan of the IRA; he denounced them back in thirty-six."

"Yes, I'm aware of that."

"I've been speaking to the Foreign Office." Monkton picked up his teacup and took the last sip. "Frankly, the Irish Government are in a bind. If they're seen to be supporting Britain, it could spark a civil war in Ireland; on the other hand, any siding with Germany would, of course, prompt a swift response from Britain. He's worried we would go in and retake the Irish ports; that's their assessment."

"So, he's trying to protect their neutrality?"

"It certainly looks like it."

"But I don't understand; why would De Valera want to discredit Sean Russell? De Valera's a staunch Republican."

"He's also a pragmatist and shrewd politician. They're looking to lessen his impact in America."

"How are they going to do that?"

"Well, according to the Irish, they believe that about ten or twelve years ago, Russell was in the employ of the Russians as an agitator. They wanted to know if we had any evidence to support this claim."

"And have we?"

"Well, we certainly haven't; I don't know about the Foreign Office."

"Hmm, it will be interesting to see how this plays out."

Thursday, June 1st.

Agnes was checking her makeup for the umpteenth time. Her dresser was fussing with her frock, especially chosen for tonight's opening performance. The good news; the theatre had sold out, but that just increased Agnes's anxiety.

Solly knocked on the dressing room door and entered, carrying a bunch of flowers.

"Half an hour, Agnes, the orchestra will be starting up in fifteen minutes."

"Oh, they're beautiful. Thank you so much."

"How are you feeling?"

"A little anxious, if I'm honest; but I'll be alright once we start."

"I've checked on the other artists and they're all ready. The dress rehearsal went well yesterday. I am sure you will be a great success."

"Oh, I hope so; it's been a long time since I did any stage work."

The minutes ticked by. Agnes remembered her first tour. Gloria, the juggler, had taken the eighteen-year-old under her wing; she was not sure how she would have managed on her own. Then she recalled Cameron, her manager and Master of Ceremonies, the larger-than-life entrepreneur who had been Agnes's greatest fan. He would always check on the artists before a show.

Agnes sipped at her honey and lemon cordial which she used to lubricate her vocal chords. She was glad Alistair was conducting the orchestra. He had been her rock.

The orchestra tuned up, then started playing some lively melodies as people left the bar and started to take their seats. As a gala evening, it was formal dress, with men in their dicky-bows and white shirts, women in their finest gowns and jewellery.

"We are about to start. Do you want to watch from the wings?" asked Solly.

"Maybe later, I'll just sit here and remember my words." She managed a smile.

Solly left the dressing room and there was movement along the corridor as the dancers readied themselves for their entrance.

Solly had booked one of the country's up and coming young comics as the M.C., a 'cheery' Cockney. He had appeared on the Variety Show several times and was very popular. Agnes had got to know him and was also a fan.

Showtime! The compere walked on to a jaunty tune and welcomed everyone. He told a few jokes, before introducing the dancers. After a magician, and the speciality act, Marie Lloyd Jnr closed the first half with several of her mother's songs. She invited the audience to join in.

Agnes had decided to watch her from the side of the stage.

Marie had inherited the voice and many of the traits of her famous mother. The audience were singing along as she reeled off several of her mother's most popular songs, and two of her own compositions. As the curtain closed, several members of the audience, stood to applaud.

Agnes was the first to congratulate her as she left the stage.

"Your mother would have been so proud of you," said Agnes as the pair embraced.

As her own curtain call approached, Agnes was feeling really nervous. Solly arrived.

"Five minutes, Agnes. I'll escort you to the stage."

"Thank you, Solly."

Agnes took the last sip of her drink and left her dressing room.

The curtain was down, and the compere took the stage. He told a couple of jokes while the scenery was prepared, then gave Agnes a big build up.

The lights dimmed and the curtain rose. Agnes was backlit, creating an ethereal effect. The orchestra started the introduction. Agnes could see Alistair smiling at her. Her nerves had gone and the unmistakable voice that had entertained millions of people on the radio over recent months, filled the auditorium.

There was a split second of silence before the applause erupted at the end of the song. Agnes bowed deeply and thanked the audience.

Her set lasted about three quarters of an hour, including the obligatory encore. The audience were standing, as Agnes invited the rest of the cast to take a final bow.

The lights came on and the customers started to leave the theatre.

"Congratulations Agnes, that was marvellous," said Solly, as she left the stage and made her way to her dressing room.

She remembered the after-show parties they used to have on her earlier tours, usually instigated by Gloria, who was always able to find a bottle or two; 'to unwind' she would always say.

Solly produced a bottle of champagne, and they were soon joined by some of the cast, including the compere. Alistair arrived from the orchestra pit.

"You were tremendous, darling," he said as he reached Agnes through the crush.

"Thank you. How do you think it went? Do we need to make any changes?"

"For a first night, I don't think it could have gone any better."

It was over an hour before Alistair and Agnes left the theatre by the stage door, they were surprised to see people stood outside, patiently waiting for autographs. Agnes dutifully signed until the taxi pulled up.

The following day, Agnes was awake early, anxious to read the reviews. The newspaper had been delivered and was sticking out of the letter box. She stood there in her silk dressing gown. Alistair joined her.

She flicked through the pages and reached the entertainment section.

The headline, 'A Triumph', greeted her. She flicked through the narrative written by the theatre critic.

"Oh darling, that is wonderful," said Alistair as he read the review over her shoulder.

A little later, there was a telephone call; it was Solly.

"Congratulations, Agnes, Duncan Favell, is not any easy man to please. He's been known to close shows in the first week. It's not often you get 'this show should run and run', from him."

"Thank you, Solly, but you must take most of the credit; it was your show. I just sang."

"And so perfectly."

Saturday, June 3rd.

Back in Keithley, William was mixing the second batch of the day and preparing it for the oven. Robert was assisting; something they had done together for many years. William had a lot on his mind.

"Tha's quiet," commented Robert, as William closed the oven door.

"Aye, got stuff in me 'ead."

"So, what's this then?"

"It's t'wedding. We've changed the date like Mam's said we should."

"So, what's the problem then?"

"Everything's rushed; there's too much to do. I've been trying to work it out."

"Well, tha's booked the church, haven't tha?"

"Aye, June 17th, but that's only two weeks away. We've not sent all invitations out yet. Nobody'll be able to come."

"Don't be daft, course they will. Tha's got the ring; I knows that, tha's showed me."

"Aye."

"Well, that's most important. What about t'reception?"

"Aye. Marjory's Mam's booked Church Hall."

"At Ingrow?"

"Aye, so what else's to be done? Tha can phone relatives

and tell them date's been changed."

"Aye, that I can."

"Well, I can help with the written invitations."

"Can tha?"

"Aye, I'm best man, that's what I'm here for... I know, after we're done today, we'll go to t'stationers and get some cards. They do them now, specially. Then we can make a list. When are tha seeing Marjorie?"

"Lunch time."

"Well, when we've finished today, we can go upstairs and make a list. Mam'll help an'all. Then we just need any relatives Marjorie's Mam wants to invite."

"Aye, ta Robert; tha's eased my mind."

"What about photographer?"

"Marjorie's Mam knows one; I think she's already spoken to him about doing it."

"What, the new date?"

"Aye."

"Well, tha can stop mythering, seems like it's all under control."

Chapter Nineteen

Friday, June 9th, 1939.

Grace was on her day off from the ambulance service and was using the time to catch up on household chores.

The telephone rang.

"Oh, Hetty, how lovely to hear from you," said Grace on picking up the handset.

"Hello, old thing. Sorry I haven't been in touch, but the move has taken up all my time."

"Yes, Chloe told Matthew you had found a house."

"Yes, moved in last week, still surrounded by boxes."

"I can't wait to see your new place."

"Well, give me a couple of weeks and you can come down, stay over if you like; I've got room."

"Hmm, I can't commit to staying overnight, the ambulance work has taken over my life. I'm already working more shifts than I intended."

"Well, that's one of the reasons I'm ringing. Have you got the address of the recruitment office? I've been thinking, I need to be doing something and I think I would like to join the ambulance service."

"Yes, of course. Oh, that's marvellous, maybe you can join the same station as me; I'm at Ealing."

"It depends on the travel, old thing; it's over an hour from Tunbridge into London Bridge. I'll need to check."

Back in Keighley, just over a week away, preparations were well advanced for the forthcoming wedding. Despite William's reservations, everything was ready and most of the invitees were able to attend. The one absence from the Marsden family would be Agnes, who would be performing that evening but had sent the couple a large hamper from Harrods as a wedding gift complete with a dinner set. Grace had confirmed she would be attending but without Matthew who was unable to leave work. James was now at Brize Norton, learning to fly, but Dorothy would accompany her mother. They would arrive by train and stay at Blossom Cottage with Mildred.

Freddie had not found work following the collapse of Molly's business but had seen an advertisement in the daily newspaper for a supervisor at one of the local mills. It was just up the road from where they lived, and the job was not dissimilar to that he was doing at Molly's. Freddie had applied.

He was at the kitchen table when the morning's postal delivery arrived. There was just one letter, postmarked 'Headley Mills'.

Jean saw Freddie open the letter. "Is that from the Mill?"

"Aye."

"What's it say?"

"Give us a chance; I'm just trying to read it." Freddie concentrated for a moment. "They want us to go for an interview, it says."

"Well, that's good news. Does it say when?"

"Aye, Monday, eleven-fifteen."

"I'll wash your best shirt and press your suit."

"Aye, ta... Have tha heard owt from tha Ma?"

"Not since last night. I hope she's feeling better she sounded dreadful. Chest cold she said. I might go and visit her later."

"Aye, but don't go bringing germs back here."

"No, I'll keep my distance."

Freddie went to get up but winced and sat down again.

"Is your leg playing up again."

"Aye, 'appen it's a bit sore this morning. I think I'll keep 'Harry' off for a bit."

Jean had christened Freddie's false leg 'Harry'. It was a private joke between them.

"Nothing from our Arthur," commented Jean. "I thought we would have heard from him by now."

"Aye, it's been over a month."

"I hope he's alright. I suppose they do have a post service from Tor Point; I mean, it's a long way."

"Aye, I suppose so. Seven hours on t'train, he said," replied Freddie.

"Well, he's not best at writing."

"Aye, that's true. We'll hear from him when he's ready."

Meanwhile, at the Secret Service Headquarters, Matthew was in his office going over reports with his assistant.

"I was reading in the newspaper about that submarine," said Chloe, in a break in conversation.

"The Thetis? Yes, it was dreadful."

"Nearly a hundred dead. Do we know what caused it?"

He looked at Chloe. "Well, I've seen the initial findings. According to the navy, it seems that the inner hatch on one of the torpedo tubes was opened while the outer hatch to the sea was also open. Goodness knows why; four ratings did manage to escape."

"I can't imagine what that must have been like for the crew," said Chloe.

Just then, the telephone rang. "Yes, right away," said Matthew, hearing the command.

"That was the Commander, something's up."

He reached the Commander's office and walked in.

"Sit down, Major, we're getting reports of letter boxes

being targeted."

"Letter boxes?"

"Yes, just had the Home Office on. Twenty so far, plus one of the sorting offices here in London they also hit a mail lorry in Birmingham."

"Hmm, I wonder why they're bombing letter boxes. Anyone hurt?"

"Seven, apparently but not serious, burns mostly."

"Do you think it has anything to do with Russell's arrest?"

"I wouldn't think so."

"What's the latest on Russell, by the way?"

"Well, it seems he was in Detroit. They had reports he was about to cross over into Canada which is why the FBI arrested him."

"What will happen? Are we going to get him extradited?"

"Good question. The Irish Americans in Congress are up in arms about it already, so there will be a huge political stink if the Government applies for extradition, and they don't want to do anything to upset the Americans. If there is a war, we're going to need their support. At the moment, the Foreign Office are just glad he's off the streets. At least, he's not spouting off his nationalist diatribe to all and sundry."

"So, they're just keeping him locked up until someone decides what to do with him?"

"That's about the size of it. The Foreign Office have had enough of his incendiarism."

Saturday, June 17th, Ingrow Parish Church.

Four o'clock. The baker's had closed early, and William was waiting anxiously at the altar. Beside him, his brother, Robert, played nervously with the ring in his pocket. After a great deal of worry, everything was ready.

The front pew was lined with relatives. William's mother,

Ivy; aunts Freda, Grace, and Molly, his cousin Dorothy, Marjorie's mother. Freddie and Jean were also there, as was Mildred. William's sister Daisy was a bridesmaid and would accompany Marjorie. Just two of his cousins from the butchers were at the church, as the shop was still open, but would join the family at the reception.

The organist played the traditional Wedding March as Marjorie made her grand entrance and the entourage walked down the aisle.

William turned and watched his bride-to-be move gracefully towards him. She looked radiant.

One of her uncles had agreed to give her away and joined them at the altar.

Twenty-five minutes later, William and Marjorie walked arm-in-arm as husband and wife.

It was just a short distance to the Village Hall where the reception would be held.

There would be no honeymoon for the moment, and the happy couple would return to their new house together for the first time as man and wife.

Monday morning. Freddie was looking smart in his best shirt and suit, his flat cap and boots completing the ensemble.

Jean straightened his tie and had a final check; he was ready.

It was a ten minutes' walk to the factory, to the end of the road and turn left. It wasn't a large mill like the ones in Keighley, but still employed around fifty people. Freddie reached the gates and walked through to reception.

Having announced his arrival, he was asked to take a seat in the small entrance area to wait. A few minutes later, a smart-looking man in a dark suit approached and introduced himself.

"Johnathan Headley, I'm one of the directors, you must be Fred Bluett?"

"Aye, folks call me Freddie."

"Ah, well follow me... Freddie."

The director led Freddie down a corridor to an office at the end.

"Please take a seat. Thank you for applying for the supervisor's role. I'll ask you a few questions, then I can show you around. I understand from your letter, you served in the war."

"Aye, I did, came back with less than I went."

The director looked confused. "Go on."

"Aye, 'appen I lost my leg."

"Oh, I'm so sorry... and you manage well enough?"

"Aye, I do."

"Good, good. So, tell me what work experience you've had."

Freddie continued to outline his work as a gardener and his brief spells at two mills before the war, then, more recently, his supervisory role at Molly's factory.

"'Appen work dried up on account of no cloth."

"Yes, it's a difficult time. Fortunately, we have a small Government contract making uniforms which means we get priority on fabric."

After half an hour's further questioning, Freddie was shown the factory and the shop floor where the manufacturing was done. The director explained the set-up.

Eventually, they returned to the director's office.

"Well, thank you for calling; I'll be writing to you shortly."

Freddie left the office and reflected on his latest interview. The director seemed happy enough, but it was difficult to say.

Monday Morning in Bloomsbury, Agnes was in her sitting room with Mary, reading another batch of fan letters handed in at the theatre, delivered by Solly the previous day. Some were heartbreaking; many expressed concern at the prospect of war and that her performances had given them strength in these 'uncertain times'.

She was drinking her honey and lemon cordial which she normally drank before a show. Her throat felt tight, and she had a 'tickly' cough which had kept her awake for much of the night.

Around eleven o'clock there was a knock on the door which her assistant answered.

"Hello, again; it's Céline, isn't it? Do come in, Agnes will be delighted to see you."

Agnes was stood in the sitting room, having heard the greeting.

"Céline, how wonderful to see you," said Agnes as the visitor entered the room.

There were hugs and cheek kisses.

"'Ello, Agnes, it is good to see you also. I 'ope I'm not, er, disturb you."

"No, no, we've just been sorting through some correspondence. Would you like a coffee?"

"Oui, zat would be so nice."

"I wondered if you would call again; I hadn't heard from you since your last visit."

Agnes coughed again and took a sip of cordial.

"No, after I saw you, I returned to Paris, to arrange some things; zen I returned 'ere again on Friday. I stay with my friend, Francine. I wanted to tell you zat I 'ave decided to come and live in London."

"Oh, but that is wonderful news."

"Oui, I have rented my, er, apartment, and now I am

looking for one 'ere in London. Paris, it is too *dangereuse*. Zay say zat 'itler, ee will invade France and ee will bomb Paris."

"Who says that?"

"My friends in Paris. Zere is much worry; zay say zere will be war."

"Oh, I do hope they are wrong. What will you do here?"

"I will maybe teach, or I can, er, 'ow you say? Translate."

"Yes, of course; I am sure there will be plenty of opportunities."

"Oui, yes, I 'ope so."

Just then, Mary brought in a tray with a coffee jug and cups.

"Are you still on zee raddio?"

"No, I finished that for the moment. I have a show on at one of the theatres in London. Three nights a week, Thursday, Friday, Saturday."

"House full every night," interjected Mary, proudly, as she poured the coffee.

Agnes started coughing again.

"You are not well?" said Céline.

"It's just a slight cough, nothing to worry about," said Agnes and took another sip of cordial.

Céline left after an hour with the promise of an early return.

Agnes's coughing had got worse, prompting concern from Mary.

"I think you should call Doctor Brittan."

"No, I don't want to trouble him. I'm sure it will go after some rest."

"But he could prescribe some linctus for you. You want to be well for Thursday's show."

Agnes thought for a moment. "Yes, actually I think you're right; can you call him for me?"

It was early afternoon when the physician arrived. Agnes had taken to her bed to rest her throat and catch up on lost sleep.

Agnes was called and walked down the stairs, slightly heady, in her silk dressing gown. The doctor was stood in the sitting room talking to Mary.

"Ah, Agnes, your assistant was just telling me you're feeling unwell."

"Hello, Doctor, no, I seemed to have developed a bit of a cough and I feel breathless."

"How long have you been experiencing these symptoms?"

"Since Saturday's show, although I feel I haven't been myself for a week or so."

"You are doing more shows I noticed in the newspaper."

"Yes, three times a week, at The Vaudeville Theatre."

"I see. Let me take a look."

He took out his stethoscope and started examining Agnes.

After a thorough examination, the doctor gave his diagnosis; his demeanour was grave.

"Well, I can rule out pneumonia, but I'm not happy with your breathing. I want to refer you to a specialist I know in Harley Street. I'll ask him to carry out an X-ray. I'm going to try to get you an appointment at the earliest opportunity."

Agnes looked at Mary. "But what do you think is the matter?"

"I don't want to speculate, Agnes. I will call the consultant this afternoon and let you know when he can see you."

"What about my shows?"

"Hmm, honestly?"

"Yes."

"I think you should cancel them for the time being."

Agnes sat down trying to take in the message. "Yes, of course; if that's what you recommend."

Agnes looked at Mary. "I must contact Solly."

Later that afternoon, Alistair returned from work. Agnes was lay on the settee in the sitting room. Mary had left for the day.

"Hello, darling, what's wrong?" he said with a concerned look.

"I don't know." Her voice was croaky and shaky.

"What's wrong with your voice?"

Agnes raised herself into a sitting position and put her head in her hands.

"I don't know. Mary called the doctor this morning." Agnes coughed. "He wants me to see a specialist in Harley Street. He's arranged an appointment for eleven o'clock tomorrow."

Alistar sat down next to her. "Tomorrow? How long have you been feeling unwell?"

"I've not been myself for a few days and then I've developed this cough." She coughed again.

"It's strange you should say that. I noticed on Saturday you were having difficulty with some of the top 'C's' which you always master with ease."

"Yes, that's true, but I hoped no one would notice."

"I don't think anyone did, but I know your voice better than anyone. Why didn't you say something?"

"I didn't think anything of it. I put it down to working three nights in a row. My voice does get tight sometimes."

"Hmm, yes, and I did notice the coughing last night."

"I'm sorry if I disturbed you."

"Don't worry. Did he give you any medicine, for the

cough?"

"Yes, Mary went and collected it from the chemist. Just some linctus; he said it would ease it." She coughed again. "My chest aches." She rubbed her chest below her neck in an attempt to ease the affliction.

"Would you like me to come with you tomorrow?"

"What about work?"

"They can manage without me for the morning; they'll rearrange my classes."

"Yes, if you think you can get away."

The following morning, Agnes and Alistair were on their way in a taxi to Harley Street to see the specialist. It was a bright June morning; the trees were in full bloom and the sun was making its presence felt. Agnes was wearing a lightweight jacket over a blouse and skirt with one of her 'Spring' hats. Despite her indisposition, she still maintained her appearance. Her coughing had improved which she had put down to the linctus and her throat felt less sore.

They reached the fashionable mews. The row of houses which had become the home of numerous physicians looked immaculate as they pulled up outside number twenty-nine. There was a small brass plaque with the name 'Charles Williams FRC' appended; above it a matching brass doorbell.

They alighted the taxi and Alistair pushed the doorbell.

In a few moments, a matronly-looking woman in a blue nurse's uniform opened the door.

"Ah, you must be Agnes Marsden."

"Yes, this is my husband."

"Please do come in; Mr Williams will be with you directly."

There was a corridor with various rooms on either side. Agnes and Alistair followed the nurse to a small waiting area at the end of the corridor. It was light and airy, the décor modern and tasteful.

There were several armchairs around the room and low wooden tables with neatly presented magazines.

The nurse left the couple.

"This is most pleasant," said Agnes.

Alistair looked around the room. "Yes, it is."

After five minutes, a distinguished-looking, middle-aged gentleman walked in from the corridor. He was wearing a suit with a dickie-bow and pocket handkerchief.

"Miss Marsden? Charles Williams. I've had your referral from Doctor Brittan, if you would like to follow me."

They walked back along the corridor and into a room to the left. There was a desk with two seats in front, and, opposite, a screen, behind which Agnes could see an examination couch.

"Doctor Brittain has sent across your notes; you're a singer, I understand?"

"Yes," replied Agnes. She looked at Alistair then back to the consultant.

The consultant was reading the notes over the top of a pair of half-rimmed glasses.

"Hmm, Doctor Brittan says you've been experiencing, he says, 'an irritating cough'."

"Yes, it's gradually worsened over recent days. The doctor gave me some linctus which has helped."

"I see, and some shortness of breath, it says here."

"Yes, although I think that's because of the coughing."

"Hmm. I see. Well, let me examine you, and then I will arrange for a chest X-ray; hopefully, it will tell us what's going on."

Agnes was invited into the examination area and the screens closed. She stripped down to her undergarments.

Alistair was still seated in front of the desk, fidgeting anxiously.

After twenty minutes, the examination was completed. Agnes was given a gown, and then the physician escorted her back down the corridor, into another room. Alistair returned to the waiting area.

It was sparce with just a desk and a few chairs, with various pieces of equipment on tables, including one with the name 'Siemens' written on the side. An assistant in a white coat was seated behind the desk who appeared to be examining some X-ray photographs.

"This is Doctor Schneider, he specialises in radiography and will conduct the X-ray examination. I'll leave you in his capable hands."

The Consultant left and Doctor Schneider took over; he spoke with a strong Eastern European accent.

After half an hour, Agnes was led back to Mr Williams room. She could see Alistair drinking a cup of tea and reading a magazine. He looked up and waved, seeing Agnes walking down the corridor; she returned to the consulting room.

"Please take a seat, Agnes," said the clinician. "I've asked them to expedite the photographs and then we can discuss your condition in more detail."

Agnes looked at him with some concern. "It's nothing serious, is it?"

"I'd sooner wait for the results of the X-rays before speculating. You can get changed now and join your husband. Nurse Painter will get you a cup of tea. I'll call you when we're ready."

Agnes went behind the screens and got dressed.

She walked back down the corridor and Alistair stood up. "Any news?" he asked.

"They're waiting the X-ray results."

"How long will that take?"

"He didn't say."

Moments later, the nurse approached. "Would you like a cup of tea, Miss Marsden?"

"Yes, thank you," replied Agnes.

"Can I just say how much my mother and I enjoy your radio show. We really miss it now that it's not on anymore. Will you be doing more performances for the BBC?"

"Thank you, that's very kind. In the autumn, that's the plan."

"Oh, I'm so pleased, my mother will be delighted." The nurse turned. "I'll just make your tea."

It was nearly two hours before Mr Williams approached from his office; his demeanour appeared sombre. "Would you like to come through?" he asked.

Agnes looked at Alistair, then the pair followed the consultant back to his room.

"Please take a seat."

Grim-faced, he picked up two X-ray photographs.

"Do you smoke at all?" he asked.

Agnes looked at Alistair. "No, not now, I've not smoked since I stopped touring. That was a long time ago. I found it irritated my throat."

"I see... but you work in smoky conditions."

"Ha, yes. Sometimes you can't see the back of the theatre." She looked at Alistair and smiled.

"Hmm, that's interesting."

"Why do you ask?"

"Hmm, I'm very sorry; it's not good news."

Agnes looked at Alistair again.

"What do you mean?"

"It's cancer, I'm afraid. It's in your oesophagus and has spread to your lungs. The reason I asked about smoking is, there's some research being done in Germany, looking at the possible link with cancer, particularly lung cancer, and smoking. I have to say, I don't believe it myself; in fact, I've often prescribed it to cure anxiety."

Agnes was speechless.

"What does it mean?" asked Alistair. "Can it be treated?"

The Consultant picked up the X-ray photos again.

"Unfortunately, not, it seems to have spread very quickly."

"But there must be something?"

"I wish I could give you hope. I can arrange for palliative care."

"Palliative care?"

"Yes, make sure your wife is comfortable."

Agnes had her head in her hands, still too numb to speak.

"Thank you, Mr Williams. What happens next?" said Alistair, trying to maintain his composure.

"I'll speak with Doctor Brittan to let him know, and I suggest that I visit you weekly. It will be quite expensive, but it will enable me to keep you informed."

"Yes, yes, whatever you think's best. I know this is a difficult question, but how long do you think we have? Weeks, months?" asked Alistair. Agnes was still numb.

"It's very difficult to say, cancer is such an unpredictable disease; that's why I suggest I visit once a week. I can prescribe some tablets which will ease any pain."

"Yes, thank you, Mr Williams. Can you ask someone to call us a taxi, please? I think we need to get home," said Alistair.

Freda Marsden was the most academically gifted of the Marsden family, due largely to the fact that she was able to continue her schooling until she was eighteen and then attend college to fulfil her ambition of being a teacher.

After qualifying, she joined a small primary school in one of the local villages and eventually rose to become its Headmistress in 1934.

The vacancy for Principal at Utley High School for girls appealed to her, after she had been approached by one of the governors to apply. The daughter of the governor in question had attended Micklethwaite Primary School and had commented favourably on Freda.

She had been in her post for three months and had set about a programme of reforms to modernise the teaching faculty in line with modern times. Her initial opinion was that many of the practices dated back to Victorian times. There was some opposition to her changes, but the staff were starting to see some benefits, and they were certainly well-received with the Board of Governors.

The school housed just over two hundred pupils, mostly from wealthy background who could afford the high fees. There were, however, a small number on scholarships. The building resembled a large stately home, donated to the community to be used as a school, by a former mill owner and benefactor in 1897. It had had several renovations over the years, but its character remained.

The Headmistress's office was in keeping with the rest of the building with its wood-panelled walls. Freda's desk was original, dating back to the Victorian era. The room added additional status to the role of Headmistress.

It would soon be the end of term and the start of the long summer break. Freda was at her desk scrutinising some students' examination answer papers to ensure consistency of marking. There was a knock on the door.

"Sorry to disturb you, Miss Marsden, but there's a

Monsignor Costa to see you."

"Monsignor Costa?"

"Yes, he apologises for arriving unannounced but wants to talk to you about our refugees."

"Very well, just give me five minutes."

The secretary left and returned a few minutes later with the visitor.

Freda got up from her chair to greet the priest, resplendent in his black robes and red zucchetto.

"Miss Marsden, I am sorry to call unannounced, thank you for seeing me." He spoke in a strong Spanish accent.

"Not at all, please take a seat. How can I help you?"

"I have been sent to England by the Archbishop of Barcelona on behalf of the new Spanish Government, to organise the er, repatriation, of the remaining refugees."

"I see."

"I understand you still have three here at this school."

"Yes, that is correct, Maria Zornoza, and her two sisters, Antonia, and Isobel."

He consulted a notebook. "Si, si."

"What will happen to them?"

"They will return to their home town."

"What about their parents?"

"Si, their mother is still alive, but their father he is, er, *muerto*, killed in the war."

"Oh, how sad. I don't know if they are aware of that, the girls. I will need to speak to their teacher. When is this taking place?"

"In two days. I am arranging for, er, an omnibus to take them to Southampton, and then I will escort them by, er, boat. There will be others who are still here, two in Bradford." He indicated to his notebook.

"To Barcelona?"

"Si."

Most of the four thousand refugees that had arrived in the UK in 1937 to escape from the Spanish Civil War had returned by the end of 1938, but the hundred or so who remained were distributed across the country. The Government did not want them in England due to the political implications – aiding a Fascist regime and refused any financial support. The children were cared for in children's homes run by the Catholic church, or by well-to-do patrons.

The Zornoza sisters had been staying with a member of the wealthy Flemming family in a large house about five miles away from the school.

"I'll need to speak to the girls, and Mrs Flemming."

"Ah, si, Mrs Flemming, she has been very helpful. We are very much thankful to her."

"What if the girls want to stay in England? They seem very settled here and speak English well now."

"It will not be possible; they are Spanish and will need to return home. Now the war is finished, it is perfectly safe."

"Very well, what do you want me to do?"

"Can you speak to the girls, er, *por favor*? I will arrange for them to be collected on Thursday morning. Er, they can be ready for ten o'clock, si?"

"Ten o'clock, Thursday. Yes, I will see to it. Was there anything else?"

"No, thank you, for seeing me at short notice. May God protect you."

"Thank you, Monsignor. May God protect the Zornoza sisters."

The priest bowed and Freda showed him to the door.

Freda was deep in thought.

She left her office and walked through to the reception

area. The secretary was typing letters behind a glass window. She saw Freda and opened the sliding window.

"Hello, Miss Marsden, what can I do for you?"

"Can you ask the Zornoza sisters to come to my office at one o'clock? Oh, and I need to see Miss Marchant at quarter to?"

"Yes, Miss Marsden."

"And can you get me Mrs Flemming, please, at Larkfield Hall."

"Yes, of course."

Freda was back in her office when the call came through.

"Mrs Flemming? It's Miss Marsden from Utley School, here. I've just received a visit from a priest from Barcelona. It appears that the girls need to return to Spain."

Freda explained the circumstances. Mrs Flemming was extremely upset.

"Is there any way they will let them stay? They are very happy here," said the woman.

"Yes, I'm aware they've been well looked after. Unfortunately, it appears not. The Government are supporting the repatriation so it's unlikely they will agree to any sort of asylum."

"But that's dreadful; what am I going to say to the girls?"

"I don't know, Mrs Flemming, but I'm seeing their teacher later before telling them."

"Oh dear, well thank you for letting me know."

Saturday, June 24th.

In London, the IRA's terror campaign continued with attacks on Banks - branches of the Midland Bank, Westminster Bank, and Lloyds Bank were targeted with a series of massive explosions.

Following the bombings, Special Branch carried out mass arrests and interrogations of the Irish community in London with the majority being released soon after.

In Parliament, the Home Secretary, Sir Samuel Hoare, introduced the Prevention of Violence Bill. The bill provided comprehensive powers for the British government to prevent the immigration of foreigners, for their deportation, and for extending to the Irish the requirement to register with the British police. Hoare referred to the S-Plan of the IRA when presenting the bill.

In his speech he detailed the number of attacks and their resulting impact. He also gave a chilling warning. According to reports, the campaign was about to intensify 'with no regard being paid to human life'. He added that the IRA campaign, which he believed was being actively stimulated by 'foreign organisations' (Germany), was being closely watched.

Matthew was in the Commander's office discussing the possible ramifications.

"Actually, we have been somewhat fortunate," said the Commander. "Considering the number of bombs that have been detonated, the loss of life could have been much higher."

"Yes, although, the terrorists have not as yet targeted populated areas or Government buildings. That could of course change," replied Matthew.

"Yes, that's true; we must not ease up on this."

"Have we had any more news on Seán Russell?" asked Matthew.

"No, not a thing. He seems to have just disappeared."

"I thought the Irish Government might have asked for his deportation."

"Hmm, well given the British Government's impotence in the matter, I think we would have welcomed that. Unfortunately, it would cause too much political fallout for us to become involved. As you know, the Irish lobby in Congress have been very vocal."

"You think one of them has aided his escape?"

"Almost certainly. The FBI have no idea where he's gone."

Chapter Twenty

The journey home from the Consultant in Harley Street was traumatic. Both Agnes and Alistair were trying to come to terms with the course of events. The implications were devastating.

On returning home, Alistair sat down with Agnes and hugged her.

"What are we going to do?" asked Agnes.

"We have to be brave and make the most of whatever time we have."

"But there're the shows, and what about you and Gwen? Who's going to look after you?"

"That's for another day. For the moment we must think about the practicalities. We need to discuss who we should tell."

Agnes was trying to compose herself and think rationally.

"Well, we need to contact Solly; he'll need to cancel the shows, then the family, and Mary."

"What about the press? They are bound to find out."

"I don't know. I'll speak to Solly."

Agnes started to cough again; this time more violently.

"I'll make you a cordial. Do you want anything to eat? You haven't eaten since breakfast."

"I'm not hungry, if I'm truly honest."

"Do you want me to call Solly?"

"Yes, but don't say anything over the telephone, ask him to call this evening. He'll need some time to cancel the shows."

Alistair went to the kitchen and returned with a warm glass of honey cordial and the bottle of linctus.

An hour passed and the couple were starting to think more clearly. Agnes's coughing had eased.

The sound of the front door opening, and Gwen arrived from school. She was surprised to see her father at home at this time. Both he and Agnes looked upset.

"Hello, how was your day?" she asked cheerily, as she took off her school jacket and hung it on the coat peg in the hall. "What are you doing home, Dad? Is everything alright?"

"You better sit down, dear," said Agnes.

"What's wrong, something's wrong, I can tell," said Gwen.

"I'm afraid we've had some rather bad news," said Alistair. "Your mother has not been feeling too well."

"Yes, she was coughing this morning before I went to school, I heard her."

"Well, we've been to see a specialist this morning."

Alistair looked at Agnes. "Your mother has cancer."

Gwen put her hand to her mouth. "No, no, that can't be right."

"I'm sorry, it is," said Agnes.

"But, but what does that mean? They can operate now."

"Unfortunately, your mother has it in her lungs and throat. There's nothing they can do."

"So, does this mean you're going to die?" Gwen started to well-up.

"Yes," said Agnes. "I'm afraid it does."

Gwen rushed to her mother and threw her arms around her shoulders.

"You can't die, Ma, you can't."

"We have got one of London's best doctors to look after your mother. He even looks after Mr Churchill. We will make sure your mother gets the best possible care," said Alistair.

The three hugged.

Gwen offered to cook the dinner while Agnes went back to bed to rest. Alistair meanwhile had called Solly, and he would call round at eight o'clock.

Alistair also called Grace who had finished her shift at the ambulance station and told her the news. She promised to tell Mildred and call round in the morning.

Gwen made some soup for Agnes - she was finding it difficult to swallow and made a macaroni cheese for her and Alistair.

After dinner, Agnes was feeling better and got dressed ready for her meeting with the agent.

Just before eight o'clock there was a knock on the door which Alistair answered.

"Come in Solly."

It was a warm evening and Solly was wearing just a light jacket over his shirt and tie.

"Thank you," he said as he removed his hat.

"Come into the sitting room," said Alistair and Solly followed.

"Hello Agnes," he said, seeing Agnes seated on the settee. "Is everything alright. I have to say, I was concerned to be called at this time. I've been getting quite worried."

"Would you like a drink?" asked Alistair.

"Not just now, thank you, Alistair. There's something wrong, you'd better tell me."

Alistair looked at Agnes.

"It's bad news I'm afraid. Agnes has cancer,"

"What!?"

"Yes, we've been to see a specialist today and he's confirmed it."

"But what does that mean?"

"It means Agnes does not have long to live."

Solly's face drained of colour. "Are you sure? I mean, they make mistakes. Would you like me to call someone?"

"No, but thank you. We have the top clinician in London on the matter," replied Alistair.

"I, I, I... just don't know what to say."

"We wanted to tell you today as you'll have a lot of arrangements to make. We need to think what we should say to the newspapers," said Agnes.

The following day, Grace was the first visitor. Agnes was still coughing but less frequently, she was well enough to get dressed and greet her sister.

There were emotional hugs.

"I just haven't been able to take it all in," said Grace. "Are they absolutely certain?"

"Yes, I'm afraid so. The doctor took some x-rays."

"But there must be a cure."

"Unfortunately not, it's in my throat and in my lungs."

"But some people go on for years."

"I don't think so in my case. I've already noticed a change in the last few days. I'm getting short of breath, and I have this dreadful cough."

Agnes coughed again as if exemplifying the condition.

"But what about the shows?"

"Solly came round last night. He's going to speak to the promoter. They may cancel, or it's possible that Marie could take over as top of the bill." She looked down. "I hate disappointing people. He's also going to send out a press release today, saying I have a throat infection and have had to pull out of my shows."

"What about the BBC?"

"Solly's speaking to Robert... Lang, the producer, this morning, to let him know."

Grace continued, her cheeks wet with tears. "Oh, I don't know what to say. Matthew and I were devasted last night. I couldn't sleep; I still can't come to terms with it."

"Did you manage to speak to Mam?"

"Yes, I did. She couldn't believe it. I asked her to let Molly and Freda know."

"Thank you, I'll telephone her this morning; I couldn't face it last night, but I needed her to know before the press get hold of it."

"How is Alistair and Gwen?"

"I don't think it's hit them properly. Gwen's gone to school, although she wanted to stay home. It's important to try to carry on as normal as far as possible; that's what we agreed last night. Alistair's gone into work, but he's coming back at lunchtime. He's going to take some time off; he needed to arrange things with the principal."

Just then there was a knock on the door. Grace went to answer it.

"Hello Mary, come in, Agnes is in the sitting room."

Mary took off her jacket and hat and joined them.

"Hello Grace, lovely to see you again. How are things at the ambulance station?" said Mary.

"We've been quite busy," replied Grace.

"And how are you feeling today, Agnes? You look better than Monday."

"You'd better sit down."

Agnes explained the outcome of her visit to the consultant.

"Oh, dear Lord... Are you sure?" said Mary.

"Yes, the consultant was recommended by Doctor Brittan. He's one of the best in the country."

"I just don't know what to say," said Mary, visibly shaken.

"No, I know; it's difficult, but I want to stay positive and make the most of the time we have. Alistair and I have been thinking about setting up some sort of foundation to help up-and-coming singers. I haven't spoken to Solly about it yet, but I thought it's something we could work on."

"Yes, yes, of course, that's an excellent idea."

"Well, I have more than enough money. I thought we could use the income from the houses, but we can discuss this with the solicitor. Which reminds me, can you set up an appointment with Mr Hyde, ask him if he will call; there will be a lot to think about."

Mary was deep in thought, not really concentrating. "Yes... Er, I'll call him, directly, but first I'll make a drink. Would you like a coffee?"

"I'll just have my cordial, thank you."

"What about you, Grace?

"Yes, please," she replied.

The activity had given Agnes fresh motivation; at least there was something positive that could come out of this. The atmosphere had changed.

Mid-morning there was another caller.

"It's Doctor Brittan," said Mary, as she escorted him into the sitting room.

Grace was seated next to Agnes and stood up as the doctor approached.

"Hello Agnes, how are you feeling today? I've spoken to Mr Wilson, and he's told me the dreadful news."

"Thank you, doctor; yes, he was quite thorough."

"Yes, he wants to keep an eye on you. He said he's going to telephone to arrange an appointment to visit. I gave him your number; I didn't think you would mind. In the meantime, I said I would call round and see if there was anything you needed; pain relief maybe."

"That's most kind of you. I don't have any pain at the moment, not as such, just this annoying cough, and the shortness of breath, which I have to say has got worse since yesterday."

"Yes, that's to be expected. I can give you some stronger medicine, but it will make you tired; you will sleep a lot."

"Thank you doctor, whatever you suggest."

The doctor carried out another examination and recommended some new drugs which Mary agreed to collect from the chemist.

Grace stayed until lunchtime before returning home and, a few minutes later, Solly called.

After accepting refreshment from Mary and enquiring after Agnes's condition, he got down to business.

"I've spoken to the promoter and he's going to cancel the run. The shows are completely sold out until the end of July, but we felt that changing the line up at this late stage would lead to more complaints. As he said, there is only one Agnes Marsden."

"Thank you, that's very kind of you to say. I'm so sorry to let the rest of the cast down."

Agnes started coughing.

"Oh, please don't think that. It's your wellbeing that must take priority."

Agnes looked down, then changed the subject. "How are your parents, by the way? I meant to ask."

"They are settling in well, thank you. They're getting help with their English, which will make a big difference, but between you and me, I think they are finding it difficult. I've had to accompany them when they go shopping. Unfortunately, they have experienced some bad comments when they speak, about their accents."

"Bad comments?"

"Yes, er, anti-German. There's a lot of ill-feeling around. Still, it's better than Germany."

Agnes started coughing again.

"I shan't stay long; I just wanted to let you know what was happening. Oh, I spoke to Robert Laing at the BBC. I have to say he was very upset. I've asked him not to say anything to the production team for the moment. We'll stick to the official press release."

"Thank you," said Agnes. "Mary, can you tell Solly about our plan? This talking is making me cough."

Mary turned to Solly and explained the idea of a foundation in Agnes's name to support talented singers and musicians."

"Some sort of bursary?" queried Solly.

Mary looked at Agnes for confirmation.

"Yes, that's the plan," said Agnes.

"I think it's a wonderful idea," said Solly.

"We're going to speak to the solicitor and see what he says. We have no idea how it will work," said Mary.

"Well, anything I can do to help, just let me know."

Early afternoon, Solly had left. Alistair had returned from work and was helping Mary in the kitchen; Agnes had taken to her bed.

"I'll just go to the chemists, and get Agnes's medicine," said Mary.

A few minutes after she had left there was another knock on the door. Alistair went to answer it.

He stood in amazement. "Mildred...? What a surprise, come in."

"Thank you, Alistair, I'm sorry to call unannounced, but

I just had to come."

A taxi driver had carried what appeared to be a heavy suitcase to the front doorstep. Alistair took over.

"Of course... Agnes is asleep at the moment, but I know she will be glad to see you."

Alistair left the suitcase in the hall as Mildred removed her hat. She was wearing a smart top and skirt, with a matching jacket.

"Come in," Alistair repeated, and led Mildred into the sitting room. "How was your journey?"

"Oh, it was quite tiresome, and the carriages are so smoky these days; I'm sure they didn't used to be so bad."

"Yes, I'm sure you are right. Let me get you a drink."

While Alistair was making tea, Agnes came down the stairs, holding onto the banister and stopping halfway to catch her breath.

"Mam, what are you doing here? I thought I heard your voice. I thought I was dreaming."

"Oh, Agnes, come here, let me look at you." They embraced warmly.

"I couldn't settle, dear, I was awake half the night. I just had to come down. I promise I won't get under your feet."

"Don't be silly; it's lovely to see you. You're always welcome."

Alistair came in from the kitchen carrying a tray. "Would you like a drink, darling?"

"Just a cordial please," replied Agnes.

"I hope you don't mind, I've brought a few clothes with me. I can always get a hotel if it's not convenient."

"I wouldn't dream of it. I'll get Mary to make up a bed when she returns. She has gone to get my medicine from the chemist. The doctor came this morning and has prescribed some painkillers."

"Oh, I hope you're not in any pain, dear."

"No, not as such, just this awful cough, and feeling breathless all the time. I was telling the doctor; it feels it's got worse over the last day or so."

"I'm so sorry, dear, I really am. Freda and Molly send their love."

"How are they?"

"They seem well enough but were very upset when I told them the news. I've not spoken to Ivy yet, but I'm sure word will get round."

"Yes, Solly's arranged a press release this morning, so it will be in the newspapers tomorrow, just saying that I have a throat infection, not cancer."

"He's your agent, you told me? The Jewish one you went to Germany with?"

"Yes, he's been wonderful. I don't know what I would have done without him."

Agnes started coughing again.

"You must rest your voice darling."

Monday, July 3rd.

Back at Broadway Buildings, the headquarters of the secret services, Matthew was with Commander Monkton in his office.

The Service had significantly increased in number in the last six months with forty-seven officers and fifty-five secretaries based in the building. Space was becoming an issue.

"I wanted you to know that there's going to be further changes around here. We're moving the GC and CS units up to Bletchley Park. SIS will remain here for the time being, but that could change."

"Yes, we knew that was on the cards. It makes sense

having the cypher teams together."

"Yes, they've installed the very latest equipment up there, including four more transmitters and six receivers."

"Well, that's going to help... I meant to ask while I'm here, has there been anything more on Seán Russell, any developments? It seems to have gone very quiet."

"Nothing; there have been all sorts of rumours. Apparently, he skipped bail. The FBI have no knowledge of his whereabouts."

Monkton's telephone rang.

"Yes, Home Secretary," he said, and listened. He had a note pad and was writing.

After a couple of minutes, he replaced the receiver. His expression was grim.

"Problems?"

"It seems our Irish friends have upped their game."

"Oh?"

"They've gone after the railways. We're getting reports of explosions in the Midlands." He picked up his notepad and read his scribble. "It seems, let me see, Nottingham, Leicester, Warwick, Derby, Birmingham, Coventry and Stafford stations have all been bombed."

"Casualties?"

"None reported, but several injured. They hit the ticket office at Leicester; it's been completely destroyed."

"What have Special Branch got to say?"

"I've not spoke to them yet. Can you get down there and arrange a briefing meeting. The Home Secretary wants a report by the end of the day."

"Yes, sir, right away. I'll take Miss Crouch with me; it will be good experience."

"Good idea."

Twenty minutes later, Matthew and Chloe were in a taxi

heading for New Scotland Yard.

Meanwhile, in Oakworth, the post had arrived. Freddie Bluet picked up two letters. Jean came out of the kitchen.

"Is that the post? Who are they from?"

"Looks like one's from t'mill. T'other's from our Arthur; it's his writing." He handed over the letter from their son to Jean and started to open the letter from the Mill. He was feeling anxious.

His face beamed in a smile. "Hey, they want us to start next Monday."

Jean looked up from Arthur's letter. It seemed several pages long.

"Oh, that's good news."

"What does our Arthur say?"

"I'm trying to read it. His hand writing's not best and his pencil needs sharpening I think... He says he's left Tor Point, that place where they were training. Hey, he says they've sent him to Portsmouth to join a ship."

"Which one? Does he say?"

"The Hood, he says; do you know it?"

"Really? Aye, I say... I know The Hood alright. It's the biggest ship in t'navy, a battle cruiser."

"He says he and the other boy sailors are up at seven o'clock cleaning the decks."

"Aye, well a bit of hard work won't hurt him."

"Then they have schooling till lunch time." Jean continued reading.

"He says he's started smoking as they're allowed to smoke, which they weren't allowed to do at Tor Point. He's made some good friends already. He says they speak different, and they tease him on his accent, but all in good fun."

"Does he say owt about going to sea?"

"No, that's it. He says he'll write again soon. I'll write back today; he says we can write to him at 'His Majesty's Ships'."

She put down the letter.

"So, what do they say... The Mill?"

"Nowt much, just want us to start next Monday; that's the seventeenth."

"That is good news."

Monday, July 17th.

Matthew was with Commander Monkton in his office.

"Just seen the reports of Oswald Moseley's First Britain meeting at Earls Court last night. thirty thousand turned up, apparently."

"Yes, a noisy gathering by all accounts, but I've spoken to the Home Office; they're not overly concerned. MI5 have been monitoring the group closely. They've had agents inside the BUF since 1934."

August 1939, in the cinemas, the Pathé Newsreels continued to promote their jingoistic rhetoric, designed to keep the country's morale high. Clips of thirteen hundred planes filling the skies in a training exercise; the King reviewing a hundred and thirty-three ships in Weymouth harbour.

On August 11th, starting at midnight, half of England went dark for four hours in a test to determine how effectively the country could shroud itself from enemy planes, a frightening experience for those affected.

The activities of the IRA, however, continued to dominate Matthew's agenda.

On August 3rd, the organisation had announced that it would continue its campaign against Britain for another two-and-a-half years. However, under the new Prevention of Violence Act, deportations of Irish nationals from Britain increased which would start to have an impact on the bombings.

August 14th, Matthew was at his desk when his telephone rang. It was the Commander.

"Ah, Major, just to let you know Seán Russell's resurfaced. He's still in America, just made another speech against Britain, more or less reiterating the message from the third of August. Interestingly, he's taken a swipe against de Valera and the Irish Parliament, calling them compromisers."

"Can't he be arrested again? I mean, he's skipped bail."

"Ha, they would, if they could find him. The Foreign Office say he's gone to ground again."

In the event, believing correctly that the threat of war had increased, De Valera had started a major crackdown on the IRA, recognising their activities threatened Irish neutrality. The Irish police made numerous arrests and a considerable amount of weaponry and American money was seized.

Following the announcement of Agnes's incapacity, back in Bloomsbury, Agnes was in the sitting room. She had been inundated with cards and letters from well-wishers. There had been plenty of press speculation on what was wrong with her, but Solly fended off questions, continuing the line that it was merely a throat infection.

The house was awash with flowers. In fact, she had received so many, she had donated any new floral arrivals to the local hospital.

Mildred was still staying with Agnes and Alistair, and had

taken charge of things, as she tended to do. Mary continued to look after the numerous letters and gifts that arrived on a daily basis.

Agnes's condition however was starting to deteriorate and cause concern.

Alistair was in the kitchen making her a drink.

"I would like to go out," she announced, as Alistair brought in her cordial.

"But you're not well enough, darling."

"Yes, and I'm not going to get any better... I would like to see the sea one more time."

Alistair hesitated for a moment. "Well, yes, if that's what you want. What did you have in mind?"

"Do you remember when we used to sit by the sea in France, when you were in hospital?"

"Yes, of course, it will stay with me for ever."

"I would like to do that again, just the two of us. We can take a taxi down to Brighton."

"But do you feel up to the journey?"

"It shouldn't take too long. I think the sea air might do me some good."

"When would you like to go?"

"Today, after lunch; it's a fine morning and this afternoon is set fair."

"Very well, I'll order a taxi for one-thirty."

Despite protests from Mildred, Agnes was insistent, and by early afternoon, Agnes and Alistair were in a taxi heading for the South Coast.

As they reached the resort, the driver called over his shoulder from the cab.

"Where would you like to go?"

"The sea-front please," shouted Alistair, and a few

minutes later the taxi was driving past the Grand Hotel. It continued further down the promenade and past the pier to a quieter part of the front.

"By this shelter, please," shouted Alistair.

The taxi pulled to a halt and Alistair assisted Agnes out of the vehicle. Alistair gave the driver a pound note. "Get yourself a cup of tea and pick us up here in an hour."

"Right, Guv, that's very generous of you," said the driver and drove away.

There was no request for autographs; the cabbie would not easily recognise Agnes. She had lost so much weight, her face looked gaunt and frail.

It was just a short walk to the shelter. Agnes's mobility was now severely restricted, the slightest movement causing her to have difficulty breathing. Alistair almost carried her to the seat that overlooked the ocean. The sun was beaming down, and the sea shimmered its reflection. Seagulls squawked and swooped, looking for titbits left by visitors.

They sat together, holding hands, looking out to sea.

"Are you warm enough, darling?" asked Alistair.

"Oh, yes the sun is quite warm. This is so lovely; I'm glad we did this. It brings back so many memories."

"Yes, I don't think I would have survived without your kindness," said Alistair.

"I'm sure you would, but I did want to protect you. It changed my life; I was all set to marry Lord Harford."

"Are you glad you didn't?"

"Oh, most definitely. It was the best decision I've ever made. You have made me very happy, darling."

"And you, me. I've never met such a kind and gifted person."

"I have been blessed, I know, but I could not have done it without you by my side." She squeezed his hand. "I'll tell you something. I knew from the first time I saw you playing that piano I wanted to be with you; do you remember, in the common room?" said Agnes.

"Yes, Debussy, how can I forget? I didn't think a nurse would have heard of Debussy. What a dreadful thing to say; it taught me a lesson about being judgemental, so patronising, on reflection."

"It's alright; it was quite a reasonable assumption, and I wasn't even a nurse, just an assistant."

"Well, I can safely say, you helped cure more men in that hospital than all the doctors. Many of us were traumatised from our experiences. You gave us hope."

"That's very kind."

She squeezed his hand again. They continued looking out to sea in silence, just like the time at Wimereux, all those years ago.

Today was a special day.

By mid-August, Agnes's conditioned had deteriorated to the extent she was confined to bed. The slightest movement had become too difficult for her lungs to support. She was finding it difficult to eat; her ability to swallow was becoming an issue and all her food was being made into a soup.

There had been daily visits from Doctor Brittain as well as weekly appearances by Mr Wilson, the consultant. The main thing was to keep Agnes comfortable.

Mildred was still staying with the family, cooking and entertaining the various visitors; it had kept her mind occupied. She called Molly and Freda back in Yorkshire at regular intervals to keep them updated.

Cards, letters and flowers continued to arrive as concern for Agnes's health grew.

Mary was a daily presence, helping deal with the

correspondence. She was in the sitting room when there was another delivery. She picked up the official-looking envelope from the doormat and opened it.

She called Alistair. "Have you seen these?"

She walked into the kitchen where Alistair was chatting with Mildred.

"What is it?"

"I don't know; it says, 'Ration Books'."

"Oh, dear Lord, I thought we had seen the last of those during the war," said Mildred.

"What does it mean?"

"There was something in the newspaper about it. We're supposed to hold onto them and wait for more information from the Government. We need to keep them safe," said Alistair.

"I expect I'll have one," said Mary.

"Every house in the country will get them," said Alistair.

On a more positive note, progress had been made in setting up the Agnes Marsden foundation, Mr Hyde, the solicitor, had established a charity to manage the donations and income. He would be one of the trustees together with Alistair, Solly and Mary, A committee would select suitable bursary recipients.

Friday, August 25th.

At Broadway House, reports had been received about an atrocity in Coventry. A bomb had been left in a bicycle outside a departmental store, killing five people and injuring numerous more. Matthew had been called to New Scotland Yard for a meeting.

Ironically, this action effectively marked the beginning of the end of the bombing campaign. The negative press both in Ireland and America had an adverse effect on support and, importantly, donations. More arrests followed, both on the British mainland and in Ireland leading to executions in Ireland. There were further bombings, but less frequently and with less damage or injury. There were no more fatalities.

Of equal concern to the British Secret Service and the Government was the announcement from Berlin, two days earlier, of the non-aggression pact between Germany and Russia which sealed the fate of Poland and made the possibility of a war a near certainty.

Parliament had been recalled and passed the Emergency Powers (Defence) Act, giving the government broad powers in order to conduct war effectively.

Planning started quickly, as arrangements were put in place for the evacuation of a million school children away from cities thought vulnerable to bombing.

It was late into the evening when Matthew received a telephone call at his desk. It was Grace.

"Matthew, I know you are probably busy, but can you come home? Agnes died half an hour ago."

Agnes's passing was widely covered in the newspapers. Letters of condolences arrived by the sack load, including a card from the King and Queen.

Her obituary in The Times was hard to read for those fortunate enough to know her.

'From humble beginnings to the brightest star of stage and radio'

Born and raised in a working-class area of Yorkshire, Agnes Marsden never eschewed her roots; throughout her career she retained that common touch that endeared her to audiences across the country.

The routine nature of her career provided a settled contrast to Agnes's early upbringing. She was born Agnes Mary Marsden in 1896 in Keighley to Albert Marsden, a master baker, and Mildred, who later became a local benefactor during the war years. Agnes was the second of four sisters and a brother who won a gallantry medal during the Battle of Ypres and died earlier this year.

Discovered at the young age of eighteen by the late impresario, Cameron Delaney, Miss Marsden was soon headlining a successful recruitment drive across the country for the army and later toured military bases in Northern France. These concerts were lauded as a major boost for morale. In 1915 she gave up singing until the end of the war to work as a nursing assistant at an officers' hospital in Wimereux, France, and later at the Endell Street Hospital in London.

She returned to the stage after hostilities had finished, starring in several West End Productions, then in the mid 1920's as a recording artist, reached a new audience, while bringing up her family. She occasionally performed with her concert pianist husband, Alistair, himself a gifted musician. She was also an occasional visitor to Buckingham Palace where she sang in front of their Majesties.

But it was her recent radio broadcast which took Agnes Marsden's career to new heights, attracting audiences into the millions with her magnetic personality and crystal-clear voice.

Only last month she was entertaining sell-out audiences at the Vaudeville Theatre until cancer cruelly took her.

Viewed as a glamorous figure, she was never less than at one with her adoring fans. News of a foundation to support struggling performers is typical of her connection with those trying for success.

She is survived by her husband, Alistair and daughter, Gwendoline.

Agnes Mary Marsden, May 14th, 1896 – August 25th, 1939

Agnes's funeral took place on Friday 1st September, the very day that Hitler invaded Poland.

The service was held in Acton at the Church of All Saints. Such was the demand, loudspeakers relayed the proceedings to the hundreds of mourners that had congregated outside. There was a poignant moment in the service when, about halfway through, Alistair made his way to the church piano – the one they used for choir practice, and played Debussy's Clare de Lune, 'especially for Agnes'.

The streets were lined with people as the funeral cortege left the church and made its way to the cemetery.

At the wake, back at the house, Mildred took charge of the proceedings. All the family were there from Yorkshire, Molly and husband, John; Freda, Grace and Matthew, who had taken a few hours off from his desk in Broadway House. Céline and Mary, Agnes's two assistants for many years, were trying to come to terms with the loss.

Sunday, September 3rd, 1939.

The Bloomsbury house seemed empty without Agnes's presence; Alistair was trying to come to terms with the situation but didn't believe he ever would. He had lost his world.

Mildred had returned to Yorkshire, and it was Gwen who made breakfast. Mary had offered to call round mid-morning to help deal with the numerous sympathy cards which continued to arrive.

Like every household in Britain, at eleven o'clock, everything stopped while they listened to the radio broadcast by the Prime Minister.

"This is London," said the announcer.

There was a feeling of nervous tension as Neville Chamberlain spoke; his voice edged with emotion.

'I am speaking to you from the Cabinet Room at 10, Downing Street.

This morning the British Ambassador in Berlin handed the German Government a final note stating that unless we heard from them by eleven O'clock that they were prepared, at once, to withdraw their troops from Poland, a state of war would exist between us. I have to tell you now that no such undertaking has been received, and that consequently, this country is at war with Germany......

We and France are to-day, in fulfilment of our obligations, going to the aid of Poland, who is so bravely resisting this wicked and unprovoked attack upon her people. We have a clear conscience. We have done all that any country could do to establish peace, but a situation, in which no word given by Germany's ruler could be trusted and no people or country could feel themselves safe, had become intolerable. And now that we have resolved to finish it, I know that you will all play your part with calmness and courage.'

THE END

Acknowledgements

A significant amount of research went into the writing of this novel, and whilst it is a fictional account, many of the scenes in this book are based on real events.

For further reading on the topic of the IRA activity in the lead up to the Second World War I can recommend 'IRA Terror on Britain's Streets 1939-1940' by Dick Kirby; and 'MI5 and Ireland 1939 – 1945' by Eunan O'Halpin, both of which provided inspiration and essential background information to enable me to describe accurately the course of events.

Alan Reynolds, November 2023

Alan Reynolds

Following a successful career in Banking, award winning author Alan Reynolds established his own training company in 2002 and has successfully managed projects across a wide range of businesses. This experience has led to an interest in psychology and human behaviour through watching interactions, studying responses and research. Leadership has also featured strongly in his training portfolios and the knowledge gained has helped build the strong characters in his books.

Alan's interest in writing started as a hobby but after completing his first novel in just three weeks, the favourable reviews he received encouraged him to take up a new career. The inspiration for this award-winning author come from real life facts which he weaves seamlessly into fast-paced, page-turning works of fiction.